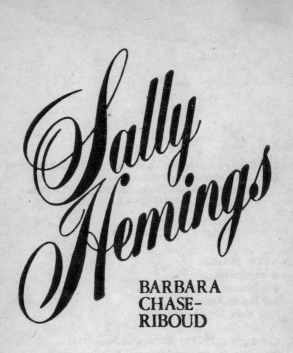

Sally Hemings

**BARBARA
CHASE-
RIBOUD**

AVON
PUBLISHERS OF BARD, CAMELOT AND DISCUS BOOKS

The Viking Press edition carries the following Library of
Congress Cataloging in Publication Data:
   1. Hemings, Sally—Fiction. 2. Jefferson, Thomas,
      Pres. U.S., 1743–1826—Fiction. I. Title.

AVON BOOKS
A division of
The Hearst Corporation
959 Eighth Avenue
New York, New York 10019

Copyright © 1979 by Barbara Chase-Riboud
Published by arrangement with The Viking Press
Library of Congress Catalog Card Number: 78-12682
ISBN: 0-380-48686-5

First Avon Printing, June, 1980

AVON TRADEMARK REG. U.S. PAT. OFF. AND IN
OTHER COUNTRIES, MARCA REGISTRADA, HECHO EN
U.S.A.

Printed in the U.S.A.

To the enigma of the historical Sally Hemings

That God forbid that made me first your slave,
I should in thought control your times of pleasure,
Or at your hand the account of hours to crave . . .
WILLIAM SHAKESPEARE

Records are destroyed. Histories are annihilated, or interpolated, or prohibited. Sometimes by popes, sometimes by emperors, sometimes by aristocratic and sometimes by democratic assemblies, . . . such had been and such is the world we live in. . . .
JOHN ADAMS

forties; immune to all the material below the north of the
valley fevers that struck eighteenth century Virginia in
their swampy, unhealthy climate, punctuated by the periodic
outbreaks of cholera; without physical blemish or con-

Contents

AUTHOR'S NOTE

There are documents included in this novel which are not only authentic, they are central to the story of Sally Hemings and Thomas Jefferson. These documents are like the sea on which their small and private boat sailed.

BCR

PART I

1830
Albemarle
County

CHAPTER 1

ALBEMARLE COUNTY, 1830

It is difficult to determine on the standard by which the manners of a nation may be tried, whether *catholic,* or *particular.* It is more difficult for a native to bring to that standard the manners of his own nation, familiarized to him by habit. There must doubtless be an unhappy influence on the manners of our people produced by the existence of slavery among us.

THOMAS JEFFERSON, *Notes on the State of Virginia,* 1790

There was a white man coming up her road, as if God had ordained it and as if he owned the road.

The woman standing in the dark square of the cabin doorway knew that this was the way white men arrived. Anyway, no slave would be driving a carriage unaccompanied. And the only freedmen for miles around were her sons, Madison and Eston. She never thought of herself as free, and now, at fifty-six, with her sons waiting politely for her to die so that they could move West (why was she so stubborn about it?), she was fixed in another time and space, belonging to another epoch, an epoch which had ended for her on the Fourth of July 1826, four years gone.

The cabin in which she stood was the most beggarly habitation for miles around. The land surrounding it was cotton-exhausted and impossible to work. Yet they worked it, her sons, with a furor and a wrenching desperation, although it was not even theirs. Freed slaves could not own land in Virginia. It was rented; expensive and worthless—eroded, hilly, evil. The cabin leaned into its own decay. Backed as it was against the boundaries of the once-famous

3

plantation of Monticello, it too now strangled in its own undergrowth.

The carriage was approaching, the iron wheels grinding against the deep ruts of the ill-kept road. She could see that it was not really a carriage but a buckboard. And what she had thought to be horses were really a very pretty pair of matched beige-and-brown mules, fat and glossy. Her eyes followed the advance of the little buckboard without surprise, as if the event that was to take place had already been explained to her, as if she knew who would be arriving in such splendor at an ex-slave's cabin door.

Actually her eyes were never surprised. They were eyes of a deep amber yellow, mark of a quadroon, which gave her whole face an illusion of transparency. Eyes that were liquid gold in an ivory mask; windows onto banked and mysterious fires that burned day and night, absorbing everything and returning nothing to the surface. The skin was drawn, but smooth. There was no way to tell her age; neither in the lines of her face nor the contours of her body —which was small and low, compact and strong, with that wiry vivacity of congenital thinness. Her head was bound in a white cloth that darkened the skin and set off the pale and beautiful mouth with its two deep dimples on either side. In her ears dangled small ruby earrings, like tiny drops of blood, incongruous next to the faded rough black-linen dress and its black apron. She was still in mourning. Her hands, which were hidden in the folds of her apron, were small, soft, and slender, unmarked by hard labor.

The buckboard had stopped at the bottom of the orchard. The man had gotten out and was making his way up the steep path to her door. As she watched the approaching stranger, her expression changed swiftly from curiosity to anger to apprehension. There were only two reasons for a white man to be coming to the cabin: either he was the census taker from the Albemarle County Courthouse or the sheriff with an eviction notice. Either would ask the same questions: her name, her age, and if she were slave or free. Well, everybody in Albemarle County, every Tidewater family for fifty miles around, knew her name; how many children she had, and by whom; knew too that as a manumitted slave she had no right by law to remain in

Virginia—unless she had been granted a special dispensation from the Virginia legislature.

If the census taker, if that's who he was, had any sense
at all, he wouldn't have had to come all the way up here
in the afternoon heat to ask her what he undoubtedly already knew: if she was Sally Hemings of Monticello.

The slave mistress of Thomas Jefferson had been famous
in Albemarle County for as long as he could remember. At
least her name was famous. Few people had actually seen
her and that was one of the reasons he was making his way
slowly up this wretched road: to meet Sally Hemings face
to face.

Not one person in a hundred would recognize "Dusky
Sally" if they saw her, he concluded. She had seldom left
Monticello in all her fifty years there, yet it seemed he had
always heard her name. His father had known both her
masters, John Wayles, the father, and Thomas Jefferson,
the lover. Nathan Langdon, who was indeed the census
taker for Albemarle County, smiled grimly. He was home.
He was home in Virginia, with its passions, its blood feuds,
its pride, its duels, its Southern honor. And glad of it. Even
in the few weeks he had been back, the energy and efficiency of his affected Northern manner had disappeared
like a lizard's skin. The heat, the languid pace of the tidy,
beautiful mules, the lurch of the old-fashioned but elegant
buggy, the reins softly caressing the palms of his hands, all
gently contributed to make him feel at home. He settled his
large frame into the cracked leather of the seat and raised
his eyes to the little cabin sitting on the boundary between
the wilderness of a ragged pine forest and the southernmost
acres of Monticello. As he did he saw a childlike figure
standing in the lopsided doorway. A woman. Sally Hemings. It must be. There were no other women out this way.

The shadowed figure in the doorway stood stock-still.
Why was it that she could never control the dread and panic
she felt at the approach of a white man? Any white man.
A familiar uneasiness settled in her stomach. There had
been only one white man she had ever welcomed. And he
was dead and buried behind this cabin on his little mountain.

At least Madison and Eston were not home. If there was trouble, she preferred to face it alone. Facing down an angry white man was a black woman's job, not a black man's unless he was prepared to die. But then this man just might be the census taker Madison had spoken about the other day.

She felt a strange calm. The sheriff would have an eviction notice, if he had anything, and a writ to run them out of the State of Virginia—which would suit her sons just fine, if they could leave peaceably.

Sally Hemings knew her presence in Virginia and that of her sons depended on the will and whim of her niece, Martha Jefferson Randolph. It was Martha who had manumitted her, and it was Martha who had persuaded her friends in the legislature to allow her to stay. Her life here depended on Martha, and Martha depended on her silence. Both had their reasons. So be it. They both had reasons to keep silent—reasons that would die with them. It was against the law for a freed slave to remain in Virginia more than a year and a day from the date of emancipation. The slave risked being sold back into slavery.

But she would die in Virginia, at Monticello, God willing, and not in some desert scalped by wild Indians. Madison and Eston were young and healthy. The West was their only chance; but she would finish her days here. Her sons would simply have to wait. It wouldn't be all that long.

The white man was approaching on foot. Weaving in and out of her apple orchards, the sun to his back. The pretty mules, shimmering in the heat, were stopped quietly at the bottom of the pathway. Sally Hemings heard the flutter of her chickens at roost in their pen, and felt the sun on her eyelids as she closed them against the glare.

Nathan Langdon had practically forgotten his fascination with Sally Hemings as he made his way toward the cabin. The strange destiny of Sally Hemings seemed less urgent to ponder than his own future, now that he was back.

His job as census taker would last only through the summer. He had to do it while helping to run Broadhurst. He was the heir now; his older brother, his father's favorite, was dead, a hole blown through him at point-blank range.

His father was grief-stricken, unable to take even the most meager duties on his shoulders.

There had been relief and gratitude when he had announced that he would stay at home and marry. Esmeralda Wilks was rich and temperamental, and she had let him know in no uncertain terms that she was tired of waiting. It was her family who had gotten him his temporary job as census taker until he could finish his studies and pass his bar examinations. He had thought about politics as well; but not only was he too "radical" for this county, he would also be in competition with his brothers and brothers-in-law. Still, he could consider this appointment as a first "political" step to bigger and better things. He would apprentice himself to Judge Miner in Charlottesville, see more of Esmeralda, comfort his father, and run Broadhurst. At least he was rid of the necessity of forever explaining himself, his family, and his state—to say nothing of the entire South—to Northern friends, acquaintances, and reformers. One thing he never wanted to explain again was the Institution of Slavery. He could give a lecture, in his sleep, on this subject. He never again intended to endure Northerners and their impertinent questions, the sententiousness of their comments, the insulting familiarity of the exchanges.

He had managed, after years of arguments, to convince his closest Northern friends that a Virginian did not automatically own "thousands of slaves," and that he did not starve and beat the ones he had; that Negroes bred in nine months like everybody else, and that neither he nor his servants had tails, two heads, indolent or oversexed dispositions.

He always felt a general outrage that these ignoramuses could so presume on his private life and that of his kin and his native territory. Sooner or later their curiosity would get the better of their manners, and they apparently found it quite natural to ask the most unwarranted and intimate questions of a total stranger, one they considered the "expert" Southerner. They would never dream of asking such questions of their own family or class. Owning Negroes seemed to them to be a license for all kinds of forwardness.

What's more, they never seemed to be satisfied. There

had always been "just one thing more I wanted to ask you."
And these Northerners, he thought furiously, had been his
friends. The well-bred and aristocratic sons of gentlemen
and capitalists. Yet their greed for information about the
South, and their fascination with slavery, knew no bounds.
What had fascinated them most, especially the ladies, was
not the economics, the humanity, or the Christianity of
the Institution, but sex. Langdon's mouth tightened in exasperation. The only thing they really wanted to know about
was the sex life of the Southern aristocrat and his slaves.
They had all heard of the thousands of New Orleans
octoroons, the dashing Washington mulattoes, the plantation quadroons, sometimes sired by the sons' fathers, and
overseers of slave-owning families. Cross-breeding was
something one didn't discuss in polite society. One didn't
discuss it at all, even in the intimacy of one's private
journal. It was something one relegated to that corner of
the mind reserved for incest, insanity, epilepsy, suicide, and
sodomy; it was sordid and unthinkable. He had never been
able to explain to these morose Northerners the particular
combination of cruelty and affection, detachment and
possessiveness that made up the relationship between master
and servant, a relationship all the more complex and
intense if they were blood kin. How could he ever explain
it to them? True, white men had begot and freed sons, even
daughters, but the basic rule of this charged and intimate
correspondence was that there was a superior and an inferior race, and to intermingle them was an error against
God, Nature, and Society. No matter how many mulattoes,
quadroons, octoroons, métis issued from lust or passion. He
also knew that freed slaves were not allowed to remain in
Virginia. Why were the Hemingses so privileged? Who had
petitioned the Virginia Legislature for special permission
for them to stay? And why? Or did they remain without
official permission? How was it possible that, at the pinnacle
of his power, Thomas Jefferson had chosen a slave when
he could have chosen any white woman alive!

His heavy shoulders moved uncomfortably in the loose
woolen jacket. He was not dressed for the heat. His
thoughts had taken him far away, so that he was startled
to find himself looking at the most beautiful woman he had
ever seen, a woman old enough and fair enough to be his

mother. It can't be, he thought wildly, unnerved by her physical beauty.

The woman was indeed beautiful. The face was unlined, the gaze fragile but unyielding. The eyes were almost emerald in the bluish shadow. The mouth was soft and childish in its contours, and vain. The body was well proportioned. She had removed the white cloth and her hair seemed to glow like a silk cap, the braid coiled around her head breaking into planes of light.

No sound came from the dark recess, and Nathan Langdon struggled to find a way of addressing this woman. How did one address a creature who did not exist, who was the negation of everything he had been taught to believe? There were no white slaves. There could be no white ex-slaves. There were no women who looked like this, who lived in a Negro cabin at the end of a dusty, weed-choked footpath out of time and memory, who had been loved by a great man who had never freed her. The smell of poverty and cooking hung in the interior. The woman's dress and apron were of poor quality black linen, faded to gray and without trimmings. A window in the room let in the afternoon light, silhouetting this figure who neither moved nor spoke.

Finally, he said, "You are? . . ."

"Sally Hemings." The voice was crisp and clear. "Are you the census taker for the county my son spoke of?"

"Yes, Ma'am. Nathan Langdon, at your service."

The simplest words seemed to explode into the atmosphere. Langdon caught his breath as the woman emerged gently from the shadow of the room into the light. In the brightness, her eyes assumed their true color, fringed with thick black lashes and by heavy eyebrows. The nose was slightly flared, the cheekbones abnormally high, the eyes wide-spaced. There were streaks of gray in the fine black hair, which, if loosened, would doubtless have reached her waist.

"You live here with your sons Eston and Madison?"

"Yes."

"Ages?"

"Mine?"

"Yours first, Ma'am, then your sons'."

"Fifty-six. My son Eston is twenty-two and Madison is twenty-five."

"All born in Albemarle County?"

"At Monticello." ·

"You are manumitted slaves, are you not? Do you have a special dispensation to remain in Virginia?"

"Yes."

"Former slaves of Martha Jefferson Randolph?"

"Of Thomas Jefferson. My sons were freed by his will in 1826."

"And you?"

"The same year."

"This cabin and land, the property of?"

"Cornelius Stooker of Charlottesville."

"Land?"

"Twelve acres."

"Yearly rent?"

"Two bales of cotton and seven bushels of corn."

"The professions of your sons?"

"Musicians . . ."

Nathan Langdon raised his eyebrows. "They farm the land as well?"

"Yes."

"No other adults living here?"

"No."

"Total?"

"Total?"

"That is, there are three adults and no children in residence, am I correct?"

"Yes, that's right."

"Other members of your family not living at home?"

"What?"

"You have other children, do you not?"

"They are listed as runaways in the Monticello Farm Book."

"How many?"

"Two—three."

"Three runaways?"

"Three."

"Five children in all?"

"Seven."

"Two deceased?"

"Yes."

"Are your sons at home?"

Sally Hemings hesitated. She was alone in the house and unprotected.

"They will be coming home shortly."

"Where are they?"

"At the university."

"Can they read?"

"Yes."

"Can you read?"

"Yes."

"Vote?" The question had come automatically to his lips. Now there was an embarrassed silence. Of course they couldn't vote. They weren't even supposed to know how to read and write. It was against the law. But then they were freed now, and there was no law saying freed slaves could not read and write. Or was there? He covered himself as best he could.

"Uh . . . property?" He flushed deeply. He was questioning her as if she were white. As if her sons were white farmers and musicians.

"Would you like a drink?" she asked suddenly. "Ginger beer, perhaps?"

"Thank you, Ma'am."

"Wait here. No. Come inside out of the sun. You have no hat on. It is finished, no?"

The strange involution of the sentence startled him. There was something foreign about her speech, as if she were thinking in a different language. It had no tremor of old age, but was delicious and young.

Nathan Langdon had to stoop to enter the somber cabin; quickly he took in the room. It was the most disconcerting interior he had ever seen. He had been in many slave and ex-slave cabins in the past weeks, so that he was not surprised by the simple handmade benches and tables, the rough plank floor, the whitewashed clay walls, the bits and pieces of hand-me-downs, broken, and repaired finery from the Big House, but as his stunned gaze took in the delicate cherrywood piano-forte, an exquisite onyx-and-bronze pendulum clock ticking away over the finely carved wooden chimney, the elegant dark-green leather chest with its brass fittings gleaming dully in the gloom, the French armchair, a huge ornate and gilded mirror, and, strangest of all, a French flag, a musket on which hung what looked like a small effigy or doll. He felt he had walked into the inner sanctum of some desperate and overwhelming mystery.

There was a large bouquet of fresh flowers, and on the floor lay a piece of white cloth, crumpled, as if discarded. In this incongruous setting, the light silhouetted the woman, and the effect was so intimate, so seductive, that Nathan Langdon instinctively took a step backward. As he did, his head almost hit the low doorframe, and Sally Hemings, in an unconscious, protective gesture, stepped forward.

"Please sit down."

"Thank you, Ma'am."

Even this invitation, so noncommittal, made Nathan blush.

"Your mules need water?"

"Why, I'd be much obliged." Langdon fell into the Southern formula for politeness. He had hardly used that term since his return. As Sally Hemings turned away from him, Langdon had the distinct impression that he recognized her; he knew he had seen this woman turn in that same way before. But where? He had lived four years in Massachusetts. It was five years since he had been in Charlottesville.

"But don't bother. . . . They'll be heading home now . . . this is my last visit."

Langdon had risen from his chair and followed her to the door, but she had already turned and was out of the cabin to fetch the water. Again, the same acute sense of recognition came back to him as the slender back disappeared into a shaded area not far from the house, where he supposed there was a well or a spring.

When she returned, she was carrying two buckets of water.

"You can take these down to those pretty mules of yours. If you'll be so kind as to leave the pails at the bend, my son Eston will see them and pick them up when he returns from work."

"I'm much obliged. Thank you. I'm sorry I missed seeing your sons, Ma'am."

"You must know them by sight. Pretty much everybody

in town knows who they are. They work around the university."

"It's been a long time since I've been home. You see, I just arrived from the North not too long ago. I don't know much of what has been going on for the past four or five years . . . but now I'm staying to help my family."

"Oh, you a lawyer? You look like one."

"Not exactly yet, but shortly. I intend to finish my studies this year at the university. I've already spent four years studying up at Harvard."

"Many of those brick buildings—and the carpentry and windows and metal work—they were done by my brothers, Robert Hemings and John Hemings, for Master Jefferson when he started to build his school. Now Madison and Eston do a lot of repairing and additions, since they are the most familiar with the original work. You see . . ."

Her voice floated like silk scarves, sweeping and billowing the simple everyday language into a honeyed intimacy. He wondered whether she was, by nature, a talkative woman. Certainly many of his visits to the isolated farmhouses in Albermarle County had ended in long bouts of conversation with lonely farm women. Yes, he sensed a loneliness, a sadness here. Charmed, Langdon kept her talking, adding little bits of gossip he had picked up in town, explaining himself and his family to her (something he had done so often at Harvard it was by now second nature). He realized she knew a great deal about what went on in Tidewater. He had always remarked that the Negroes had a wonderful art of communicating among themselves. Information and gossip would run several hundred miles in a week; but where had she learned the art of conversation that would do justice to a lady in these backwoods?

They spoke late into the afternoon, the fair, blue-eyed youth and his mysterious hostess. He, with his feet planted solidly on the floor, hunched forward in his seat, elbows on knees, his large hands folded loosely in front of him. She, also leaning away from her chair, swayed slightly with the conversation, or suddenly propelled herself backward as her girlish laughter responded to some amusing tidbit of gossip. She knew everything and everybody, despite the fact she hadn't been near the town in years.

The lovely face glowed with the pleasure of unaccustomed male company. The pretty hands gesticulated, folded and unfolded, or moved to fondle a large oval locket that hung on a velvet ribbon around her neck—her only adornment except for the ruby earrings—but obviously a valuable and beautifully executed jewel.

Surely I'll have leave to come again after such a long conversation, thought Langdon. He tried to find more anecdotes and gossip to please her. Never in all his drawing-room experiences had he striven so hard to entertain a woman. When she laughed he was hopelessly flattered. Would her sons appear? Langdon wondered. He wanted to see what they looked like. Madison and Eston Hemings. Their names brought the reality of the outside world back to him. The pails of water stood like sentinels on each side of the door, unattended.

Piedmont, like the rest of Virginia, was caught up in the political and racial torment of the times, Nathan mused. Already, the distant thunder of the coming conflict could be heard if one cared to listen. Virginia had tightened its slave laws the past years, measures which invariably affected the freedmen as well. The large cities in the South, including Charlottesville and Richmond, were armed camps. There was the scent of violence in the air, and families were already divided on the slave issue. Tensions were high, and repressions against the black population had increased tenfold. It had been deemed a crime since 1814 to teach a slave to read. There were curfews as well as passports and grade-shotted cannon for those who didn't respect it. There were kidnappings and lynchings, and daily public whippings for even accidental infractions.

In this year alone more than seventeen resolutions concerning slavery had been introduced and debated in the House of Burgesses. The spread of slavery was fiercely fought state by state, territory by territory. A sinister stillness had taken hold of the soft, low-lying countryside from Williamsburg to Richmond. Wrapped in an unnatural suffocating calm, the elements seemed to be waiting for some sign.

Langdon finally gave up waiting for Eston and Madison. As the shadows lengthened, Sally Hemings gracefully brought the conversation to an end, and, before he knew it, he was out of the cabin and on his way down the footpath toward his buckboard and thirsty mules.

The census taker had spent all afternoon in her cabin. How strange, she thought, he had spoken to her as if she had been a white woman. She watched him disappear and reappear among her apple trees as he made his way toward his buggy carrying the two pails of water. She saw the tall figure emerge at the bend beyond the orchard, approach his mule team, and water them. Then he set down the pails and got into his buggy. She expected him to drive away, but he sat there for a long while. She watched him as the sun got lower in the sky and the silence broke with the beginnings of night sounds. Still he did not move. Maybe he's waiting for the boys. Maybe he has questions to ask Eston as the head of the family. But what could they be? Nobody was interested in their lives. A few dates in a Farm Book, a price in an account book, a bill of sale, a number in the ledgers of a census taker. No more. At least no more than she was telling.

Her silence was what had kept her alive and sane in this world where everything had been taken from her except these last two sons. And even they knew little about her life. Slaves revealed as little as possible about their origin and background to their children. It was an old trick. Not to speak was not to put into words the hopelessness of having no future and no past. But now, her sons had that future. It was only she who had none. And the past . . . what did she really feel about the past?

Sally Hemings continued to watch the census taker as he sat motionless in his wagon. Why could he not bring himself to drive away?

Nathan Langdon had descended the steep footpath leading away from the Hemings's cabin. He had felt the woman's eyes on him, felt the backward pull of her silence and her peculiar sadness. He could not rid himself of the feeling that once, before today, somewhere, he had seen her. He acknowledged an eerie recognition in their meeting. He smiled. Fate? Reincarnation? How many nights at Harvard had he spent discussing just such nonsense. He was an atheist, like Jefferson. No God could have a hand in anyone's affairs on this earth, for if He did, how could He make such a mess of things?

Monticello, he thought. It had to be Monticello. He had been in the mansion only once in his life, as a student when Jefferson was already a very old man. It must have been in '25, before he had left for Boston. A cousin of his had invited him to sit in the presence of the great man at dinner.

The memory was still vivid. The straight, thin, enormously tall man with the burning eyes and thick white hair, was pale and still freckled, though age had given his face a delicate transparency, and the famous voice had turned edgy and slightly petulant. Thomas Jefferson had dominated the dinner and the company of younger men with vast and brilliant monologues, virtuoso pieces almost like music, which were occasionally interrupted by sullen and inexplicable silences when his thoughts seemed to be elsewhere. But his rejoinders were always precise and to the point. He dearly loved a metaphor, an elegantly turned phrase, and had a genius for storytelling. People around the table spoke a little louder than normal, as is often the case with old people, but, so far as he knew, there had been nothing wrong with Jefferson's hearing or any of his faculties. Even then, at eighty, Thomas Jefferson was known to ride twenty or thirty miles a day. He, Langdon, had sat awed and silent while the conversation had ranged from the tobacco crop to Italian and French wines; the annexation of Cuba; the Monroe Doctrine; the Second Missouri Compromise; and the raging political struggle over the extension of slavery in Illinois.

At the end of the meal, over which his daughter Martha Randolph had presided, Jefferson had been taken with malaise, Langdon remembered. He had floundered in midsentence, gagged, and turned pale, then abruptly pushed back his chair, almost tipping it over. His daughter had quickly taken charge, and, with the help of one of the guests had led the old man from the table. As the company milled around the dining room, Langdon had glimpsed Jefferson being handed over to another woman, who had led him away. Sally Hemings? The small figure had been dwarfed by him; the small sleek head had not reached the stooped shoulders of the fainting man. He remembered, too, a fleeting glimpse of a coiled braid.

The picture was so sharp; it startled Langdon out of his reverie. He leaned down and absently stroked the warm living flesh of his mules, as if to bring himself back to the present. Then he got out his ledgers. He "knew" everyone in Albemarle County—by sex, age, religion, and occupation; by property, political party, race, and condition of servitude. But the two people he thought about at the moment didn't figure on his list.

One had been rich, famous, powerful, covered with honors, and years in the greatest office of the land, respected and loved. He was dead and buried. A permanent fixture in American history. The other had been a slave. A woman despised for her color and her caste; and yet still alive, and so had to be counted.

He opened to a new page in his ledger. If Sally Hemings was who and what people said she was, then Thomas Jefferson had broken the law of Virginia. A law punishable by fine and imprisonment. And he, Langdon, was an official of the United States government and a Virginian. He hesitated for a moment and then wrote:

Eston Hemings, Male, 22. Head of Family. Occupation: Musician. Race: White

Madison Hemings, Male 25. Occupation: Carpenter. Race: White.

Sally Hemings, Female, between 50 and 60. Without occupation. Race: White.

Whatever he thought of Thomas Jefferson, author of the Declaration of Independence, third president of the United States, there was one thing he, Nathan Langdon, was determined that Thomas Jefferson would not be guilty of: the crime of miscegenation.

CHAPTER 2

MONTICELLO, 1815

The whole commerce between master and slave is a perpetual exercise of the most boisterous passions, the most unremitting despotism on the one part, and degrading submissions on the other. Our children see this, and learn to imitate it; for man is an imitative animal. This quality is the germ of all education in him. From his cradle to his grave he is learning to do what he sees others do. If a parent could find no motive either in his philanthropy or his self-love, for restraining the intemperance of passion towards his slave, it should always be a sufficient one that his child is present.

THOMAS JEFFERSON, *Notes on the State of Virginia,* 1790

MR. FRANCIS C. GRAY
March 4, 1815   *Monticello*
Sir,

You asked me in conversation, what constituted a mulatto by our law. And I believe I told you four crossings with the whites. I looked afterwards into our law, and found it to be in these words: "Every person, other than a Negro of whose grandfathers or grandmothers anyone shall have been a Negro, shall be deemed a mulatto, and so every such person who shall have one-fourth part or more of Negro blood, shall in like manner be deemed a mulatto"; L. Virga 1792, December 17: the case put in the first member of this paragraph of the law is *exempli gratia.* The latter contains the true canon, which is that one-fourth of Negro blood, mixed with any portion of white, constitutes the mulatto. As the issue has one-half of the blood of each parent, and the blood of each of these may be made up of a variety of fractional mixtures, the estimate of their compound in some cases may be intricate, it becomes a mathematical problem of the same class with those of the mixtures of different liquors or different metals; as in these, therefore, the algebraical notation is the most convenient and intelligible. Let us express the pure blood of the white in capital letters of the printed alphabet, the pure blood of the negro in the small letters of the printed alphabet, and any given mixture of either, by way of abridgment in MS. letters.

Let the first crossing be of a, pure negro, with A, pure white. The unit of blood of the issue being composed of the half of that of each parent, will be $\frac{a}{2}+\frac{A}{2}$. Call it, for abbreviation, h (half blood).

Let the second crossing be of h and B, the blood of the issue will be $\frac{h}{2}+\frac{B}{2}$, or substituting for $\frac{h}{2}$ its equivalent, it will be $\frac{a}{4}+\frac{A}{4}+\frac{B}{2}$, call it q (quarteroon) being $\frac{1}{4}$ negro blood.

Let the third crossing be of q and C, their offspring will be $\frac{q}{2}+\frac{C}{2}=\frac{a}{8}+\frac{A}{8}+\frac{B}{4}+\frac{C}{2}$, call this e (eighth), who having less than $\frac{1}{4}$ of a, or of pure negro blood, to wit $\frac{1}{8}$ only, is no longer a mulatto, so that a third cross clears the blood.

From these elements let us examine their compounds. For example, let h and q cohabit, their issue will be $\frac{h}{2}+\frac{q}{2}=\frac{a}{4}+\frac{a}{8}+\frac{A}{8}+\frac{B}{4}=\frac{3a}{8}+\frac{3A}{8}+\frac{B}{4}$, wherein we find $\frac{3}{8}$ of a, or negro blood.

Let h and e cohabit, their issue will be $\frac{h}{2}+\frac{e}{2}=\frac{a}{4}+\frac{A}{4}+\frac{a}{16}+\frac{A}{16}+\frac{B}{8}+\frac{c}{4}=\frac{5a}{16}+\frac{5A}{16}+\frac{B}{8}+\frac{c}{4}$, wherein $\frac{5}{16}$ a makes still a mulatto.

Let q and e cohabit, the half of the blood of each will be $\frac{q}{2}+\frac{e}{2}=\frac{a}{8}+\frac{A}{8}+\frac{B}{4}+\frac{a}{16}+\frac{A}{16}+\frac{B}{8}-\frac{C}{4}=\frac{3a}{16}+\frac{3A}{16}+\frac{3B}{8}+\frac{C}{4}$, wherein $\frac{3}{16}$ of a is no longer a mulatto, and thus may every compound be noted and summed, the sum of the fractions composing the blood of the issue being always equal to unit. It is understood in natural history that a fourth cross of one race of animals with another gives an issue equivalent for all sensible purposes to the original blood. Thus a Merino ram being crossed, first with a country ewe, second with his daughter, third with his granddaughter, and fourth with the great-granddaughter, the last issue is deemed pure Merino, having in fact but $\frac{1}{16}$ of the country blood. Our canon considers two crosses with the pure white and a third with any degree of mixture, however small, as clearing the issue of the negro blood. But observe, that this does not re-establish freedom, which depends on the condition of the mother, the principle of the civil law, *partus sequitur ventrem*, being adopted here.

But if *e* emancipated, he becomes a free white man, and a citizen of the United States to all intents and purposes. So much for this trifle by way of correction.

His long legs under the full-length gray frockcoat shifted position, itching for the feel of his horse Eagle between them. He was seventy-two years old. His presidency was six years behind him and those six years had been spent here at home, in retirement, surrounded by those he loved most in the world; his women, his children, his grandchildren, his slaves, his neighbors, his kin. Restless, he rose from his writing table to his full height, the face ascetic and serene in the bright light. He sat down again, and his left hand took up his pen, and as it did, the copying machine he had invented by which a letter written manually with one pen was simultaneously traced with another by a series of connected levers, called a polygraph, followed the movements of his hand. This would be the last letter of the morning.

He looked out of his study windows: it was a view in which nothing mean or small could exist, he thought. That was why he had chosen the site, which commanded the Blue Ridge Mountains: it was one of the boldest and most beautiful horizons in the world. His house, which he called Monticello, giving it the soft Italian pronunciation, stood upon a plain formed by cutting off the top of the mountain.

The light this morning is so pure and delineating, he thought, touched with the soft promise of spring that turns the mountains their deepest blue.

He stared for a moment more at the west lawn, noting several figures gamboling on it—children, he supposed. He smiled. Whoever they were, black or white, they belonged to Monticello. And to him.

He turned his eyes away and picked up his pen. Absently, he massaged his wrist before signing: *Thomas Jefferson.*

CHAPTER 3

ALBEMARLE COUNTY, 1830

But generally it is not sufficient. The parent storms, the child looks on, catches the lineaments of wrath, puts on the same airs in the circle of smaller slaves, gives a loose to his worst of passions, and thus nursed, educated, and daily exercised in tyranny, cannot but be stamped by it with odious peculiarities. The man must be a prodigy who can retain his manners and morals undepraved by such circumstances.

THOMAS JEFFERSON, *Notes on the State of Virginia*, 1790

"Mama, what did you talk about all that time?"

"I don't know, Eston, different things, gossip mostly."

"You mean a white gentleman traveled all the way from Charlottesville to come up here and gossip with you? What did he want? What kind of information? And how do you know he weren't one of those journalists?"

This was Madison Hemings speaking. His voice had a perpetual edge of violence and irritation.

The question sent a flush of surprise up the back of Sally Hemings's neck. As a matter of fact, she had no idea at all if he was a journalist or not. He didn't seem or speak like one, or at least her idea of one, since she had never met a journalist in her entire life. Therefore, she wasn't sure. Besides it was evident from his knowledge of local families and his accent that he was from these parts.

"I told you, Madison, I was afraid it might have been the sheriff and when I saw that it wasn't, well, I was just so relieved I guess I just believed anything. He had to be one or the other, and if he was white and wasn't the sheriff, then he had to be the census taker. He said he was the census taker, and didn't you tell me the census man would be coming round these days? I just assumed he was telling the truth."

"Mama, you believe everything a nice white gentleman tells you! You had no business letting a strange man, white or black, into my house!"

"Our house, Madison," Eston said. "And leave Mama alone. You just scared it might have been the sheriff. I told you Martha Jefferson Randolph is not to be trusted. She hates all of us, and always has."

"Leave Martha out of it, Eston," Madison said. "She had her reasons for helping us—if you can call this run-down, no-dirt farm 'help.' She's no better off herself, living down there in Pottsville, in that dinky house with all her children, and Thomas Mann Randolph, dead as crazy and drunk as a loon. I'm not shedding any tears for Martha Randolph! She didn't have to marry that bastard!"

Of all her children, she thought, Madison was the most difficult, and because he was the one who reminded her of her brother James, she favored him in a way. He, of all her children, was in the most danger. Eston, with his placid nature and good looks, would always get by as a black man or as a white one.

"Mama, admit you were wrong to let him in! He could be a journalist pretending to be the census taker just nosing around for dirt to print," Madison went on.

"You can surely find out if he is the real census taker," his mother answered. "Just ask in town. He said his name was Nathan Langdon and he was born at Broadhurst. He has six brothers and sisters, and his father is old Samuel Langdon and his Uncle John was a friend of Thomas Jefferson. He is fair with a dark beard and about six feet tall, light for a young man, about twenty-seven or -eight. He is going to marry a Wilks girl from Norfolk by the name of Esmeralda, and he just came back from Boston and Harvard, cause his pa is sick and his fiancée upset about his taking so long to come back. Then too, his brother . . . killed in a duel . . ."

"Mama, you found all that out!"

"I was the last count to be made for the day and he was hot and tired. I guess he just stayed on longer than he intended."

"Was he waiting for us to come home?"

"Not really. He asked about you both; and wanted to know how he could reach you for some work his father needs done at the plantation. I told him he could find you after curfew if he needed to."

"You mean you invited him back?"

"Well, that was the least I could do, he's—"

"White, Mama! I don't want him in the house. Any business he has with me, he can find me at the university. Any business with anybody can be conducted at the front door. And you were alone. . . . What if—"

"Madison, for heaven sakes. Not all white men are rapists!"

"No? Just remember Stokes's wife, stuck out there past the Channing place. . . . Didn't happen less than two months ago. A free colored man's wife, free colored man's property doesn't mean anything in this county. They don't want free coloreds in Virginia. They've made that pretty clear. One false step—even one—and you are in a chain gang heading for Georgia or South Carolina, papers or no papers. Just sudden like that. Nobody ever found out what happened to Willy Dubois. Where'd he go? In the dead of night? After curfew. Just disappeared, leaving hearth and home, wife, mother, and five children. Now just where did he go? I don't want any strange men in this house, Mama, black or white. You hear me, Eston?"

"I hear you," Eston said, moving over protectively to his mother.

Eston Hemings was a beautiful man. He was huge, over six feet four, with bright red hair and a continent of pale freckles on a clear milky skin that showed no trace of a beard. He had enormous hands that could carve the most delicate designs—flowers, scrolls, fruit—in any wood that grew, and could wrench the most beautiful notes out of his instruments—the pianoforte and the Italian violin. His features were regular and delicate, like his mother's, with a high wide rather long nose and a generous sensual mouth. Already there were laugh marks around his pale-blue eyes. He was broad of shoulder with a surprisingly long and girl-like neck.

Eston knew that when Madison was like this, something bad had happened to him in town. Maybe he would

tell them, and maybe he wouldn't. Madison had a damned
irritating way of doing everything. He was the darkest in
the family, and his cool slender grace, his animal vitality
and cockiness, seemed an affront to both races. He was
always getting into trouble: rows with shopkeepers over
bills, with foremen over plans, with masons over blueprints,
with other carpenters over techniques, with the landlord,
with the bank, with the tax collector. With everybody, nigh
on. Madison should leave for the Territories, thought Eston.
Now. Before he really got into some scrape he wouldn't
be able to get out of. Eston knew why Mama would never
leave here. He could take care of Mama alone. He wasn't
in love. He wasn't trying to prove to some freeborn girl
how great a man he was.

Madison Hemings felt the gentle but firm pressure of his
brother's rough hand steering him toward the back door of
the cabin and the cool fragrant night air. The gentle, in-
sistent pressure calmed and soothed him. He clamped shut
his jaw in an effort to stop tears of rage.

Why was he so upset? Why had he yelled at his mother?
The real reason, he knew, was fear. . . . He was scared to
death that something was going to happen to ruin their
fragile existence, before they even got a chance to live it.
He didn't want to tell anyone about what had happened to
him today in town. Not even Eston. Eston could feel his
brother's neck muscles tense, but he said nothing.

Outside, they faced the dying red sun sinking below the
delicate line of the peach trees they had planted more than
a year ago. Beyond that lay the boundaries of Monticello.
Normally a thick whitewashed birch fence cut across the
dark green of the pine woods, marking the end of the
plantation on the southwest side. But the fences were now
mostly down, and those standing were a dirty disinherited
gray. The crossbeams lay on the nettle-packed ground
where they had fallen.

Madison stared at this unkempt frontier. It seemed to
be the line between his former life and this one. He
would never understand why his mother refused to leave
this place; why she deliberately chose a rented house so
close to Monticello. Was it that she wanted to be reminded,
every minute of every day, of her former servitude, of her
concubinage?

His mother had never told him anything of his origins. He knew that slave women never told their offspring anything. So slave children learned what they could when they could, in bits and pieces from older slaves, mammies, white people's conversations, and the bitterness of what they learned was all the more wounding. It intensified the shame without alleviating the burden. He remembered the shock of learning from some old crone that he was the son of the master. Even his grandmother hadn't told him! He was their son; yet neither father nor mother seemed to love him for it! He had tried to understand. He had stood for hours looking at his pale-yellow face in the polished silver mirrors of the Big House. He would run down to this very frontier, far from the Big House, and butt his head against the white-birch fencing until the blood came, because he couldn't understand why his father didn't love him. Madison stared at the fence posts now, as if he expected to see the stains of his childish blood still on them.

Madison looked up. He and Eston watched their mother slip under the high gray railing of the frontier of Monticello. Gathering her skirts as she went, she was walking up the mountains toward the cemeteries.

When she was upset or angry she could usually be found either by the grave of Thomas Jefferson or that of her mother, Elizabeth Hemings. They divided her loyalties in death as they had in life. When her sons saw her turn eastward, they knew she was heading toward the slave cemetery and their grandmother.

CHAPTER 4

ALBEMARLE COUNTY, 1830

And with what execration should the statesman be loaded, who permitting one half the citizens thus to trample on the rights of the other, transforms those into despots, and these into enemies, destroys the morals of the one part, and the amor patriae of the other. For if a slave can have a country in this world, it must be any other in preference to that in which he is born to live and labour for another: in which he must lock up the faculties of his nature, contribute as far as depends on his individual endeavours to the evanishment of the human race, or entail his own miserable condition on the endless generations proceeding from him.

THOMAS JEFFERSON, *Notes on the State of Virginia*, 1790

Sally Hemings closed her eyes and sank down at the foot of the neat rectangle marked off by smooth stones and planted with primroses. Fresh grass was growing within its boundaries. A wooden cross that had been lovingly carved by Eston Hemings had replaced the original tombstone. It didn't seem possible that twenty-three years had passed since one of the two pillars of her life had crumbled. Elizabeth Hemings had died on August 22, 1807, at the age of seventy-two. She had outlived her daughter's father, John Wayles, by over twenty-five years. It had not been an easy death. It had taken the whole, humid fever-infested month of August to kill her. Two months before she had died, she had stopping eating and had taken to her bed. But even starvation had been slow to weaken the fabulous constitution that had survived almost three-quarters of a century of slavery and the birth of fourteen children. Resistant to all the infections that killed childbearing women in their

27

forties; immune to all the malarial fevers, the typhoid and
yellow fevers that struck eighteenth-century Virginians in
their swampy, unhealthy climate; untouched by the periodic
outbreaks of cholera; without physical blemish or congenital weakness, she had survived everything, including
her own biography.

Against her closed eyelids Sally Hemings could still see
the oppressive, insect-filled interior of that slave cabin
where she and Martha Randolph had watched her mother
strain toward death with the same prodigious will that had
sustained her in life. In the sweltering heat of that room
she and Martha had sat in a strange and southern circle of
complicity: the concubine, daughter, the mistress and
the slave; the aunt and the niece. The three women
reflected the intricate and convoluted ties that bound them
one to the other: blood, love, servitude, hate, womanhood,
time. All flowed together in the vehement heat of that day
when Elizabeth Hemings, struggling, frantically seeking an
exit from the life she had endured, had whispered, "Put
your hand on my chest and push down; my heart won't
stop beating."

Monticello, August 22, 1807

"I never knew of but one white man who bore the name
of Hemings. He was an Englishman and my father. My
mother was a full-blooded African and a native of that
country. My father was a Captain of an English sailing
vessel. Captain Hemings, my mama told me, was a hunter
of beasts like her father, except that he hunted in the sea
and his prey was the whale.

"He sailed between England and Williamsburg, then a
great port. When the Captain heard of my birth, he determined to buy me and my mother, who belonged to John
Wayles. He approached Master Wayles with an extraordinary high offer for us, but amalgamation was just beginning and Master Wayles wanted to see how I would
turn out. He refused my father's offer. Captain Hemings
begged, pleaded, threatened, and finally they had words.
All to no avail; my master refused to sell. My father,
thwarted in the purchase but determined to own his own

flesh and blood, then resolved to take us by stealth. His ship was sailing; everything was in readiness. But we were betrayed by fellow slaves, and John Wayles took us up to the Big House and locked us in. Captain Hemings's ship sailed without us.

"We were kept at the Big House, but my mother never recovered. She kept running away. I must have run away six times before I could walk! Her master warned her that the next time she did it she would be punished not by the regular beating she got every time they sent her back, but by the legal punishment for runaways: branding of an 'R,' for runaway, on the cheek.

"She ran away again, and John Wayles ordered the punishment. It was the overseer that was to do it. My mama screamed and hollered and fought. She was a strong woman, my mother, and it took four men to hold her. But when the brand approached her skin, John Wayles's hand shot out against that iron. He had meant to knock it from the hand of the overseer, but the blow only spoiled his aim, and the brand came down on mama's right breast instead of her face. The slaves witnessing the punishment thought Master Wayles was going to kill that overseer.

"My mother never ran away again. There is something about a brand in the flesh that will stay with you until death. You never forget. Beatings you can forget. But not the scar. Especially a woman. My mother went to the fields, and I was kept at the Big House.

"Then one day when I was about fourteen going on fifteen, my mistress took me by the hair. I mean she just took a whole handful of my hair and half dragged me down to the tobacco fields. And there she left me, just left me. I never saw her face again, for when I returned to the Big House, she was long dead. I stayed in the fields. I was given to a slave named Abe for Abraham, and bore him six children.

"Twelve years later, John Wayles took me as his slave mistress, despite the fact I had already bore six children for Abe, who went and died on me. John Wayles had seen three wives die. The first, Martha Eppes Wayles, died within three weeks of her daughter Martha's birth. The second wife, a Miss Cocke, bore four daughters, three of

whom—Elizabeth, Tabitha, and Anne—grew to maturity.
After she died, he married Elizabeth Lomax, who survived
only eleven months. When that last one died, he took me
into the Big House as concubine. I had grown up in the Big
House, and now I came back as housekeeper. I was twenty-
six-years old, the year was 1762, and Martha Wayles was
thirteen. In 1772, John Wayles was still dealing in slaves,
buying, selling, and breeding them. By that time I had
borne him four children: Robert, James, Peter, and Critta.
In 1767, when Martha was eighteen, she married her cousin
and left Bermuda Hundred, only to return less than two
years later a widow. She stayed at home until she married
Thomas Jefferson three years later on a snowy January
first. I served the passions of John Wayles and ran his
household for eleven years, from the time I was twenty-six
until he died in 1773, three months after the birth of his
last child, Sally. My life was connected with his white
children, especially Martha, as well as my own children
by him. I loved them all.

"I cared for them all. Like they were mine. The younger
girls didn't remember, but Martha always remembered. Of
all the white children, I loved her most. I followed her to
Monticello; I nursed her in her illnesses and saw her die a
little after every birth, trying for a son for Thomas Jefferson. For her darling. And he let her try and let her kill
herself trying, then mourned her—monstrous—as did I.

"Somehow, I could never forgive him when he knew
he was killing her; when he knew after the first child she
had no business trying again. Her body going give out. But
he was hit even harder than me. We struggled, we did, both
of us to gain our equilibrium. I cried and he burned.
Burned all her things. All her letters. Her portraits. Her
diary. Her clothes. Everything. Weren't right to destroy
what was hers like that. That was rage. Rage against God,
and rage against God is blasphemous. He could get angrier
than any man I knew. For a while, I thought he was going
to get so mad he was going to kill himself.

"But I couldn't think about self-murder 'cause I had all
those children. I had ten of my twelve children with me
when I went to Martha. John Wayles died not freeing me,
nor any of my children. I told all my daughters, beautiful

things all of you, don't love no masta if he don't promise
in writing to free your children. Don't do it. Get killed
first, get beaten first. The best is not to love them in the
first place. Love your own color. That brings pain enough.
Love your own color if you can, and if you're chosen, get
that freedom for your children. I didn't get mine, nor for
my children. I can't say he promised it to me, so I can't say
he didn't keep his promise. He never promised and I never
asked. I just expected. A terrible thing for a slave to do.
Expect.

"Found myself at Monticello, property of Thomas Jefferson. I just said to myself I weren't going to die of it. I'd
just get on with caring for Martha and my children and
hers. I couldn't let go, you see, I just had too many heads
to hold. My last two children were born at Monticello. One
by a slave husband Smith. The other, I don't like to speak
about. Got raped is what happened. And not just once.
Nothing to do about it. He was a white carpenter named
John Nelson. Nothing to do but to have the child and to
love it. It wasn't his fault how he got here. He was my
last. My baby. When I was almost fifty.

"Despite all the misery, and the bondage and the hard
work, I loved life. The idea, you see, was to survive. Not
go under with grief: the game was to last out the day and
the night and garner enough strength for the next. And,
Lord, I needed that strength. First, I had Bermuda Hundred
to run, that huge sprawling house and all them slaves.
Then I had Monticello. The house was smaller, but Thomas
Jefferson was always tearing it up, rebuilding, so I could
never get that plantation running like I wanted. Every time
things would quiet down and I would get the house and
the servants all orderly, why he would come back from
Philadelphia or New York and we would be in the brick
and plaster again. Reduce me to tears, it did. Poor Martha
never did see her house finished. She was poorly a lot of
the time and she hated when he was away. She hated that
politics anyway. But she loved the man. She loved him. I
kept telling her to hold on. To try and garner her strength.
Not to try to keep up with him, because Thomas Jefferson
would live to be a hundred. Strongest man I ever did see.
Twenty, thirty miles on horseback every day. He was like

me in temperament, except he sometimes got his moods or
his 'depressions,' as Martha would call them. He liked his
privacy, too. Didn't want Martha sticking her head out
too much either. He was a jealous and possessive man. And
he had a temper—oh, he was sweetness and light—but I
saw it. He had a monumental temper when he was riled.
Even when it didn't come out. He thought it weren't
dignified . . . but he had it. I could sometimes smell that
brimstone inside him. Sometimes he would just look at me
smelling it, and laugh. He stayed out of my way. He stayed
out of my household affairs, so we got on. I liked him, I
did. And I guess he did love my Martha in his way. But he
never did understand women, really.

"When his mother died in 1776, why he did the same
thing he did later with his wife's belongings when *she* died;
he burned everything—letters, portraits, mementos—everything. He didn't want anyone to know him, yet I never saw
a man who so much needed to be known and loved. Well,
Martha Wayles loved him, and so do you Sally. I can pass
down to you what I knowed about Thomas Jefferson,
which ain't much. But nobody can teach you how not to be
hurt when you love a white man.

"I say 'love' if that's what can pass between a slave and
a free white man, or a slave and free white woman. I
loved Martha like a mother, and I loved Wayles like a wife.
Trouble was I didn't ask for nothing, and nothing's what
I got in the end. When I realized who I was or what I was,
I made up my mind I might be called a slave, but I wasn't
going to live no slavish life. I wasn't going to go out of my
way to be no slave. I tried to pass that on to all my children. One thing I always insisted was that we had a family
name—Hemings. Hemings. And I wanted all my children
to be addressed by it. Made them remember they had a
surname! I tried to get them interested in life. In seeing
what was going to happen next. Even slaves have things
happen to them. Even in a slave's world, something got to
be happening all the time. I believe in life-preserving and
love.

"I believe in having a secret life with secret plans and
secret dreams. Just like having a little vegetable garden to
yourself out back of your cabin like mine. You got to work

it at night or real early in the morning, but it's yours. Same
with dreams. Maybe you got to work them late at night or
real early in the morning, but nobody can take them out
of your head lest they kill you and if you work ain't nobody going to kill you, cause you too valuable. Lord, God,
I would fight the suicides."

All through the sweltering summer afternoons, Elizabeth
Hemings ran out her life with words. They flowed on until
dusk and until she was too exhausted to speak. Many of
the stories, Sally Hemings and Martha Randolph had
heard a dozen times, yet they clung to Elizabeth Hemings
as to a floating log in a rapid. And Elizabeth Hemings
carried them faster and faster down her particular river of
memory. Rivulets of incidents, old family jokes, intrigues,
feuds, births, and deaths, trickled through the ramblings of
each afternoon.

She reached back further and further, her hands hovering
over the quilts as if she were choosing the bits and pieces
of a mosaic in colored glass, each cut glass reflecting other
past events which brought on still other images of her life.
Sally Hemings thought that she would never be able to
remember her own life so well, and Martha Randolph too
was amazed at the richness of this slave's recollections. For
the two women tending her, there had never been a time
when there was not an Elizabeth Hemings.

"After John Wayles's death, all of us slaves were divided
up amongst the inheritance of the four living daughters,
Martha and her three half sisters. Martha took me and ten
of my children. The other two went with Tibby. I didn't
come here to Monticello until after your birth, Patsy. Came
with Sally, who was two years old, and the baby Thenia.

"Thomas Jefferson was a rich man in those days. Yea,
rich. He inherited one hundred thirty-five slaves from John
Wayles, including us Hemingses, and eleven thousand
acres. He had four plantations: Monticello, which wasn't
much to begin with, but with all his building became the
most beautiful; Poplar Forest, where we all went after
them British came 'round for us; Elk Island; and Elkhill.
Life was sweet for Martha up until all the trouble about the

independency came along. First thing, Thomas Jefferson out defending a mulatto who claimed freedom because his great-grandmother was a white woman who had him by a black slave father. Masta Jefferson saying the sins of the father shouldn't be visited on the third generation, or generations without end, and that that boy was free because he was the great-grandson of a free white woman, and it is the mother who determines slavery in Virginia. He lost. Didn't no Virginian wants to hear nothing about no white lady having no black children. Used to sell any white woman and her child into slavery for it: five or ten years for the mother, and thirty for the child. They used to believe, back in those days, a white lady have one black baby, all her babies coming black. Now, if that were so, why didn't it apply just as well to us? Then came this Stamp Act. I heard all about that. This ruckus up in Boston with white men disguised as black folks and Indians throwing tea into the water, and first thing, Thomas Jefferson finds this thrilling and writes a 'revolutionary document,' as Martha called it. Telling the English where they could go and what they could do, which made him a traitor to the Crown and liable to get himself hung and quartered. Poor Martha was fit to be tied. She told me all the terrible dangerous things her husband was doing, running risks of losing his fortune, his name, and his head.

"But Masta Jefferson was right happy. He racing around feeling good, smiling, writing, speechifying. Then he got one of them headaches like he got after his mama died. Headaches and dysentery were his two ailments. All coming from his nerves and that hot temper. Then he left home with my son Robert for Philadelphia. He went to the Continental Congress with all them famous men of those revolutionary times. His little girl died at eighteen months, and Masta came racing home, but it was too late then. Martha grieved something terrible and Masta Jefferson begged her to come back with him to Philadelphia, but she wouldn't go. Masta Jefferson went on back to Philadelphia and wrote his Declaration of Independency which made him the most famous man in Virginia, maybe in all the colonies. Martha didn't care. She didn't want no revolution, but she didn't say nothing to her husband but once.

"Only that Christmas in '75 she pleaded with him to give up politics. There was the death of little Jane still grieving her, and she pleaded with him to give up politics, to give up making war on England. Of course by this time it was too late; I could have told her that. Masta Jefferson was not going to give up his politicking for no mortal. She mostly couldn't stand the separations. She said she wasn't like Abigail Adams, who loved politics and who pushed her husband. Yet she wouldn't go to Philadelphia with him even when she was well. She fought and pleaded, but he struggled. It was a hard thing to ask an ambitious man like him to give up his life's work. Well, England was getting riled up and sending troops and commanders and generals, and landed them mostly where they liked. It got around amongst the slaves that the English was taking slaves into their army and offering them their freedom and giving them uniforms. It seems they had three hundred in the army in Maryland with 'Liberty to Slaves' on their breasts. I sure would have liked to have seen that. Black men in uniform with rifles, and before you known it, we was at war.

"The second year of the war, Martha finally bore a son for her husband. He lived only until June fourteenth, and we buried him without a name. Only Patsy lived now, and I thought Martha was going to lose her mind. She had lost three children, counting her son by her first marriage. I had seen women lose five, seven, ten children before they was two years old. There's nothing in this life harder than burying your own children. I thank God it never happened to me. Oh, I've buried two now, but they were full-grown men.

"Martha got with child again as soon as she could, and the next year she had Polly, who was blessed to live. At least she lived long enough to marry. But Martha was slow coming back this time. She was scared of dying, scared of losing Polly, scared of losing another child, and scared of having another.

"Masta Jefferson started in rebuilding again Monticello. Things weren't going too well for him. It seems we were losing this war he started. He was governor of Virginia now, with his seat of government in Williamsburg, but he

weren't made to be no war general. The generals and
officers that did come to Monticello during those times was
mostly German and English, prisoners of war, at least
that's what they was called. But, they was treated like
guests. Many a musical evening and dinner took place for
foreign gentlemen fighting against us. One German lady,
wife of a general, followed her husband clean to our shores
and was lodged at Monticello along with him. Twenty-two
slaves run away from Monticello to join the English army,
eleven of them women. Lord, then come the day British
dragoons came looking for Governor Jefferson, saying they
wanted to put a pair of silver handcuffs on him. Searched
the house they did from top to bottom and took off poor
Isaac to the army, with his mother there screaming and
crying. I guess this decided Martha to move to Williamsburg with the masta and then to Richmond, where she
again got pregnant. This left the plantation for me and my
son Martin to run alone. Never knowing when the soldiers
would show up or nothing. Coping with slaves running to
join the English right and left, and taking everything they
could eat and anything that weren't nailed down. In
November eighty, Martha come home and Lucy Elizabeth,
the first, was born."

"Lord, here come the British again. They showed up
again in June eighty-one. Jack Jouett rode all night to
reach Monticello with the news that the British general,
Tarlton as I recall, was coming to capture Thomas Jefferson. Jouett was all cut up from the thickets. He carried
them scars on him to his grave. He was in a *state* that
morning. I cleaned him up and got something to eat in
him and then off he rode. Masta Jefferson sent off Martha
and Patsy and Polly and all the white people to Poplar
Forest. You remember that, Patsy? Sally, you stayed with
me. You was scared and trembling something terrible.
Thomas Jefferson sat and had his breakfast at his leisure
and then when he saw through his telescope that the
English was coming up the mountain, he got his horse
saddled and rode off toward Carter's mountain. I was the
one who met the English at the door. But I made Martin
open it for me. But before that we was running around

getting the silver together for Caesar, who was hiding it under the floorboards. The English was banging on the door and Martin, he let the plank drop on poor Caesar, leaving him under the house, trapped underneath the floorboards. He told me later that he could hear them boards groaning and creaking under them dragoons' feet. One of the soldiers put a gun to Martin's chest and said he'd fire if Martin didn't tell him in what direction Masta Jefferson had rode out. Martin said 'Fire away then!' And poor little Sally thought she was about to see her half brother shot dead, and she started screaming, but they didn't shoot anybody. They rode out the next day just as nice as yous please, not taking anything and leaving me and Martin in charge. If I had thought, we could have hid Thomas Jefferson in Caesar's place! I've often laughed with the masta about that.

"Masta Jefferson, he didn't have no more heart for governing after that. Them militia weren't fighting properly, breaking and running and deserting, and half of them couldn't shoot straight no-how. Wouldn't let the slaves fight, those Virginians, although slaves was fighting on both sides in Maryland and Pennsylvania and Carolina. But those militia boys, they was just farmers and yeomen and backwoodsmen. They didn't know anything about fighting a real army with real uniforms and all. It was just a mess. Then to top it all off, Masta Jefferson fell off Caractacus and was laid up for six weeks. He's had six horses in his life. He loves them bay horses, especially that tall horse with white hind feet. Well, anyway, he was a changed man after the British raided the capital. Martha, she was in heaven and hell—that is she was with child again, even after all the troubles we had after Lucy Elizabeth. This here was her seventh pregnancy. I didn't leave her for the whole nine months, and Masta Jefferson neither.

"He put his office up in the little room next to hers at Monticello to wait it out. Started writing a new book on Virginia. Heard it said he didn't care much for black folks mixing with white folks. Anyway, about that time Masta Jefferson sent Martin out after that slave boy Custer, who had run off to Williamsburg—never did catch him. In May of eighty-two, Martha gave birth to another girl child and

named it after the one she had lost, Lucy Elizabeth. I
didn't say nothing, but I didn't want that name for that
child. It seemed to be a bad omen, and I was right. Lucy
survived until the age of four, but Martha didn't live to
see her face but for another seventeen months. Martha
knew she was dying, and I knew it, and Masta Jefferson,
he knew it, but nobody said nothing until the end. Lord,
when he see her die . . . And she not yet thirty-four."

Elizabeth Hemings gazed from under the half-closed
eyelids at the two women watching her die. Martha was
stubborn about coming to sit with her. It was her duty as
mistress of the house to attend to dying slaves.

Those two sat there like they were made of wood, Elizabeth Hemings thought. They had always had a talent for
stillness. She had never been able to sit still. She was doing
her best to die, before they murdered her, but she was
dying hard. She always knew she would have a hard time
dying. There they sat, and she lay, the three of them, waiting for death. They had all lived their lives according to
the rules: the rules of master and slave, man and woman,
husband and wife, lover and mistress. The one who had
called the rules and who had made the game was gone
riding, loath to associate himself with all this women business of dying and watching other people die. She knew
these two would mourn him when his time came, more than
they would ever mourn her, and could she blame them?
They had been birth'd and trained for that. She herself had
trained her own daughter, her favorite child, to the triple
bondage of slave, woman, and concubine, as one trains a
blooded horse to its rider, never questioning the rights of
the rider. If she hadn't done that, her daughter would
never have come home from Paris.

Lordy, yes. She had procured for her master. She had
made him a present of what she had loved most in the
world. How could she have known that her vision of the
perfect slave would coincide with his vision of the perfect
woman? And Sally Hemings loved Thomas Jefferson. That
was the tragedy. Love, not slavery. And God knew how
much slavery there was in love . . .

Oh, the small degree of love she had felt for John Wayles
had given her some measure of privilege, of barter, of

freedom, of pride, of comfort. . . . No, her daughter's was
a love of which she had had only an inkling. Sally had no
worldly pride, no independence, no idea of justice. She was
still childish, rancorless, detached, except for that which
concerned what she loved. Sally was not even conscious of
injuries inflicted upon her, and of the self-possession it took
to forgive, she had not one grain of that.

The old woman continued to examine the placid and
unlined face of her favorite daughter. She wanted to scream
at her to run away. But it was too late. Much too late.
Nothing could change now. If only she had understood in
the beginning that her daughter had been constituted for
love the way some women are constituted for breeding.
Her life had left no trace on her body or her spirit. She
could absorb everything. Not like poor tormented Martha
Randolph with her twelve children by her insane and
drunken husband, and her passion for a father she could
never quite please. Martha with her awkward body, and her
plain looks, and her quick temper hidden under migraine
headaches, like her father.

Elizabeth Hemings felt a sudden mixture of love and
contempt for them both. She turned her head away from
them and fell silent.

The pause seemed longer than necessary, and Sally
Hemings automatically continued: "I was forty-seven and
Sally was thirteen, Martha she was twelve," and waited for
the discourse to continue. But Elizabeth Hemings did not
pick up the thread of her tale.

"Mama?"

"She's dead, Sally." Martha's voice was like a rock under
her.

Martha tried to rise, fell back, and then, with a moan,
threw herself over Elizabeth Hemings's still body.

Sally Hemings remained seated, staring at Martha as if
she had gone mad. Her mother couldn't be dead. Her
mother had something eminently important to tell her. She
had waited all these weeks to hear it. Like the keys to the
mansion, it was information that had to be passed on
from black woman to black woman, just as she would pass
it on to her own children. Her mother couldn't be dead
because she didn't know the secret. Her mother had taken
it along with her slavehood to the grave.

She felt a chill. Her mother's face was calm, smiling. She had murdered herself before they had done it for her.

"Mama!"

Sally Hemings tore Martha's encompassing arms from around Elizabeth Hemings and began to shake the frail body of her mother.

Even Martha, who was strong, could not unlock the two women. It was Thomas Jefferson, who, with all his force, finally wrenched his mistress away from her mother and carried her in his arms from the cabin, as the other slave women began the ritual wail which echoed from cabin to cabin, following them along Mulberry Row, as he strode grimly back with her to the Big House.

Elizabeth Hemings had a fine funeral. All her children, grandchildren, and their children were summoned to Monticello from the neighboring plantations. One hundred and four descendants, all answering to the surname of Hemings, came to pay their last respects. Black. Brown. Yellow. White. All slaves.

HERE LIES THE BELOVED
ELIZABETH (BET) HEMINGS
OF
MONTICELLO
BORN 1735   DIED 1807

"Mama—" She paused as if she expected an answer. "I'm so lonely."

The last sound came from her throat like the rasp of a night cricket. Sally Hemings stretched across the rectangle of earth and pressed her face into the cool young April grass.

CHAPTER 5

ALBEMARLE COUNTY, JUNE 1831

> With the morals of the people, their industry also is
> destroyed. For in a warm climate, no man will labour for
> himself who can make another labour for him. This is so
> true, that of the proprietors of slaves a very small propor-
> tion indeed are ever seen to labour. And can the liberties
> of a nation be thought secure when we have removed
> their only firm basis, a conviction in the minds of the
> people that these liberties are of the gift of God? That
> they are not to be violated but with his wrath?
>
> THOMAS JEFFERSON, *Notes on the State of Virginia*, 1790

It had been more than a year since the census taker's first
visit. Several months had passed before he appeared again,
but thereafter Nathan Langdon's visits to Sally Hemings
had become almost regular. Madison and Eston had finally
accepted the presence of this tall lanky Virginian. They
had become friends of a sort. Langdon never arrived
empty-handed. There was always the town news, a book,
or a newspaper, or a pamphlet, or some exotic fruit off one
of the West India boats, some New England sweets, or a
tool catalogue for Eston. Today he had brought something
special.

Nathan Langdon entered and sat in the battered armchair while his hostess placed herself opposite him. She
had prepared something to drink, and the silver platter,
with its silver pitcher, was no more incongruous than his
"unofficial" visits to the recluse Sally Hemings. In the
rounded curve of the silver pitcher lay reflections, mauve
and green, of the room. There was also a pool of yellow
light in the center of the tray, heavy and still. The woman

before him had raised her arm to pour into the small
goblet.

The South had anchored these two people into predetermined, unbridgeable positions. Yet all they both represented
was suddenly shrouded in such ambiguity that it made
them ill at ease. The light made this forbidden woman almost ethereal, and, for a moment, Langdon imagined their
separate worlds coming together. He was filled with a sense
of forboding intimacy.

"What is it?" asked his hostess, eyeing the package he was
offering her.

"New poems by Lord Byron. Straight off the ship from
London!"

"I have never read much poetry. . . . A little in French
when I was in Paris. My teacher used to give us lines to
memorize. . . ."

"Byron is the most famous English poet living."

"Thank you, Nathan. How I envy those who can express
themselves with words."

"Most people express themselves with too many words
. . . such as Southern lawyers. Verbosity is not lacking in
any Virginian. And what they can't talk about, they write
in their journals. Even I have succumbed to it."

"You keep a journal, Nathan?"

"Since I went North. I felt it was my duty to record the
horrors of the North as seen by a true Virginian for my
compatriots who didn't dare cross the boundaries between
Heaven and Hell. . . . I called it 'Reflections of a Virginia
Gentleman on the Manners and Morals of Boston Society.'
I fancied myself a Southern de Tocqueville. . . .

"During your stay in France, didn't you keep a journal?"

"I?" Sally Hemings smiled. "I was fifteen and though I
spent most of my time inside the ministry, I did see a great
deal that I felt I wanted to record. I was also there during
the storming of the Bastille in 1789. My brother James saw
much more than I did. He ventured outside and mixed with
the crowds. It was like being in the middle of a rapid, he
said. I will never forget that day."

"And you kept a record of it?"

"A childish record, but a record nevertheless."

"It should be a precious document."

"My diary, a precious document? For me, perhaps.

Maria gave it to me on the boat sailing to France. I could hardly write at the time. . . . I have since copied those first attempts over. . . ." Sally Hemings stopped talking. She wanted to change the subject. Did he think she could be persuaded to share her most private possession?

She frowned. When she had decided to receive the census taker as a "caller" rather than as a representative of the class and power that governed her life, she had done so impulsively, responding to a strength and warmth she sensed in him. He had never asked to visit, nor had he been invited; yet week after week, he appeared at the cabin. Why she continued a relationship which she knew to be dangerous to her sons, she didn't know. And now she felt trapped. What was it that made her look forward to his visits? Vanity? Yes, she enjoyed the attentions of a young man, his strivings to please her. Loneliness? Perhaps. Langdon seemed to infuse a confidence in her she had never known before.

In the long afternoons of recounting her past, she had discovered that she had indeed had a life: a life full of deep and complex feelings. When he had questioned her, she had answered him in the only manner she was capable of: truthfully. Searching for the right tone, the exact phrase evoking as accurately as she could what she remembered. A sort of conspiracy had developed between them. There were times she didn't even feel like mentioning his visits to Eston and Madison. After all these years, she thought, how could she again be anticipating a man's visit? She found herself careful of her clothes, of her hair.

The secretive nature of their relationship seemed almost fitting. Had it not always been thus with her? Always the forbidden? It would have been more fitting, she thought, if, instead of exchanging thoughts, they exchanged pleasures. This would have been much more acceptable than what they were doing; for thoughts, feelings, and memories were all a slave, or ex-slave, had to call her own. Even Thomas Jefferson had bowed to that rule. He had loved her as a woman and owned her as a slave, but her thoughts had always remained beyond his or anyone's control.

Nathan Langdon realized he had crossed the invisible barrier Sally Hemings had put between them and she smiled back at him.

"My writing upsets me. It reminds me that so many years have elapsed since anything has happened in my life."

"Do you know of the famous poetess who lived in Boston, named Phillis Wheatley? She was an ex-slave and highly praised for her poetry."

"No, I have never heard of her."

"I hear the abolitionists publish her widely." .

"Even in the South?"

"Oh, publications slip in. Many people read and like her poetry and don't know that she was black and an ex-slave."

"You should say 'freedwoman,' not ex-slave, Nathan. You make it sound like a punishment instead of a liberty."

Nathan Langdon stared at the small face gazing intently into his. He wondered how these conversations would sound to an eavesdropper of his own color. In the beginning, he had posed simple questions, staying away from the subject of slavery. Yet as this had been the central element of her life, it was impossible not to touch on it in a thousand ways. As Sally Hemings's life story was unfolding, both the narrator and the listener had been overwhelmed by the weight and breadth of it. Langdon was awed at the intricacy of the information he was receiving. He was also well aware that it was compromising him both politically and emotionally. He had by now become hopelessly attached to this woman. More than that he had become involved with her.

He was spellbound by the fading echoes of her existence as bits and pieces came to him.

Sally Hemings regretted her confidences to Nathan, yet on the days that he didn't come she was disappointed. She still prepared for his visits carefully, reaching in her memory for incidents or names that would impress or amuse him. Despite herself, she spoke more and more openly. She opened drawer after drawer of memories, which she rearranged, changed, aired, discussed, and counted, like linen. Her volatile performances, for that was what they were now, excited and fascinated Langdon.

"They were just men," she would say with a smile when she spoke of those heroes already carved in marble (all except the dubious Aaron Burr). She and her sisters and her uncles and her mother and her mother before her had all been an unseen army, treated as if they could not see, hear, or feel. Yet their contact with the whiteworld they served had been devastatingly intimate, subversively real.

Clinging to her words, Nathan followed the complicated plots and the many famous characters, slave and free, devotedly. Now, Langdon hardly asked a question. There was no need. Words followed in an unending stream. Sally Hemings spoke with a kind of desperation, willing him to understand. Sometimes she would take on the accent of the person she was describing. She was a talented mime. She didn't realize that while she was merely recounting her past to Nathan Langdon, she was in fact uncovering a person she had never known from a life she had had no sense of. From these afternoons emerged a new Sally Hemings.

CHAPTER 6

ALBEMARLE COUNTY, 1831

> Indeed I tremble for my country when I reflect that God is just: that his justice cannot sleep for ever: that considering numbers, nature and natural means only, a revolution of the wheel of fortune, an exchange of situation, is among possible events: that it may become probable by devine interference!
>
> THOMAS JEFFERSON, *Notes on the State of Virginia*, 1790

Nathan Langdon had run into the close-mouthed, protective silence of Tidewater society concerning the Hemings affair, as well as the "official" family denial by the Randolphs. But everyone knew the reason the Hemingses were left in peace; the reason Sally Hemings would not budge from the frontier of Monticello. For Nathan Langdon, the Hemings affair was a parenthesis in the Institution; it neither condemned nor knighted it. He felt that there was something sinister in this blatant misuse of a master's absolute power. But then, did one have absolute power when one was in love? That Sally Hemings was a victim was certain. Her submissiveness was what had made her the perfect slave, but, to his mind, the perfect woman as well. To misuse his moral or physical power over a woman, however, was abhorrent to him. A man's power over a woman was like the master's power over a slave. It came from an innate superiority.

"You would think my life depended on my telling you everything, Nathan." She paused. Perhaps it did, she thought. She stared at the man she had just addressed. Langdon returned her quizzical glance with one of such tenderness that Sally Hemings was forced to lower her

eyes, but not before returning the look in a way that told
Langdon he was not the first to have fallen in love with
Sally Hemings. He had the impression that this woman had
never really used her beauty to manipulate men. Was it
because, as a slave, she had had no concept of power? Or
was it because, as a slave, her beauty simply had held no
threat and was thus neutral both to herself and others? Had
she used this power in Paris? Over Jefferson? He flushed.
He would soon be a married man, he thought ruefully, and
instead of concentrating on Esmeralda, he was obsessed
with a slave and her strange reclusive life and its secrets.

Langdon had been well aware for some time now of his
physical attraction to this woman.

It was almost ritualistic by now to admire the slick black
hair she never unwound, and to imagine it racing in one
thick coil, like a black wave down her back. Now he was
admiring the tender curve of her neck bending toward the
pages of the book. The quiet folds of that indentation between her thighs, the sheen of old silk, filled him with a
kind of fainting sickness. Would he ever dare to lay his
head on those folds? Shocked as he was by his own
thoughts, he tried to face them honestly. How many other
Southern white men had dreamed similar dreams? He felt
foolish and giddy. This pale, almost white woman was connected with darkness, with dark recesses, with dark flesh.
Those first memories of comfort and warmth that all white
Southerners share.

There had been a long pause in their conversation, and
Langdon looked up to find Sally Hemings staring at him in
a strange, intense way.

She seemed distracted as she rose and came toward him.

Sally Hemings, trained since birth in obedience, had
heard the silent command of Nathan's mind and body and
had obeyed. In her loneliness and weariness she had failed
to remember the first lesson of black womanhood: never
touch a white man.

She knew that in Virginia, her color alone was a provocation to any white man. An invitation. And any gesture or
familiarity on the part of the slave woman, no matter how
maternal, how pure, was inviting disaster. She knew this,
but she forgot. A mistake that was to cost her dearly.

She took one of his hands in hers, and with the other she pressed his face into the folds of her dress. It was the first and last time Nathan Langdon would experience such a feeling of pure happiness. Sally Hemings's blunder, as offhand and unconscious as it was, awoke in Langdon an unbearable jealousy of a dead man.

"I begin to be jealous."

"Of a dead man?"

"Jefferson lives. Didn't you know that? That is the chorus of a new patriotic song."

"He lives for me."

"How do you think Langdon got so well into the good graces of Mama, knowing how particular she is?"

"I don't know how he did it, Mad, but he's here and it don't look like he's going to budge any time soon."

Eston hoped Madison was not going to make a scene. His mother was happy.

"What I don't understand, Eston, is why the hell ne comes up here all the time. What does he stand to gain? We ain't got nothing worth stealing! Or do we?"

"Our mama!" Eston laughed.

"Eston!" Madison was shocked.

"Oh Mad, I didn't mean he would try anything! And I don't think he's out to *get* anything. I just mean she's fond of him. I think she's kind of taken him under her wing, like . . . like a son. . . ."

Eston wished that last word had not come out of his mouth.

"A son!" exploded Madison. "She's GOT two white sons who haven't even seen fit to let us know if they're living or dead! That's not two white sons too many?"

"I think Mama knows where they are, and how they are. She just doesn't want to talk about it."

"Well, Nathan Langdon is hardly some poor ex-darky, passing for white, that Mama has to protect, you know. He's Tidewater, and even if his family ain't rich anymore, they still got their place in society. . . . What's he doing up here? He's got a fiancée; he's passed his law examinations; and he has started out on his own. And you saying he needs our mama for a friend? That he can't do without Sally Hemings? He's picked up some strange ideas up North!"

"I know it's strange, Mad, but I really think he can't do without her."

"Eston, sometimes you haven't got the common sense of a jackrabbit. He's using Mama. Nathan Langdon is eaten up with curiosity about Thomas Jefferson, that's all. It's fascination with our *father*, not with Sally Hemings!"

"He also has political ambitions, Mad. He wouldn't risk any kind of compromise over mama."

"Wouldn't he now? You know his visits up here don't go unremarked."

"Nobody's crying scandal."

"Not yet. Because nobody knows, Eston, how damn often he comes up here!"

Madison held the pale eyes of his brother.

"You know it ain't right, Eston."

Madison was right, thought Eston. Besides, there was something of the master that he resented in Langdon, despite his genuine affection for him. They had had many long conversations together, but he despised Langdon's proprietary air with his mother. His presumed intimacy.

"All I know, Mad, is that she is happier seeing him than not. There's probably no harm in it."

"That still don't make it right. Don't make it correct. If mama was white, Eston, there'd be a lot of tongues wagging about a widow and a young engaged gentleman!"

"But she ain't white, Madison. And neither are we. We can't stop him."

Eston stared at Madison. Twenty-one years later, at the age of forty-four, Eston would indeed be what he was not. He, and his family consisting of a wife and three children, would cross the color line from black to white and take the name of his natural father, becoming Eston H. Jefferson.

The two men eyed each other. They would give anything never to see Nathan Langdon again, but they didn't dare say such a thing in front of their mother. Whatever she chose to do was correct in their eyes. Neither would acknowledge that there was a double standard for black women and white men. Madison turned to look out the window and saw the small resolute figure of his mother

approaching the house through the peach orchard. A flash
of tenderness and pity made Madison shift his gaze back
to his brother.

"Nathan Langdon, you are not as cynical and complicated as you like to appear."

"Do I like to appear complicated? Am I complicated?"

"No, but this . . . situation is complicated, and unhealthy.
You should be spending your time with young people,
not—"

"A historical monument?"

"Whose?"

"His!"

"What?"

"No, yours. Your monument to yourself. We must erect
it with your life as you have lived it . . . and write about it.
He has enough monuments. It's yours I'm concerned with."

"I need no monument."

"Let me decide that."

It was the seriousness in his voice, not the arrogance,
that turned Sally Hemings's eyes on him. His tone had been
sharp, as if she had caused him pain.

"I would allow you to decide everything, Nathan, if it
were possible. If I could," she said softly.

"I could, if I knew you. If I didn't come knocking at
your door each time and find a stranger. A new stranger,
not even the old one. You change like a chameleon."

"It's not I who change, but you. You come each time
expecting an answer. And there isn't one."

"I expect to find the answer to Sally Hemings."

"My answer to that is that you have the answer to me.
You know me better than anyone ever has, Nathan. It's
just that you expect too much. You expect explanations I
can't give. The only thing I can give is that knowledge of
myself you already possess. It is my gift to you for all the
happiness you've brought me."

"Happiness? . . ."

"I have as much affection for you as for my own sons."

"Yet you've never told your sons your—their—history?"

"I've never told them for a reason—that reason is that
they are safer without it, Nathan."

"And I'm in danger?"

"You are white, Nathan. That puts you mostly out of danger. But you would be, if you try to use the knowledge I've given you. You are in danger if it has changed you."

"Of course it has changed me. You have changed me."

"I know. That's what makes me sad."

"The change is for the better."

"Change is hardly ever for the better, I've learned. I want you to be happy."

"Not at your expense."

"Love is always at another's expense."

"Love is doing something for that person. Changing things."

"But there is nothing you can do for me. You can't change the past."

"I can change myself."

"But don't you see; that's the danger. You change yourself, and first thing you want is to change me, then those around you—your family, your life, the South, everything. There is danger when you contradict your roots, what is considered 'right,' what is accepted."

"I said you were a dangerous lady, and you laughed," Langdon said.

"I just don't want to see you hurt. Not by others and not by me. All these months, there have been remarks about us."

"I know that."

"And there are Eston and Madison to consider."

Langdon suddenly sensed Sally Hemings slipping out of his grasp. Several times in the past he had had this sensation of panic.

"Damn Eston and Madison!" he said. "What about you? What do you want?"

"I've never had what I wanted, Nathan. Never."

"Why?" he asked, like a stubborn child.

"Because . . ."

Sally Hemings did not continue, and she smiled at this childish exchange. There was something naïve and touching about Nathan. Some basic innocence white men seemed to take in, she would have said, "With their mother's milk," had it not been for the fact that that "milk" had been black. There were times she believed that white skin was more than a protective covering—nothing ever really seemed to penetrate it.

"This time you will," Nathan said.

The violent temper Sally Hemings had striven all her life to conceal flashed to the surface; she suddenly wanted to slap his face hard, to bury herself in his chest, and scream curses at him.

"No, I won't," she answered vehemently. She wanted to hurt him. "It will end, Nathan . . . and I shall miss you."

"There is no reason on earth why it should end."

There was every reason on earth, she thought.

"Let's not talk about it," she said.

They both looked away at this. To put the possibility of an ending in words was tempting fate with their fragile happiness. The same fate that had brought the lonely woman and the lonely young man together in the first place. Langdon knew he must break the tension.

"Besides," he said lightly, "if I stopped coming to see you, where would you get your weekly gossip and slander? Madison has no imagination, and Eston has no malice."

They both smiled at this. Eston's good nature and Madison's bad temper had become a private joke between them. Nathan Langdon felt a rush of affection: everything was all right again.

He smiled and rose.

"You're leaving?"

"I must. I only stopped for a minute." He looked at his watch. "I am going to miss the post."

"Oh, Nathan, I've kept you again."

"No," he said sharply. "I wanted to come. I hadn't seen you in more than a week. But I haven't had any time since this new lawsuit started."

"How is it progressing?"

"Badly. I'm up against one of the slickest, most outrageous liars I've ever had the misfortune to represent. He changes his story every day. At least I can say that the adversary is consistent—consistently lying. . . ."

"Nathan, how are you supposed to defend someone who lies?"

"It can be done. Liars can be defended brilliantly and honest men can be destroyed. You should know that—

you've seen many an honest man lose . . . especially in politics."

"Promise me." Sally Hemings suddenly reached out and touched Nathan's sleeve. A flicker of memory, like a grain of sand, made her blink.

"Yes?" he said, his voice low. But the moment passed.

"Promise me you'll bring the latest ending to the Randolph saga of the 'look-alike chickens coming home to roost'!"

The young man burst into laughter. Then he said softly, "I promise."

"No excuses. . . ."

"Please, Ma'am, am I the kind of gentleman who would bring excuses when I could bring mayhem and scandal? By the way, the latest Andrew Jackson joke is that when he puts on his reading spectacles, he turns out the lights!"

With that he was already out the door. She watched him descend the steep pathway to where his horse waited, and waited until she could see him no more.

CHAPTER 7

ALBEMARLE COUNTY, AUGUST 1831

> The Almighty has no attribute which can take sides with
> us in such a contest.—But it is impossible to be temperate
> and to pursue this subject through the various considera-
> tions of policy, of morals, of history natural and civil. We
> must be contented to hope they will force their way into
> every one's mind. I think a change already perceptible,
> since the origin of the present revolution.
> THOMAS JEFFERSON, *Notes on the State of Virginia*, 1790

The summer was passing and Sally Hemings's thoughts
were enclosed in a soft, weary happiness. Slowly, out of
an almost invisible but very deep wound, in an unceasing
stream, thoughts and feelings welled up and spilled out. She
felt herself floating, felt an odd excitement in answering
Nathan Langdon's questions, and even while speaking was
divided between pleasure and torment. She had lived a life;
she was startled to perceive that life. As if it had been kept
in a long underground passage which ascended now and
again into the midst of tremendous events called History.
History, which had left her alone in a vast, unfamiliar, un-
wanted wasteland.

Furtively, she looked across at Nathan Langdon. He
really was quite an ordinary man, yet it was only with him
that she felt this new sense of her existence. Had he given
her that, or had she taken it herself? It was so hard to
know.

"What are you thinking?" he said from the shadows.

"My own thoughts," she answered.

Nathan sensed a resistance, even an irritation. He knew
the mood. Since summer he had treaded softly with Sally

54

Hemings. He remained silent and let the moment pass. There would be other moments, a long series of moments in which to unravel the mystery of Sally Hemings. He would bide his time.

Nathan Langdon sighed in the stillness. It was an afternoon like many he had spent with this ex-slave. He felt himself sliding deeper and deeper into compromise with his race and his class and less and less inclined to shake himself out of a numbing lethargy, an insidious guilt that kept him peering into the faces of his slaves, his servants, his mother, his brothers, his fiancée. For what? He didn't know. He really didn't know anymore why he had returned to Charlottesville. He had certainly begun to question his earthly destiny. When Esmeralda and his mother had begged him to come, it had been with relief that he had returned South to take up the responsibilities of his family. He had made little headway in Boston. The possibility of success in the North for a Southerner, without means or influential friends, was dubious. He also knew that he was wanting in the bitter, energetic ambitions of most of his Northern schoolmates, but he had blamed this on his "Southerness." Yet his luck had been no better here in Charlottesville, where he could hardly call himself a stranger. He found it difficult to slip back into "Virginian" ways. He had acquired sharper edges in the North. At least he liked to think so. The coying slickness of Southern manners now stuck in his gullet. The only thing he had accomplished in the past year had been his job as census taker. That had ended now, he thought, and he hadn't succeeded in extending his connections or his business. He had tried to form a partnership which had not worked out well. His clerkship with Judge Miner was over and he had not been invited to stay on. He had always had a desire for public life; to shape national conduct seemed to him the highest form of achievement, he mused, but he had no money and what influence there was had to be shared with his two brothers, who also had political ambitions. There was little that was public in his solitary room, or his solitary office, or his solitary visits to Sally Hemings. He didn't think consciously of his unhappiness, or of what Sally Hemings might have to do with it. If he had, he might

have prevented what happened that peaceful August afternoon.

It was several days after the much-awaited eclipse of the
sun.

It was the same August 31, 1831, that the slave Nat
Turner, property of Putnam Moore and born the property
of Benjamin Turner, and his aide-de-camp, the slave Will
Francis, born the property of Nathaniel Francis, were, with
a small army of sixty or seventy men and one woman, all
born slaves, sweeping through the County of Southampton,
Virginia, and in two days and one night, murdering every
white man, woman, and child that had crossed their path,
systematically burning everything as they killed. Fifty-five
men, women, and children would perish this day because
of the one favor of God they held highest and in common:
being white. Turner's goal was the arsenal in Richmond
where, he, hoping to have gathered around him an army
of hundreds of runaway slaves, had planned to organize
an uprising of all the slaves of Virginia, in the name of the
Father, the Son, and the Holy Ghost. He would fail.

"If your brother doesn't want it, why don't you take on
the case, Nathan?"

Langdon shifted nervously in his chair. He hadn't come
to see Sally Hemings today to be challenged. Confronted
with a difficult decision. One that basically went against his
grain. The Hemingses were one thing. Mulattoes were
another.

"He didn't say he didn't want it. He said it couldn't be
won in a Virginia court of law."

"I know the atmosphere, with all these new laws, is
tense, Nathan, but perhaps you . . ."

Who did she think he was, thought Langdon, Thomas
Jefferson?

"The case, as I said, is un-winnable. It will be one of
those trials that is decided even before it begins."

"As are all trials concerning mulattoes in Virginia," said
Sally Hemings. She had almost forgotten. If Virginia courts
condoned murder, they wouldn't blink an eye at fraud.

"Yes, most."

"And you can't help him?"

"I would, if I could."

"Mr. Jefferson once tried to defend a mulatto when he was young. . . ."

"And he lost." Nathan Langdon said this not without pleasure.

"He lost, to be sure, but he tried." Sally Hemings was trembling. She rarely asked for anything. She hadn't realized how difficult it was. "It took courage at the time," she said, and looked intently at Langdon. It had been the wrong thing to say.

"Courage or foolhardiness? You must know that with the situation as it is now, any mulatto who sets foot in a court is going to lose just for having the temerity to do so."

Sally Hemings was still looking at Nathan Langdon. There was something in her gaze that profoundly irritated Langdon. Something childish and stubborn. Or was it only his anger and terror at being compared with the great Jefferson, the constant references to him as if he were a touchstone, a holy relic? . . .

"But this case is different, Nathan. This man was never a slave. He was freeborn to begin with. You see, Mas . . . Mr. . . . Jefferson's case was one of a slave who sued for freedom on the grounds that his mother was white, and a child by Virginia law inherits the condition of his mother. But this man was born free because his mother was freed before he was born and left the state. His father recognized him in court in Philadelphia, and he should have the same rights as any citizen of the United States, being born outside Virginia, to inherit property. In this instance, his property is his own slave kin! Brothers and sisters and uncles!"

"He is still legally a mulatto, therefore he cannot testify against his white cousins in the case. It is no longer a question of slavery but that of a black man testifying against a white man."

Sally Hemings was silent. Nathan Langdon felt the gall rise in his throat. Women. She still wanted a hero. The heroic age was over. Didn't she know that? Ended with James Madison. This was the age of mediocrity, small-mindedness, caution, calculation, money-grubbing. The age of the common man. An age that deserved what it got: Jackson, not Jefferson. Then he heard her say:

"Think if it were Madison or Eston."

"It could never be Madison or Eston."

"Why not?"

"Madison and Eston," Langdon said very deliberately, "are white. I made them white. Legally. They can testify against anybody on earth."

"White?"

"In the census. I listed them and you as white."

There was a stunned silence. Outside, only the sounds summer makes. "It takes more than a census taker to turn black into white." Her voice had an ominous quality to it: a sudden chill that should have warned him.

"After all, by Thomas Jefferson's definition, you are white."

"By Thomas Jefferson's life, I'm a slave."

"Think how much easier it is for you now, staying in Virginia with all that's going on . . . not to have that sword of expulsion hanging over your head! I . . . decided."

"*You* decided." He couldn't tell whether she was going to laugh or scream. "*You* decided! For fifty-four years I've been Thomas Jefferson's creature, and now . . . now *you* decide it's time for me to be yours. *Yours!*" She began to laugh. "It's Judgment Day! Instead of being black and a slave, I'm now free and *white*."

Her eyes showed something of that lurid yellow that had frightened him on his first visit.

If he had been a good lawyer, or even a competent one, Langdon would at this point before it was too late have laughed and tried to turn the whole thing into a joke. Or he would have lied by saying she had completely misunderstood. But Nathan Langdon was not a good lawyer. He blundered on, insisting, explaining. Perspiration was forming on his high forehead. There were undertones, nuances, secrets he hadn't calculated and that he had no way of gauging.

Her laughter had shattered what composure he had left. Instead of reading her face, in which was reflected shock, disbelief, horror, as well as a plea for rectification, he went on pleading his already lost cause, repeating himself with a kind of childish despair. Surely she knew he had meant well. That he had done it for her!

The shrillness of her laughter had given it a loud, raucous, almost drunken quality. Then suddenly it stopped.

"Why did you have to tell me? Why couldn't you have kept quiet? What did you think you were doing—playing God?"

"I did it for you and your sons."

"Don't be a fool, Nathan. You didn't do it for me. You didn't even know me. You did it for him. To make him not guilty. To shield him . . . so that he wouldn't have a slave wife!"

Her eyes had turned darker. A strand of black hair had escaped from its knot. He wanted to go down on his knees and hide himself in the folds of that skirt again. Surely, it was going to be all right. Surely, he wasn't going to lose her over this.

"Forgive me, I didn't realize . . ."

"Forgive you because you didn't realize . . . That's what black folks are here for. To forgive white folks because they didn't realize. Forgive me. Forgive me. My father said it. My lover said it. My white sons will say it. Yes, I forgive you. All of you, and your insufferable arrogance. But I never want to see you again."

"Please . . ."

"You are not welcome here anymore."

"I beg you . . ."

"If you come back, Nathan, I'll have Madison throw you out." She went on before he could cut in again. "I'm tired, Nathan. I'm tired of white men playing God with my flesh and my spirit and my children and my life, which is running out. I thought you understood that. You've left me nothing of my own. Not even my color! I've been asked to give, and give, and give, and now I can't give any more. I can't forgive another man, Nathan. I'm sorry."

He had made one of those blunders of enormous consequence that only a fool or the very young makes. One that afterwards plays again and again in the mind like a set piece in a game of chess long after the match has been lost. It would seem to him incredible, later, that such a small miscalculation, flung so nonchalantly on the board, would have cost the game.

"Oh, God," he groaned. "Tell me what to do. I'll do anything. Pay any price."

"That's what all white men say." There was dullness and pity and contempt in her voice. "You are just like all the rest. You haven't understood anything of what I've told you all these months. You still think I exist by your leave. You always will."

The bitterness shocked him. She meant what she said. He had not understood.

"Please, I love you."

"That's what all men say. That's what he said. That's what he said!"

Suddenly, there was no Sally Hemings. No Nathan Langdon. There was only unfathomable, uncontrolled black rage that went far beyond the terrified young man who skimmed and rocked on its surface like a storm-tossed skiff.

Sally Hemings rose like some outraged goddess in her sanctuary, now defiled. Like pure crystal light, her rage, he felt, could maim or kill at will. There was something diabolical and possessed in the scream that echoed after Nathan Langdon as he fled from her.

That sound would remain for him one of the bitterest and cruelest memories of his life.

For a long time, Sally Hemings stared at the receding figure of Nathan Langdon. Then her head snapped back. There was a pressure in her skull that seemed to push her neck forward and made her want to lower it.

When she looked down, there were spots of blood on her apron. Blood. Her nose was bleeding. She lifted the white apron and buried her face in it. Blindly she whirled and entered the darkness. She let her apron drop.

She owned nothing, except the past. And now, even that had been taken from her. She had been raped of the only thing a slave possessed: her mind, her thoughts, her feelings, her history. Among all the decisions of her life, she realized, not one was ever meant for herself.

Sally Hemings was trembling. She went to her dark-green chest. This moment she knew had been coming ever since that April day the census taker had arrived at her door, interrupting her solitude, disturbing her memories, changing her color. She took out a small linen portfolio, opened it, and stared at the yellowing, unframed sheet within. It was a pencil drawing, a portrait of her as a girl in Paris. She had never shown this drawing to anyone—not to her sons, not to Nathan Langdon, not to Thomas Jefferson. She had never reasoned why. Except that somehow, on this small scrap of paper, John Trumbull seemed to have captured something that made her see herself for the first time. This was the sole image of herself that belonged only to her.

For a long time she studied the delicate lines on the aging paper. Had she ever been this young? Could she ever believe, invisible as she was, betrayed, and drowning in this sea of loneliness, the generations passed from her, that she had loved? . . . *Had loved the enemy.* . . .

She turned and strode to the fire. Sacrifice. For one instant of pain, she hesitated, and then she threw her image into the fire. Blood. A blood sacrifice.

For one moment her eyes went to the small bundle of cloth and clay on the mantel. What more did the gods want? She strode again to the chest and stared down at the yellowing diaries.

"In order to burn them I would have to forget you."

There was a slight smile on her lips as she began to burn paper. She burned through the afternoon. The last to go were her diaries. As she knelt, tearing the pages one by one, her eyes shone like a cat's in the light of the fire, her face was streaked with tears. George . . . George. Like George. A human sacrifice. She destroyed all but the last diary. There was still one more thing she had to do. She tried to rise. Her long black hair had loosened and fell like a nun's chaplet over her shoulders to her knees. She no longer had the strength to pull herself up, so she continued kneeling in an attitude of prayer, her diary open to the last page on her bloody apron. There, before her, in small neat script, was the account of hours: every visit with its date and length of stay Thomas Jefferson had made to Monticello from the time she had returned to Virginia with him. Re-enslaving herself. Thirty-eight years. Thirty-eight years of minutes, hours, months. A certainty that her fate was something more than a personal one overtook her.

Like an abbess at her devotions, she repeated each date. The last inscription was not the date of his death, but the date of his last return to Monticello, twenty-six years before.

She would make this act her very own, she thought:

neither black nor white, neither slave nor free, neither loved nor loving.

She burned it. She felt a deep calm. She no longer feared anything; not death itself. She had crossed that line. Even if they hanged her.

As for Nathan Langdon, he had helped her leave her life. She never intended to see him again.

CHAPTER 8

JERUSALEM, 1831

> The spirit of the master is abating, that of the slave rising from the dust, his condition mollifying, the way I hope preparing, under the auspices of heaven, for a total emancipation. . . .
>
> THOMAS JEFFERSON, *Notes on the State of Virginia*, 1790

There was not one black person to be seen as Sally Hemings stood in the white mob disguised by her color, shoulder to shoulder with other tense women and men who had come to Jerusalem. It had taken her and Eston one week to get to this place; yet she had felt compelled to be here in the chill of this November day, a long, once elegant cloak covering her from head to foot.

The remnants of Nat Turner's army, twenty-eight in all, had been destroyed or apprehended, and thirteen of them, including the woman, had been executed—all without confessing. There remained only Nat Turner; only Nat Turner had confessed, and this was his trial. As reports and rumors of Turner's revolt had spread through Virginia, Sally Hemings had been so affected by it that she, who for almost thirty years, had never ventured outside the boundaries of Monticello, now stood in this place, in awful danger, against the will of her sons.

It was as if Nat Turner's giant hand (for she thought of him as being immense) had placed her in this heaving crowd that seemed to rest in the hollow of some enormous bloody bosom, now calmed and stroked by the awe of true massacre.

She felt as if this man had taken her hand and lifted her out of the loneliness after Nathan Langdon, after the destruction of her diaries. Now, alone, she faced the truth of her life: she had loved the enemy. She had denied and denied the mesmerizing violence of Turner and his avengers that had been around her and in front of her and a part of her forever. Nat Turner was the nullifier of her life.

The silence was deep and sensual; she felt the fear and hatred and dread of her blackness like twin asps at her breast. She had begged and pleaded and finally forced Eston to bring her here without being able to give a reason, but now she knew there was one: to force back invisibility forever, to confront her life. The danger was immense. Blacks, slave or free, all over Virginia, were hidden, crouched behind locked doors or plantation masters. Reprisals had been heavy, sweeping through counties as far away as Alberdale, as far south as North Carolina. Already more than a hundred blacks had been killed in the orgy of revenge that followed the two-day insurrection. Fifty-five whites had been killed. The number glowed before her. Blacks had perished because of the color of their skin, but for whites to perish for the same reason was revolution!

They were not invincible!

It was like the day she had stood in the yellow salon in Paris and listened to her brother James describe what was going on in the streets of the city. Blue blood had proved as red as peasant. White blood could flow as easily as black. Virginia had begun to bleed. This day's wound was staunched for the moment, but, like some royal disease, it would result in a never-ending hemorrhaging. Invincibility, Sally Hemings knew better than most, was in the mind. Her head whirled. She saw now the contradiction of her life. The weight of every moment of it. The weight of power was being exchanged. Just as, for two delirious days, the power of life and death had passed from white hands to black, so the power over her life and death passed at last from her dead master's hand to her own.

The thought rocked her back on her heels. She swayed slightly, and as she did the crowd stirred with her as the courthouse door opened. Sally Hemings clutched her son's arm with both hands as Turner stepped, stumbled, and was half-dragged into the dappled sunlight.

Eston's arm trembled under her clutching hands. They were without doubt the only black witnesses to this awful moment.

The pale woman standing beside her bastard son had thought she knew all about real power. Sally Hemings had spent forty years of her life in daily contact with one of the most powerful men in America. She had seen his friends and his enemies sweep in and out of their mansion in quest of power or in homage of it. She had never understood until now, however, why men lusted after it with such ferocity; why they fought, killed, slandered, flattered, begged, worshipped, begot sons in its name. All the Burrs, the Hamiltons, and the Washingtons that she had seen come and go had never been able to convey the meaning of it as well as this black man about to have terrible things done to him. He was now being dragged, spit upon, and kicked. He seemed half-crazy; wounded, a hunted animal, caught. Yes, this man's dignity had become real power to her. There was something almost obscene about seeing it here, so naked. This man had killed her enemies. For her! He had taken them on and fought them to his last breath. For her! He had stood while she had done nothing for herself all these years except submit. She wanted to cover the convicted man with her cloak. To blot out a vision of herself more terrible than she had ever imagined. She felt herself sinking into this white world as into a watery grave.

She raised a hand above her head as one does in drowning, but it was really to signal Nat Turner that he was not alone. Her hand was dragged down by her distraught son, in whose blue eyes she saw tears of fear and loathing.

Nathan Langdon made his way through the restless ugly crowd. He had ridden two days from Washington City to get here. He was haggard and uncoordinated in his movements; his face showed the same savage and perpetual bewilderment that had clouded his features since his precipitous departure from the Hemingses' cabin three months ago.

He shoved and pushed at random, but it was like trying to move some great mountain of flesh. People felt neither pressure nor pain. Shoulders and elbows knocked and prodded into tissue without the least response from the victim. Langdon even found he was shoving women in his frenzy to reach the courthouse before it adjourned and spewed out the criminals.

It was a nasty day, with sudden bursts of occasional sunlight. It seemed the right climate for the drama of the trial.

He too had been compelled to this place for reasons he only dimly perceived. He knew they had something to do with Sally Hemings. He was here to find out something about her, but also about himself; about Virginia, about slaves and insurrection and murder. People from all over the Tidewater region were calling Turner's rebellion an aberration, yet all Langdon's instincts told him this was not so. This event was logical and inevitable. There was no mayhem here. Here was systemized homicide as the perfect and indelible equation to slavery. There had been talk of slave armies, thousands of men marching on Jerusalem, killing and raping and burning by the hundreds. The governor of Virginia had even begun to muster an army to meet the insurgents, and there had been talk of the federal army marching from Fort Lauredale in Maryland. Panic had seized the capital, yet Turner had been captured less than fourteen miles from where he had started his crusade.

The race from Washington City to arrive in time for Nat Turner's condemnation—one couldn't call it a trial, since he had confessed beforehand—had also been a sudden decision. Sally Hemings' words had echoed in his head like the rhythm of his horse galloping toward Jerusalem: "You haven't understood anything! You haven't understood anything!" He smelled the restless, straining crowd, the odor of death like singed hair, the overexcited bodies swaying in some kind of primitive dance of retribution. . . .

Turner was mad! Of course he was. Being an atheist, Langdon had only contempt for religious fanatics. It was Will Francis, Turner's aide-de-camp, who fascinated him, for here was pure, unadulterated logic, unclouded by biblical hysterics. My God! What was he thinking? How could he be rationalizing insurrection? What had become of him? His eyes narrowed against the brief glare of the sun, but soon the ray disappeared behind the clouds.

But Francis, ah, Francis . . . Francis had killed more than twenty-five of the fifty-five people murdered.

Langdon was sweating under his greatcoat as he burrowed his way toward the red brick courthouse. He now had no hope of reaching the courtroom or getting inside, although he had used what little influence he had to get a seat.

He had to see Nat Turner and Will Francis with his own eyes. His very life depended on it. If Nat Turner existed, then all he had been taught to believe was false.

Nat Turner was the nullifier of his life! Nathan's personal bewilderment flowed toward the larger drama.

Nathan Langdon had thought of Nat Turner as gigantic and black. But the man who was dragged into sight was of medium size, not more than five feet eight, slender, and a light-brown color. This visionary had made a full confession of his crimes. Crimes committed in the name of justice. God knows how many innocents in Virginia would pay, thought Nathan. He had to urge the Hemingses to leave Virginia with their mother. She was no longer safe here.

Nathan passed so close to Sally Hemings that day he could have touched her cloak. Not in his wildest speculations would he have imagined, however, that the delicate recluse would be in this heaving, bloodthirsty mob. He had been promised that this could never happen, and that was what he had intended to tell his sons. Now he wouldn't be able. He stared intently at the dark figure being dragged through the crowd. Women and men were spitting, screaming, and cursing—especially the women. The man seemed but a sack of flesh; all spirit had fled him.

Later, Nathan learned that Nat Turner's body had been skinned; grease made of the fat, and souvenir money pouches made of the skin.

Eston Hemings knew his mother was in a near-hysterical state by now, and looked around wildly to find a way out of the crowd. They were jammed tight into this solid block of humanity. There was no escape. His mother was screaming that Turner was accusing her of something, but that she was not guilty. He could not make out what it was she was saying over the din of people. He bit his lip in exasperation. He was terrified. His bowels were gripped with spasms as if he were about to be seized and herded with the insurgents.

He knew in his heart he was as guilty as Turner. They were all guilty. Every slave or ex-slave had as much murder in his heart. His terror broke loose and spread through the crowd, mixing with the miasma of stagnant hate that rose from the packed bodies. Nausea overcame him. His mother —he must get her away from here. He must get himself away. Not only away from here, but out of Virginia, out of the slave states. Madison was right. As long as there were slaves, there would be murder, and as long as there was murder, retaliation could fall on anything and anyone who was exposed. That included all Hemingses.

Eston turned his back on the courthouse and Nat Turner, placing himself in front of his mother to protect her. He put both his arms around her and leaned back using all the muscles at his command to secure a little breathing space around her head. Her pale face was transfixed; small beads of perspiration stood out on her forehead; she drew her cloak around her. Her mouth was slightly open, and her eyes glinted.

Eston understood now why she had made the long and dangerous journey to Jerusalem. Her obsession with Turner's rebellion, his trial, his execution—all was finally clear to him. With the same intensity that had made her refuse to see Nathan Langdon, she had devoured every scrap of information she could obtain about Nat Turner. If Nathan Langdon had given a meaning to his mother's life, then Nat Turner had taken it away. He doubted if Langdon would even recognize her now. He had seen his mother change from a young woman to an old one, the amber eyes turn a dull brown, the jet-black hair streak with gray, almost overnight, the slender body dehydrate and fold like parchmant. The glow of continual fever gave her an iridescent glow like that of a religious fanatic. But to what or to whom?

Sally Hemings sat for hours now staring into space. She would either talk to herself or fall silent for days. She had agreed to leave Monticello. But Eston worried that she would not survive the hardship of the journey West. He saw life running out of this proud, passionate, and secret woman.

Eston continued to fight to give his mother breathing space, but she seemed transplanted to another space, another time.

"O God," she whispered, "now forgive me for ever loving him." And Eston wondered which man she meant.

PART II

1787
Paris

CHAPTER 9

ABOARD THE *GREENHELM*, JUNE 1787

I am more and more convinced that Man is a dangerous
creature, and that power whether vested in many or few
is ever grasping, and like the grave cries give, give.

ABIGAIL ADAMS

I never hoped for mercy . . . for more than fifty years I
have lived in an enemy country.

JOHN ADAMS

I believed myself to be happy. As a child I *was* happy. I
was brought up around the Big House at Monticello, and I
loved those around me: my mother and uncles, Martha,
Maria, Master Jefferson. Like all slaves, I was told nothing
of my origins, which little by little I pieced together. Once,
when I was eight or nine, my brother James and Martha
went off to play and left me behind. I don't remember the
reason, only that I felt abandoned and was crying.

Master Jefferson came upon me and tried to comfort me.
He said being sad was a waste of time and the best thing
to do when you were sad was to write down everything you
saw about yourself, even the tiniest detail, and then to think
about them one by one. By the time you had got halfway
through the list, he said, you wouldn't remember the origin
of your misery anymore. He left then and returned with a
smooth pine board and some charcoal. He sat beside me
and we made a list of all the plants, flowers, trees, and
vegetables we could see in the kitchen garden and beyond;
all the fish we could imagine in the little river by the north-
west boundary; all the animals we could imagine living in
the pines of the southwest boundary. It was my earliest
recollection of him, and, that moment knowing neither

past nor future, I felt only an immense calm and safety in his presence that rested on my shoulders like a warm cloak.

When Martha and James came back and found us together, Martha flew into a rage of jealousy, took off her boot, and started to hit me with it. The heel of Martha's boot came down above my temple and raked the skin and broke it. More blood than was warranted by the wound streamed down my cheek. It mingled with my tears of confusion and grief.

Out of desolation, I ground my teeth to keep from crying and brought my petticoat up to my ear to stem the flow of blood. But he was there before me. He held my head and pressed his handkerchief to the wound. Then he picked up Martha in his arms to keep her from hitting me again.

I remember her bright head meeting level with his great height in a blaze of red. He had flung her over his shoulder, but his eyes met mine in an attempt to console me, too. I despised Martha for being jealous of those few minutes I had had, when she had him as a father forever. . . . That day made me a list-maker. And a diary-keeper. I would continue to be one all my life.

The *Greenhelm*, June 17, 1787

It was June seventeenth. I remember that day we were five weeks out of Norfolk, and we were, as Captain Ramsay would have said, "becalmed." There was not a sniff of wind; all the great square sails were furled and bound. The sun was hot on my head, and even now, if I close my eyes, I can still see the reflection of the sun on that smooth sea, like the field of white clover that runs down the back toward the river boundary of Monticello. I had found a wonderful hiding place, and intended to keep it for myself. It was high up on the forward mast, well, not so high up, but it was quite a dangerous climb. There was a little niche where I could watch what was going on below without anyone seeing me. I used to go up there and take off my bonnet. I can still hear little Polly screaming not to take her bonnet off, for if she got freckles in the sun, her father had written, he wouldn't love her anymore. Well, I would take my bonnet off and let my hair down and feel

it curl round my waist. At home I was made to wear it tied
up. My charge, Maria Jefferson, known as Polly, had done
nothing but cry and cuff me for the past ten days. We, that
is, her cousin Jack Eppes, Mistress Eppes, and myself, had
lured her on the ship by deceiving her, and she still wasn't
over it. She hadn't wanted to leave her Aunt Eppes to go to
her father. Now she found herself on a strange ship with
me, on her way to a foreign country to see a father she
didn't remember, who said he wouldn't love her if she got
freckles! From the time she had awakened, hours out of the
port, she never stopped screaming about being shanghaied.
I was just fourteen and Polly was nine. On the ship she
had been left with me, who was as scared as she, and who
felt just as abandoned. We were on our way to Paris,
France, and her father, Thomas Jefferson, the minister to
that kingdom. But by then, the worst was over. She had
liked the captain, Mr. Ramsay, who had taken charge of
her. She clung to him.

We were the only females on the ship and were made
much of by the five other male passengers and the captain.
For me, it was the beginning of my real history. From the
moment I stepped onto that ship as nurse for Polly, everything that had happened to me before seemed to recede
and grow smaller, until nothing remained except the sweep
of the sea and the vastness of the sky and those unexpected
days of freedom.

I was still quite childish at fourteen, although I looked
older than my age. My childhood days at Monticello—the
little school, run for the white children and the house
servants, taught by Mrs. Carr; old Cook's underground
kitchens with all their intrigues and noise and heat—faded
away in the bright sea-sun. I missed my mother. I thought
for a while she was going to take Polly to Paris herself, but
finally my mother had decided on me. It had been a queer
choice.

It was Mammy Isabel who was supposed to have gone
with Polly. When Mistress Eppes arrived to fetch her to
Norfolk, it became known that Mammy Isabel was well
gone with her eighth child and wasn't fit to travel. Mistress
Eppes, who was altogether distracted anyway about losing

Polly and sending her so far away against her will, was
beside herself. First, because Polly really didn't want to go;
and second, because there was no one to take her.

My mother had suddenly turned and looked at me and
said, "Sally will go. She'll have James to look out for her."
And before Mrs. Eppes could get her breath to ask if I
had had my smallpox, or how old I was, Mama swept me
out of the parlor, down the hall, and out through the
kitchens, leaving Cook with her mouth wide open, ready,
but unable to get her two cents in. I was breathless and
scared. I had never been a nurse or a lady's maid or anything. Most I had been before then was a child! But Mama,
she kept right on going, I can remember her skirts
whistling, up the back stairs, into the linen room in the
back, out with a straw trunk and three cases, then back to
her own chests of linen to find chemises and petticoats and
stockings and bolts of cloth for dresses. Nothing Isabel had
for the voyage fit me, even the underwear, so, in less than
a week, everything had to be made new.

I was going and we couldn't miss the ship that was waiting in Norfolk. Master Jefferson was not going to tolerate
any more delays. I suppose my mother could have found
someone to fit into Isabel's things. After all, there were
some three hundred and sixty-four slaves she could pick
from, at least half were female and grown. But something
pressed her to send me. To this day I don't know why. If
it was fate, then she had a hand in it.

"It will be Sally, then. I can't think anymore," Mistress
Eppes had said, finally and belatedly, for her voice was lost
in the preparations of my departure.

I was leaving Monticello, the only home I knew, for a
strange country.

Monticello, the most beautiful place in the world. The
grass was greener, the scent of flowers keener, the blossoms
bigger, the air clearer, the animals more healthy, the rigs
more elegant, the cooking better, the slaves happier, the
master—whom I had not seen since I was ten—kinder than
any other place. Of course, I had never been outside the
boundaries of Monticello. I was born at Bermuda Hundred,
the plantation of my father, but he died three months after

I was born, and the next year I came with my mother to live at Monticello, perched on its mountain, looking onto the Blue Ridge Mountains. My mother loved it more than I. It was always cool, with a breeze even in the hottest summer, and had a great hall that carried the freshness through the house. With horse and carriage, it took almost one hour to reach the main gate from the road.

Master Jefferson spent much of his time away from the plantation, in Philadelphia or New York, but every time he came home he would tear something down or build something new or rebuild something. He always arrived with his plans, and he would summon my brothers James and Robert and the white workmen, and they would start to work.

The slave cabins dotted the hillside in back of the Big House; they climbed up the hill like white morning glories gone wild with the smoke drifting out of the chimney fires. Along the back of the main house was a long covered walk, looking onto the kitchens, the meat house, smokehouse, icehouse, laundries, storehouses, and servants' quarters. This was my mother's domain. She oversaw twenty-five or more house servants.

We never had the number of servants a big plantation had. Master Jefferson didn't want it, and as Mistress Jefferson was frequently ill, she couldn't have managed to run them. My mother could have, of course, but there didn't seem to be much point in having a footman behind every chair and no mistress.

And, of course, there were always everybody's children, black and white, running everywhere. Once Master Eppes came rushing in to find Master Jefferson, tripped over a baby in the hallway, and slid seven feet on the parquet that had just been waxed for the fourth time that day. Fractured his rib, I remember. My mother usually kept everybody in the back and made do with Martin and Big George when the master was home.

My mother was beautiful. She was not very tall, but well formed and light mahogany in color. Her skin changed colors on different days; sometimes there was a rose tint and sometimes a yellow tint. She had her "dark" days and her "light" days. She used to say that my father would always remark on her color every morning. Once I surprised her in the fields just standing perfectly still like a statue among the tall wheat; her skin had taken on the same color, her eyes were blazing, and there were two tears running down her cheeks, but there had been no sounds of weeping.

A great calm had settled on our ship. Another day and still there was no wind, so we lingered, sitting on the tranquil sea, like a turtle in its shell. Sailors and passengers alike were lulled by the silence, the absence of movement. Games were organized and promenades. We made friends with the sailors who would make us gifts of little soft animals, creatures made out of rope and hemp. Polly and I used to "fish" over the side of the ship, which amused the sailors, who would ask us if we had caught any "catfish." One fat, red little sailor with a blond beard and green eyes made me the figure of a little dog in the image of a certain race they had in France. He made it out of hemp, and around the neck, tail, and legs was a mass of curls shaped like shrubbery. I later learned this race of dog was called "*caniche*" and was in fashion with the Paris gentry. I tied a ribbon on mine and called him George Washington. I would climb up to my hiding place, my "Monticello," with Washington, and there I would sit, making lists in my loneliness, to pass the time.

Blue. Sky. Water without wind. No clouds. Sixteen sails. Three flags. Birds. Seven Masts. Sun. A long railing of polished brass. God. Silver on blue. 85 spokes in in the railing. 48 sailors on the ship. 3 cooks. 1 surgeon. 2 mates. 1 adjunct. 4 officers. 1 Captain. Captain Ramsey. The cargo; sugar. tobacco. rice. barley. molasses. peanuts.

Inventory of Polly's trunks: 2 fans; 2 masks; 4 pairs of ruffles; 7 girdles consisting of 2 white, 2 dark blue, 1 rose, 1 yellow, 1 black; 6 linen drawers; 6 silk drawers; 13 chemises; 14 night gowns; 14 night caps; 6 day caps; 2 straw bonnets; 2 silk bonnets; 1 irish lace cap; 4 shawls; 1 fur cape; 5 woolen underdresses; 6 woolen

shirts; 1 angora shawl; 2 woolen scarfs; 6 flannel petticoats; 1 silver mirror; 1 silver comb; 1 silver powder
holder; a silver perfume flask; 1 pair of curling irons;
16 dolls; 5 books; 1 jewel case containing 2 pairs of
earrings, 1 pearl brooch, 1 garnet brooch, 1 garnet
ring, 1 silver butterfly, 1 sapphire and diamond stick-
pin; 25 handerkerchiefs; 3 silk scarves, 2 wigs, 4 cans
of black tea; 1 writing chest with ink, quills and paper;
1 folio of sheet music; 4 crates of dried fruits and pre-
serves; 1 medicine chest; 1 sack grains and seeds; 1
flute; 1 pocketbook; 2 purses; 41 costumes for dolls; 6
fine flowered aprons; 4 quilted petticoats; 2 pairs of
paste buckles; 1 crepe shawl with flowers printed in
color; 3 pairs of doeskin gloves; 1 muff; 2 bonnets of
muslin made over reeds; 1 white Holland ball gown.

Inventory of my trunk: 2 cotton petticoats; 1 quilted
petticoat; 6 dresses; 1 blue muslin; 1 straw bonnet; 2
pairs worsted stockings; 4 linen aprons; 2 girdles; 12
chemises; 6 drawers; 4 caps; 6 head rags; 1 pair of
shoes; 2 night shirts; 3 woolen underdresses; 4 linen
underdresses; 3 damask shawls, one with ruffles; 1
wooden crucifix carved by John; 1 medicine chest in
wood; 4 ribbons; 2 girdles; 1 woolen shawl; 1 wooden
comb; 1 wooden hairbrush; 1 flute.

On the thirteenth day, we got under way again. It had
been still the whole day, when suddenly a breeze whipped
the ribbons of our bonnets as Polly and I strolled on
deck and suddenly sailors came from everywhere, running
and leaping in a noisy slippery dance. The sails were
lowered and swelled before our eyes and the ship shuddered,
rolling under us like a galloping horse. In about an hour,
we had begun to take on speed and what a beautiful sight
were the waves we made, frothing in the setting sun, the
last streaks of light quarreling with the dark that finally
came dropping like a black cloth. From then on, we made
good time. I started looking forward to the future instead
of being homesick for the past. That night we celebrated
the trade winds.

Everyone dressed for dinner, and Captain Ramsay put on his dress uniform and fairly took our breath away. It was of a bright- but deep-blue hue, a velvet jacket with golden tassels on the shoulders hung with golden cords. The lapels were red satin, with a matching waistcoat. His cravat and shirt were a snowy white, with lace at the cuffs, and his small cloths were also white with blue stockings. His hair was powdered and tied with a blue ribbon, and his shoes were black patent-leather, with silver buckles. His buttons were of silver and he had a silver watch and a great sword in a silver harness and a blue sapphire on his hand. I will never forget the splendor of Captain Ramsay. Little Polly had found her first love. Oh, he was a splendid man, Captain Ramsay, and Polly did adore him! I think it was because she no longered remembered her father.

I remembered her father well, but Polly had been only four when he had left, and she had no recollection of him at all. All that she had known, as love and family, she had left in Norfolk with her aunt's family. I felt sorry for Polly. I loved her in a way I never loved her sister Martha. Martha was one year older than I, yet I was her aunt, just as I was Polly's. We had grown up together at Monticello, fought, played, rode, and laughed together. I was with her when Mistress Jefferson, my half sister, died. A long, pale, hot afternoon, stinking and mosquito-filled. We had tried to keep the bugs off her, taking turns fanning her. The doctor came at the end, but Master Jefferson wouldn't let him bleed her. My mother had dropped all her household duties to nurse her mistress. Master Jefferson had moved his study next to her bedroom and had not left her for the whole time it took her to die. Monticello, which had always been a house full of people, babies, guests, kin, and animals, seemed to empty out, and there was just my mother, Master Jefferson, Martha, Polly, and me, and the rest of the servants. At the end, my master had fainted dead away. He remained unconscious for so long his family thought he had died with her. The last thing she had made him promise was never to marry again.

It was my mother who had bathed her and laid her out and wept over her. The mistress had been like a daughter

to my mother, even though they had been, like Martha
and me, almost contemporaries. Whatever accommodations
they had had to make in their lives because of my mother's
concubinage, they seemed to have made long ago, because
they genuinely loved each other. Mama combed her long
hair out onto the pillow. Mama wept and wept and
cleaned her and put on her jewels, draped the room and
filled it with fresh flowers, and wept. She wouldn't let anyone else touch the body. She had tended Master Jefferson
as well, who seemed to have lost his senses and his will to
live. She cooked his meals and practically fed them to him,
nursed him until he was able to go out riding again. Then
he had ridden like the wind for days and days until he was
exhausted. Martha rode with him sometimes, but mostly
he was alone. And mostly Martha was alone. She couldn't
reach her father in his terrible grief, so she turned to me.
Or rather we turned to each other. We didn't cry over
Martha Jefferson's death, but then Master Jefferson and
Elizabeth Hemings wept enough for all of us. Martha and
I seemed to enter into some kind of covenant; tearlessness.
We were shocked by the conduct of the grown-ups. Somehow it didn't seem dignified. One day Martha, who was
called Patsy to differentiate her from her mother, held up
a mirror to my face and said: "You look more like her
than I do. I look like my father."

In seven more days we were to reach England. I was
happier with every passing day. Everything in my former
life grew smaller as we put more and more ocean between
our ship and Virginia. Monticello became farther and
farther away.

I felt myself breaking a barrier, leaving childhood for
adulthood. I already knew that I looked much older than
my age, and something happened on board which brought
home to me the fact that I was no longer a child.

It was June nineteenth, and Polly was busy playing
cards and learning curse words from Captain Ramsay. The
sea was navy blue, with lacy frills of soft waves made by a
gentle easterly wind. The sky was bright blue without a
cloud. We had had nothing but good weather. When I

told the captain that I too would have loved just one storm at sea, he had laughed and said beautiful girls shouldn't make wishes that beautiful girls might regret, as beautiful girls usually got what they wanted in life. Considering my place in life, I thought he was making fun of me, and my eyes filled with tears. I started to speak, but he had already turned away, occupied with his affairs.

Later that day, one of the five gentlemen passengers, Monsieur LaFaurie, a Frenchman, spoke to me for the first time. I was delighted, for on my own I could not have addressed him. I was anxious to ask him about Paris, the French people. We had often had French visitors at Monticello. My mother always took special care with the food on those occasions, since she said the French put great store in what they ate. And always Mistress Jefferson took special care with what she wore because, as with their food, she said, the French cared a great deal about what they put on their backs. This, I found out, was a contagious disease, for never was I so consumed with envy for clothes and despondent not to have them as in Paris.

It seemed to me too that the French were very careful about the way they spoke, for Monsieur LaFaurie hemmed and hawed for over an hour before he finally asked me: Why did people refer to me as being a Negro slave? Since obviously I was neither a Negro nor a slave. "Why, you are whiter than I," I remember him saying in astonishment.

I could have told him that I was a slave not because of my color, but because my mother was a slave and her mother before her. But I was, I found myself lying, a Spanish orphan from New Orleans (that sounded distant and foreign enough), engaged as a lady's maid for Miss Jefferson. I was on the seven seas, far from Monticello, and I let my imagination take me through a most convincing childhood. I had had much practice with Martha at home, making up imaginary childhoods.

But, of course, he asked Captain Ramsay later, who told him the truth, plus my age. He also gave me a scolding I would never forget. After the gentlemen had had their brandy and cigars, Captain Ramsay sent for me.

"Sally, I want to know why you deliberately lied and misled Monsieur LaFaurie this morning."

"Because he wouldn't have believed me if I had told the truth."

"I can't believe that a slave at Monticello has been brought up to lie. Your master would be shocked, and what an example to set for young Miss Jefferson!" He sighed and waited for me to say something. When I didn't, he continued. "You know it is very difficult to have two female passengers on this ship. Of course, Miss Jefferson is a child, but you are not, and you should be careful how you conduct yourself. I know that at home you have all kinds of freedom and license and that you are . . . are . . . are even encouraged . . . but you must remember in the close quarters of a ship, you cannot . . . I will not permit that you give . . . provocation to my gentleman passengers. You may look sixteen, but I know you are but fourteen, and you invite . . . something you are not prepared for, to be sure. . . . You are a child, and I might add a not very well-brought up slave and servant, and if you have not been taught as yet your place in life, then I will confine you to your cabin until we reach shore."

All my pretensions of womanhood dropped like so many petals. I had wanted to impress Monsieur LaFaurie because he hadn't treated me any differently for being "black." I supposed French people didn't know any better.

"I have not said anything to Miss Jefferson, nor do I intend to. Nor do I intend to punish you myself. That is, if you behave yourself. Am I understood?"

"Yes, Master."

"Now, another thing, Miss Hemings. You have the habit of sitting on the first platform of the forward mast. Sitting there, you may not be aware, but you are in *full view* of the sailors working beneath the upper deck. You cannot see them, but they can see you. You sit there for hours, and undo your hair and let it stream down your back, and this is dire provocation for the sailors who call you the 'siren.' I know you don't know what that means, but let me say, for a sailor, a siren . . . is someone who makes . . . who provokes."

"What's that?"

"Provocation . . . flirting . . . frolicking," he said.

I almost fainted with shame. Captain Ramsay, who had
been getting redder and redder, paused, and I began to
sob. I was suddenly lonely and miserable.

For the first time in my life I realized that I was truly
alone. I had never had a father, and might never see my
mother again. I had no rights before society, whatever
Monsieur LaFaurie said. I had no rights even over my own
body, which was changing and unnatural to me. I could be
coveted or punished at the whim of any white man, not just
my master. No kin of mine could protect me, for they had
no rights either. This horrified, tobacco-smelling white man
before me could beat me or confine me or take me to his
bed and I had no redress: no man would step forward to
protect me, and I had no right to protect myself if I could.

I was a slave. A female slave. I felt sick.

Poor Captain Ramsay was utterly undone. He sat me
down. Then he stood me up again. He poured me a glass of
some kind of spirits and made me drink it. But it did nothing against that great dark desolation that crouched in my
soul that day.

We would get to Paris; Polly would find her father, but
I would not find mine. I was a slave. Captain Ramsay sat
with me in the dark cabin a long, long time. He said how
sorry he was for having been so stern. He hadn't realized
how innocent I was, how young. He tried to take me in
his arms, but I let out a scream of terror. So we sat there
like two stones, me with tears rolling down my cheeks.
Finally, he let out a big tobaccoish sigh and got up. He
paced around for a while, lit a cigar, and stared out of the
porthole, so that I saw only the broad blue of his back.

After a time he left, saying he was going to fetch Miss
Jefferson. Polly finally came much later, bringing Washington with her, and she took me in her arms.

The next two days, Polly and I spent the afternoons
listening to stories about Paris from Monsieur LaFaurie.
It didn't seem possible that such a city could exist on the
same planet with Charlottesville, Virginia. We never tired
of hearing the descriptions of the ladies and their dresses,
the coiffures, the gardens of the Tuileries and Versailles,

the palaces of the king, the Royal Palace, Marly, Fon-
tainebleau. I dreaded that I would be sent back to Virginia
once Polly was safely delivered to London. Polly said she
wouldn't allow it, but I had already learned not to put too
much faith in the promises of mistresses.

Captain Ramsay announced that we would reach our
destination the next day, the twenty-sixth of June, and little
Polly understood that she would be separated from Captain
Ramsay, to whom she had become so attached. She too
made everybody laugh by announcing that she would not
leave the ship until she had her storm at sea. That she felt
cheated, after being practically kidnapped onto this ship,
not to have had a real storm and waves *that* high. Captain
Ramsay laughed and said he would ask the cook if he
would "stir" up a storm for Polly that night.

The last night I dressed Polly in white muslin and put her
hair up. I dressed myself in red with a dark blue girdle and
I let my hair out and tied it with a red ribbon. The gentlemen seemed quite pleased. Captain Ramsay seemed relieved
that I was myself again, and all the officers and gentlemen
rose when we left the table.

The next morning we saw birds and smelled land. After
a long voyage even the inexperienced can small land.
Everybody was up early so as not to miss the first glimpse
of the shore and the famous Cliffs of Dover. We were to
go up the Thames to London. We had spent six weeks on
the sea. I had stored up those six weeks of freedom, of
being at no one's beck and call, making lists in my diary
and entries in my heart. I had read and I had written and I
had dreamed. And I had grown up.

When land was sighted, a great cheer went up from
everybody on deck, and Captain Ramsay appeared resplendent in still another new dress uniform. He was a vain
and beautiful man! The sailors too had on their best tunics.
The ship's orchestra started playing a very gay tune as the
banks of the river closed in on us. We slipped along the
narrow channel toward the port of London Town.

I had never seen such a place filled with more white
people than I had ever imagined in one place. Not one

black face anywhere. It was for me a strange and new sensation. There were no slaves. This was another world.

We had dressed in white that day. Polly was trembling in agitation, and clinging to Captain Ramsay as he led us down the gangplank toward a bright-yellow carriage with magnificent horses, in front of which stood a couple dressed in black. The couple was Abigail and John Adams. They had come to fetch us. They seemed a pretty couple as we approached them. They looked stern and straight in front of their pretty carriage, with a splendid liveried footman atop in scarlet. Abigail Adams was small but still slightly taller than her husband, slim and in black silk. Her husband, holding her arm, was short, round, and portly, with a large square head that seemed especially bald because of the abundance of his side-whiskers. His face was ruddy, his mouth strong, his eyes direct, and his expression happy.

I followed slightly behind Polly and Captain Ramsay, and stood apart while the greetings were exchanged. The Adams couple seemed to know Captain Ramsay and greeted him warmly. I could tell from the set of Polly's body that she was about to burst into tears. She was clinging to Captain Ramsay with both hands, as he and the handsome couple tried to coax her into the waiting vehicle. She called my name in terror and Abigail Adams, in one swift movement, turned her gaze toward me.

I got a good look at her, too. She had an oval face with a long regular nose, a pointed, almost fleshless chin, and a thin mouth. It was her eyes that made her face; they were tear-bright and sparkling, closely spaced and quick, like the eyes of a small animal. From beneath her bonnet sprang bright-red curls. Her eyebrows were arched high, giving her whole face a mischievous look. It was a face that had no age, although at the time she was middle-aged. Her color was high, as in people with that color hair, and, as she turned, there were two bright spots of exasperation on her cheeks.

"And who are you, Miss?"

"I am Mistress Polly's slave, Ma'am."

Several expressions passed quickly across her face, but the one that settled there was one I already knew well: that of a rich white lady eyeing a poor darky slave. She looked first at her astonished husband, then at Captain Ramsay, who still had hold of one of Polly's hands while I had taken the other in mine.

"What!" she said.

It was the first time, I am sure, Abigail Adams had ever seen or addressed a slave of her own country.

CHAPTER 10

LONDON, JULY 1787

I cannot feel but sorry that some of the most Manly Sentiments in the Declaration are Expunged from the printed copy. Perhaps wise reasons induced it. . . .

ABIGAIL ADAMS, 1776

I have had for a fortnight, a little daughter of Mr. Jefferson's, who arrived here with a young Negro girl, her servant from Virginia.

ABIGAIL ADAMS, JULY 1787

"A white slave!" Abigail Adams would never get over the shock of seeing the image of Thomas Jefferson's late wife descending the gangplank of Captain Ramsay's ship in the guise of a Negro slave.

"So it seems. Since we are hosts to one."

"I won't have a slave, black or white, under my roof. It's . . . abhorrent to me."

"I know, Abigail, but the child is here, and we cannot do much about it until we have further instructions. Now, if she had been middle-aged and black . . ."

"Oh, John. It's not that . . . or maybe it is that, I don't know. Her color only underlines the horror of her condition because it's our color. But, even more serious, I can't in good conscience entrust the care of a child to another child. The girl is a child, a beautiful one, but one with undoubtedly no training as a nurse or even a maid. Why, she needs more care than Polly herself!"

"She seems very sweet—clean and good-natured."

"I insist she go back to Virginia. She is of no use to me

88

and I don't see how she could possibly be of any earthly
use to Mr. Jefferson."

John Adams shifted his rotund body in the stiff, uncom-
fortable, new English furniture they had ransomed their
lives to buy, and looked at his wife. She was the very
essence of his life and his good fortune. The long years of
separation—first when he left for the Continental Congress
in Philadelphia, then to Europe—were over now, forever.
He would never leave Abigail again. His life was comfortable, happy, and so well-run with her here in London.
He refused to let anything to mar this perfect felicity. He
knew Abigail could be stubborn in matters which she considered principles. She was a staunch abolitionist, as he
was, but without any of his compromising instincts. God—
the child did look like Jefferson's dead wife Martha,
thought John Adams. Years later, they would learn that
Sally Hemings was Thomas Jefferson's half-sister-in-law.

"Abigail, we can't do anything until we have instructions
from Thomas Jefferson. Which, I should think, will be
forthcoming."

"Mr. Jefferson! Where is he? Why isn't he here to fetch
his daughter? I've already written him about Sally."

"Well, we'll have to wait for an answer then."

"Captain Ramsay's ship sails shortly. She ought to be on
it."

Abigail was being particularly stubborn about this,
thought John Adams. Why? The poor girl had just endured
a long sea voyage.

"First of all, Abigail, if Sally leaves before Jefferson
arrives, Polly will be stricken with grief. She is wholly attached to Sally, who is her only link with the loved ones
she's left in Virginia. She's a sensitive child. She'll be upset.
You don't want that, surely?"

"I would do anything for Polly's happiness. I have taken
her to my heart, John—so gay, so fragile, so beautiful. Like
Nabby as a child. But when Mr. Jefferson comes—"

"If he comes. Meanwhile, we can't deprive Polly of
Sally. Besides, I don't like the idea of sending Sally back
unescorted on another dangerous journey. We haven't the
right. She is, after all, under our protection until her
master comes. Jefferson himself may be expecting her. He

may have sent for her, for all we know. We can't dispose of her. She is," Adams continued wryly, "his own property, and we have no legal right to tamper with his rights over her."

"Property!" Abigail Adams stifled an outraged cry. John was baiting her, to be sure, in his lawyerly way, but she couldn't help it, the word fled to the top of her head and burst there like a shell. It was the most iniquitous scheme God had ever invented! How she wished there wasn't a slave in the States! They had fought and won for themselves what they were daily robbing and plundering from those who had just as good a right to freedom as they did; who had set foot on the soil of their blessed nation at the same time their forebears had; who had fallen in battle against England first!

"You know, my dear," Adams continued, "if Sally does get to Paris with Polly, she is, by French law, free. Slavery has been abolished on French soil. By sending her back, we may be depriving her of her only chance for emancipation. She has only to claim it." John Adams knew this would clinch his argument and he had saved it until last. His wife had an acute sense of justice, which he cherished and admired, and slavery had a moral and physical repugnance for her. She felt, as he did, that it corrupted not only the fiber of the best class of the South but threatened the very existence of the nation.

"I didn't know that, John." Abigail was stunned by this news. Had it been fate, then, that had chosen Sally out of the hundreds of Monticello slaves for this potential blessing?

"It is true, Abigail. Think about it."

But Abigail was thinking about something else. She had a strange sense of foreboding, and the obvious origins and extraordinary beauty of Sally Hemings did nothing to dilute her alarm.

Those Southern white planters lived like the patriarchs of old. Even as she thought this, she realized that her own motives were not entirely pure. It was not only the presence of a slave in her household, however temporary, that was so upsetting.

Abigail Adams was nothing if not honest. It was an honesty so total and so dulcet it gave her whole person a kind of brilliant transparency that more than made up for her lack of physical beauty. The maid was a charming and docile child. But the maid was also an affront to white womanhood, she thought, a living and most visible proof of the double standard of white male conduct. The master-slave relationship appalled her not only because the dignity of both master and slave were destroyed but the exercise of total power over other human beings who lived in the closest possible intimacy with them provoked the kind of reciprocal sensuality Abigail Adams both feared in herself, recognized as part of human nature, and read in the face of Sally Hemings. This girl was both a provocation and a victim, she thought. In her still unformed personality there resided the innate arrogance of the totally possessed . . . an elusive disinterestedness that was both an insult and an invitation. How to explain these ambiguous feelings to a man? How to explain powerlessness to any man who had never experienced it? Abigail Adams bit her lip and finally looked up at her husband. "Why didn't you tell me before of this chance for her in France?"

"I hadn't thought of it, actually. There is something disloyal to Jefferson about it."

"I know. And I would sooner be disloyal to myself than to him. But . . . shouldn't we tell her?"

"We'll talk about it again, Abigail. We have nothing to decide just yet. We can decide later. Jefferson, at any rate, knows the law."

"No, I don't think we should discuss it again, John. Let fate decide."

John Adams knew from the tone of his wife's voice, and from her face, that he had won. It was the moment for concessions.

"Of course, you should do whatever you think best," he said. "This is your domain."

"She is devoted to Polly. If we can improve her lot in life, we have the duty to do so, now that I know what Paris might mean to her . . ." Abigail's voice trailed off. She knew her feelings about Sally Hemings. What she didn't know was Sally Hemings's feelings about her. She would have preferred outright hostility in a slave. A sense of injustice . . . of rebellion . . . but this mixture of abject love, indifference, and unquestioning, nay luxurious acceptance, disturbed the neatness of her soul. There was a feral self-satisfaction in the submissiveness of this adolescent, she thought, that was more than that of a servant. It was demeaning to a woman and addicting to a man.

"Besides," her husband's voice continued, "it is pleasant to hear an American accent among the servants."

John Adams liked Sally Hemings. He liked her reserve and the limpid good character he sensed in her. And her voice: he had never heard a more pleasing one—fresh, lovely, and melodious.

Abigail Adams said nothing. She had no desire, she thought to herself, to upset her domestic tranquility over so trivial a matter. Her nine years of separation from John Adams had marked in her a feverish desire for harmony. She had spent those years alone, running the farm and raising the children, six of those years separated from him by the Atlantic Ocean. After so long a wait, so deep a commitment to public service, so passionate an attachment of the heart, she thought, she looked forward only to peace and love in her middle years. Besides, she herself would discuss the problem with Jefferson when he arrived. They were old friends, weren't they? They understood each other, and her admiration for him knew no bounds. He was one of the choice of the earth. She remembered their happy days in Paris together, just after she had been reunited with John, and she remembered the awe of her son, seventeen-year-old John Quincy, who had come with them, for the great Thomas Jefferson.

The affection Abigail Adams lavished on Polly didn't extend to me, although I was also of a tender age and I too had left everything I loved behind me. She was kind to me, but with every effort I made I seemed to provoke more than please her.

Abigail Adams was a Yankee, the first I had ever met. She knew nothing about slavery. I doubt if she had seen a slave before. She knew only that she did not want "one" under her roof. When I came to understand that it was my origins she disliked and not my person, I began to respect and even like her, although I knew she was determined to send me back to Virginia.

Master Adams seemed to understand better. I know he was the one who argued against sending me back to Virginia. But Abigail Adams was adamant. Back to Virginia I would go. So I spent my days in the great house on Grosvenor Square under a cloud of apprehension. Captain Ramsay's ship was making ready to return to America, and Master Jefferson had not yet come for his daughter and me.

I had learned as a slave never to hope, never to anticipate, and never to resist, so I lived from day to day with the other servants, trying to please Mistress Adams—taking care of Polly and keeping as quiet as possible. I took every opportunity to get out of the house and see London, which appeared to me both terrifying and wonderful. Paris, I thought, could not be greater than this!

When we traveled on foot, the carriages and *porte-chaises* of the gentry would pass us as we made our way past the great town houses, which were palaces compared with the mansions I knew in Virginia. I had never seen such beautiful people, clothes, and carriages. The London ladies walked a great deal and very fast. I was used to long walks at Monticello, so I managed many miles a day through London. The sides of the streets were laid with flat stones, and the streets were filthy, but they were always crowded with people laughing and cursing.

Finally, the word came that Master Jefferson was not coming for Polly and me, but that he was sending his *valet de chambre*, Monsieur Petit. Abigail Adams was fit to be tied and Polly refused to leave. With Polly so upset, there was no longer any question of my returning to Virginia. Why Master Jefferson did not come to fetch Polly, I learned later, but for Mistress Adams it was unforgivable.

Abigail Adams's thoughts centered on Jefferson. That his sex was naturally tyrannical was a truth so thoroughly established as to admit of no dispute, but men who wished to be happy, she muttered to herself, should be willing to give up the harsh title of "Master," and all such power of life and death over female souls.

Jefferson wasn't a cruel man, Abigail Adams thought, not by any measure. He was especially tender and gallant with the female sex. Why, then, this cavalier attitude and heartlessness toward his own small dear child, whom he hadn't seen since she was four. Why had be submitted her to the perils of a long sea voyage, uprooted her from those she loved and knew, only to insult her by sending a servant to fetch her! What could be holding Thomas Jefferson in Paris?

"I have written Thomas Jefferson and told him how deeply I regretted his not coming in person for his daughter." John Adams was also trying to calm the furor of his wife.

"I've endured all kinds of heartbreak because of long separations, John. The canceled visits, sickness in solitude away from my heart's partner, and other cruel infractions on my hopes and plans deemed necessary by duty or misfortune . . . have swallowed my grief in silence and self-abdication. But this I will not abide!"

"I'm afraid Adrien Petit is arriving to fetch her."

"Well, he'll have to leave without her if she doesn't want to go," said Abigail Adams stubbornly.

John Adams gazed at his wife in silence. There was something too excessive in her reaction to little Polly's plight. Mightn't she be overreacting, compensating for her own secret hurts all these years? Was she projecting onto this situation her own concealed rage at having been "abandoned" by him, John Adams, in the name of Public Duty and the fate of the newborn United States? He had left her alone so many years. . . . Had he seriously neglected his children in favor of his country? One thing was certain. He would never leave Abigail again.

True to her word, Mistress Adams made Monsieur Petit cool his heels for two weeks, while Polly refused to leave with a man "she couldn't understand." But no more messages came from Master Jefferson. And Petit was unmovable. He would not leave without us; he had his orders.

Finally, through the combined efforts of Mistress Nabby, Master Adams, and me, Polly Jefferson was finally detached from the skirts of Mistress Abigail Adams and bundled into the carriage that would take us on our road to Paris.

CHAPTER 11

PARIS, JULY 1787

I leave to time the unfolding of a drama. I leave to posterity to reflect upon times past; and I leave them characters to contemplate.

ABIGAIL ADAMS, 1801

Thomas Jefferson stood in the tall rectangle of the French window looking onto his gardens at the Hôtel de Langeac and guessed at the hour. His tall frame stirred in the soft light and the nervous fingers of Jefferson's left hand groped for his timepiece. Then, after a moment's hesitation, he lowered his left hand and, with difficulty, raised his right hand to his waistcoat and extracted his watch. For a brief second, he pressed his right wrist against his breast as if in salutation and then he brought the left hand up to cover the exposed wrist and hand which were slightly twisted inward, the hand having an atrophied look. Slowly his left hand caressed his injured right one, his pale eyes blinking away the pain. A slight smile played at the corners of his fine mouth. As he had guessed, it was almost five.

If Petit and Polly had started out early enough from London, they would be in Dover by now. The thought of London made him pensive. There was still no news of Maria's arrival. How long had he been waiting for word from her? It seemed like years. He dared not move from Paris lest he miss her. Jefferson turned and walked away from the glowing greenery and the multicolored flower beds framed by the windows of his salon. A slender man, with a stiff air, accentuated now by the way he held his injured wrist, Jefferson's eyes were his finest feature. A sapphire blue of dazzling clarity, they seemed to look out upon the world like twin mountain peaks from his great height, frosted and glacial, tinged with melancholy, with lashes the same color as his red-gold hair. His complexion was fair, the fine skin almost transparent under a rash of fine reddish-brown freckles that gave him a youthful, innocent look. The face was aristocratic and handsome with its long, slightly turned-up nose, sensual mouth, and firm, protruding, dimpled chin.

He did not consider himself vain, but he was quite pleased with the likeness the sculptor Houdon had begun of him. He had seen the plaster for the first time a few days before.

Entering his forty-fourth year, Thomas Jefferson had become, since he had been in Paris, almost dandyish in his manner of dressing, favoring creamy lace and sapphire-blue worsted. Even his injury had a certain romantic elegance. After his mysterious fall last year, which had deprived him of the use of his right hand, he had been forced to re-educate himself, and he now wrote almost as well with his left hand as he did with his right. But he was in pain at the moment. Both the wrist and the steady throbbing in his head had not abated since yesterday noon. He would force himself to work tonight. It did not seem possible that Petit and Polly could arrive before the day after next. He was very fond of his *valet de chambre*. He did feel slightly guilty that he had not sent James to London when he had learned that his sister Sally had been sent to accompany Polly from Virginia. He had hesitated, knowing the Adamses' disposition toward Negro slaves; and knowing James's own temperament, he felt safer with Petit. Of course, he could have sent them both, but the extra cost, simply to please James, seemed excessive, especially now when the ministry and his expensive obligations were taking all of his official funds.

He stood absently in the middle of his magnificent oval salon with its painting of "Dawn" by Berthélemy on the ceiling, backlit by the late-afternoon sun, a figure in black with white linen and a blue waistcoat, the fair hair pulled back in a pigtail and lightly powdered.

When a servant in pale-yellow livery entered, he was startled. He had forgotten he had asked for the medicines and hot water to bathe his wrist at precisely five. Thomas Jefferson looked into the eyes of his slave James Hemings as if he were contemplating a mathematical equation.

James Hemings had not seen his sister in four years. She had been ten and he eighteen when he had left Monticello as body servant to Thomas Jefferson. He loved her more than any of his family and now that in two or three days she would be in Paris, the waiting was unbearable. She would bring the sweet breath of Monticello and all that it represented for him—family and the slavehood he had never forgotten.

He knew he could disclaim his bondage any time he wished on French soil. No one could hold him in slavery and now no one could hold her, either. What providence!

Thinking himself on the brink of freedom, he could even look on his master now with a certain affection. He did feel affection for Thomas Jefferson. His master had been more of a father to him than his real father, John Wayles, had ever been. When he and his brothers and sisters had not been freed, as Wayles had promised, and were sent to Monticello as part of his half-sister's inheritance, he had been nine years old. Old enough to work. Old enough to grasp the dream they had been deprived of. His mother, with all her wiles and cleverness, her airs of superiority and her concubinage, had failed. She had failed in the only way that matters to a slave concubine: she had not made his father love her enough to free his children by her.

When James entered the room, he found Thomas Jefferson standing, as if he had forgotten something. He had been in this mood for days now. He was, James knew, expecting word from London on the arrival of Lady Maria Cosway. The servant felt a wave of affection and pity for his master as he saw him there cradling his wounded wrist. Thomas Jefferson was not a happy man, thought James, despite all his fame and riches and celebrated friends. He was lonely. The death of his wife had made it impossible for him to believe again in happiness or good fortune. Moreover, his master missed his home more than he admitted.

Personally, James never intended to see Monticello again, nor Virginia for that matter, but he could understand pain and homesickness, especially since the sudden death of Jefferson's third daughter, Lucy. Now Thomas Jefferson's two remaining children would both be with him, and he, James, would be reunited with his beloved sister. As if they shared the same thought, Jefferson gave him a strange look, then smiled and squeezed his arm. Without a word, Jefferson sat in one of the armchairs and let his servant bathe and massage his wrist.

Two days later, a public coach drew up to the gates of the *hôtel*, and Petit, a little girl, and a very young woman stepped out. Polly Jefferson burst into tears at the sight of her father, whom she didn't recognize, while her maid paled at the sight of her brother. The two girls clung to each other, and finally the two of them embraced James Hemings, as Polly would not let go of her maid.

The joy of seeing the beauty and purity of his sister's face moved James deeply. She was well dressed, he thought, in new black silk that showed off her pale complexion and her dark hair, and she was fully formed. Her eyes were a pure liquid gold, a color he had not seen on anyone else. He took her in his arms and watched as, shyly, his master approached his daughter and pulled her away from her slave. James knew that the paleness of Jefferson's face was an indication of great emotion. Thomas Jefferson was intimidated by his own daughter. Later, he said he would not have known her if he had met her on the street, nor she him.

Polly Jefferson was to make him pay for those four lost years, and Thomas Jefferson paid gladly. He ruled his daughters, as he did everyone, with a fastidious tyranny. It fell hardest on Martha, who loved him most, but all of them were to feel the weight of that demand and its fetters of steel.

But that day they were a happy and reunited family. Martha, home from her convent, was dazzled by the beauty of her little sister and her maid. After much kissing and embracing, Thomas Jefferson and his two daughters went inside. Brother and sister remained behind in the sunshine. Only Petit remained apart from this "family" celebration.

How strange were the ways of Americans and their servants, he was thinking. James had explained to the Frenchman that they were literally the same family. This had shocked Petit, for he was the perfect servant: discreet in his service, correct, loyal in his protection of the ruling class and their privileges.

As they kissed and embraced, Adrien Petit saw more clearly than any of them the farce and the tragedy of that reunion.

Before the week was over, Polly Jefferson was in the Abbaye de Panthémont with her sister Martha. Sally Hemings was installed at the ministry and being taught by James's tutor, Mr. Perrault, and Petit began to teach her to be a ladies' maid.

Jefferson remembered everything and asked questions about everyone, white and black. Sally Hemings, through her mother, knew everything that had gone on in the intervening years. She delighted him with her stories, her reports on the crops and gardens. She took over from James the duties of nurse, and every day, her small but surprisingly strong hands would bathe and massage his wrist while she kept up a steady stream of conversation in her soft Virginia accent, a relief to his ears from the harsh beauty of the French he had become so accustomed to. Nothing seemed to be too trivial for him to ask about.

"Tell me everything," he begged. "Who has died, who has married, who has hanged himself because they cannot marry?"

The mansion where she would live now, explained James to his sister, was called the Hôtel de Langeac. James had moved there with his master about a year after they had arrived in Paris, where his master was minister plenipotentiary and ambassador to the French king, Louis XVI. The Hôtel de Langeac was situated halfway up the Champs-Elysées, one of the main thoroughfares leading out of the city. It went up to and then down the bridge leading to Neuilly and thence to Saint Germain-en-Laye, Marly, and the king's palace of Versailles. The *hôtel* (which James explained to her was the French name for a private mansion) adjoined the Grille de Chaillot, a large and beautiful wrought-iron and gilded-bronze gate that marked the limits of the city and was one of its exits and entrances at which the city tolls were levied.

The mansion itself was in creamy white stone with sculptured friezes. The main gate led into a spacious court-yard. To the right were the steps that led up to the front door. To the left of the reception hall was a sweeping pink marble staircase that led to the upper stories. On the ground floor was a circular room with a skylight, and adjoining it was an oval drawing room, one of the most beautiful of the mansion, from which steps led into the garden. It was the ceiling of this oval room which was decorated with the painting of Jean-Simon Berthélemy's "Dawn," the master's favorite.

James led his stunned sister through the elegant, beautiful rooms. On the second floor were the master apartments, with their spacious sun-filled bedrooms, each the size of the drawing room at Monticello, and each with its dressing room and bathroom attached with a hammered-copper and porcelain bathing tub. Then, with great excitement, James showed his sister the "lieux anglais," or water closets, the latest invention and most modern installation imaginable. The young girl marveled at what she had until now called with awe "The Big House." Monticello. She burst into laughter.

The furnishings were as luxurious as the architecture; the dining room was in the same yellow silk as James's livery; the oval salon in blue and green velvet; tapestries and wall hangings abounded, delicately carved armchairs, satin bed-steads, gleaming rosewood and teak desks. She had never seen so many paintings and statuary, Persian rugs and ornate mirrors, bright parquet floors. There were immense bouquets of flowers, bronze clocks ticking; crystal chandeliers that held hundreds of candles.

The sweetness of her voice echoed down the endless corridors of the hôtel where she would pass almost two years of her life and would become accustomed to the precise and languorous sound of the French which now enveloped her.

CHAPTER 12

PARIS, DECEMBER 1787

Yet will I be dumb and silent and not open my mouth
because thou Oh Lord hast done it.

ABIGAIL ADAMS

"Slavery is outlawed in France. We are on French soil.
That means we are emancipated. Free."

"I don't believe you," whispered Sally Hemings, as if
they were being overheard in the empty pantry under the
kitchens.

"It is true!"

"You make so many jokes, James, tell so many far-
fetched stories. . . ."

"Why don't you ask your master, if you won't take your
brother's word? Ask a white man."

"Have you ever asked him?"

"I don't have to ask what I know to be true. There are
white men in Paris and London and Boston who are working for the freedom of Negro slaves everywhere, but
Thomas Jefferson isn't one of them."

"It seems so unbelievable."

"It's not, not if you have the courage to claim what is
yours by right."

"It would hurt him to know we were talking like this. He
is all we have."

"All we have!" James Hemings slapped his sister's face.
It was an instinctive gesture, directed more against his own
rage than at her disbelief. The effect on her was immediate.
Her eyes welled tears and she stopped listening. The
enormity of what her brother had said struck her with the

same force as had his hand. She had never contemplated freedom. Freedom, to Sally Hemings, was a vague, glimmering place no one ever returned from to prove it really existed. Before she realized it, she spoke her thought aloud. "What do 'free' people do?"

"They work for themselves and their families," James answered. "They get paid for their labor. They go where they want and do what they want according to the nature and demand of their trade. They vote. They hold property. No one can imprison them, brand them, beat them, kill them with impunity, and no one can sell them." James Hemings tried to control his anger and tried to explain as he would to a child, for he remembered that his sister was still a child.

"Free people marry and have children, who belong to them and for whom they are responsible and who in turn take care of them in old age. Free people do what they want without asking permission of any man. Many are like us, mulatto, métis, or quadroon, but there are black freedmen as well. In the French Indies, one can buy one's freedom by accumulating enough money to buy oneself back. A few slaves have even done it in America." James took a deep breath and continued. "Freedmen protect their home and hearth and children and wife. They congregate with their friends when and where they wish. They choose their holidays and travel without permission from anyone. They have rights and are protected before the law. Free people have family names that they pass from father to son. They have property, and they can learn to read and write."

"But we already know how to read and write, and we have a family name!" said Sally Hemings. She clung to the one thing she understood.

"Not our family name—a white man's family name, and what good does it do us to read and write? To read and write is to be able to rise in the world, not to amuse one's master or mistress by reciting like a trained monkey, or reading to them when they are too lazy to do it for themselves. We must refuse to go back to Virginia and prepare ourselves for the days we are commanded to do so."

"Stay in France?"

"Or Europe. There are other countries besides France."

"What would I do?"

"Let me worry about that."

"They have children that really belong to them? They cannot be sold? Explain it to me again. From the beginning."

"In the beginning . . ." James smiled. He smiled and lifted her up in his arms. "Little sister, you are going to learn; learn to walk, then learn to run! Then you will learn some other things as well. Your French is not bad. . . . And that voice!"

Sally Hemings smiled uncertainly. She found it difficult to follow James's changes in mood. His ideas, which would spill out of him in a torrent of words, admonishments, curses, lessons, and silences, always frightened her. The catlike eyes would gleam with malice one minute and brim with adoration the next. Sometimes he would let loose such a cyclone of abuse that the air itself seemed to shrivel. He had done this at home as well, provoking gales of laughter from the gathered entourage. Her mother had been glad to see him leave with Master Jefferson; at least it was less likely he would end up swinging on the end of a rope in Paris than in Albemarle County. Her half brother Robert called James's swearing raunchy, polecat, ornery, low-life, filthy swearing, and the whole family would burst out laughing, since Robert would find himself swearing at swearing. Then someone would break down and plead for one of his imitations, for no one at Monticello possessed the art of mimicry better than James. He had the ability to make people laugh and make their blood run cold at the same time. He would choose his words carefully and would work himself up into a malicious frenzy. This was what he was doing now. He was taking her carefully through an insurrectionist garden, having her smell first this flower, then another, leading her gently toward the strong scents, the bolder colors, the mandrake, and the poison. Little by little, he led her where he wanted her to go, stopping to explain an idea. All these ideas were new to her, and James had to explain to her over and over.

He made her study seriously, she read anything she could get hold of. They were already planning what to tell their master when the time came.

Sally Hemings acquiesced to everything. She was borne along on the tide of her brother's vision and excitement. After a long lesson, she would make her way to her room, lie on her narrow bed, and stare at the ceiling.

James Hemings knew that it was lonely for his sister in the ministry. There was no one her age, and she had no official duties besides that of bathing her master's injured wrist. Except for an occasional errand, or a visit to the convent, she spent most of her time strolling in the gardens, or reading.

She applied herself to learning everything she could, the rudiments of dressmaking, hairdressing, and clothes-cleaning. In a few months the backwater-country slave had learned to speak the language well. Brother and sister were now speaking French together. They would also at times combine their Virginia-slave English with French, inventing their own secret language. But with Thomas Jefferson, Sally Hemings spoke only her soft Virginia-accented English. Thomas Jefferson sought his slave's company more and more. They seemed drawn to each other, master and slave, by mysterious threads that Sally Hemings did not completely understand. Thomas Jefferson indulged her as a child rather than as a servant, laughing when Petit remarked that it didn't matter if she was useless around the ministry; she was such a joy to be with and to look at. And often he would gaze at her, staring without realizing it, or without realizing that he was being watched.

Both James Hemings and Adrien Petit saw this affection develop. Petit, observing with the cynicism of his race and his caste, and James like a blind man in a lighted room he had been away from Virginia and slavery too long.

"James?"

"Yes?"

"Do you remember our father at all?"

"Master Wayles? Sure I remember him, I was nearly ten when he died."

"What was he like? Was he kind to Mama?"

"I suppose you could call him kind. He never mistreated her and she had the run of the house, nay, the whole plantation. He was never there."

"What happened to her husband?"

"He died. At least I think he died. I never knew Mama to say anything about him."

"And her other children—those who didn't come with us to Monticello?"

"There were two who became the property of our half sister Tibby Wayles."

"And Mama's mother, our grandmother?"

"Knew her too at Bermuda Hundred. An Afric she was. The most beautiful woman on the plantation, and she was old when I saw her. She had run away many times. She had an 'R' for runaway branded on her chest—it should have marked her cheek, but at the last moment our father didn't have the heart to do it."

"Mama never speaks of her."

"I know."

"And on the other side, our father's mother?"

"He was an old man, our father. He died a few months after you were born. I never saw anybody who looked like his mother."

"So strange to have blood in your veins and not know where it comes from."

"Yes. Not like the Bible, where you can say he was the son of . . . who was the son of . . . who was the son of . . . That's what you mean?"

"Yes," she said, "yes, that's what I mean. If I could know that the son of the son of my son would have some knowledge of me, would have something . . . a portrait of me or a mother or grandmother who remembered me . . . if something of mine, some object or some memory could touch him years and years and years from now . . . That he would know who I am. Who I was. That it wouldn't all be silence."

There was so much fervor in Sally Hemings's voice that it stopped James from making a derogatory remark about ancestors. She was right in a way. Blood was magic. To be able to trace it back was the most precious thing they had lost. He thought about the plantation and the old people with their fetishes. They knew blood was magic, a link to the past, a curse or a blessing on its inheritors, a fearful potent magic. Even their mother, Elizabeth Hemings, was not completely free of ancestor worship. She knew a few spells herself. He smiled bitterly. If only she had used them at the right moment.

The two young people looked at each other, their eyes meeting in frail comprehension.

"Yes," James said, "it is as if part of you is recovered if you claim ancestors and expect descendants."

"But if we don't know them—can't find them or their graves or anything?"

"Then it is very bad voodoo. Very bad spirits. The gods are angry and turn away from us."

It was enough for white people to know that they were "sons of God" straight down from heaven. No intervening generations to cloud their divinity; their blood was "pure," yet they deigned to mix it with the blood of Africa, a blood laden with the responsibility of a million years.

"And if our gods are angry, can we go to their God?"

"It seems we started off wrong 'cause of somebody called Ham. And so we are damned to be waterbearers and wood-choppers and servants because, all of a sudden, we are back with blood curses. We arrive here in trouble. Everybody else starts out with a new soul, only we come here with the curse of Ham around our necks. No purity for us. Christ didn't get around to it."

"And the Afric gods say this, too?"

"Of course not. They haven't even heard of Jesus. He hasn't been around long enough to even make the acquaintance of those gods. Frankly, if people get the gods they deserve, then white people sure got theirs because He's the meanest God I ever heard of. And the more He loves you, the harder it is on you. So He must really love us!"

James threw back his head and let out a roar of laughter.

James Hemings had the narcissistic energy of a forest animal. Almost as tall as his master, he was lean and muscled. His body gave him a European rather than an American look: the coal-black wavy hair, the thin flared nose, even the dark-ivory color seemed less exotic here against the rich brocades and silks of French interiors than in the simpler trappings of Monticello. His face was a harder replica of his sister's. The shadow of his heavy beard and eyebrows shaded his face with a kind of violence entirely absent from hers. The generous mouth was almost always engaged in complaining and turned down in perpetual discontent. Yet, instead of giving his face a somber, even disagreeable aspect, his bad nature took on a melancholy and romantic tinge. Both black and white had always indulged him in this, and everyone said that he had a handsome, even noble face, despite its latent anger, which could be dispersed with one delicious smile. This had saved him from many a reprimand and several beatings.

His arrogance and adventurous nature stood him in good stead as a cook, and his long, beautiful hands had begun to shape masterly cakes and pastries. He was now in the midst of his third apprenticeship. The first had been with a *traiteur* named Combeaux. He was calm and patient in the kitchen. Meticulous and infinitely careful. Never did he lose his temper while cooking—the mark of a true chef. Adrien Petit recognized this, and although he was hazy on the dictates and protocol of American slavery, he had already indicated to "Jim-mi" that he would be welcomed in several French households when, as James put it, "the time came."

One day, six months after her arrival in Paris, Sally Hemings passed the gilded mirror in the entrance of the Hôtel de Langeac and caught a glimpse of herself. She was pleased with what she saw. She had completely recovered from her mild case of smallpox, an experience that had terrified her and through which James and Petit and Master Jefferson had nursed and indulged her. She had had only a few eruptions on her face, but those had caused her untold misery. The doctor had been kind, and her ordeal had left her without a mark on face or body.

Her provincial air and homemade country clothes had disappeared with the fever and her new skills in dressmaking. The clear liquid gold of her eyes gazed serenely at her image in the polished silver. She was satisfied.

Her lips turned up in a smile and two dimples flashed for an instant on either side of her mouth. Abigail Adams had been right. It was more criminal to be out of fashion in Paris than to be seen naked. To which the Parisians were not averse, as Mistress Adams had noted . . .

The French ladies, she thought, as she looked at herself in the mirror, displayed such an art with powder, rouge, wigs, perfumes, and elaborate clothes that you couldn't be sure they weren't the famous dolls of Mademoiselle Bertin, dressmaker to the queen, that traveled from court to court all over Europe, dressed in the last fashion.

The French ladies spent a great deal of time making themselves beautiful, she mused. The French ladies also possessed a most voluptuous room installed only for bathing, called a *salle de bain*. She repeated the expression out loud. The French ladies would even sometimes receive visitors there! They would empty a pint of milk into the water to cloud it, and called it a *bain de lait*. The French ladies . . .

The young girl repeated the new French expressions she was learning, savoring them each time anew. She laughed outright. She was happier than she had ever been in her life.

She was learning new and independent ways of thinking and behaving. Her eyes no longer slid off the glances of whites. She was able to look white people in the eye, even to address them in French or English without hesitation.

Humming to herself, she smoothed the folds of her new dress, pulled the hood of the soft woolen cloak she wore over her head, and stepped out into the crisp December air.

In December a young painter from Massachusetts named John Trumbull arrived at the mansion. I liked him from the beginning. He was to spend some time with us, sketching the French officers who had fought in our Revolution and doing a portrait of my master for the painting commemorating the Declaration of Independence. He was tall and thin, with dark round eyes that seemed to see everything and consume what they saw. Things, he told me, were lines and planes to him, light and shadow. I asked him if he saw me this way and he replied by making several sketches. He showed them to me.

"This cannot be me," I said to him.

"But it is. You have only to look in the mirror."

I tried to please everybody: my master, my brother, and the girls; but it was not always easy. James had always been demanding and quick of temper, and now he had taken on all the airs of the French servants. He took me in charge and rationed my contacts with the other servants. Polly had wanted me to accompany her to the convent, where the young ladies were allowed to keep their maids, but Master Jefferson was against it. He, too, was making more and more demands on my time and guarded me jealously from the outside world.

As consolation for my disappointment at not being allowed to stay at the convent—it was a calm, beautiful place, which I had loved at first sight—he had allowed me to study with Monsieur Perrault, James's tutor in French.

"You have a lovely voice, Sally. Married to the French language properly spoken, it will be extraordinary. Extraordinary." It was the first compliment I had ever received outside of my slave family and I had blushed. But Monsieur Perrault went on, without apparently noticing.

"It is not so much in the tone as in the timbre. Like a musical instrument. A pity you have had no musical training. I am sure you should sing. And you, 'Jim-mi,' at least you've learned how to swear in French to perfection. A notable necessity for a chef."

Monsieur Perrault had looked from me to James. I knew he was really very fond of "Jim-mi" despite his "*sottises*" and "*mauvais traitements.*" James was horrible to his tutor, but diligent in his studies, preparing himself for his "future." He never said exactly what this future consisted of. It was a "secret," only to be revealed at the "right" moment.

There were only nine months between us, and Patsy and I were preoccupied with the changes taking place within ourselves. I was almost fifteen, she sixteen. Polly was still a child, but she had all the beauty and grace denied her sister. Martha had long resigned herself to not being beautiful but she was still unhappy about being in a country, and a society, that placed such importance on it. Because she was plain, several beautiful ladies befriended Martha, as she was no threat to them. She was the image of her father, and almost as tall as he. She towered over most of the men who were introduced to her. She had bright-red hair like her father, and freckles, which were her despair. Still she had a kind of touching grace, and she was an excellent horsewoman. She had her admirers, but

she rarely went out in company. Sometimes she returned
home for a special party or dinner, but during my first
months in Paris, Master Jefferson was occupied with the
mysterious Maria Cosway and rarely saw his daughters,
except for Sunday dinner and an occasional tea at the
Comtesse de Noailles. So, I would often visit Martha and
Maria at the convent and bring the latest gossip, of which
I got an earful from James and the other servants. Martha
was annoyed by her father's infatuation with Maria Cosway
and repeatedly told me so. Her jealousy was bitter, and
I was later to feel its cruelty. I was just as envious of Maria
Cosway—her exquisite manners, her magnificent gowns,
and haughty condescending and languishing airs. She came
to see Master Jefferson with a proprietary attitude that
made James mimic her behind her back, and the servants
raise their eyebrows. Only Petit knew the real story, and he
was as close-mouthed about it as old Martin back at
Monticello.

"I wish she would go back to her husband!" This seemed
to explode from Martha's very soul, and I realized that
Paris gossip didn't stop at the convent gates.

"She is very beautiful."

"But so old! She must be at least twenty-five!"

We sat in silence charged with malice. How could men
be so anxious to pursue such decrepit creatures? I thought.
They seemed to be made out of some soft, pudding-like
material that had nothing to do with muscles and bones.
What would they do if they had to run?

I remembered the joy I felt when, picking up my skirts,
I would race as fast as I could down the Champs-Elysées,
across the fields, toward the bridge of Neuilly, looking
behind to make sure no one was watching. I would run
until I had a stitch in my side and then pause, listening to
the pumping of my heart, the quickness of my breath. . . .

We did not know that at that very moment Maria Cosway, the object of all our jealous envy, was already on her
way back to her husband, having quit Paris that very day
for good.

Martha then turned to me and whispered, "There was a
gentleman a few days ago . . . you know, who killed himself because he thought his wife didn't love him. They had
been married ten years. . . . I believe that if every husband

in Paris was to do as much, there would be nothing but
widows left." And then suddenly, with an emotion I
didn't understand at the time, she said, "I wish with all my
soul the poor Negroes were all freed. It grieves my heart!"

CHAPTER 13

PARIS, MARCH 1788

> Thou canst not prove a villain, impossible. I therefore still
> insist upon it, that I neither do nor can fear thee.
>
> ABIGAIL ADAMS

Perhaps I had always known that he would claim me. Had
not the same happened to my mother and my sisters?

I watched him secretly to see if he knew, but I realized
he would know only when the moment had arrived. I
could hasten or delay that moment, but I was powerless to
prevent it.

Once I went with Martha and her father to Notre Dame
Cathedral to hear a mass by Cardinal Beaugrave. Both
Martha and I were so overwhelmed by the beauty of the
cathedral and the mass that we burst into tears. When I
accompanied James on his excursions to the city, he would
speak of what our life would be together, once we had our
freedom. He would speak wildly and with arrogance, as if
what he dreamed could be had at the wave of a hand.
Perhaps so, but I knew as sure as death that I belonged to
Thomas Jefferson.

I hardly strayed from the mansion on the Champs-
Elysées. My first nine months in Paris had been happy
ones, and now I tried to prolong that happiness, plunging
into my studies, grateful and hardly believing my good
fortune, honing the knowledge I had acquired and forgetting the sword that hung over my head.

Everyone was homesick for Virginia as one gray, damp
Parisian day followed the other in monotonous succession.
Even the famous Paris rats had disappeared, frozen into

the sewers under the Seine on which the nobility and bourgeois skated. There was fire after fire on the outskirts of the city as entire shantytowns went up in smoke. The men were bored, and an oppressiveness hung over the days as we roamed the mansion, each in our little orbit. I remember the silence of those short days when candles burned at noon.

In January, an unheard-of freeze took hold of the city and confined us to the mansion. We knew that the poor people of Paris had begun to die of the cold and of starvation.

Haughty French officers came and went; Trumbull sketched them for his painting of the Surrender of Cornwallis at Yorktown. James became more and more mysterious, speaking of "freedom" and "revolution" and "liberty." Each time he would speak in this way, I remained silent. A sense of fatality took hold of me. I was the center of a drama; yet no one else seemed to know it. Only the painter Trumbull, with his great black eyes, seemed to have a sense of what was happening.

"Do you like it?"

"Oh yes, Master. It is very fine."

I had come to serve his tea. He was finishing his study of my master for his painting of the Declaration of Independence. I gazed at the portrait. It showed a man of high countenance, young with a long and serious face, a high brow with soft curling red hair covering it and a wide unsmiling mouth that made him appear rather stern. It was a good resemblance.

I often sought John Trumbull's company. He was a gentle man. Sometimes I would be impatiently waved away. When, later, he had finished his work in Paris and was folding his easel in preparation for his departure, I felt more alone than ever. I could not confide my fears to James. I thought of Petit, who liked me, but he was devoted to his master, unlikely to thwart him in anything he desired. As for the other women in the house, I was afraid of them and realized they would have no sympathy with a so common and sought-after situation. Above all, I was separated from Polly and Patsy by their innocence. I was alone, in a strange world, as I waited for a sign.

Spring came.

The ice on the Seine cracked, and its black water seeped between the glistening white. The days became longer and the candles went out. The rats came back and the brilliant stones of Paris shone again in the pale sunlight, which had timidly reappeared.

I was fifteen years old.

"I'm going away, Sally. To Amsterdam with Mr. Adams and then to the Rhineland. I'll be gone for six weeks. I want you to study hard while I'm away."

"Yes, Master."

Away. I hadn't counted on that. More waiting.

"Don't look so sad, my Sally. It is only for a little while."

"Yes, Master."

"Your friend John Trumbull recommends the journey highly."

The tall somber image of Master Trumbull distracted my thoughts for a moment.

"When I leave, you will stay with Madame Dupré near the convent on rue de Seine. You can visit Polly and Patsy, and I have arranged that you may spend Sundays at the convent. Mr. Perrault will come to give you your lessons during the week."

"Yes, Master."

"I'm giving all the staff a holiday. It is not proper that you stay here . . . alone."

"Yes, Master."

"I shall miss you, Sally."

"Yes, Master."

"Sally, is that all you have to say?"

"Yes, Master."

"Sally, I shall miss you. I promise . . ."

"Promise me!"

The words burst out of me, more a sob than an exclamation. I could bear the waiting no longer. I drew my head up and looked long into his eyes. Deep in the centers was a dark pinprick. My own reflection.

Yes, I thought, the time has come.

A thousand times a day fear would overwhelm me. Blood would rush to my head, and often I would clutch a velvet hanging or the back of a silk-covered *fauteuil*. I stopped seeing Polly and Patsy. I dared not leave the house lest he

send for me. At night I fell asleep sitting upright on the
side of my bed. My body would be turned away from the
door, but my head and shoulders would be turned toward
it. There was no lock, and I would not have dared turn the
key had there been one. I would not face the door lest I
invite its opening, yet I could not turn completely away.
Thus I sat watch through the night.

Lord keep me from sinking down.

Lord keep me from sinking down.

Lord keep me from sinking down. I would repeat to
myself, until in the early hours of the morning, exhausted,
I would sleep.

The night before his departure, he sent for me, but he
did not appear. I fell asleep in his room, and when I awoke
an immense shadow blocked my vision.

I had no idea how long he had been standing there. Now
that he had come, I felt no fear, only an overwhelming
tenderness. His presence for me was command enough; I
took control of him. I bent forward and pressed a kiss on
the trembling hands that encompassed mine, and the contact of my lips with his flesh was so violent that I lost all
memory of what came afterward. I felt around me an
exploding flower, not just of passion, but of long deprivation, a hunger for things forbidden, for darkness and un-
reason, the passion of rage against the death of the other I
so resembled. For in this moment I became one with her,
and it was not my name that sprang from him but that of
my half sister.

At once he left me, surveying me from above with the
eyes of a man afraid of heights scanning a valley from a
tower. Then his body tensed and rushed toward me as if
he had found a way to break his fall.

Thus did Thomas Jefferson give himself into my keeping.

When I awoke the bed was empty beside me. I slipped
from the abandoned bed and stared at the gray rectangles
of light from the tall windows barred by the shadows of the
balconies. In the strange, majestic room, I gathered my
clothes from the four corners where they had been flung in
the violence of the night. I stared at the sheet and then
quickly, without thinking, covered the bed with its counterpane. The feeble groping for James's dream had been erased
by the force of a man's body and a man's will.

I washed and dressed, and quickly left the house by the front door. The morning was cool, but the day would be fair. Frost was still on the trees and bushes of the garden, but tiny sparks of green had begun to appear.

I started to walk slowly toward the Pont de Neuilly. I had taken my brother's heavy cloak, yet I trembled uncontrollably either from shock or cold, I don't remember. To my surprise, I recognized ahead of me his solitary figure breaking pane after pane of silvery light. Even at this dawn hour, and for every dawn to come. Thomas Jefferson had risen before me and had chosen the cold bitter morning to walk abroad.

I was filled with confusion. Should I turn back? Hurry to greet him? Stay as I was now, fifty paces behind him? Call out to him? I followed for a long moment, dreading that he would, for some reason, turn around and see me, but he kept his eyes ahead. I fell farther and farther behind as his long legs strode through the Elysian fields spread out before him. The bottom of James's cloak, wet with dew, dragged behind me. I was seized with a terrible yearning. I thought of my mother and her mother before her. Nothing would ever be the same again. Nothing would ever free me of him. Nothing would erase those strange words of love which I had to believe in my weakness.

"*Je t'aime*," he had said.

In his terror, he had used that most potent of weapons, the ruler of the mighty as well as the helpless. And I had answered, without any other words passing between us.

"*Merci, monsieur.*"

CHAPTER 14

SPRING, 1788

Nothing escapes the apprehension of those who have
everything to lose.

ABIGAIL ADAMS

James discovered the concubinage of his sister that morning when he turned back the counterpane of his master's
bed. He had waited, first outside the door of the bedroom
and then in the gray shadows of the arc made by the
curved marble stairway of the Hôtel de Langeac in the
early dawn. He had seen Thomas Jefferson descend the
grand staircase and carefully unlatch the front door and
step out into the courtyard of the mansion. For one
moment, the rosy light loomed against the blackness of the
arch. Then the door had slammed shut. James had waited
for a length of time he could not measure when Sally Hemings came down the same stairs. She had turned, almost
facing him and wearing his heavy black cloak and had gone
out the front door.

Sally Hemings's brother now stood in his master's empty
room under the painted ceiling of "night." He was twenty-
three years old. Of those twenty-three years, fourteen had
been spent serving, loving, and tending Thomas Jefferson.
Like some demigod who descended from the heavens to
mingle with mortals, he had ascended, leaving that which
had to be cleaned up to his servants. James's master had left
Paris.

He was in throes of some powerful emotion, yet he
couldn't sort out which emotion it was. James Hemings
was a virgin. His master and his sister had gone beyond

the pale of his existence. He gathered the stained sheets in his arms. The complexity of his new feelings paralyzed him. Violence, like an ague, shook him. What should he do? How should he conduct himself as a free man? Kill?

"Help me," whispered James. "God, help me."

He didn't—would never—have the courage to kill Thomas Jefferson.

From that day on, James dreamed of those spots of blood. The whole bed would turn red as he touched it, staining his own hands as if he had plunged them into the entrails of a living creature. He would struggle to take the sheets off the bed, but they would heave and swirl, and sickening sounds would come from them. Terrified, he would back away, but the sheets would pursue him, leaping at his throat like a wild animal, enveloping him in a slimy embrace. In the ensuing struggle, he would be hurled into the fire burning in the room's hearth. His hands and feet, still swaddled in the sticky sheets, would begin to burn. Then his arms and legs. Then his private parts. Finally, only his torso would remain with a blackened and charred head, the mouth opened in a horrible but soundless scream. The head would begin to spin itself in agony until it literally spun itself off the burning body and lay in the ashes which filled its mouth and eyes and nostrils, strangling and suffocating him.

That same dream would come back time and again, and would remain with him until the day he died. The first time he had awakened to find himself being shaken by a pale Petit, terrified by his screams.

"Jim-mi. There is nothing to be afraid of. *Réveille-toi, mon garçon.* It's only a nightmare. Wake up, son."

"No, not like that! Glide. GLIDE! You're not supposed to lift your feet from the floor!"

"I'm *not* lifting my feet from the floor!"

"You are too. You walk like a duck! Look at Sally. She does it perfectly; better than either of us."

"That's because I've watched the *frotteur* do it every day for a year now! Just think of waxing floors with your feet like he does and you'll have it."

"Waxing floors! Will you just imagine the queen of France waxing floors!"

"I'd never thought of it! Marie-Antoinette, *'La Frotteuse.'* "

The three girls dressed in their undergarments and perspiring, collapsed into loud laughter, falling onto the deep featherbed in Sally Hemings's room at Madame Dupré's boardinghouse.

Martha and Maria had doffed their crimson convent uniforms, which lay in a heap on the polished floors. Sally Hemings had been in her chemise, being fitted for a new dress, when the girls arrived. Martha and Maria had begun to visit their maid regularly in her comfortable and cozy rooms. There was absolutely no privacy for the girls in the convent, the fifty pensioners slept in two immense rooms without curtains, the other rooms being reserved for drawing rooms and classrooms. Sally Hemings was overjoyed and welcomed the company of her two playmates. Released from the oppressive Hôtel de Langeac, from the smoldering power of Jefferson's sensuality, and the bitterness of her brother James, she had found relief, joy, and affection in the adolescent company of Marie and Martha. Her initiation into womanhood forgotten, she basked in her temporary return to childhood.

Often she would leave her rooming house and walk the several blocks to the Abbaye de Panthémont, entering through the chapel on the rue de Grenelle and stepping into the courtyard filled with crimson-uniformed ladies of the gentry. As this was not only a school for girls, but a retreat for spinsters, abandoned wives, and ladies of the court in temporary seclusion, the ways and gossip of Versailles and the court found their way here with rapidity, and girls were playing a game now popular at the school: attempting to imitate the famous walk of the queen, Marie-Antoinette, the "most beautiful walk in France."

With the voluminous hoop skirts in fashion called *robes à paniers*, which completely hid the bottom half of a lady's body, the desired effect of moving oneself from one place to the other was that of floating disembodied along the galleries and antechambers of palaces like ships on water, rather than humans on legs and feet. The effect was obtained by never lifting the feet from the floor, but by gliding them forward and slightly outward along the surface of the floor in a skating movement, and keeping the tightly corseted upper part of the body erect and rigidly immobile. The walk was practiced by both the ladies and gentlemen at the court of Versailles, but no one in the kingdom achieved the desired effect with greater success than the stately, full-bosomed queen herself.

"One of the ladies at Panthémont said that she had never seen such a sight as the queen sailing along the gallery of mirrors. One could see nothing in the throng of courtiers but a forest of waving plumes a foot and a half taller than her ladies' heads," Martha said. She turned to Sally Hemings.

"Can you imagine such a thing, Sally? Oh, how I would love to see it just once, the court of Versailles. Papa has promised to take me to the public galleries when he returns. Anyone may enter, you know, and the gardens as well are public, and you may come across the queen herself walking with her ladies. Of course, we shall have an *entrée* in the person of the Comtesse de Tessé, who is a lady in waiting to the queen. I will find her gliding like a swan among the pools and fountains of Versailles, and I will drop my best curtsy, and Papa will kiss her hand and . . . Can you imagine!"

Martha Jefferson shook the bare shoulders of her maid gently and affectionately, tossing the mane of bright hair behind her. Sally Hemings nodded to Martha and let her petticoats drop. At any rate, she could walk like a queen, if nothing else.

She fell back into the arms of Martha, pretending to slip, and as she did she let out a whoop: "Her majesty has just glided onto her royal *derrière*. . . ." They all collapsed into new gales of laughter. This brought Madame Dupré to the door of her boarder.

"Girls, ladies, you would think I had a regiment of hussars in my house!"

Madame Dupré was the proprietor of a small rooming house on the rue de Seine. She had been instructed to board the maid of the American minister's daughters while he was away on a trip to Amsterdam and the Rhineland. She had agreed to do this for the sum of twenty-one francs a week plus laundry and dressmaking. The gentle, lovely

girl, who had arrived at her door two weeks ago accompanied by the minister himself, had pleased her. As she
had not been instructed otherwise, Madame Dupré treated
Sally Hemings as she would have treated any maid of an
aristocrat: that is, a young girl of a poor family with no
dowry who enters the service of a great family as a lady's
maid and companion to the daughters of such a family in
return for room, board, and protection. Obviously the
minister thought enough of her not to leave her alone in
the company of his servants when he went abroad. . . .

Madame Dupré had no way of knowing that Sally
Hemings was a slave. She had no way of knowing either
that a "maid" in Virginia was a polite way of indicating
someone who was black. Sally Hemings' complexion told
Madame Dupré nothing, except that she was dark. She
would even have said swarthy, but a little strange; the
particular tint of the young girl's skin was not the same as
she had noted in the Italian or Spanish complexion. It was
rather an extraordinary shade of buff, without the profu-
sion of down that usually accompanied the ladies of that
hue. She was a bit surprised at the meanness of her wardrobe. Certainly if one was poor, one had to know how to
sew in order to dress oneself, but then she was to remedy
these shortcomings by instructing her in dressmaking and
making sure that she had the minimum uniforms of a lady's
maid. Certainly her manners and gentleness and soft,
charmingly accented French bespoke a certain breeding,
and with a little grooming, thought Madame Dupré, she
would surely attract a gentleman of property and improve
her station in life in the time-honored manner of becoming
the mistress or (why not?) the wife of a modest member
of the gentry. She, of course, had had no instructions along
these lines, but as she liked the child, Madame Dupré
decided she would do all she could to improve her while
she was in her charge. Besides, through her mistresses, Sally
Hemings had access to the Abbaye de Panthémont, where
only the finest ladies and young girls retired or were educated. She had only to imitate her betters, she concluded.

When Madame Dupré saw what the girls had been doing,
she joined the laughter. The queen's extraordinary walk
was renowned throughout the kingdom, and when little

Sallie showed her version of it, she had to admit it was both seductive and accurate.

"My, that is quite good. Now do me a curtsy, all of you —*comme il faut*. I have come to serve you tea, but you had better put your clothes back on before the servant sees you in the state of nature."

The three girls stood up and Madame Dupré looked at the virginal young bodies pressed close to her. The eldest Mademoiselle Jefferson was so tall she towered over everyone. Some American ladies were immense, and this one certainly took after her father. She had a fine complexion: milk and roses at the same time, except that it was marred by the same freckles that dotted the countenance of the minister. She remarked on Martha's lovely hair. It was hanging down in a mass of thick auburn waves to her waist. Her eyes were without color or lashes and too close together, and her chin, she felt, was impossible: long and jutting, with the promise of unyielding stubbornness so disagreeable to men. Yet the luxurious curls managed to soften the lines of her face and long nose, and her mouth was delicate, firm, and good humored, bespeaking justice if not generosity, and the body was slim, well made, and bursting with good health.

As for the young Mademoiselle Jefferson, she and her maid resembled each other uncannily. Madame Dupré continued her inventory. They were both remarkably beautiful, both dark with hazel eyes, the maid's being a peculiar but fascinating shade of yellow. They both had deep dimples, prized by French ladies, and soft wide mouths with that touch of sullenness found in ardent characters. The maid reflected the promise in body of the mistress, who was still a child; perfect mat skin, long thick dark hair, and fragile yet compact body with a deep bosom and full hips.

Yes, thought Madame Dupré, with a little luck, *Sallie* will make her fortune in Paris . . . if she has the luck to attract a gentleman.

The first time James Hemings came to visit his sister at Madame Dupré's, she fell into his arms with a cry of relief. She had not seen him since she had left the *hôtel* that March day almost three weeks ago. James Hemings was still reeling from the shock of his sister's seduction, but he determined to show nothing but tenderness and solicitude. He had three or four weeks at the most to convince her that her master had compromised all claims to her love and loyalty by his forcing of her, and that now was the time to claim her rights as a free woman on French soil. Once the demigod was back, his powerful compelling presence would again dominate their lives, and their only chance would be lost, perhaps forever.

He had brought her a letter that had arrived for her from her master.

She had taken the letter from him with trembling hands but had not read it, hiding it in her petticoat pocket. They had then gone out for a walk, as they had so many times before in Paris. Free of uniforms and even the semblance of servanthood, they had roamed the streets and the grand boulevards crammed with new buildings. American Revolutionary ideas were everywhere, and they met them in a form hitherto never encountered by either of them: the newspaper and the broadside.

There were regular newspapers printed every day which, even under the king's Censure Bureau, were wildly critical and full of republican ideas. Anyone with the money to buy or rent or who owned a printing press was free to print and distribute what he liked. These were called broadsides. Anyone doing this was liable, of course, afterward to be arrested by the king's censors for *lèse-majesté*, but no one prevented the broadside from being printed and distributed, even if the author was in the Bastille. It was around the Palais Royal that most of the newspaper vendors congregated and it was usually here, in the magnificent gardens of the palace with its famous meridian cannon fired by the rays of the sun at noon, that brother and sister spent part of their promenade.

The public gardens of the Palais Royal teemed with every manner of man, woman, and beast—from veiled noblewomen on their way to assignations to street prostitutes painted in the gaudy red rouge and white powder in fashion. There were priests and hawkers, lemonade and food vendors, cavaliers and officers of the king's regiment, beggars and pickpockets, raving orators, and all manner of dubious-looking characters. In the center of the gardens was the Duc d'Orléans's new glass-domed circus, the latest wonder of Paris. It was here, amid the pamphlets, engravings, newspapers, broadsides, rumors, and posters, that brother and sister discovered the shadow of things to come.

Each week a letter had come, hand-delivered by James, and each week Sally Hemings had silently hidden it in her petticoats and gone walking in Paris with James. Each week James sought to steal the mind and body of his sister from her master, while she half-listened to his pleas and warnings about her life, too stunned to think of anything except the letter that had arrived.

They were the first letters that anyone had ever addressed to her in all her fifteen years. They had taken on a magic, these letters addressed to "Mademoiselle Sally Hemings." She was unable to explain to James her fascination with the power of these words. Her name had stood independent of her will on the thick white paper. Again and again, she had touched the black letters of the fastidious, elegant handwriting imagining this person "Sally Hemings" to whom they were addressed.

Even not being able to answer these summons, because he was not long enough in each city, seemed right: the magic hold was never broken by the effort it would have taken to answer and thus claim the title by which she was addressed. Instead she had only to wait, to receive, to acquiesce.

The letters themselves, when tremblingly she opened them after James's departure and read the dozen or so lines, were as ordinary as those her master wrote to his daughters, which she also read when they came to visit her. If she expected billets-doux, she got none. Instead, there was a steady stream of fatherly advice, kindly, distant, a little cold, which took on the air of a monologue, since no response was possible. Yet the young girl read and reread her letters. She kept them in a silk envelope she had sewn especially for them. Without knowing why, she showed them to no one, nor did she speak of their existence.

Sally Hemings smiled at her latest geography lessons interspaced with "be a good girl." "Study . . . depend on yourself . . . visit with Patsy and Polly . . . love me. . . ."

These fatherly letters disappointed her. How strange these terse letters that arrived from mysterious German cities so remote from her imagination, she thought.

Then, one day, a new letter arrived. It was dutifully brought to her by James to her rooms and dutifully hidden in her petticoats until she returned from their walk to read it alone, and dutifully opened and held toward the light in order to decipher the minuscule, almost illegible writing. When she finished reading it, she sat down weakly, her legs no longer able to support her, and steadied the letter trembling in her hands on her lap. Again she strained over the tiny cramped writing, as if her life had depended on it, and finally she clutched it to her bosom with a cry.

The message was clear. And because it was written, it had for Sally Hemings the binding power of a holy writ.

CHAPTER 15

PARIS, APRIL 1788

"... but may I ask if the same temperament and the same
Sensibility which constitutes a poet and a painter will not
be apt to make a lover and a Debauchee?"

ABIGAIL ADAMS

Thomas Jefferson woke with the alarm of someone who
does not know where he is. The alarm was physical as well
as metaphysical. He hadn't remembered for a moment not
only where he was but who he was. He had traveled so
many miles. . . . He sighed. He was staring at Jean-Simon
Berthélemy's painting of "Night" on his own sculptured
ceiling over his own bed, in his own room in his own
Hôtel de Langeac, and not in some Prussian inn lying in
his white-linen envelope among strangers. He raised himself
on one elbow and stared at the sleeping girl beside him. He
had gone to fetch his slave from her rooms as soon as he
had arrived in Paris. She was on her side, turned away
from him, her long dark hair fanning out from her body.
The white sheets darkened her skin, like a pale sky darkens
clouds. He lifted the covers from her and slowly pulled
them away from her body. Then he bent his bright head
and ran his tongue along the delicate backbone. The taste
of honey and pine hit the back of his throat.

"*Mon Dieu . . .*" he murmured, and sank back into his
satin pillows. Possessively he drew the girl closer to him
and arranged her head on his naked chest. She slept. Without waking her, he caressed the tangled hair. There was
a small crescent-shaped scar in the silky down at the
beginning of her hairline. A dim recollection made it seem
that this scar had something to do with him, but he couldn't

remember what. Tenderly he rubbed the slightly raised whiteness of it with the tips of his fingers.

Landscape after landscape rushed before him as if he were riding in the jostling coaches and carriages of his Rhine journey.

He had described to the girl again and again the long, lonely voyage through the Low Countries to the north and finally Prussia and the Rhine Valley. His description of the vast, magical Black Forest had transported the young girl into a world of dragons, princesses, and fairy tales. His imaginary carriage slowed now, so that innumerable scenes of rustic beauty floated before his eyes in stately sequence. On the second of April he had arrived at Düsseldorf and had gone straight to the painting gallery. It was there that he had seen the Van der Werff painting that had so moved him: the Biblical story of Sarah giving the slave Hagar to Abraham. That same afternoon he had written to Sally in Paris. Had it really been a sign, he wondered?

"Abraham's wife Sarah had borne him no children. Now, she had an Egyptian slave-girl whose name was Hagar, and she said to Abraham, Take my slave-girl; perhaps I shall found a family through her. Abraham agreed to what his wife said; so Sarah, Abraham's wife, brought her slave girl Hagar the Egyptian, and gave her to her husband Abraham as concubine."

He straightened a lock of her hair. He was a rational man. It was unreasonable, he thought, loving for once what he saw and felt without wanting or trying to give a reason, and not caring much if there was one. God knows he would agree to be Abraham . . . though the consequence would be that he be dead five thousand years . . . and he had no desire to die . . . not now. Sometimes her face took him back to his happiest days. His eyes rested again on the sleeping slave. Her youth, the deepness and serenity of her sleep, stirred him. To be that young . . . Love is never a surprise to the young; but to him! He almost laughed, then remembered she slept. He shifted position carefully and drew her closer to him. After Düsseldorf, he had thought of her often with a growing sense of fatality. Was it not incredible that she was here at all, in Paris, in his arms?

Was it not strange and unaccountable the circumstances of her arrival here, of her very birth? That fateful Wayles legacy so intertwined with the past, and now with the future? Future? What possible future except hate and guilt could they possibly have, he reminded himself.

He closed his eyes and drifted back to the Rhine Valley, sailing down the wide flat ribbon of it from Cologne to Hanau and Heidelberg. His return had had a dreamlike and hurried aspect about it after Düsseldorf. By the middle of April he had been in Strasbourg, where he had recrossed the Rhine into France. He had hurried then, remembering for the first time the bitter toil and poverty of the German peasants. Why had he suddenly been so touched by the women—disheveled, worn beyond their years?

His slave stirred and opened her eyes. The low morning sun caught their golden color and flecked green and brown into them. His heart pounded as she reached for him.

His face still held such terror for her. She pulled back from the lips that had brushed hers and looked into the hooded and melancholy eyes with their fair brows, and then at the wide mouth with its slightly upturned corners. Her master's thick, wavy hair fell around his shoulders. There was a mat of reddish hair on his chest. Sally Hemings's eyes took in the mysterious stubble of red beard and the fine age-lines around the eyes and the stern mouth. There were marks of age at his throat, a slight indentation of flesh, and suddenly she felt a piercing flash of pity for him.

CHAPTER 16

SUMMER, 1788

For nothing is ours that another can deprive us of.
THOMAS JEFFERSON

Lent was over and the promenade of the Champs-Elysées bristled with multicolored flower borders. Tulips and dahlias, lilies of the valley and crocuses, spread like Oriental carpets escorting the golden carriages and prancing horses of the Paris gentry come forth to show themselves and salute spring.

From the upper window of the Hôtel de Langeac I could see the place Louis XV at the end of the Champs-Elysées and, beyond the place, the gardens of the Tuileries filled with tiny moving figures. They reminded me of butterflies swarming among the stone façades and the flower borders.

The gilt-carriages moved down the famous chestnut-tree-shaded promenade. I trembled at the change in my own small world. From his daughters' maid I had become the pampered and adored mistress of Thomas Jefferson. I was one insignificant secret amongst the many buried under the surface of this spring procession.

It was the summer of my fifteenth year that I saw Marly for the first time, and like my master who had been transformed by a painting in Düsseldorf, I was transformed by Marly. I too saw what I wanted to see. Nothing would ever be the same for me again. Marly had been the favorite palace of the Sun King, Louis XIV, his retreat and hermitage from the glories of Versailles. It seemed to float above the earth, in its own nature, its own sky, its own water, its own sun. More than any of the other palaces of the kings of France, this was the most magical one. Imagine a young woman come with her love to Marly, standing beside him, and looking at all this beauty for the first time.

Marly stood planted in the wild blue forest of Saint-Germain-en-Laye. The gardens, canals, terraces, and labyrinths stretched for miles. On each side of the magnificent palace were six summer pavilions connected by walkways embowered with jasmine and honeysuckle. Water fell in cascades from the top of a hill behind the castle, forming a reservoir where swans floated. One fountain sprouted so high, the spray was lost from sight. In the main canal, glistening marble horses mounted by bronze men cavorted; and here and there one could see tiny gems which were ladies moving along the paths and gardens.

The only sound was wind and water; all human sound had been reduced by the vast scale to silence or whispered murmurings. From the top of the hill where the reservoir of Marly's waterworks stood, the day had furnished a rainbow. As the great mechanical wheels raised the water of the river, a pale arc of color hung above it and faded into the colors surrounding us—the silver white of the fountains, the multicolored flowerbeds; the cream-and-blue shadow of the stone facades, the pearl-gray of the gravel underfoot—pastel colors; pink and lemon, delicate greens and blues, so unlike the harsh, hard colors of Virginia.

That day convinced me that there was no Virginia. No slavehood. There was no destiny, it seemed, that did not include this place, this hour, this Marly.

I looked at the tall figure standing beside me. No. Not tall. Immense. Like some glorious eagle overlooking Marly. I studied the familiar profile. My fifteen-year-old heart burst with pride. I could pale that face with longing. I could part that beautiful mouth with desire. I could fill those eyes with agony or joy.

I thought of Martha and her peers tittering and giggling in their fine watered silks and gauzes, the greedy restlessness and ignorance of them! Prancing by in their convent red; gossiping, silly girls who knew nothing of men. Their feverish fantasies and sickening pride revolted me. I neither despised them nor was jealous of them. I merely pitied them. What did they know about being a woman?

I remembered a scene I had witnessed with Martha at the abbey less than a year before, the mysterious and strangely seductive ceremony of ordination for novices. I watched those girls, most of them my age, their faces and bodies pressed into the cold, humid, unyielding stone: their wedding day, the soft fine wool of their habits spread around them like spilled milk. They married God as one married a man. And if one loved a man as one loved God, was it so different? Did it really matter if it was God or man, as long as it was not both?

I put my hands on my face and pressed my eyes red-gold, as if the image blinded me. I opened them again. Marly was still there. And so was he. Smiling down at me from the vast distance between us.

On the thirteenth of July, 1788, there fell, on the very edge of harvest, the most frightful and abnormal hailstorm ever remembered, completely destroying the crops of the year which had already been much damaged by a long drought. For sixty leagues around Paris, it was said, the ruin was total. The legendary Estates General, that had not met in one hundred and sixty years, would meet again the following May. The king had surrendered. Paris was exultant. Martha and Polly came home from the convent, and an ominous calm fell over the city.

I had had no female companion at the Hôtel de Langeac. And so, although I did not feel that I could confide in her, Martha, when she came home from her convent, became for me a refuge from the masculine world of the ministry, and from my powerful lover. His impulsiveness, his vagueness, interspersed with melancholy silences, his inexplicable bursts of passion overwhelmed and often confused me. Later, I would conquer his moods; but at that time I turned to Martha. She was my link with home, with my mother, perhaps with other women. She returned my affection that summer with a warmth we were never to recapture again. I would accompany Martha on her calls to her school friends before they left for their summer estates. We would stroll along the busy and crowded rue Saint-Honoré, dodging the hackney coaches, or along the chestnut-shaded cobblestones of the quai Pont Neuf, looking. We would walk side by side, arm in arm. A lady and her maid, a slave and her mistress, an aunt and her niece, the virgin and the concubine.

Then, one day, the first shadow of what was to pass fell between us. As in all aristocratic households of the day, hair was dressed daily by professional hairdressers who came to the house. There were more than three thousand of them in Paris alone. The one appointed to the Hôtel de Langeac, after dressing my master's hair, would go to the convent to do Polly and Martha's coiffures. There was a second hairdresser whose duty it was to dress the hair of the servants. There was not a fine household in Paris that did not avail itself of the services of two or three hair-dressers every day.

As if in silent recognition, my master's hairdresser began to dress my hair. Martha had no knowledge of this until one day it was whispered to her by a friend that her hair-dresser was also her maid's hairdresser, an unheard of breach of etiquette.

"Is it true that Antoine does your hair?" We were out walking. Her clear eyes were puzzled, not angry. I returned her gaze. It was one of the last times we looked into each other's eyes.

"Pierre complained that he had too many heads to do with the increase in staff, and Antoine said he didn't mind doing my hair, since he could not come directly to you any-way." If Martha had thought about it, this would be un-thinkable. Hairdressers placed more importance on rank and etiquette than the queen herself.

"I don't think it's fitting," Martha answered.

"Well, it's convenient, Mistress."

"I shall ask Father about it."

"I wouldn't do that if I were you, Mistress. He is so annoyed at Antoine anyway that he will surely fire him, and where to get another as good?"

"I won't do anything if Antoine stops doing your hair."

"What harm is there, Mistress? Besides, he does James's too," I lied. I wanted to keep my hairdresser.

"He does?"

"Yes."

"Oh . . . In that case . . . I guess it's all right. I'm sur-prised Antoine would . . . If Father says so . . ."

"Master says so," I continued to lie.

It was the first of many lies I would tell to the white
women in my life. From that day on, I would lie to her
and to others. Poor Antoine became a milestone between
me and Martha.

"My dear . . . you mustn't worry if I seem . . . strange
sometimes." Thomas Jefferson's voice had the familiar
hesitancy of his public speaking. "This is so unexpected
and for me, so unbidden. And you are . . . so young and
yet so sure. . . . You seem as old as Eve to me, my wise
one."

It was part game and part true, he thought. There really
didn't seem to be any differences in their ages. Sometimes
he wondered who was the child. He felt so young. His
naked back was to the silken draperies of his rooms on
the street side of the apartments. His huge body was framed
in the rectangles of barred, balconied windows.

He reached and cupped the head of his mistress in his
giant hands and stared across at her, pressing her tiny
skull between them. Her smallness always stirred him. He
gave a short harsh laugh.

"I don't know what to do with you!"

"Don't do anything, Master," she replied, "and it will
be done."

"Thy will?"

"Thine."

Thomas Jefferson fondled the delicate skin at the back of
his slave's neck under the coiled hair. She was indeed his
creature. Both in body and in spirit. He had formed and
shaped her himself, this wild flower, into something that
bordered on the aristocratic—or at least the unique, an
exotic hybrid of exquisite beauty and fascination. Her
training and tutoring was beginning to show, her musical
education as well. Her voice was low, true, with a lilting
sweetness that was unforgettable. Her appreciation of
beautiful things gratified him. She had even begun to speak
her native tongue differently, and her French was perfect.
He possessed something he had created from beginning to
end, without interference or objections or corrections. In a
way, he had birthed her. As much as he had his daughter.
He had created her in his own image of womanly perfec-

tion, this speck of dust, this handful of clay from Monticello.

"I love you," he said.

"I have always loved you," said his mistress, but he was no longer listening. He had already gone from her, not physically but mentally, as he often did.

Sally Hemings watched secretly the proud, haughty face in a hundred moods for a trace of herself, yet never once had the face she knew as hers—this passionate, hungry, wounded face that had just been so close—ever betrayed him in public. That other face, the public one, was the face of her enemy, her master. But this one she owned. . . .

Once, in the privacy of her attic room, she had pulled down her bodice and stared at the smooth skin, expecting somehow to see the branded scar "C" for concubine on her flesh just as the famous La Motte had recently been branded with a "V" for *voleuse* on her shoulder, and her grandmother with the "R" for runaway on her breast. But there had been nothing but smooth skin.

When would he free her? she wondered. What if she asked him now . . . here? . . . She couldn't, she was ashamed. The pallor, the soft eyes, the ribbon undone, the mouth softened by her kisses . . . He was smiling lazily at her. Even now after their moment of passion, there was a violence and a constraint about him that made her tremble. It was then she realized that he liked owning her. She looked back at him. The face that just a short while ago had been hers was now closed. It belonged to the world.

My anxious lover would sometimes touch me or smooth my hair as if I were a touchstone, a relic of Monticello, a living symbol of all the love and happiness that he had invested in his patrimony. Late at night, when the house was silent and Paris slept, he would tell me of his new plans for Monticello, of changes in the Big House, of redesigned gardens and vineyards with German and French grapes, and olive trees not native to Virginia. For him, the Blue Ridge Mountain region was Eden, and even Paris, the most beautiful of all cities, could not replace it.

This I understood even as he spoke of his retirement, of his leave of absence, and our return to Paris. When he spoke of these things, he never made it clear if I was to stay in Paris to wait for him, return to Virginia and be reenslaved, or be freed at once by his hand. I did not yet ask which of these alternatives he contemplated, but when I brought up my own plans, laid with James and based on freedom in France, he would become silent and morose, or suddenly leave the room.

Just as he willed the Revolution that was growing to be a peaceful one, so did he will that my conversion from slave to lover be also without violence. He saw the Revolution through the eyes of a man who had found unexpected happiness and who was determined to avoid unexpected grief at any cost.

"Have you told him I want to speak to him?"

"Yes," I lied. I had begun to lie to James.

"He knows that we are aware that under French law, he cannot hold us against our will?"

We were speaking French. James had an abrupt and excitable manner of speaking in which every other word came out as if underlined.

"Yes." I lied. I didn't know if he knew or not.

"*Did* you *tell* him about the *proposition* of the Prince de Conti's *maître d'hôtel?*"

"Yes."

"*Well*, what did *he* say?"

"He said he would speak to the prince at the first occasion."

"Has he told you, sister, that he has written to ask the Congress for a leave of absence to return to Virginia, and is waiting for an answer?" James had lapsed back into English.

"Yes," I lied. I was shocked; he had not told me anything.

"Don't you *think* it is *time* to claim our *liberty?*" He had reverted to French.

"You mean to ask to be freed? Shouldn't we wait until the date is set for our return?"

"So that *he* can *pack* us up with *his* other *possessions?*"

"You have said that we are not owned. We have gotten wages since last January. He has recognized that this is not Virginia. . . ."

"*You* can *say* that *this* is not *Virginia? Mon Dieu!*"

I blushed, but I kept my head high. "He's given me his word."

"In writing?"

"He's promised."

"And *you* will *leave?*"

"I'm ready when you are."

James turned his hard gray eyes on me. "And you've *told* him you will *leave* him?"

"Yes," I lied.

"He will *never* forgive you. He will *accuse* you of betraying him."

"I know." This time I didn't lie. The specter of my master's cold fury, his outraged injury, which I had witnessed once or twice, struck terror in my breast.

"*He* . . . wouldn't *do* you *harm?*"

I thought a moment of my impulsive lover. Yes, I thought, he was capable of hurting me.

"Of course not," I said. "He is the kindest and most gentle of men."

"Why, *why* could he *not* have *taken* a . . . white mistress, if he *must* have *one*, like all *his* friends?"

"I don't know."

Jealousy struck me, unexpected and hot. James and I had never spoken of my concubinage.

"How should I know why he does or doesn't! Do you think he tells me what goes on in his mind? Do you think his secrets concern me?" I stopped short.

I felt sick with this new emotion. The pain of it overwhelmed me, almost carrying me to my knees. He was mine! Mine. So this was jealousy. This is what I would live with from now on.

"Time is running out," James said to me in English. He seemed to be sorry for what he had said.

"You believe that there will be an insurrection . . . a revolution? Our master says not."

"There will be an insurrection. But this was not what I meant," he said gently.

"I'm careful," I whispered.

"Ask Marie-Louise downstairs to help you. She knows what to do and she likes you. . . . There are ways."

I looked at my brother. There was no more boy left in

him. He was lean and hard. It was a violent hardness of body. His eyes beneath their long black lashes were disillusioned and bitter. He had been seventeen when he left Virginia. Had it been in Paris that he had known his first woman? And who had she been? A countess whose eye he had caught? A prostitute? Whoever it had been, I was convinced, she had been white.

I lowered my head. I had never thought of such things before. We knew so little of each other—men knew so little of women and women so little of men. I had no idea where he spent his money and free time. Who his friends were. We had barely spoken to each other since I had returned to the ministry, and we had never, until now, spoken of the one important event of my life.

Whoever this man my brother was, he was a man. And no matter what happened to him, he would never be caught like me in the throes of a love which now held me against my will. But, no matter what, I would break that will, I believed. I would reclaim my body, my heart, and I would be careful. . . . I would not be deprived of my one chance in life. I would not fail my brother, I vowed. When the time came, I would run.

CHAPTER 17

PARIS, APRIL 1789

> But if they come to him, and say Acknowledge a lie:
> Really it seems to me the one reason which could justify
> revolting . . . It has been the soul of all revolts among men.
> Not HUNGER alone produced even the French Revolu-
> tion: No, but a feeling of . . . insupportable all-prevading
> FALSEHOOD.
>
> THOMAS CARLYLE

James Hemings untied the roasted golden-brown suckling
pig and stepped back to avoid the rich dark juices that
spluttered out onto the chopping block of his kitchens at
the Hôtel de Langeac. He had filled the suckling pig with
a mixed stuffing of herbs, walnuts, mushrooms, and ground
meat. Around the roast pig, he placed the candied fruits
and flowers glazed with sugar. Julien, the French chef,
nodded curtly. His apprentice was now a master cook.
James stood staring at his dish.

A year had passed since Thomas Jefferson had taken his
sister as concubine. Only he saw the dark side of her station: she was still a slave. The master had taken up his
political and social life as if nothing had happened, he had
simply added Sally Hemings to his bed.

He, James, had become a master cook and his sister had
become a master whore, he thought with bitterness. Not
that anyone cared, he reminded himself. Her existence, and
her romance did not seem to carry any weight in the network of gossip exchanged between the servants, the
lackeys, the hairdressers, and coachmen of the great
Parisian *hôtels* in this spring of 1789. This spring there was

only news of the political situation. Riots, court intrigues,
manifestos that flew from the courtyards to the kitchens
and the backstairs of one *hôtel* to another with the efficiency
of the Tidewater slave network. An aristocrat's liaison with
a lady's maid was after all so common, he thought, so lacking in interest, that it was beneath the notice of even the
lowliest scullery maid. For this forlorn silence, James was
grateful.

Of course, the servants in the house all knew that the
beautiful young girl, supposedly the maid of one of his
daughters, was in fact Jefferson's mistress. But as far as
James could discern, this fact had escaped the intelligence
of the white Americans connected with the household: Mr.
Short, Mr. Humphreys, Jefferson's two daughters. The
master was more than ever a loving father, a sweet-
tempered lord, a kind and compassionate aristocrat, a
gallant appreciator of beautiful women. His many migraines
stopped, his melancholy abated, and he seemed to be unconscious of the undertow of civil discontent which racked
France. "The Revolution is completed," he was fond of
saying over and over.

As for most of the visitors who wandered in and out of
the ministry, they had never set eyes on his sister, nor even
known of her existence. If any of the elegant French ladies
had remarked her, they certainly would have dismissed
their famous friend's *divertissement* with an amused shrug.
His hope that his master's interest in his sister would be
transitory and "in the French fashion" had turned out to
be in vain. He might play at being French, James thought,
but his nature was Virginian, passionate, proud, possessive,
tenacious; violent feelings ran under that polite and remote
surface. If anything, he had noted that his master's obsession with Sally Hemings had grown rather than waned
in the past year. His master, thought James, showed no
lessening of the tyrannical possessiveness and watchful
interest in her dependence on him. She seemed to be a
prisoner in this house. And his sister was reveling in it;
she had blossomed under this jealous power. The last
childish contours of her body had dropped away, leaving
the low-burning smolder of a woman's maturity far beyond

her sixteen years. The final shape of her face with its high, flat cheekbones and wide-spaced eyes had hardened and lost some of its innocence. A small, exquisite, heavy-breasted, slim-waisted body had emerged from the coltish and countrified adolescent of a year ago. She had honed her natural grace and inborn elegance on the examples of the most fashionable ladies of Panthémont and Paris on whom she spied incessantly and indecently, and had developed a lust for clothes and a taste for finery that went with such examples.

She had lessons in French, in music, in dressmaking. In her seclusion, slave was better read than most ladies. Yet she had resisted all his pleadings to use her power over the senses of their master to achieve her freedom and his. She assumed that all would be taken care of in time. That love would make her free.

James knew better. Men didn't free what they loved. He had surprised Thomas Jefferson more than once looking at Sally Hemings as he had often seen him contemplating some of his rare objects, those he meant to keep. It was the look of a man who both coveted and had the means to possess what he coveted.

How many times had he seen this look as the steady stream of precious objects flowed from the workshops and auction houses of Paris and were set before his master in unending abundance. Urns and flatware from the silversmith, lamps from the jeweler Daguerre. Damask and silk bolts of cloth. Rare and extravagant Persian rugs. Delicate clocks and timepieces from Caillouet; scientific instruments from Noseda; musical instruments from Kewarien; porcelain from Sevres; paintings and sculpture from Paillet's Auction House; gilt chairs, velvet armchairs from Dupuis; pastel carved and painted *boiseries*, rare mineral samples, and as always, book after book bound in soft morocco leather or fine linen came in processions. One by one they had become his master's possessions. A look of tender greed would flash across his tense thin face like a bright star and then his long slender oversized hand would reach out and touch the object presented to him, bringing it under his domination.

He pitied his sister in her enraptured beauty and delusion. She was nubile and Jefferson was virile. It was only a matter of time before her fate as a woman caught up with her.

James Hemings absently gestured to the lackey who had been standing in front of him patiently waiting for the platter to be ready. It was the sixth and last meat dish of the meal and now, along with the other cooks, James hurried to fill the vegetable platters while calculating how much time he had to finish the six desserts that would be served.

It was the third large noisy party of the week. It seemed to him that there had been nothing but an endless round of dinners, teas, suppers, balls, operas, and concerts all season. All of Paris seemed to be in the throes of one long season of pleasure, ignoring the undertow of civil discontent which lapped at the satin and brocade skirts and high-heeled red shoes of his master's aristocratic friends. "The Revolution is completed," his master insisted as each new crumb was thrown by the nobles to the discontented. It must be because of his sister, thought James. Jefferson bathed in happiness and was determined to ignore the political intelligence all around him. His confidence knew no bounds. His elegant dinners had become famous in Paris thanks to his, James's, cooking. Leonard, the footman, had just delivered the entire list of guests now seated around his master's table devouring the dinner it had taken fourteen hours to prepare.

There was Lafayette, rouged and red-heeled dandy, a hero to both the Americans who had made their Revolution and to the French who were starting theirs. He was surely the guest of honor. He had been the subject of lively debate in all of Paris since his command had been taken away from him by the king. There was Buffon, the famous scientist and hero of the French philosophers; the Baron and Baronne de Staël, arbitrators of style and taste in Paris. There was the Abbé Morellet, who with his friends the Abbés Chalut and Arnaud, was preparing a French edition of his master's *Notes on the State of Virginia*. A famous mathematician, the Marquis de Condorcet—the whitest man James had ever seen—was also there with his wife, Sophie, a celebrated beauty. And, finally, the Duc and Duchesse de la Rochefoucauld completed the table.

James was disappointed. Missing was one of his favorites, Monsieur de la Tude, who dined out on his adventures of having spent thirty-five years on and off in the Bastille and a dungeon of Versailles, and had lived to tell of it. The last time, it had been for making up verses about Madame de Pompadour. He recounted his life as a convict more as a good story than a tragedy, and so ate well and often on his tales.

James Hemings loaded the desserts onto their platters. There were at least four women upstairs in the pale-yellow-and-gold high-ceilinged dining room, he reminded himself, who were having illicit affairs with men who were not their lawful husbands and who were also present. The young wife of the Duc de la Rochefoucauld was having an affair with the pleasant but dull Mr. Short, his master's faithful secretary, Madame de Hunolstein with General Lafayette. The poet Saint-Lambert lived with his mistress the Comtesse d'Houdetot and her husband in a happy *ménage à trois*. . . . At least Madame de Staël's latest lover was not at the table, he thought. He counted the succession on his fingers. The Baronne Germaine Necker de Staël was twenty-three years old and had been married for three years to the Swedish ambassador. Her first lover had been Charles de Talleyrand, now the Bishop of Autun. Her present lover was Comte Louis de Narbonne, who was said to be the illegitimate son of King Louis XV by his own daughter, Madame Adelaïde. And if his own sister, mused James, had entered the room to do some small task—which she often did in order to spy on her master's brilliant gatherings —then there would be five concubines in the same room, he concluded bitterly.

Why didn't he leave this place? What bond held him here in the underworld when above him, rank and privilege and riches consumed his labor? Twenty-three years of servitude. . . . Why didn't he doff his starched chef's bonnet, take off his apron, walk out, and be gone by one of the forty-seven gates of Paris? Why, why was he unable to do this? Why could he not take his freedom like a man, instead of crouching and waiting to be given it like a slave? No, not like a slave, for James Hemings wanted his master to acknowledge his existence and his debt, instead of simply allowing him to "stroll" away. He wanted him to give back what he had taken. Until then James Hemings knew he could never leave. He would never steal himself.

It was still early April, not long after one of his master's elegant dinner parties. This Sunday night was one of the rare nights Thomas Jefferson had neither a dinner to give nor one to attend. As was the custom, he dined *"en famille"* with his daughters before they returned to the convent.

James Hemings stood behind Martha Jefferson's chair in the small octagonal salon, which served as a dining room for family dinners. There had been much gentle laughter and now, as James Hemings, contrary to French protocol, poured the demi-tasses of strong coffee at the table and offered one to Martha, he discreetly studied the eldest daughter of his master.

It was to Martha that James always directed his services and his sympathy. He saw her rarely now. They had grown up together, Martha and he. He was seven years older than Martha, and more than any of the other Hemings boys, he had been the right age to play the role of elder brother. He had played this role well and lovingly. They had ridden together over the plantation fields and forests, exploring the woods around Monticello, fishing and eating wild berries. It was he who always helped her up after her frequent tumbles off her pony. Whenever she had lost some treasures, it was he who always found them for her. He and his uncle had built her dollhouse, carved its furniture. He had been the one who had driven her pony cart, keeping it spic and span with coats of blue and white paint. When they played, he let himself be tormented, teased, kissed, and generally used, misused, as well as loved by her, as he would in turn do the same to her. Even when she had reached the age of twelve and their relationship would have, according to the mores of the South, come to an end, they had remained in their roles as brother and sister, passing these last four years in the same familiarity of their earlier years.

Martha, like her younger sister, was listening intently to her father.

"My dear Martha, do you not look forward to the tranquil pleasures of America and find them preferable to the empty bustle of Paris?"

Sally Hemings entered the room and stood quietly apart from the group from which she was excluded. Was he going to announce that they were going home? Had the permission finally come to leave?

Thomas Jefferson flashed his frank and charming smile. "For to what does the bustle tend?"

The small group exhaled. This was not the announcement they were all waiting for.

"At eleven o'clock, it is day *chez madame*. The curtains are drawn. Propped on bolsters and pillows and her head scratched into a little order, the bulletins of the sick are read, and *billets* of the well, she writes to some of her acquaintances and receives the visits of others. If the morning is not very thronged, she is able to get out and hobble around the cage of the Palais Royal. . . . As for royalty and royal courts, they should be regarded as you would the Tower of London or the menagerie of Versailles with their lions and tigers and other beasts of prey, and standing in the same relation to their fellows—a slight acquaintance with them will suffice to show you that, under the most imposing exterior, they are the weakest and the worst part of mankind. . . . Furthermore, she must hobble quickly, for the *coiffeur*'s turn is come, and a tremendous turn it is! Happy if he does not make her arrive when dinner is half over! The torpitude of digestion is a little past, when she flutters for a half hour through the streets, by way of paying visits, and then to the spectacles. These finished, another half hour is devoted to dodging in and out of doors of her very sincere friends, and away to supper. After supper, cards, bed, rise at noon the next day, and tread, like a millhouse, the same trodden circle over again. Thus the days of life are consumed, one by one, without an object beyond the present moment; ever flying from ennui

of that, yet carrying it with us; eternally in pursuit of
happiness, which keeps eternally ahead of us."

Martha Jefferson laughed her low melodious laugh, one
of her few charms, but she glanced at her father with some
apprehension. There was a touch of melancholy to his
amusing recital, a wistfulness with an edge; she even
detected some bitterness. Was he tiring of Paris life? Homesick? Was he displeased with the kind of education she was
receiving at the convent? Did he think, heaven forbid, that
she was becoming like those women he described? She
frowned. The mere shadow of her father's disapproval sent
a wave of misery through her. She stared at him, cup
raised, but his face was almost devoid of expression, except
for a slight crinkling around the eyes.

He looked up at James as the servant poured another
cup of coffee.

"And if death or bankruptcy happens to trip us out of
the circle . . . think of poor Monsieur Saint-James—taking
asylum in the Bastille as protection against his irate creditors. Well, poor Monsieur Saint-James's bankruptcy is
merely the matter for the buzz of an evening and is completely forgotten the next morning . . . like mine would be."

"Oh, Papa," Martha replied.

Could he really have enough of the glamorous elegant
lady friends she so envied? Women who spent their lives
in just the manner he described? Not just mistresses like
Madame de Pompadour or Du Barry, but women like
Madame de Deffand and Madame Geoffrin, ladies of
intellect with the most famous salons of the day like . . .
Madame de Staël, Madame Sullivan, the Duchesse
d'Anville.

She and little Polly stared at him as he continued. Sally
Hemings was listening, hoping not to be sent from the
room.

"In America, on the other hand, the society of your
husband, the cares of children, the arrangements of the
house, the improvements of the grounds fill every moment
with useful and healthy activity. Every exertion is en-
couraging, because it also joins the promise of some future
good. Leisure is spending time with real friends, whose

affections are not thinned to cobwebs by being spread over a thousand objects."

The staid and faithful adolescent that was Martha Jefferson thought of the flighty Maria Cosway and she suppressed a smile. So, she thought, her father was over his infatuation at last with that dangerous and seductive creature.

"This is the picture, in the light it is presented to my mind. Now let me have it in yours. If we do not concur this year, we shall the next or, if not then, in a year or two more. You see I am determined not to suppose myself mistaken. . . ."

Mistaken about what? Martha Jefferson wondered in alarm. What was it he was trying to tell her? He seemed to be almost pleading with her. Didn't he know he could ask anything on earth of her? That her only wish in life was to make him happy? She would agree to any sacrifice he asked of her. If he wanted her to give up her aristocratic friends . . . if he wanted to leave Paris tonight, she was ready.

"Papa! Really! You sound like you want to drop everything and turn into a hermit. Goodness knows, you already go all the time to your hermitage at Valerian . . . you don't want to give up society completely, do you?"

Although her tone was light, Martha's eyes were troubled and she glanced quickly at Polly, who was staring at her father, then she looked at James. What was he asking her to accept, James thought bitterly, sensing rather than seeing the small, silent, discreet figure of his sister.

Martha's face became even paler under the white powder that covered the freckles James Hemings had known and practically counted since childhood. She is going to disagree with her father, he thought, and he held his breath.

"I agree, Papa, that many of the fashionable pursuits of the Parisian ladies are rather frivolous and become uninteresting to a reflective mind . . . but the picture you have exhibited, dearest Papa, is surely overcharged. You have thrown a strong light upon all that is ridiculous in their characters and you have buried their qualities in the shade. These women, *your friends*, are not ordinary women. They are a race apart, with all the dispassion, the irony, the intuitive sense of measure and moderation of their breed. The state of society in different countries requires corresponding manners and qualifications. Those of the French women are by no means calculated for the meridian of America. . . ."

Martha paused. She had been choosing her words carefully. What did he want to hear? she wondered. Conscious of the silence in the room and the impervious expression on her father's face, she continued:

"You must admit, Papa, that the Frenchwomen are more accomplished and understand the intercourse of society better than in any other country. Their education is of a higher caliber. True, the women of France interfere with the politics of the country and often give a decided turn to the fate of the empires. . . . They have obtained that rank and consideration in society which our sex is entitled to and to which they in vain contend for in other countries . . . including our own! Perhaps," Martha said timidly, "I went too far."

At this, her father burst into laughter. "My dear, I've never heard a better speech in defense of the rights of womanhood. Bravo! Mrs. Bingham couldn't have put it better!"

Thomas Jefferson almost involuntarily glanced to where Sally Hemings stood. Although there was no visible agitation on his master's face, his natural high color, now ruddy in the glow of the candles, James Hemings knew his master well enough to know that he was not at all pleased with his daughter's outburst. She, on the other hand, was visibly frightened.

Martha Jefferson sighed. She was relieved that her father had taken her inexplicable outburst as he had, but she knew he didn't agree with her. His displeasure was concealed as usual behind that benign expression she knew so well. Why had she let herself be carried away like that? Had it been because of the strange urgency in her father's voice? He was hiding something from her, and even the thought of his secret gave her a pang of jealousy. If only he would treat her as a woman instead of a child . . . at least as he treated those frivolous Frenchwomen he was so busy condemning.

She would ask for nothing more. She no longer wished to be shielded, shut out of his private thoughts.

The handsome trio rose and moved into the small salon. All were in motion, except for Sally Hemings. She felt at that moment great admiration for Martha. James pulled out Martha's chair and as she turned, her bewildered eyes met those of her maid. The two young girls held each other's eyes until the benevolent glance of Thomas Jefferson flicked between them.

It was a week later that Martha found herself standing in her maid's room in the attic of the Hôtel de Langeac. Not being able to find Sally Hemings, she had climbed the steep back stairs to the servants' quarters with the dozen chemises and bloomers that needed mending. Now she stood in the center of the small cramped room transfixed, her elaborate coiffure almost touching the low ceiling and making her stoop unconsciously. The room was crammed with silk and muslin dresses and petticoats. There were delicate chiffon shawls and laces piled in one corner on a chair. The moment before, she had opened a large green morocco leather trunk at the foot of the narrow bed. In it she had found dozens of pairs of silk stockings, kid gloves, ribbons, plumes, delicately embroidered cambric underclothes and petticoats, and pairs upon pairs of silk and leather shoes.

She turned and fingered the dress nearest her. It was of fine yellow silk with delicate white stripes and embroidered white roses. She was so transfixed that she had not noticed her maid's presence behind her as she stood rooted there, silent in utter consternation. Martha turned, brushing the skirt of one of the dresses out of the way, and stared at her maid. She took in the coiffured hair, and the pale-blue silk dress over green petticoats. This dress too was new. She had never seen it before.

"Where did you get all this?" she asked in something like awe.

Sally Hemings paled but did not answer immediately. Anger had overwhelmed her at seeing her friend in her room without permission and without an invitation. Then she realized that Martha was not her friend, but her mistress

and that she had every right to enter at will the room of
her slave—to finger and touch those precious possessions
she found there because by all rights they did belong to
her.

"I said, where did you get all this?"

"It . . . it's mine. It belongs to me, Mistress. It doesn't
concern you."

"Doesn't concern me! Doesn't concern me! Since when
does the fact that my *maid* has the wardrobe of a lady not
concern me? I asked you where you got all these things. Did
you *steal* them?"

"No."

"No, who?"

"No, Mistress."

"Then someone *gave* you all this?"

"Yes, Mistress."

"Who?"

"I cannot say, Mistress, please . . . don't ask me. . . .
Some I bought with my wages. . . ."

"Wages?"

"Yes, Mistress."

"Since when have you been receiving wages?"

"Since last year. . . . Twenty-four francs a month."

"Even a hundred years' salary would not buy these . . .
these exquisite things. Tell me"—Martha's mouth set itself
in a hard line; the ways of French society were no mystery
to her—"it is a lover, is it not?"

"I don't know what you mean, Mistress."

"*You know perfectly well what I mean! I mean you have
a man as a lover.* You have attracted the eye of a gentleman and you have . . . become his mistress!"

"I—"

"You think I don't know of such things! After four
years at Panthémont. Tell me or I'll beat it out of you!"

"Yes." Sally Hemings's eyes glowed fierce and dry. Her
fear had been replaced with outrage. If Martha struck her,
she was ready to strike back and her small hands curled into
fists of revolt.

"I demand to know who it is."

Martha Jefferson had suddenly taken on all the airs and
long-forgotten drawl of a Virginia-plantation mistress. She

took her servant's chin and lifted her face so that she could look into her eyes. "I demand to know who the gentleman . . . or rather rascal . . . is!"

"I cannot tell you." She turned her head away from the revolting female hand that touched her.

"Then I will tell Papa."

At this the maid turned her head back toward her mistress and for the last time looked directly into her eyes.

"I wouldn't do that if I were you."

Something in the tone of the young girl's voice stopped Martha Jefferson; she stared at her for a long time.

"*Mon Dieu!* What would your mother say, Sally Hemings!"

"It is not what my mother would say, Mistress, but what yours would say."

Sally Hemings waited for the storm to break over her head. Martha Jefferson was strong. She towered over her slave, and Sally Hemings almost threw up her arms to protect herself. Only pride made her stand and stare up at her owner. Only pride made her still the trembling of her body and cool it with an icy indifference that bordered on hatred. Why, she thought, should I bother to lie to this white woman? Simply because I am expected to calm and soothe her fears? Look how she flounders at the least resistance.

Martha Jefferson waited for the name of her maid's lover, but her maid remained silent.

Once, just this once, let her lie to herself. With this, Sally Hemings turned her back on the intruder who had violated her sanctuary, her only place of privacy. Even this room was not her own. Let her lie to herself, she thought. And she left Martha standing in the midst of her treasures, a pair of white satin slippers clutched in her hand.

April 18, 1789, The Abbaye Royale of Panthémont

My dearest and most adored Papa,

I respectfully and formally request your permission to enter into the Holy Orders of the Abbaye Panthémont as a suppliant and a novice in preparation

eventually to take vows as a nun in the Roman Catholic
Church and the convent of Panthémont.

I realize this may be a shock to you, but I assure
you, dearest Papa, that I have not taken this decision
lightly and have been in daily correspondence with the
Papal Nuncio, Comte Duganani, and in daily prayers
and consultation with the Abbess Madame Mézières
as regards this matter. I cannot and will not reconcile
what I have learned of the world and its frivolous and
disreverent and unchristian attitudes with what *I know*
to be the precepts and the Holy Commandments of
God and Righteousness. I would rather not *live* in a
world where I must be witness to and condone by
compliance such transgressions, or *know* and not prevent the punishments for such cruel disregard for His
teachings.

I embrace you with an Exultant and Joyful heart
and Fervent prayers for your accord in this matter
and for the Happiness of my Cherished Papa. . . .

Your loving Daughter

James Hemings knew what had been in the note he had
delivered to the mansion on the Champs-Elysées several
weeks after Martha's last visit. He had not read the letter,
so he could not know if his sister was mentioned by name
or by function. He only knew that Martha Jefferson had
decided and had told him with passionate tears of joy in
her eyes that she wanted to become a nun and enter the
convent of the Abbaye de Panthémont. He had listened to
her speechlessly as she had told him of her decision.

When James Hemings had entered his master's cabinet
he watched Thomas Jefferson casually read the note from
his daughter. James waited in silence. But Thomas Jefferson
did not betray any emotion; he sat down at his writing table
and wrote quickly, and then rang for Petit. The carriage
was ordered to be hitched and brought to the front courtyard. He beckoned James to come with him. They rode
into Paris together until they reached the rue Royale. They

went from shop to shop buying linen for Martha Jefferson. At the end of the morning, James, walking behind his master, was carrying armloads of fine silks, laces, and chiffons. In anticipation of Martha's birthday, he had even bought a sapphire ring. He had also bought a silver locket for Sally Hemings. They had spent two hundred and seventy-four francs that morning.

Two days later, James accompanied his master to the Panthémont Convent, the back of the carriage filled with the purchases. James followed as Jefferson moved quickly into the inner courts of the convent, where he was met by a pale and trembling Martha. James tried to signal some comfort, but she had eyes only for her father. Never had his master's smile been so benevolent, never his manner so tender and charming, never had he shown in public such a fatherly attitude toward his eldest daughter, thought James. Thomas Jefferson kissed her hand and then her cheek, and then turning to the abbess who had entered the somber courts, he disappeared with her into her apartments. Martha and James waited outside the closed oak doors of the abbess's office. When Jefferson emerged, he was smiling. He told Martha that he had come for her.

Martha Jefferson looked up at the handsome, smiling man who was her father. His auburn hair was flecked with white, giving it a sandy color when it was not powdered, and it was not this day. It was tied in a queue at his neck with a blue ribbon and hung down his back over the Prussian blue of his frock coat fitted perfectly over his broad shoulders. The long powerful legs were encased in pale ivory chamois and he too had on the red-heeled patent leather pumps of the aristocracy. His long chin was set, his eyes clear and guileless as a summer day. His attitude was one of a determined, but attentive suitor. He smiled, showing small white even teeth and without a word, Martha Jefferson took the proferred arm of her father and mounted the double steps into his carriage, the door of which was held open for her by James.

James Hemings closed the door and mounted beside the coachman. The elegant English carriage of lilac and yellow trimmed in dark gray turned and rattled out of the lonely cobbled courtyard onto the rue de Grenelle. Martha settled back behind the white lace curtains into the brimstone-colored silk upholstery. She looked with wonder at the piles of presents and packages on the seat beside her. Never, as long as she lived, would she mention this incident again. She pulled back the silk tassels and took a last look at the white facade of the Abbaye de Panthémont drenched in the rosy spring sunlight.

The education of Martha Jefferson was ended.

CHAPTER 18

SUMMER, 1789

I hold it, that a little rebellion, now and then, is a good thing, and is necessary in the political world as storms are in the physical.

THOMAS JEFFERSON

The twelfth of July 1789 was a Sunday. There had been riots and food was becoming more and more scarce. The dismissal of the minister, the defiance of the National Assembly, the stubbornness of the king, all conveyed a sense of impending disaster those first weeks of July. Now, the streets were all plastered with enormous-sized *De Par le Roi* inviting peaceable citizens to remain indoors.

From my window, I could look down the length of the Champs-Elysées—eight hundred and twenty double steps according to my master—to the place Louis XV. I could also see, around the bronze statue of Louis XV, the dragoons and hussars assembling in their red-and-white-and-yellow uniforms. All sorts of rumors ran rampant, and James went to the Palais Royal every day to see what he could find out. At twelve, the cannon went off as usual when the sun passed its meridian, but this day, its low thunder struck gloom and disquiet in the hearts of almost everyone.

Through my master's telescope I watched in the distance as a growing crowd, festooned with green cockades, grew and like a flight of locusts filled the place Louis XV. There were some people armed with axes, staves, others with picks and pitchforks. I knew James was somewhere in Paris.

Perhaps even in the very mob which was now entering the square. I saw the crowd being charged upon by the German Hussars; I heard noises of shots, sabers flashed clearly, and puffs of smoke from muskets rose like tiny clouds over the heads of the men. Then the crowd exploded along what streets and alleys they could, and suddenly the square was empty with the soldiers pursuing agitators and Sunday strollers alike up the avenues. It was a fascinating spectacle and I sat by the window all day.

When darkness fell, all the roads out of the city, including our own Champs-Elysées, were blocked by pickets and barriers. There were stalled carriages and vehicles of all sorts. Traffic, wheel to wheel, immobile from the tollgate all the way to the place Louis XV.

On Monday, Paris was like a tomb. When James and my master went out to investigate, they found that no one had reported for work; all had joined the rebellion. Everything was closed, except for wine and bread shops. James was sent to prowl the Palais Royal he knew so well and to report back to the mansion. When he returned late that evening, he told us that the people were busily sewing cockades to be worn, not the green of d'Artois, but the red and blue of Paris, on a white background which stood for the constitution. They called it the *"Tricolore."* Our ministry was ecstatic. The people of Paris had chosen the colors of the American Revolution.

Outside our house, the streets were deserted and silent. That evening, by a special new order, every window was lit in every house. I tried to imagine Paris, a maze of winding narrow streets, deserted, crossed by the large boulevards also deserted, except for the shadows of the National Guard patrolling with their torches and flares. All the lights of Paris, no more than a gathering of fireflies compared to the blazing lights of Versailles, where the National Assembly sat through the night. We slept little and by dawn on Tuesday both James and Thomas Jefferson had abandoned the mansion.

While the Hôtel de Langeac was locked and barred, the hot July sun rose and the National Guard prepared to march on the Hôtel des Invalides. By the end of the day, the Bastille, the fortress dungeon which was the very

symbol of the king's unlimited power, had been stormed
and taken.

James was an eyewitness to that event, which had marked
the turning point of the rebellion. Later on, James, like
Monsieur de la Tude, would often drink and dine on the
tale of the storming of the Bastille. That night, in the oval
salon of the *hôtel*, servants and masters alike were held in
thrall to the present. Even James's own highly developed
imagination could not embellish the drama of that siege.
How much he actually saw and how much he heard about,
I would never know, nor would any of his audience, but
as he told his tale, we fully sensed the extent of the drama.
We sat, Martha, Polly, Mr. Short, Petit, our professors,
and all the other servants, spellbound while, in his strangely
accented French, he recounted the Fourteenth of July.

He had slipped out of the mansion in the middle of the
night and joined his comrades at one of the cafés near the
Palais Royal. He had slept on the floor for the rest of the
night, rising again at six. Hot rum had been served. Someone had pinned a tricolor cockade on him, the women had
stayed up all night sewing. He had taken a butcher's knife
from the kitchen as his only arm, and now he joined the
milling militia as they surged halfway up the Champs-
Elysées and turned toward the Invalides, where someone
had said there were arms to be had. James, still in the light-
yellow livery of the Hôtel de Langeac, unwashed, already
lightheaded on the morning's rum like the rest, became one
with the thousands of marching men and women. A strange
elation had stolen over him, he said, his heart had beat in
rhythm with that of his neighbor, as if everyone were one
huge crawling animal of which he felt one particle of skin,
one strand of hair.

The mob arrived at the walls of the Invalides, and the
garrison did not fire upon them as the walls were scaled and
the gates flung open. They had rushed in, spreading through
all the rooms and passages of the great building. A roar
went up as the place where weapons had been found was
seized. Those nearest snatched, struggled, and clutched at
them. There was no order, no leaders, no officers as James
looked around him and saw thousands of firelocks hoisted
onto thousands of shoulders with the cry of "On to the
Bastille!" The dreaded prison-tomb with walls nine feet

thick which was the Bastille had been battered down, the
drawbridge lifted and manned with a cannon since Sunday.
Since early morning the cry had been, "On to the Bastille!"
and as the cry went up again the whole suburb of Saint-
Antoine was marching as one man. The people, now armed,
turned as a flock of wild geese, homing toward the eight
grim towers that one could see over the rooftops of Paris
from almost every point in the city. The new army arrived
at the drawbridge of the Bastille at one o'clock. By five
o'clock, all the soldiers were covered with blood. The
wounded and the dead were being carried into the houses
along the rue de la Cerisaie. For four hours the crowd
howled before the gates.

Cannon and musket shots from the towers hit at random,
crumpling men and women who sank and then were crushed
under the weight of others pressing forward. The crowd increased until it spilled down and over the quais of the Pont
Neuf. Then, without warning, a cry rumbled back like a
wave over the sweating, bleating heads . . . the Bastille had
surrendered.

The Bastille was taken. The Bastille had fallen.

James threw up his arms. We were all hanging on to his
every word. The forward motion of the mob, like a wave,
surged headlong toward its goal, and had not the National
Guard wheeled around and leveled its guns against its own,
the mob would have plunged suicidally by the thousands
into the moat of the prison. The governor of the Bastille
tried to kill himself but was taken prisoner. His captors
meant to take him to the Hôtel de Ville through the cursing, clutching crowd; only his bloody scalp, held up in a
victorious hand, arrived. The head, aloft on a pike, was
now traveling through the streets. The rest of him had
been torn to pieces.

The evening sun was setting, and James, feverish and
exhausted, battered and dirty, fell quiet as did his awed
audience. The word of the fall of the Bastille had begun to
spread over Paris, and, amid gunfire, we heard the sound
of music. The people of Paris were dancing in the streets.

We put James to bed and, despite the bath, the smell of
the gunpowder hovered over him. He sat propped up on his
pillows grinning. His eyes seemed to say this: This slave

from Virginia's made history today. This slave ran with the
Revolution! His eyes said to me: I am mine. We are going
to take ourselves to freedom. If God let me do this, then
He will leave us take our freedom without running. Take
ourselves, without stealing. We are going to be free. Everything is changed.

He smiled and I smiled back.

CHAPTER 19

SEPTEMBER 1789

> ... a man's moral sense must be unusually strong if slavery does not make him a thief.
>
> THOMAS JEFFERSON, *Paris* 1788

It was amidst the ceremonies and processions that followed the fall of the Bastille that I found I was with child.

"*Tu es enceinte*," said Marie-Louise. She looked at me with kindness and exasperation as I stared at her in disbelief. She had warned me and now she was afraid all her concoctions of parsley, rue, and camphor, or any of her other remedies would be of no avail.

I roamed the streets in a daze, weakened by the cramps in my stomach and the constant nausea. Te Deums filled Notre Dame every day, and procession followed procession, with gay young women in white muslin tied with tricolor sashes moving among the crowds. The processions and the bread lines grew longer. One day I decided never to return to the mansion.

I took refuge with Madame Dupré on the rue de Seine.

She guessed at once what had happened; she took me in her arms, and urged me to return to the safety and comfort of the Hôtel de Langeac.

"Sooner or later," she said, "you will be forced to abandon your child. Paris is notorious for that." She paused. "There are three thousand abandoned children a year in Paris. Surely you don't want to add to that sad number?"

"But you don't understand," I replied, "this is not just a

bastard child, it is a slave bastard. It will belong to my master, Monsieur Jefferson."

"But of course it is his!"

"No, Madame, that is not what I mean. I mean it is his not only by blood but by property. It is his property to do with what he likes, just as he can do with me what he likes. I am not free, Madame."

There was a long silence as Madame Dupré tried to assimilate this information.

"You mean you are a slave, like the Africans in Martinique and Santo Domingo?"

"Not like the Africans. I *am* African. I am black."

At this, Madame Dupré seized me and dragged me into the light of the window. She looked searchingly at my face and body, at my hands and nails. At the texture of my hair.

"Then you are a métis?"

"Yes."

"Go back to him. Go back and demand your freedom and that of his child. Demand it in writing and stay here in Paris. You will find a protector. I promise you that. On French soil you are free and you shall stay free. But return to him. Give him the chance to express his instincts as a father and a lover. You may be surprised. He loves you."

"I don't want to be loved. I want to be free."

"Do you really, my child? You love him as well, and there is no freedom in that."

She looked at me with her wise, cynical eyes and shook me gently by the shoulders.

"*Rentre à la maison,*" she said to me. "Go home. *Tu veux rentrer, n'est-ce pas?*"

"*Oui,*" I answered, "I want to go home."

A week after my departure I returned to the mansion. I had stolen myself and now I tried to replace the stolen object quietly, as if it had never been taken from its owner. I entered through the courtyard and servant quarters in trembling expectation of meeting my brother James, but it was Petit that I met in the reception hall. He looked at me without surprise, but with studied annoyance. What havoc I must have wrought in the household to have put any expression, let alone anger, on those cold features . . . as I searched his face, looking for a clue as to what awaited me, a warm expression stole over his face.

"Do not be alarmed, but . . . he is ill. He has been in the grip of a migraine headache for almost a week with no relief. . . . James has gone again to fetch Dr. Gem."

I remembered from Monticello the violence of these sudden headaches that were powerful enough to render my master senseless. I tried to remember what remedies had been used at Monticello to ease him.

"Petit," I said, forgetting my own predicament, "it is possible to get camphor and ice and . . ."

"We've tried everything . . . Mademoiselle . . . except your return. . . . I pray that it will relieve him."

"Why did he not look for me?"

"I do not know."

"And James?"

"He ransacked Paris for you."

"But I was at Madame Dupré's!"

"She swore you were not. She even let him enter and search the rooms."

I smiled. How had she managed to fool James with me installed in her attic?

"Come," he said, not unkindly. "You'll have to face him sometime." Then, turning toward me just as we arrived in front of the apartment, he said, as if in explanation of the state in which I would find my master:

"You dealt him a blow I would not have thought possible." Now he seized my shoulders gently and turned me toward the door.

I entered the apartment. The curtains were tightly shut and my eyes were unaccustomed to the darkness. In the room, there was the same undefinable odor of gunpowder that had stalked the streets of Paris three weeks before. I recoiled as it smote me, and turned to flee. His voice sounded and held me there.

"Why did you do that to me?"

The long ashen figure, fully dressed, sat up on the bed, and the face I looked into was one of such desolation my heart almost stopped. The voice was husky and scarred. The fury was barely controlled.

"Why did you do that to me?" he repeated evenly.

"I'm with child. That is why I ran away."

I threw this at him, meaning to convey to him all the despair and loneliness of the past week of rebellion, but instead a fierce joy took hold of me.

"Sally . . ."

"I will not give birth to a slave! I am free now. I will never birth slaves!"

A flush of color came into his deathly-pale face. I stood apart from him—some yards—afraid to approach, stubborn, and poised for flight. It was he who then fell back in pain. I wavered, but held my ground.

"I know . . . that I cannot hold you against your will. Our . . . your child I consider free and will always consider free. You have my word. I recognize that you are free, as free as your heart permits."

I was lost. My heart was his, and he knew it. I faltered, cornered, weak.

"I want him born on French soil. . . ."

"We must go home, Sally, but it is only temporary. We will return."

"That is not enough . . . I want—"

He began to speak very softly to me, drawing me nearer and nearer. Making me strain to hear until I knelt beside him. His voice was low and sweet, as if he were maning a young wild falcon to the block. There were tears streaming down his face and promises on his lips.

His promises mingled along with mine in the sultry darkness. No, I would not leave him again. No, I would not die in childbirth. No, I would not claim my freedom.

Yes, my children would all be free. When? At twenty-one. Twenty-one. Five years more than I had been on this earth.

His voice and his face hovered over me, held me. He touched and pained me with his terrible loneliness. Never would I cause such pain again. My own needs, my own loneliness, seemed nothing compared to his—his needs were so much mightier than my small ones, his space in the world so much more vast and important than any place I could imagine for myself. Slowly, I succumbed to his will.

"Promise me you will not abandon me again."

"I promise, Master."

"I swear to cherish you and never desert you."
"Yes, Master."
"I promise solemnly that your children will be freed," he said.
"As God is your witness?"
"As God is my witness."
"Bolt the door," he said.

We returned once more to Marly, my master and I. We stood side by side on its heights and looked down for the last time, feasting on the panorama. The September landscape was deep and still; I fixed this vision in my mind, vowing to return to it. Here, I still believed, anything was possible. I vowed to keep this dream.

I sensed the same languor invading us both: it was like the rustling of leaves, deep and continuous, barely audible except to the soul; a sweetness that surprised both of us, for I knew he felt it, yet it never occurred to either of us to speak of it. There would always be such silences between us, partly from prudery or because of our temperaments, but also because there were so many things that must remain unsaid. All our lives. I turned toward the immense figure in dark blue standing silently beside me, and between me and the world. I was beginning to understand this strange, impulsive, melancholy man, full of contradictions and secrets, this man who owned me, my family, and my unborn child.

How did it matter that he was master and I slave? That he loved me and risked much for me? That he took more space in the world than most men did, did not concern me, neither his fame nor his power. I cherished him.

My hand was taken in his. I let it lie where it had been placed. The future and our happiness, like Marly, stretched out before me, total and shoreless. The surrounding fragrance drugged me, and made me careless of what awaited me just beyond my view.

slave and her mistress, an aunt and her niece, the virg
and the concubine.

Then, one day, the first shadow of what was to pass
between us. As in all aristocratic households of the d
hair was dressed daily by professional hairdressers w

CHAPTER 20

THE *WAYWARD*, OCTOBER 1789

I feel no ambition . . . I know the voice of Fame to be a
mere weathercock unstable as water and fleeting as a
shadow. Yet I have pride, I know I have a large portion
of it.

ABIGAIL ADAMS

The passports with the king's signature had been delivered.
Thomas Jefferson, his two daughters, and his two servants
were going home. Everything was to leave on Sunday by
river diligence for Le Havre.

Petit checked the list again. If he had calculated right,
there were eighty-two crates. And his master claimed he
was only going back for a visit! Petit shrugged. He was
responsible for the safe arrival of the baggage at Le Havre,
not Monsieur Jefferson's future plans.

He edged his way toward the south corner of the courtyard, where three carpenters were at work on the packing
crates for the great phaeton to be shipped back. The
carriage itself, which would be driven to Le Havre, stood
in solitary splendor outside the stable door. Poor Trumbull,
thought Petit. That carriage had almost driven him to
distraction. His master had ordered it from London through
his good services.

It had taken more than a year to build, with all the
changes and additions that had been made, but it was
undoubtedly one of the finest, most original carriages in
France; and in Virginia it would, without a doubt, cause an
absolute sensation. Petit walked around the carriage, admiring it, and flecked a speck of dust off the shining lilac

body. At once the coachman growled to a standing position. Petit only smiled and bowed with great ceremony. He was not supposed to touch the carriage. . . . It was a new crane-neck carriage. How splendid. Petit turned back to supervise, not without pride, the hampers of wine to be taken back to Virginia.

Adrian Petit looked down at his list:

	No.	
	1.	Hamper 24. Meurs.—12 Sauterne—12 Rochegude—12 Frontignan
	2.	do. 24. do. —12 do. —12 do. —12 do.
	3.	Hamper 6 lb. Maccaroni, 29. lb. Parmesan, 10 lb. raisins, 20 lb. amandes douces, 10 lb. brugnols, 5 lb. dates, 24 bott. vinegar, 21 do. oil, 6 amandes ameres.
	4.	box. saddle—models of machines, &c
Monticello	5. 6. 8. 9.	boxes plants.
	10.	box. books, 7¾ cub. feet.
	11.	box. books, 3 cub. feet—kitchen furniture, &c
	12.	box. bust T.
	13.	box. bust T.
	14.	box. pictures.
	15.	box. guitar.
	16.	box. clock.
Richmd.	17.	box. books, viz. Encyclop. maps 3⅓ cub. foot.
	18.	box. Pedestal for Fayette's bust
	19.	box. Harpsichord.
	20.	Hamper. 12 Sauterne. 13 Rochegude. 12 Frontig, 12 Monrach. 12 Champ.
Eppingtn.	21.	box bedstead
	22.	box bedstead
	23.	bale. mattrasses
Wmsburg.	24.	box books for G.W. 2½ cub. feet.
Hampton	25.	box. harness
Seastores	26.	hamper. 24 Meurs. 12 Sauterne. 12 Rochegude. 10 Frontignan
	27.	hamper 6 lb. Maccaroni. 18 lb. Parmesan. 10 lb. amande douce. 6 lb. amandes ameres. 10 lb. brugnol. 5 lb. dates. 12 bott. vineg. 10 bott.oil, 4 canister of tea.
Philada.	28.	box. books for Dr. Franklin, 10 cub. feet.

29. box.books, 6 cub. feet. Madison
30. hamper. 12 Rocheg. 12 Sautern. 12 Champ. 13 Monrache. 15 Frontignan
31. hamper. 12 do. 12 do. 12 do. 12 do. 14. do.

N. York { 32. box. 2 busts of P. Jones for Mr. Jay and Genl. Irvin.
33. do.⎫ gl. St. Clair, Mr. Ross of Philada. C.
34. do.⎬ Thomson. Col. Wadsworth. J. Madison,
35. do.⎭ Col. Carrington
36. box. 6 officers fusils.

37. Trunk servts. clothes
38. Trunk. clothes

Phaeton box ⎫ wearing apparel
Phaeton trunk ⎬ traveling conveniences
Brn. leather trunk ⎭ papers
Phaeton boot, servants wearing apparel
Chariot Boot ⎫
Chariot Box ⎪
Chariot trunk ⎬ wearing apparel
French hair Trunk ⎪
box covered with oil cloth ⎭
painted wooden box ⎫ Servts. wearing
leathern portmanteau ⎭ apparel
Phaeton
Chariot

No. 1. | 4 melon apricots
2. | 1. white fig (Angelic fig)
[. . .] { 3. | 1 rose bay, double blossomed
4. | 2 rose bay, common
5. | 1. Service tree Sorbus aucuparia
6. | 5. Larch. Pinus Larix
7. | 3. St. John's bread, or Caroub Ceratonia siliqua
8. | 4. Arbutus unedo, Strawberry tree.
9. | 2. cork oaks
10. | 1 buckthorn, Rhamnus Paliurus
11. | 1 Pistachia Terebinthus
12. | Mimosa arborea
13. | 4. Mimosa Farnesiana
14. | 2. St. John's bread, or Caroub &c.
15. | 1. double blossomed peach Amygdalus flore pleno
16. | 2. Budleya globosa
17. | 1 Grewia occidentalis
18. | 1 large fig
19. | 1 Amygdalus orientalis

20.	2. white fig.
21.	4 Cresanne pears
22.	2. Royal
23.	10 St. Germains
24.	3 Virgouleuse
1	1. Daphne Cneorum
	5 ivy
1	2 Sweetbriar
	Whins
	3 Italian poplar
	Alpine Strawberry

He shuddered at the thought of the long sea voyage.
Water, any body of water bigger than the reflecting pools
at Versailles, terrified him. Discreetly he crossed himself.

He glanced again at James Hemings, who was busily
supervising the closing of the wine crates, making sure that
no bottles found their way out of the crates and into the
blouses of the workmen. James, who was in his shirtsleeves,
sweated over these crates and the trunks, piling up in the
noisy courtyard of the Hôtel de Langeac. The Hôtel de
Langeac was not the only fashionable *hôtel* whose courtyard bustled and burst that day with packing crates and
trunks. Recent events had been the signal for the first great
exodus of aristocrats toward England, Belgium, and Austria.

He shook his head. He was sorry that Jim-mi was returning to Virginia. So much fire and intelligence wasted on
servitude. He, Petit, knew himself to be valuable as a
second in command, much like an aide-de-camp to a general. He knew his worth. He was an incorruptible, and
silent. *Voilà tout*; his entire life. As for James, he was of
another race. Like a thoroughbred horse, he would never
survive as a servant, as a slave. Besides, he was now a first-
class chef and could surely command the best place and the
best salary. But James, for reasons Petit could not fathom,
had decided to return to Virginia with his sister who was
carrying the child of his master, according to Marie-Louise.
Petit was sure that James would never again see the shores
of France. From one of the upper windows overlooking the
courtyard, Petit saw Martha Jefferson. She was calling to
James, waving him frantically into the house. Again Petit
shook his head. It was only with the return of Sally to the

mansion that he had learned the true relationship between
the Hemingses and the Jeffersons. James was Martha Jefferson's uncle! The whole Byzantine story of this strange
American family had finally been related to him in great
detail by Jim-mi. He, who was quite inured to the bizarre
nature of French aristocrats, had been profoundly shocked
at this odd genealogy.

That blue and black blood would mix was nothing more
than the nature of things, but that it would continue into
the second and now the third generation seemed to him
beyond propriety, even aristocratic propriety!

There was something uncivilized, raw, and brutal about
it. On one hand, they hated and despised blacks, and, on
the other, they were the objects of the most violent and
emotional desires and obsessions. . . . That the defection of
a chambermaid could bring low a man like Thomas Jefferson . . . Adrien Petit pursed his lips in distaste.

He would never understand this American family.

James Hemings felt as if he had been raped. His face
held the same blankness of defeat. Men raped men, he
thought, as well as women. . . .

He had had his "explanation" with his master and had
been left humiliated and outmaneuvered. All his resistance
had dissolved in the face of his enemy. His master as a
diplomat was as unconventional, imaginative, resourceful,
and tough as the best Old World courtiers. His arguments
were turned against him, his reasoning inside out. He had
become tongue-tied. How could he have been so abject! He
had practically thanked Thomas Jefferson when he had
said that he, James, would be freed by his grace as soon as
he had trained another cook at Monticello to take his place.
This, his master had argued, was the least James could do
to repay the training and education of these past years.
And he had accepted. He would have been a "monster," a
"serpent at my breast," a "traitor" if he had refused.
James, like his sister, was now locked in a promise of more
years of servitude. But he clung obstinately to one shred of
what he considered his essential dignity.

I will never steal myself! he thought. He has no right to

force me to do so . . . to make a criminal and an outlaw out of me who has served him for so long and with such loyalty. He must free me legally and openly.

The disappointment of his return burned his chest. Suddenly, tears splashed onto the large leather trunk he was filling with silver. With an uncontrollable sob he flung himself behind the bulk of the crates.

But there were two people who saw him crying: the discreet and ever-watchful Petit, and, from her window, Martha Jefferson.

Neither James nor Sally Hemings could shake a sense of doom as the small party set forth for Le Havre and England. As for their master, he was buoyant and optimistic, giving instructions to William Short about his return to France in a few months. But all four young people stood there in silence, each in his own anguish. Martha, because her father seemed at last willing to separate himself from her and Polly and return alone to France. James, because he, despite all his vows to the contrary, had further servitude to look forward to. If Sally Hemings was apprehensive about returning to Virginia, she was also doubting her lover's promises that they would return together to France.

Even before their arrival in Le Havre two days later there was a bad omen: the axle on the phaeton broke, and they were stranded on the road for hours.

The day after they finally arrived, a vicious storm broke out and continued unabated for six days. Hail and slashing rains and cold sleet, accompanied by unseasonable thunder and lightning—everything the heavens had to offer—came pouring down. The unceasing wind that whistled day and night brought everyone to the edge of endurance. Only Thomas Jefferson remained calm and cheerful, and on the fourth of October, during a lull in the storm, he had their baggage put on the packet for England. But again they were delayed when the storm suddenly returned.

Two days later in a tempest of wind and rain, Jefferson set out with James in search of a pair of shepherd dogs to take with him to America. In an almost manic mood, they trudged over ten miles in the filthy weather, clambering over cliffs and up goat paths, peering into caves and hovels in search of shepherds who might sell them the animals. It seemed never to occur to his master, thought James, that no shepherd nor anyone else in their right mind would be abroad in such storms. Yet his master continued, reckless and singing into the wind in his clear firm tenor. James, his clothing soaked, his eyes red-rimmed by the wind, his feet aching from the rocks and stones of the rugged landscape trudged behind him: a gaunt Sancho to Jefferson's Quixote. Then they saw it. A bundle of rags, whipped by the wind and rain, but with the bulk of a human body. As they approached, James, with his keener eyesight, drew back. It was a human body, a corpse they verified as they stood over the rain-soaked and bloated body. It was a man, who not long before they arrived, had shot himself. The body was still warm, the face so shredded and torn that identification could never be made from it. The hands and nails were bloody, almost as if the dying man had clawed at his own face in agony or, thought James, to render himself anonymous, as if he wanted to wipe his existence off the earth and leave no trace of his identity to the world. Thomas Jefferson and James Hemings stood staring at the sodden bundle of flesh and rags. James, white faced and trembling with terror, saw his own recurring dream before him causing a whistle of fear in his throat. Yet, he thought, they must move the body to a safe dry place. In panic he looked around searching for a cave or a ledge to which they could drag the dead man. But his master had recoiled in horror, his long legs already taking him down the mountain almost at a run. James called after him, but the wind or his own fear had left him voiceless. James turned and left the pitiful corpse to the shepherds who would surely find it as soon as the storm abated. He made his way down the mountain catching up with his hurrying master. They had not found the dogs. And now, James's dream took hold of him, turning him rigid with fright as the master and slave fought their way back to the inn, their breath snapping against the gale. By the time they reached safety, Thomas Jefferson was half dragging, half carrying his hysterical slave. When they reached the warmth of the fire in their rooms, the alarm of both Martha and Sally was visible.

Thomas Jefferson watched as the two women threw

themselves on James, tearing at his outer clothing, drying his face and hands with their petticoats, pulling at his sodden boots.

"We didn't find the dogs. . . ." Jefferson began stupidly, and then turned and walked out of the room. He undressed alone, without the help of his servant or his mistress late that night after the excitement of the discovery of the dead man had died away.

It was a bad omen, James repeated again and again to his sister. They should not leave France. Why . . . why were they leaving with him? Out of displaced loyalty, out of pride, out of belief in the promises of a man who would not hesitate to sell them if necessary. Sally Hemings sat staring into the fire of her brother's room. She had promised not to leave him alone this night. She had believed up until now, that they would return, but now all the doubts of the past weeks returned. Yet she dared not voice them to James, just as he dared not tell her when his terrible nightmare had commenced.

On the eighth of October the gale had dropped and the packet stood out of Le Havre for Cowes, where we would board the ship for home. It was not until the seventeenth that we reached our destination because of contrary winds, and as we approached the Isle of Wight, we encountered a virtual armada of sailing ships, all collected there and unable to sail because of the storm. More than thirty tall ships lay at anchor as our packet approached the shore.

We were met by John Trumbull, who had been waiting for us to arrive for two weeks. He had farewell letters from the master's friends in London and parting gifts for all of us. Together we stood and looked out at all the ships anchored in the somber gray sea. I stood near the slender, black-eyed, black-haired figure of John Trumbull, whose affectation of dressing only in black, but of the richest, most elegant cloth, made him stand out amongst the multi-colored, brightly dyed velvets and satins of the large group of waiting passengers on the shore.

As if sensing my inner turmoil, Master Trumbull turned to me, fixing his endearing, slightly amiss gaze upon me. "Are you going home, 'Sallyhemings'?" he asked me. We both smiled. The way he said my name was our own private joke. When he had asked me my name that winter now two years past, I had replied, as my mother had taught me, with my first and last names. Master Trumbull thought it all one name, and had continued even after I had laughingly corrected him to call me "Sallyhemings." Now all the affection he stirred in me turned into a kind of self-pity.

"We will be coming back," I said.

"Indeed?"

"Yes, it is promised. Virginia is only . . . an interval."

"I hope you are right," replied John Trumbull. He frowned, and I knew what he was thinking.

"And you?" I asked.

"Oh, I doubt that I will return to London. I must make my way in my own country." And in his usual wordy fashion he went on: "To earn a living as an artist is no easy matter. If my affairs were as I would wish, I would stay, and accept the offer of your employer to replace Mr. Short as his private secretary. Nothing would make me feel more honored, but, as an artist, I need the patronage of my countrymen—that is, if I am ever to proceed in my work. My future depends on my reception in America and as that shall be cold or cordial, I shall only decide then whether or not to abandon my country, or perhaps my profession. I hope for better things than perpetual though voluntary exile. I do hope that America will encourage me in producing monuments, not only of heroes but of those events on which their title to the gratitude of the nation is founded."

I had great affection for this man. He was a sentimental and dreamy young artist, as bone-proud as my brother James. Both clung to their small eccentricities and ob-sessions. To stand alone with only a frail sable-hair brush in hand to meet the world took a lot of courage, I thought. I guarded the sketches he had done of me with my life.

"At any rate, Sallyhemings, just in case we don't meet again, I have something for you. I did it these past weeks."

Master Trumbull was looking down at me.

"Mr. Short suggested it would be a gallant thing to make a copy of my portrait of Thomas Jefferson for Martha,

which I have done, as I had already done for other . . .
London ladies. And for some reason, one afternoon, I did
another."

He took something from his pocket and offered it to me.
I could not believe my eyes. It was a replica of Martha's
new miniature of her father, taken from the portrait made
for Master Trumbull's painting of the Declaration of
Independence. I did not trust myself to speak.

"Sallyhemings. Don't I even get an 'Ah' or an 'Oh' over
the brilliant likeness, the fine shading, the delicate color,
the inimitable expression?" He smiled.

"God bless you, John Trumbull."

"I sincerely hope he will, Sallyhemings . . . and you
too," he whispered softly. And he was gone.

I clutched the tiny painting to my breast, and looked out
over the harbor. Beyond was the sea, rolling and unfathomable. All the great ships in the harbor had their huge sails
unfurled like the wings of the sky-darkening flocks of sea
gulls that circled overhead, waiting for the wind.

It was a warm and clear twenty-third of November,
1789, when we landed at Norfolk, Virginia. My child
stirred, and James let out a string of curses as we stepped
off our ship and back into slavehood. The docks were
crowded with hustling, sweating bodies of the dockworkers
of every hue, from yellow to blue-black. All slaves. The
provincially dressed whites who mingled with them seemed
pocks on a sea of colored flesh. The low slurred slave
dialect reached my ears without meaning and the Virginia
accent sounded harsh and uncouth to my ears so long
attuned to French.

For some moments I stood bewildered and foreign in
my own country. Only my master seemed to comprehend
my confusion. He took my arm gently and led me through
the melee of orders and shouts that accompanied the un-
loading of the vessels, toward an inn where I could rest. But
before we had gone more than twenty paces, a delegation
of Norfolk citizens accosted him, excitedly greeting him
as the new secretary of state of the United States of America. Stunned, I was quickly thrust aside. The first promise
had been broken.

The looks directed my way were polite and curious until it was discovered I was maid to Master Jefferson's daughters. Then the looks ceased to be those directed at a living person and became the looks one fastens on a crate or a sack of meal. I felt faint with the shock of those looks, so well remembered but also so long forgotten. It was Polly who took my hand and held it tightly until the carriages and horses had been arranged for and we were safe inside. Trembling, I was helped into the rented phaeton by James, who was also energetically supervising the loading of our hand baggage, his own distress lost in the rush of activity. My master was still being held by the press of the anxious, noisy delegation.

In the darkness of the carriage, I pulled my veil over my face, and let Polly sink her head on my shoulder. We both slept, I think, because it was hours before the carriages started up for Monticello.

It took us a month to get home. The slave telegraph, I knew, would communicate not only our arrival but every detail of our journey—our whereabouts, our baggage, clothes, state of health . . . including and above all, my impending confinement, which I could no longer conceal. My mother would know long before I reached home.

At Eppington, a more official notice of his appointment, from the United States government, awaited Thomas Jefferson, and finally, at Shadwell, the nearest plantation, four weeks later, the Monticello slaves poured down the mountain to meet us. It was a scene that I would remember forever. The dream of Marly was gone. I knew I would never see Paris again.

The slaves had discovered the approaching carriage as soon as it had reached Shadwell and had come as one body; a flux of undulating black and brown and copper and yellow and white bodies flowing toward us, covered with cheerful ragged clothing. I recognized the unbleached Monticello woven woolen shirts of the field hands, the red-and-blue gingham head rags of the house servants, the brown and black linen dresses of the housemaids with stiff white aprons, the rough, shapeless Mother Hubbards of the female field hands, punctuated now with a red or blue blanket, now with a brightly dyed coat.

Old, shapeless felt hats and beavers were thrown into the air or waved wildly, skirts and petticoats were snatched up, showing bare feet. Most of the men were coatless as the day was warm and bright. The slaves were shouting. Some were singing, waving handkerchiefs and red bandannas; the cries and cheers were a blanket of sounds following us up the mountain. The horses were unhitched and the carriage was opened and we were received into the arms of the singing crowd, my master's servants and my fellow slaves. I sat horrified. Maria and Martha were caught up as well in the pandemonium, lifted out of the carriage, and carried by strong arms into the crowd.

They were happy. This adulation pleased my master, and the veneer of French refinement seemed to be rubbed off by the press of warm flesh.

Only James and I remained untouched by the celebration: James out of shame and bitterness; I out of fear. A wave of nausea overwhelmed me, the nausea of defeat as well as of pregnancy.

I recognized Hemingses among the crowd. And standing in the doorway, rising like a giant accusing finger above the tumult and shouting, was my mother, her hands on her hips, filling the doorway of the mansion like the stone frescoes on the façade of the Hôtel de Langeac.

Suddenly, eager hands reached for me within the carriage; I would have to face the multitude. I put the miniature which hung around my neck on a velvet ribbon, inside my dress, lest it be torn off me in the excitement. The black velvet pressed against my neck with a special softness . . . it seemed to be speaking to me, slowly. If I was ashamed to be home, no one would know it except me. I appeared at the door of the carriage, my veil lifted, a smile on my face, tears rolling down my cheeks. A murmur of "ahs" went out, like the rings of a tossed pebble upon water. "Dashing Sally" had come home! Gently I was lifted from black arms to black arms, my voluminous yellow cloak wrapped tightly around me hid the new life I carried. Joy at seeing Monticello again washed over me.

Then I saw the small figure in the doorway turn her back and walk into the Big House. The wind bit deep into my face as I was handed from slave to slave into the darkness of the now empty doorway.

She would have chosen freedom.

"Mama!" I cried against all the other cries and commotion. But, if she heard me, she did not turn back.

"Mama!" I screamed again and again.

It was years before she answered that call.

Within three months, I had my first child and named him Thomas; my master had gone to New York with James, to take up his post as secretary of state; Martha had married her cousin, Thomas Mann, and left the mansion; Polly had gone to live with her beloved Aunt Eppes, a hundred miles away; and I was left alone, having just passed my seventeenth birthday, the mistress of Monticello.

PART III

1833
The Census
Taker

ith all the dispassion, the irony, the insu-
ure and moderation of their breed. The
different countries requires corresponding
ifications. Those of the French women are
iated for the meridian of America

CHAPTER 21

WASHINGTON CITY, 1833

And what, therefore, is loyalty proper, the life breath of
all Society, but an effluence of Hero-Worship, submissive
admiration for the truly great? Society is founded on
Hero-Worship. . . . What we may call Heroarchy—
Government of Heroes.
THOMAS CARLYLE, Lecture on "Heroes and Hero-Worship,"
Albemarle Street, London, 1840

John Quincy Adams took another look at the tall blond
young man with the clear innocent eyes. He certainly knows
a lot, he thought, and he is out for blood in the name of
his lady. . . . Quincy Adams was undecided. Jefferson and
his father had finally patched up their long feud, in the face
of impending death, but his mother, Abigail, had never
forgiven Jefferson for Sally Hemings, nor for James Callender and Callender's attacks on her husband. Should he
give in to a sudden urge to voice his true opinions of
Jefferson, though he never engaged in gossiping? He
wondered whether this once he should let the chance to
recount a fascinating parable of Jeffersonian duplicity get
the better of his principles.

There was something ironic, almost biblical in Nathan
Langdon's strange addendum to the story of Sally Hemings.
The closing of the circle, and final contradiction of turning
her white for the sake of history. . . . Sally, he thought,
probably had a fine sense of the ironic. The peasant-slave
philosophy of her youth would have blended well with the
cynicism of the French education she had received while in
Paris. If he told this young man what he could not find in
the Federalist papers, he would only corroborate what Sally

Hemings herself had already revealed. How extraordinary that she had broken her silence at all, he thought.

"Well, I can't say I know the whole story, but our family was closest to the truth of it. What I do know, however, is confidential, and I should categorically deny everything if it is repeated." The rugged and ponderous Quincy Adams suddenly had the look of a mischievous boy. "The enigma of Sally Hemings and Thomas Jefferson will never be completely solved. My parents were very close to Jefferson. What I know, and I know that what I know is true, I learned from them. Despite their difference with the president at the time, they tried to stay out of the scandal as much as they could. It was a tragic campaign. . . ."

"I know, some of the newspaper articles, and the pamphlets, were inexcusably virulent."

Quincy Adams looked up over his spectacles. Could Nathan be hinting at his own poetic efforts at pornography? His miserable ballad referring to Sally had even bubbled up out of proportion during his own electoral campaign of 1828. Quincy Adams did not immediately take up the conversation. The Sally Hemings scandal had unfolded when he was young, and scrupulous enough to believe that the lives of public men should be led in accordance with their professed opinions . . . as his father's had, he thought, thanks in great measure to his mother. He turned in his armchair and gazed out onto the cow pasture that stretched from the unfinished, unpaved Pennsylvania Avenue to the Potomac River. He was thoroughly ashamed of that awful poem.

He would admit that he had greatly admired Jefferson, Adams mused, for his erudition, his interest in science and letters, but that he had always mistrusted his political principles, and disliked many of his personal traits, including much stretching of the truth in favor of the well-turned phrases or the elegant aphorism. Jefferson's affected simplicity irked him, too, when everyone knew his great wealth (if the number of slaves one owned could decently be counted as wealth). Then, too, he continued to think to himself, Jefferson's tendency to live beyond his quite sufficient means offended his Yankee sense of thrift, and he also disdained any man unable to give his ideas a clear synthesis. Jefferson's ideas were scattered in the most voluminous collection of letters of the century, yet nowhere in that morass of words, he thought, did Jefferson state clearly his political or moral principles in a way that corresponded to his political and personal actions.

Quincy Adams's inner voice continued. Why had Thomas Jefferson, a staunch abolitionist up until 1790, suddenly lost all fastidiousness about slavery? Certainly during his presidency, at least the second term, he had had the political and moral power to turn the country around on this subject. Yet, from that time on he had sunk deeper and deeper into compromise with his beliefs, and into a lethargy that couldn't be blamed entirely on the Virginia sun. Sally Hemings? Is that what turned him into a hypocritical gradualist, with no plan for accommodating the second race of America?

Nathan Langdon stirred politely, but Quincy Adams, unconcerned, continued his inner monologue.

That Jefferson had loved Sally Hemings he had no doubt. Whether Sally Hemings had loved Jefferson was less clear, since she had had no choice. That was the tragedy. That such an unnatural love may have changed the course of history, undoubtedly preventing Jefferson from using his power and genius to turn the tide against slavery instead of being an accomplice to all its darkest and most passionate aspects, was tragic indeed. . . . Why had Jefferson revised his stand against slavery when he returned from Paris? What had bound Jefferson to such a deep and lasting contradiction? He had not believed in God; therefore, all his ideas of obligation or retribution were bounded by this world. His duties to his neighbor had been under no stronger guarantee than the laws of the land and the opinions of society. The tendency of this on a great mind was to produce insincerity and duplicity. Duplicity had been Thomas Jefferson's besetting weakness.

Nathan Langdon uncrossed his legs and turned his gaze on the silent ex-president. He had come a long way in Washington since his first hesitant steps less than two years before. After his rupture with Sally Hemings he had lost his bearings. The humiliating memory of his broken engagement and his departure from home and family had almost been wiped out by the exhilaration of Washington. All aspects of his life had become resolved and clear, except one: Sally Hemings. Only she remained a haunting obsession. It was only now, after more than a year of working for John Quincy Adams, that he had dared bring up the subject—one that even after all these years had arisen in Quincy Adams's own presidential campaign. He wanted that story, told in a lonely cabin at the foot of a mountain, corroborated. He was determined to do it.

Nathan waited. If there was one thing he had learned in Washington these past eighteen months, it was that when a politician starts off with a disclaimer, you were about to get the unvarnished truth. He faced Quincy Adams, not speaking, using his now perfected technique of never breaking the silence of another man.

"Sally Hemings was indeed in Paris with Jefferson for about two years . . ." John Quincy began.

Nathan Langdon listened, hopeful yet almost afraid of what he was about to hear.

". . . but my mother's worst fears were realized, I'm afraid, since both James and Sally returned with Jefferson to Virginia after their two years in Paris. Her status at Monticello and those of her children were much above his other slaves. When I visited Monticello, I was startled to encounter one or several of them, for they were all house servants and practically advertised their paternity. It was mostly Northerners like myself who noticed. Southerners, especially Southern ladies, seemed to take it for granted. Or, should I say they were so inured to the situation they didn't even blink an eye? I greatly admired their *sang-froid* . . . but then you would know about such things, having been brought up there."

"As for Jefferson, there was absolutely no embarrassment on his part and none evidenced by his daughters or family. All the children seemed to be brought up together. So great were his powers of self-deception that I doubt if he even noticed the stares of his guests—at least those who were not privy to Southern mores—at the resemblance of his slave children to his grandchildren. Yet as you know, so strong are the bonds of silence concerning this Southern taboo, and so ferocious the penalty for acknowledging even *en famille* the concubinal arrangements of Southern gentlemen when the partner is of the dusky race, that it was only when Jefferson sought a second term as president that the scandal broke. Of course, as I said, Virginians had their own private reasons for leaving Jefferson and Sally alone—their *own* dusky partners . . . Jefferson's cousin and enemy, Chief Justice John Marshall, for example. . . ."

Nathan Langdon smiled. John Quincy Adams was warming to his story as it began to touch politics rather than sentiment. Nathan had had no idea about Chief Justice Marshall.

"My mother and father kept their peace, out of embarrassment and loyalty, and in my father's case, a deep love. But my mother could never forgive Jefferson—either privately or publicly—for what she considered a betrayal of Sally, his daughters, and herself. For you must remember, the publicity, when it came, had to be borne not only by Jefferson but by his friends, family, and daughters. It was political suicide. Political suicide," he repeated, shaking his head. Then he went on:

"My father blamed this extraordinary and tragic story on the damnable institution of chattel slavery, and he was right. Nothing is more important to the ultimate survival of this country than the abolishment of slavery. I have introduced in the House a petition for the abolishment of slavery and the slave trade on behalf of the Pennsylvania Quakers . . . I intend to do it again and again. To force the government to face and discuss this abomination. The end of the slave trade and slavery is inevitable. What is at stake is whether it will come peacefully and legislated, or in a river of blood, in the not too distant future. You, my friend, will doubtless live to see it. So will the children of Sally Hemings. I have an abhorrence of slavery, but just how bad it is no one can imagine without understanding the details."

"I know," said Nathan Langdon softly. All those women's voices he had heard on the day of Turner's trial suddenly filled his head, the room.

"This subject of slavery," continued Quincy Adams, "to my great sorrow and mortification, is absorbing all my faculties!" Adams stared gloomily ahead. He had not meant to speak with such passion. The story he had just told had dredged up the most disturbing emotions and passions. But he was stuck with it. And what did it matter now, thirty years later? One didn't cure the evils of this world by repeating them. He had been president when Jefferson had died. Today Sally Hemings probably wanted to be left alone, to die in peace and anonymity. It was with a certain anxiety that Quincy Adams met the startled, almost childish gaze of Langdon.

"You know, Nathan, you should read Thomas Jefferson's autobiography." Adams spoke again to the young man. "It is regrettable that it ends on the twenty-first of March, 1790, the day he arrived in New York to take up his post as secretary of state. It should have begun there. . . . It seems as if Jefferson made some pact with himself not to speak of himself. But every man, great or small, needs one place where he can explain himself.

"From 1790 to the end of Jefferson's presidency, his ardent passion for the rights of man, his patriotism, the depth of his understanding, the extent and variety of his knowledge, the constant awareness of public opinion, and finally the pliability of principle which he accommodated to his own designs—all these facets of his character emerged during those twenty years. And with them were combined a rare mixture of philosophy and epicurean morals, of burning ambition and stoic self-control, of deep duplicity and generous sensibility, between which qualities, and a treacherous and inventive memory, his conduct appears a tissue of inconsistency."

Adams thought back on the appropriate conclusion he had written in his private diary: "When genius pandered to the will, deceiving others meant one must have begun by deceiving oneself." It was power that was the great deceiver, and those who wielded it were the first to be deceived. How well he knew. It was Jefferson himself who had been the first deceived. He had deceived himself into believing he could love a woman he held in slavery. He had deceived Sally Hemings into believing a man that held her in such servitude could love her. Adams wondered suddenly if she had realized this finally, or had she loved him to the end?

Langdon had gotten what he wanted. But he could not help seeking more.

"But—from what I've read—there must have been a terrible row during his first term about Sally Hemings. Why did Jefferson risk losing the second term?"

A vision of those golden eyes flashed in Langdon's mind, and he imagined for a second what he would have done for them. Despite himself he blushed deeply.

"Why did he persist in the face of such humiliation?" asked Nathan Langdon. Quincy Adams smiled.

"It was all in the family, you might say, Nathan, never to be touched by anything from the outside. Washington Irving described it best. 'In a large Virginia estate, the mansion is the seat of government, with its numerous dependencies such as kitchens, smokehouses, workshops and stables. In this mansion, the planter is supreme: his overseer is his prime minister, he has his legion of house Negroes for domestic service, his host of field Negroes, a standing army; a national treasury for the culture of tobacco and cotton. All this forms a kingdom. A plantation produces everything within itself for ordinary use and luxuries, fashion, elegance is carried on with London and Paris, up the Potomac like foreign trade. . . . Everything, you understand, comes from the plantation.' " Quincy Adams paused. "The absolute power of life and death over other mortals, that was the very air he breathed. It gave him, the great democrat, a magisterial view of the world. Therefore, my dear boy, nothing could humiliate Thomas Jefferson. He was, you might say, Olympian."

CHAPTER 22

NEW YORK CITY, 1834

Hero-Worship is the deepest root of all; . . . I say great men are still admirable: I say there is, at bottom, nothing else admirable; . . . It is to this hour and at all hours, the vivifying influence in Man's life.
THOMAS CARLYLE, Lecture on "Heroes and Hero-Worship," Albemarle Street, London, 1840

"The only thing I know about Sally Hemings is that she was for a time the most famous lady of color in the United States."

Nathan Langdon squinted through the haze of blue smoke surrounding the voice of Aaron Burr. Now that he was here, in the presence of the legendary vice-president with all his messages and letters and introductions, Nathan Langdon was not all sure he really wanted to speak of Sally Hemings to him.

It had been more than a year since he had spoken with John Quincy Adams about her and now he had impulsively sought out her old enemy, Burr. Langdon, now securely ensconced in the inner sanctum of the political machine that ran Washington, was a "Washington lawyer" who would serve whatever politician and party paid him the best.

Aaron Burr, whom he had met several times before, had greeted him like a long lost son: "Why, Nathan, my boy. What brings you to New York City?"

There was something repellent about the tiny old man propped up in his bed, surrounded by his books. Burr was embroiled, as usual, in controversy and notoriety; this time,

his own divorce at seventy-eight from his fifty-eight-year-old
bride of one year for infidelities and fraud.

"You're not related to her, are you?" Burr asked as he
pushed his spectacles down from his forehead onto his
sharp nose and peered through them.

Irritated at himself, Nathan Langdon felt a blush coming on. Aaron Burr always did have the famous knack of
smelling out a motive. Now, he was zeroing in for the kill.

"Don't tell me you're a son of Thomas Jefferson!"

"Colonel Burr, sir!"

"How am I to guess," he replied crankily, "when one
side of the blanket inevitably resembles the other . . . and I
should know."

"I have met . . . two of her sons, and I believe that there
is a third somewhere in New York. I would hope to find a
trace of him, for his mother's sake."

"For his mother's sake? Then you know Sally Hemings?
I had heard that she had been sold on the auction block,
along with her daughter, after Jefferson died bankrupt."

"No, she was freed in 1826 and remained in Virginia,
where she still resides with two of her sons. I . . . I met the
family in my official capacity as census taker of Albemarle
County."

"Really? How old is she now?"

"She was fifty-six when I first met her, so that makes her
sixty now."

"Is that all?"

"Yes."

"My God! How old would Thomas Jefferson be now?"

"Ninety-three."

"The age I feel today."

"You look very well, sir."

"And you are the worst liar I've met. How do you ever
get your clients off?"

"Usually I don't, sir." Langdon laughed. Despite himself, he was beginning to warm to the old man who had an
aura, even now, of brimstone and danger.

There was something in the way he had said Sally
Hemings's name that made Langdon hesitate to go any
further into his relationship with her. Aaron Burr was not,
after all, John Quincy Adams. The quick elflike face, the

thin wasted body, the still undiminished reputation, gave
him an indisputable power of intimidation.

Langdon had delivered a packet of letters from Burr's
friends in Washington yesterday, and had spent the better
part of this afternoon with him as well.

Burr had told Langdon, when the ex-census taker had
guided him onto the subject that still obsessed him, that he
had only seen Sally Hemings once in Philadelphia at
Thomas Jefferson's inauguration as vice-president. He had
never been intimate enough with the president (to say the
least) to have been invited more than once or twice to
Monticello, and there she had not been in evidence.

"But with all the clutter I found upon entering the house,
I could have missed her in between the stuffed moose and
the statue of Cleopatra. Walking into his entranceway was
like walking into the inside of his head. Everything a confusion of relics, of conjecture about things he knew nothing
about, loose ends and solid marble. There were Indian
relics; bad paintings, including a crucifixion owned by a
man who didn't believe Jesus was divine; heads and horns
of an elk, of a deer; a map of Missouri drawn by Indians
(before he and Meriwether Lewis stole it from them);
buffalo hides, bows and arrows, poisoned lances (better
than treason trials), peace pipes, wampum belts, several
Indian dresses and cooking utensils; and a colossal bust of
himself on a truncated column which made him ten feet
tall and gave me a good mouse-eye's view. The column, I
remember, had the twelve tribes of Israel and the twelve
signs of the zodiac upon it; and besides the full-size reclin-
ing statue of Cleopatra (after she had applied the asp),
there were busts of Voltaire, Turgot, John Paul Jones,
George Washington, General Lafayette, and a model of one
of the pyramids!

"In the salon, I remember, were busts of Alexander the
Great; Napoleon, whom he professed to despise; and, quite
aptly, a 'Sleeping Venus' (white, not black). This was, of
course, when I was his vice-president. But if I didn't see
her at that time, I certainly witnessed several interesting
happenings! The guest next to me practically fell off his
chair when the spitting image of Thomas Jefferson came in
carrying the soup! But this couldn't have been the famous

'Tom,' for he was too old. I think I heard him called James or Jamey. At any rate, the place was crawling with white slaves, literally, since many of them were very young children who seemed to have the complete run of the house. As you know, after that time, the president and I had a slight disagreement. . . ."

Nathan Langdon was shocked even now. To refer to charges of treason as "a slight disagreement. . . ."

"You look shocked, my boy." Aaron Burr loved to shock people and then console them. "If you look at it from my point of view, I was simply twenty years before my time. We must kick the Spanish out, annex half of Mexico, and fight a war to make it stick. All begun by our illustrious President Jackson, twenty years . . . after *I* planned it. And not a word of credit . . . or thanks!"

Nathan Langdon laughed. He was irresistible, this old man!

"I wouldn't call a trial for treason a 'slight disagreement'!"

"It was a trial, not a conviction, my boy. The jury returned a verdict of 'not guilty because not proven guilty' the first time, and the second trial for the misdemeanor was a straight 'not guilty.' People seem to forget that! The government had no case, and they knew it. Even Hay admitted he couldn't hang me. He sought further treason indictments in Ohio. At any rate, sooner or later Jefferson, with the aid of a complacent and well-rewarded judge, would have gotten his verdict of guilty. After all, John Marshall couldn't follow me through the seventeen states trying me. So, fearing Jefferson's pertinacity in my pursuit, I went into hiding and eventually made my way back to Europe, coming home during the war to resume my law practice. I ran into John Trumbull, the painter, and his poor wife while I was in London."

John Trumbull, Nathan thought. The one man who had made drawings of Sally Hemings as a young girl.

"Is he in New York now?" he asked.

"Oh, yes, you know he became quite a staunch Federalist. He's the president of the American Academy, and he has managed to get his paintings in every federal building in Washington." Aaron Burr pushed his spectacles back up on his high-domed forehead. "Would you like to meet him?"

"Yes, sir," replied Langdon, "if it's not too much trouble."

Aaron Burr would be quite content to give the young man a letter of introduction. The talk about Sally Hemings had brought back his undying hatred of Thomas Jefferson, and had reminded him of the one great mistake of his life: trusting Jefferson to keep his word as a gentleman. What he had always hated about Jefferson was his hypocrisy. It had cost him, Aaron Burr, the presidency, he thought. Jefferson would lie with the whore politics, then rise from her bed, scream that he had been infected with syphilis, and refuse to pay. . . .

"What do you really want to know about Sally Hemings, and why?"

"Everything. Nothing. It is something I stumbled onto, and now—" Nathan Langdon stopped, disconcerted.

"Strange, I had a beloved sister called Sally . . . who protected me from many a beating at the hands of my guardian. When I ran away from home the first time, I was four and she six. She threw herself between me and the rod, a pattern which was to continue all our lives. We had only each other, having lost both our parents and grand-parents by then. But, if ever a woman left me cold, and there are not many who did, Sally Hemings was one. Beautiful, yes. I saw her in her prime." Aaron Burr gazed at Langdon, who was hanging on his every word. "She was possibly the most beautiful woman I'd ever seen, black or white, slave or free, duchess or maid, with the exception of my daughter Theodosia. But there was a cloying self-satisfaction about her that I detested. A hypocrisy that matched her lover's. Leave it to Thomas Jefferson to find the only woman in the South capable of being self-righteous about concubinage. . . ."

"Sir, being an ascetic, Jefferson can't have relished the role of a debauchee."

"My dear sir, scratch an ascetic and you unearth a sensualist! He loved words and used them like an artist; he loved wine, music, food, flowers, beautiful objects, luxurious surroundings, fine books, tapestries, paintings, horses, land.

What is eliminated from that classic list of the sensualist? If you count his love affairs with buildings, gardens, scientific instruments, and his own written word, I would say that he, not I, is the profligate. I may go down in history remembered only with the smoking dueling pistol in my hand; but, really, I am a most dispassionate individual. Behind that cold façade he was the passionate one. His hatred for me and all his political enemies was uncontrolled, almost feminine. You could say he was an inconsummate politician, rather than a consummate one. And all this . . . this ardor was consummated, if you like, in the most extraordinary political document of the century: the Declaration of Independence. This, not Sally Hemings, nor any other woman, was his great moment of passion. His pathological hatred for the English and everything English, including the English in himself, impregnated him with a felicity of language he never again achieved. Reread it, Nathan. In the original version, that document grips you like a woman. It is pure passion. That's why it sings, and that's why it moves people. What red-blooded American could resist such a ravishing and virile image of himself?

"Pure genius, my boy. I rather unimaginatively stuck to women. As for Sally Hemings . . . she came with the plantation."

"Sir, you forget she was a slave. She had no choice."

"Oh, come now, Nathan. This was Virginia, not Mississippi. And this was a Virginian gentleman, not some redneck overseer. Even token resistance would have been enough. If she was her mother's daughter, she probably *seduced* him. Now, *there* was a woman, Elizabeth Hemings. She must have been close to fifty when I saw her, and she looked twenty-five: superb, a Nefertiti with *real* traces of Africa on her brow, and a carriage worthy of a queen. She made you glad you had them, though I would have been trembling in my boots if I had had to prove it to her! No, Sally Hemings was too snobbish, too glacial, too busy playing Joan of Arc and putting on airs to suit me. How old was she in Paris?"

"Fifteen," answered Langdon.

"Then she definitely seduced him. What forty-year-old man in his right mind can resist a healthy fifteen-year-old

girl?" Aaron Burr smiled to himself. The profound shock
on Nathan Langdon's face told him all he wanted to know.
This young man had become involved with Sally Hemings
in an emotional way, probably having to do with Thomas
Jefferson, a case of hero-worship . . . He had that hangdog
look of a rejected lover. Why? if she had accepted him in
the first place. Aaron Burr was intrigued. What would
somebody as proud and haughty, as jealous of her preroga-
tives as Sally Hemings, and as famous, want with a pip-
squeak like Nathan Langdon? He decided to try another
technique.

"She's in no danger or difficulty because of what happened so many years ago? Surely there is someone to
protect her?"

"That's just what I tried to do! Protect her! I was not
even sure she was in Virginia legally, and that's why I
declared her white . . . you see—"

Aaron Burr didn't see at all, but he intended to. He
raised himself up on his pillows in the disordered, book-
strewn bed to which he had been confined since his second
stroke. How had he managed to get her declared white? Or
had he done it himself? To absolve the great man from the
"crime" of miscegenation, he assumed. This was fascinating! This cipher had been playing God, and Sally Hemings
(knowing a lot about a god, having lived with him for
thirty-eight years) had found him out. Fascinating!

Bastards Aaron Burr knew quite a bit about, he thought,
having fathered several, but this was a special kind of
bastardy. Something deeper than mere illegitimacy. Many
great men, including himself, had illegitimate children, yet
the special loss of a son or daughter to an entire race had
something mythical about it. How fatal and touching this
story was, and how ironic that it should be Jefferson, the
image-maker, the definer of America, the nation's most
articulate voice!

Aaron Burr lay back on his pillows. Nathan Langdon
was silent. They sat staring at each other for what seemed
like a long time. "Was it Voltaire, dear lad, who said,
'There is no history, only fictions of varying degrees of
plausibility'?

"Here is a true fable. If only we could unravel the beauty

of it from the obscenity and disgrace that has surrounded
its revelation. . . . I remember the papers."

"You find it beautiful?"

"Yes," said Aaron Burr. "I can forgive Thomas Jefferson
a lot of things because of it."

Nathan Langdon gazed into the large dark eyes which
had always been famous for their intensity, and were now,
in their twilight, somehow more terrible than ever. Sally
Hemings had spoken of them: "What I remember most of
him," she had said, "were his eyes, of such size and darkness as to strike terror in the hearts of anyone except the
very brave. There was something lewd about their power."
Now Burr looked narrowly at the young Washington
lawyer.

"Yes," Burr said, "he was lucky in a way. If a man
arrives at love, no matter how, when, or why—love beyond
convention—then he has already lived well. Does not every
man dream of some overwhelming, unfathomable love?
But few have the courage to risk it, to keep it, or to honor
it. If he did, then Jefferson has once more amazed me."

Nathan Langdon turned from the wistful, smoldering
eyes and bowed his head. Lucky. He had never thought of
Thomas Jefferson as "lucky." Nathan's own sense of failure
oppressed him. He was appraising, not without bitterness,
his lack of wealth, his mediocrity as a lawyer, and, yes, as a
man as well. Had he not lost the two women he really
cared about? Had he not lost all sense of proportion, he
thought? For the sake of erasing miscegenation from the
crimes of a famous man, he had annihilated his own sense
of worth as well. He repeated to himself that Jefferson's
biographers were already at work. He would emerge two
hundred years from now, spanking clean, shorn of even the
few shreds of humanity that had managed to cling to him
despite all his efforts to conceal them from the public eye.
. . . As for the Hemings family, half of which had already
sunk into the unwary arms of white America, no one would
ever know how they really felt about their lives. . . .

Nathan promised to pay his host another visit, but
Aaron Burr knew he would not. It didn't matter.

"Tell my friends I am in a position to deliver any
messages they may have for any of their departed loved

ones, as long as they are in the same location that everyone is sure I'll be repairing to quite soon. . . ."

Nathan Langdon smiled.

"As soon as I get there I'll give your best to Thomas Jefferson," he added with a wry smile.

CHAPTER 23

NEW YORK CITY, 1834

We all love great men. That man in some sense or other
worships heroes: that we all of us reverence and must ever
reverence great men: this is, to me, the living rock amid
all rushing—down whatsoever—the one fixed point in
modern revolutionary history, otherwise bottomless and
shoreless.
THOMAS CARLYLE, *lecture on Heroes and Hero-Worship*,
Albemarle Street, London, May 5, 1840.

"Mr. Nathan Langdon to see Colonel Trumbull, sir."

Nathan Langdon, days after his meeting with Aaron
Burr, was introduced into the company of the now famous
and fashionable "artist and patriot," John Trumbull. The
announcement had been made by a gray-faced, gray-
liveried servant, who bowed out as if he were in the
presence of royalty.

Nathan almost stood at attention as he introduced himself to the formidable personage that appeared before him.
Trumbull was handsome, erect, and slim, with a military
bearing, radiating a bitter but unmistakable arrogance and
self-confidence. He could better say that he had introduced
himself into the company of the Founding Fathers, since
flanking John Trumbull were copies of two of his most
famous paintings: *The Declaration of Independence* and
The Resignation of Washington. He found himself staring
not only at Sally Hemings' old friend from the Hôtel de
Langeac, now himself transformed into a national monument, but at George Washington, John Adams, Thomas
Jefferson, Benjamin Franklin, and all the other illustrious
names. John Trumbull seemed to blend into and arrange
himself as if he were part of the famous assembly of his

paintings, and in the glow of the immense skylights that
bathed his rooms at the academy, the effect was impressive
and not at all coincidental. John Trumbull felt, in fact, that
he was well placed in the company of his paintings. He had
devoted his long life to painting the glorious deeds and the
famous names of the Revolution, he reminded himself
every day. Although he had spent only a total of eighteen
months in the Revolutionary Army, and nineteen days as
aide-de-camp to General Washington, he had cashed in
on his military career since his return to the United States.
He had insisted on being addressed, Virginia style, by his
military title, a title he had come by belatedly and not without considerable vexation and humiliation, he remembered.
Nathan, who had only Sally Hemings's description of
Trumbull as a gentle romantic portrait painter, was completely taken aback.

"Colonel, please excuse my staring . . . but I pass the
originals of these paintings every day in the Rotunda of
the Capitol. They are so familiar to me they seem part of
my life. To come across them in New York is quite a
shock."

"Well, Mr. Langdon, when one enters the atelier of an
artist, one can expect to find the unexpected. Otherwise it
is a mediocre artist that you have come in contact with."
John Trumbull fixed his dark, peculiarly asymmetrical gaze
on his visitor. "I have done several versions of my large
painting in the Rotunda. By the way, how are they holding
up? I haven't seem them in several years." He went on
without waiting for Langdon's reply. "Yes, indeed, I have
devoted fifty-five years of my life and my entire artistic
career to memorializing our glorious Revolution, and those
who took part. I was, of course, in an extraordinarily
fortunate position to do so, being General Washington's
aide-de-camp. . . ."

Nathan Langdon thought, even at the risk of seeming
rude, he had better come quickly to the point, as it was
obvious John Trumbull's career as aide-de-camp to General
Washington was about to be recounted as part of the tour
of his painting studio.

"Colonel, which of the paintings were you working on
when you visited Paris in 1788 to do the portrait of Thomas
Jefferson?" he asked.

John Trumbull was startled at the sudden turn in what was usually a smooth and well-rehearsed recital.

"Well, I was working on the *Declaration*, of course, but also on the *Surrender of Lord Cornwallis at Yorktown*, and I needed portraits of all the French officers who took part in that event. It was December 1787 when I arrived at the Hôtel de Langeac, President Jefferson's home, and I took with me the prepared canvas of *Yorktown* and painted a dozen portraits of the French officers while I was there. Those that had participated in the battle or were present at the surrender. I remember it was the end of February before I was finished."

Nathan Langdon listened in amazement to the roll call of the French officers trip easily off the tongue of the tall, pompous old man. If he remembered all this, he would surely remember what happened that winter at the Hôtel de Langeac.

"It is, sir, in connection with that visit to Mr. Jefferson's ministry in that particular year that I have come to see you."

"Really? Are you a relative of one of the officers in the painting? And you would like his portrait? I do many miniatures for family and friends from my historical paintings." John Trumbull waited deferentially, and tried to guess, from the manner and clothes of the gentleman, how much he could reasonably ask for a portrait of the young man's uncle, or father, or whatever. He had frightened off many a prospective customer with his high prices. But what did they think? That artists lived on air? He had received only twelve thousand dollars apiece for his Capitol paintings from that tight-fisted Congress, and he had had to completely repair and reinstall the paintings twice. The heartache . . . the trials of those blasted paintings, he thought. The size of them alone, twelve feet high and nineteen feet long, had almost killed him with his one-eyed vision. And then the damp and mildew from the new masonry and the swampy humidity of Washington's climate . . . These paintings were supposed to last as long as the Republic! God knows if they will, with all the abuse they get! He turned back to his young visitor. Normally he asked one hundred dollars for a head, one hundred and fifty for a head with hands, two hundred and fifty for half-length, and five hundred whole length. A full fifty percent below his famous competitor . . .

"The topic I had in mind, Colonel Trumbull, was only marginal to your work in Paris and touched you only casually, I think. While you were there, you did, I believe, some pencil sketches and a watercolor of a young girl who was maid to the Jefferson ladies . . . one Sally Hemings."

Nathan Langdon glanced nervously up at the hooded blue eyes of Thomas Jefferson gazing serenely, not at him, thank goodness, but toward the venerable figure of John Hancock.

Then he heard Trumbull saying:

"Sketches? Of a servant? In Paris? At the Hôtel de Langeac? Not of Jefferson?"

Of course he remembered the little maid from Virginia, thought John Trumbull, the exquisite maid with the superb bone structure and the extraordinary complexion, little Sallyhemings. . . . But that didn't mean he should admit it to this young man. So many years ago. She would have to be an old woman now. But still beautiful, if his artist's eye had not deceived him. Yes, she had sailed back to Virginia with Jefferson the very same day he had sailed back to New York. The last time he had seen her was where? In Cowes, when he had given her the miniature of Jefferson. Ah, he had been a romantic young man in those days. Now, how much should he admit to this young man? And who was he anyway? And what did he want with his sketches of Sally Hemings?

"I do remember now. Perfectly. I did several sketches of an exquisite girl at the ministry of Thomas Jefferson, the maid of Polly Jefferson. I gave one of them to her."

John Trumbull gazed at the visitor. Who was this Nathan Langdon and what did he want?

"Let us sit down, Mr. Langdon. I will order tea to be served. You say you would like to commission a miniature. Why?"

"Let us just say I am an agent for a private person who would like a miniature of . . . his mother."

Nathan Langdon held his breath. He had taken a bold step. Either the old gentleman would feign ignorance or the prospect of a commission would bring him around to talk. He had had no intention of commissioning a painting, but he wondered why he had not thought of it before. He would like very much to have an image of Sally Hemings for himself.

"If you care to, Mr. Langdon, you may tell me what you know, and how you came to know it. But first you must give me your word as a gentleman that you are not of the press."

Again the disclaimer, thought Nathan Langdon, always the disclaimer . . .

"I give you my word."

"And that this discussion will never be repeated to a living soul. You promise this as a gentleman."

"I do."

Nathan Langdon felt much as he had felt that first afternoon in the cabin of Sally Hemings, except that here there were no shadows, no darkness. The surroundings were all light—the bright, elegant studio in the prestigious American Academy, immense, immaculate, filled with portraits of the great and the famous. A subtle and not unpleasant odor of turpentine and paint blended with the steaming English tea served in delicate cups of Sèvres China by the liveried servant. The old man settled into a comfortable English armchair and listened to the young lawyer's extraordinary tale.

When Langdon had finished, John Trumbull sat as still as a great eagle, alert to the slightest gesture. The strange, almost cross-eyed effect came from the fact that the painter had been blind in one eye since childhood.

"You are a Southerner, Mr. Langdon?"

"Yes."

"And an abolitionist, I take it?"

Nathan Langdon flushed. Had he ever really thought in those terms?

"Of course," Nathan Langdon answered.

"You know, of course, my position. It is strange that antislavery has come to be identified with political partisanship and, I might say, with the conservatives of this country. We were the ones who got the slave trading from Africa outlawed, even if the smuggling continues and more Africans still reach our shores. The enslaving of the inhabitants of Africa in the name of Christianity, especially in the name of Christianity, is not only criminal, it is intolerable in our nation. 'Is not the enslaving of these people the most charitable act in the world?' " he intoned, bitterly mimicking the pious tones he had heard on so many lips. " 'With no other end in view than to bring those poor creatures to Christian ground and within hearing of the gospel, we spare no expense of time or money, we send many thousands of miles across the dangerous seas, and think all our toil and pains well rewarded. We endure the greatest fatigues of body and much unavoidable trouble of conscience in carrying on this pious design. We deprive them of their liberty, we force them away from their friends, their country, everything that is dear to them. . . . And are they not bound by all the ties of gratitude to devote their entire lives to our service, as the only reward that can be adequate to our abundant charity?' Ah!" he thundered, "I could forgive anything but doing what we did in the name of Christianity! At least we can't accuse Thomas Jefferson of hypocrisy, can we? He didn't believe in Christianity."

Suddenly, John Trumbull got up and walked to the back of the immense studio. He was gone for a long time, and when he returned he had in his hand four small sheets of paper. In silence, the two men looked at the delicate pencil renderings of a young girl in the dress of forty years before. The sketches were quick, almost futile, with none of the pompousness Nathan Langdon so detested in the large paintings of John Trumbull.

The pose of the first sheet was guileless, the young girl with her hair down, her face cradled in one hand, her elbows supported by the arm of the chair in which she was seated. She looked out of the picture with enormous, wide-spaced, light eyes. The second sketch was a three-quarter half-portrait, where there was the ghost of a smile and symmetrical dimples. The third was of the girl in profile, standing in front of a bouquet of flowers. The long neck stretched slightly forward and bent, and tendrils of dark hair had escaped from the twisted knot piled high on her head. The final sketch, smaller than the others, was a fresh and delicate watercolor. The girl's tiny hand was touching her black hair absently, and she was gazing out of the picture.

Nathan Langdon's hand trembled as he held each of the

sketches. They were drawings of almost unbearable tenderness and delicacy. His throat constricted. How lovely she had been! He turned his back to John Trumbull.

The painter, who had spent his life looking and learning from people's faces, turned away when he saw the expression on the young man's face. John Trumbull had cast his lot with the great and the famous in every way except one. Like Thomas Jefferson, only in his heart had he erred against his class . . . and no one was ever going to find out about that from his lips, he thought. What, he asked himself, would Langdon know, having listened only to Sally Hemings, of the pain a man feels who falls in love with a forbidden woman? Of not being able to protect her . . . of always being something of a coward in her eyes because of it. . . . Trumbull had loved his beautiful, illiterate and socially unacceptable wife, Sarah, now dead. How he had known that love for a woman ultimately unprotected against the hurts of society.

Even Jefferson had not been able to protect his Sally, any more than he had been able to protect his Sarah, he thought. And what of their children? His illegitimate son now hated him and was lost to him forever, just as Jefferson's sons were. It was true, he had no fondness for Jefferson. Jefferson's atheism, his want of credibility, his stupidities in military matters, his unconstitutional embargo, had long ago wiped out their friendship. But for the sake of his Sarah and *his* Sally, not a word of this affair of the heart would ever escape his lips, certainly not to a young whippersnapper like this Langdon.

What did he know about loving and risk! Real risk! Jefferson had risked everything for her. . . . What had Langdon ever done for Sally Hemings except to turn her white in fright!

Nathan Langdon, as if sensing John Trumbull's thoughts, suddenly understood the awful power a woman could wield over a man. He remembered with what overpowering sensuality and force he had been drawn into the embrace of Sally Hemings that day . . .

"I'm afraid, Mr. Langdon, that I cannot accept your commission to do a miniature of this . . . person, for her . . . uh . . . son."

"But, sir. . . ." Nathan Langdon turned in alarm.

A look of contempt passed over the face of the proud old man. Such unmilitary behavior! "First of all, I am sure that the person in the sketches and the person of whom you speak are not the same. She was not a slave. I refuse all comment on your incredible story and, of course, all confirmation."

Nathan Langdon looked dumbfounded.

What a stupid boy for a lawyer, thought John Trumbull.

"Mr. Langdon, the greatest motive I had, or have, for engaging in or for continuing my pursuit of painting is the wish to commemorate the great events of our country's Revolution, to preserve and diffuse the memory of the noblest series of actions which have ever presented themselves in the history of man. This is an enormous responsibility, Mr. Langdon, and I carry it out to the best of my ability as an artist. The history of private passions has no place in public history." He paused. "A painting of Sally Hemings by John Trumbull is simply not possible."

"I would be willing to purchase it unsigned. It would not have to be listed in any of your catalogues."

"Mr. Langdon, I have an understanding with Yale University. All my paintings have been bought by them for an annuity."

"Even an *unsigned* John Trumbull?"

"An unsigned painting has no value, except to us."

John Trumbull felt almost sorry for Nathan Langdon.

"I regret, sir. What you ask is impossible. There can never be a portrait of Sally Hemings."

John Trumbull rose. "I thank you for your visit."

When Nathan Langdon had left, John Trumbull stood for some moments in the middle of his vast studio looking at the sketches of Sally Hemings, so beautiful, so fragile. In their small way, they were subversive, unimportant perhaps, but subversive nevertheless. John Trumbull turned and stared at his paintings. The bright, diffused light of the windows above caught the old man's face; if he felt anything at this moment, the light did not reveal it. With great ceremony, John Trumbull tore the sketches of Sally Hemings into small pieces and let them fall to the floor. There was silence in the room. John Trumbull stood as if listening for something. But there was not one nay from the painted life-size figures surrounding him.

PART IV

1795-1809
Monticello

CHAPTER 24

SPRING 1795

I set out on this ground which I suppose to be self-evident
that the earth belongs to the living; that the dead have
neither powers nor rights over it.

THOMAS JEFFERSON to James Madison,
September 6, 1789

Lord Thomas was a nice young gentleman
He rode a many a town
He courted a girl they called Fair Ellender
And one called Sally Brown.

Is this your wife, Lord Thomas, she cries!
She is most wonderous brown.
When you could have married as fair a young girl
As ever the sun shone on.

They buried the Brown Girl in his arms,
Fair Ellender at his feet.
They laid the Brown Girl in his arms
And let her go to sleep.

Traditional Ballads of Virginia,
Compiled by Arthur Kyle Davis, Jr.

It was a long time before my mother answered that first call
from the carriage that brought me back to Virginia and
slavery. And when she did, her words had been: "You got
a son, Sally Hemings. A wee darling perfect thing." As she
had taken Thomas Jefferson Hemings from my body, she
had forgiven me at the same time. She focused all her love
and hopes on him. "Get that freedom for your children,"
she repeated like a litany. "And get it for yourself while
you're at it," she added. "Don't nothing in life count more

207

than that." She had looked at me with a mixture of pity
and exasperation. "Not even love."

That had been five years ago and now it was the spring
of 1795, one year since my master had returned from
Philadelphia to retirement, since he had come home to me.
It had been the happiest year for us both. So happy, it had
made up for everything. The return to Virginia and slavery
had been a shock to me. I felt isolated at Monticello, and
slights and injuries were my daily lot. Even my master
seemed helpless against these hurts. His acceptance of the
post of secretary of state had been a tragedy for me. We
were to have stayed only a short time here, then return to
our beloved Paris. In Paris, we had both forgotten what it
meant to be white or black, master or slave.

I no longer knew whether to believe him now when he
vowed never to engage in politics again. This retirement
might not last. The temptations of power were too great.
But the hurts and humiliations of the past three years were
also deeply etched in his soul. He had "retired" in a sulk
from Philadelphia. He was in bad grace with President
Washington, who no longer spoke to him; defeated by
Hamilton; publicly attacked by the Federalists. Everything
had passed: the excise, the Bank, the treaty with Britain.
He was back home to lick his wounds.

Our letters these three years had been numerous, and
often in French. He had bid me to burn his, but I had not
done so. He burned mine, I suspected, yet I took much
care in writing them, especially those in French. And the
magic of the written word still awed me. Yet for all his
letters of love, I was uneasy without his presence. Not just
lonely, but unsure of myself. I seemed nothing without him
and everything in his eyes. My tutoring and, more than anything else, my music, had continued after my return to
Monticello, and so the creature he had begun to create and
shape in Paris had finally been ready to receive him when
he rode home from his political wars. I rested easier now
that he was home, but I still needed to ask.

"Daughter, you ought to know if he loves you or not. If
you don't know, then he don't. I know he thinks he loves
you, and maybe that's all a woman can expect from a man
—that he believes it. . . . A woman knows. A woman
knows when a man loves her . . . even a slave woman. It's

been six years. . . . A white man don't keep a black concubine for six years without loving her. He loved your sister and he lost her, and now he loves you."

My mother had changed little in the past thirteen years. She had kept her low, compact figure, her slimness, her unlined and perfect skin, her iron constitution. She was now fifty-nine years old and she still ran Monticello, despite my position. Her beautiful, vigorous body still demanded and got the services of lovers of both colors. I knew that I would never take another lover. I loved only my master. A dangerous and stupid thing for a slave. . . . God knows, I knew that. Five years had passed since the birth of the child I had carried in my womb across the water from France. Five years that had brought me another child. My mother returned my gaze. Had she already guessed it? If I had not been bound to Monticello before, this child fathered on my last birthday was the hostage to the fading memories of Paris and freedom.

"You trapped," she said. "Just like I was before you. But I never had the chance you had. And that will haunt you, daughter, haunt you. Remember, you put yourself in danger when you returned to Virginia. Danger of life and limb, and, God forbid, of being sold. Did you forget about that over there in France? That you returned to the same burden as the blackest, most ignorant field hand? You forgot the first lesson of slavery, your blackness. And you forgot the second, loving somebody you ain't got no business loving. . . . The man you got has no business loving, either. He's put himself in danger as well—don't forget that when you start feeling sorry for yourself. In danger from his own white folks, loving somebody, he, with all his money and power, ain't got no right to love."

"Do you think he'll marry again?"

My mother jumped to her feet. "Lord Almighty! You wishing for a white mistress? Your father didn't marry again, did he? I ain't never wished for no white mistress, and thank God I never had one. When there were white mistresses at Poplar Hill, I was in the fields. When I came into the Big House, they were all dead. And you wishing for one? Martha Randolph ain't enough trouble for you? Let me tell you, daughter, white Southern ladies don't seem to mind who sleeps with they husbands, but they mighty touchy 'bout who sleeps with they fathers! I remember my own trials with them Wayleses daughters. Lord! You think a white mistress wouldn't sell you so quick your head would turn? You and your children? Or kill you? Or maim you? Or ruin that beautiful face? You think it's never happened before? You think they don't know what they men doing with their female slaves? You think they believe their slaves gettin' whiter by contamination? You think because we're black, they don't feel jealousy? They love the same way. They birth the same way, and they lusts the same way. Why you think they dress themselves up in all those fine, low-cut gowns? They love their men, and they hate us. Don't forget that, daughter. There ain't that much difference between a white and a black female. And," she added, "in case you wonderin', ain't no difference a'tall between white mens and black mens. They all think what they got twixt they legs is Heaven, and what we got twixt ourn is Hell."

My prison was vast and golden. There were his vegetable gardens, his thousands of fruit trees, his forests full of Virginia pine, birch, oak, and linden.

Monticello was five thousand acres in length and width, and across the river were scattered six thousand more divided between his plantations of Tuffton, Lego, Shadwell, Broadhurst, Pantops, Beaver Creek, and at Martha's Edgehill. The mountain was enveloped in deep forest, all the way to the clearing at the top, on which the mansion stood, with its lawns and gardens and shade trees. From that point, like the spokes of a wheel, radiated his fields and valleys, his streams and rivers, his tobacco, his cotton, his wheat, his cattle, and his slaves. The forest was threaded as if with silk cords with the forty miles of bridle paths over which my master rode without fail every afternoon. I could see bent backs scattered among the white and green of his lands. He had raced up the mountain to me and now he raced over the hills of Monticello each day always singing. His hands, capable of the most delicate drawings, the most exquisite caresses, now gripped the reins of his thoroughbred horse. He was strong. He was home. He enjoyed his life at Monticello. He read and wrote in the morning, he rode and tended his plantations in the after-

noons. His lust for politics had slackened; even his appetite
for the newpapers and local gossip had waned.

The great six-foot body had remained the same in lean-
ness and strength through the years. So had his high color.
I could now see the beginning of gray in his thick red hair
and the lines around his mouth were a little deeper. The
heavy-lidded eyes were the same intense sapphire blue I
had always known. I wanted to cut off his queue, but he
still wore his hair long and tied with a blue ribbon. It fell
to his shoulders in loose curls over the fine white cravat I
wound every morning around his neck. The only impatience
I ever saw him manifest was with his horses. He would
subdue them with a whip at the slightest sign of restlessness. He chose his bays for speed and spirit, then mistreated them, making them dangerous animals. His delight
in them frightened me. He seemed to court disaster. I never
really knew if he would come back to me whole or broken
to pieces. His treatment of his mounts upset Jupiter, but I
thought better horseflesh than slave flesh. Apart from that,
my master seemed peaceful and content with his life here.

There were twenty-five house slaves on the mountain,
not including the blacksmiths, grooms, carpenters, nailery
boys, weavers, and shepherds. First there was my mother,
Elizabeth Hemings, housekeeper. Of her "dark" Hemingses,
there were Martin the butler, and Bett, Nance, and Mary,
who were housemaids. Four more of her dark Hemingses
had been inherited by my half sister Tabitha Wayles Skipwell. And then there were her "light" Hemingses, whose
father had been John Wayles: Robert, James, Peter, Critta,
and myself. Of the white Hemingses, Thenia and her children fathered by Samuel Carr, my master's nephew, were
missing, sold to James Monroe. And last year, Robert
Hemings had bought his freedom in order to live with his
wife in Richmond. Finally there was John Hemings, my
mother's last son and my half brother, whose father was a
white carpenter called Nelson. Some of us had children so
that there were third-generation Hemingses on the mountain as well: Critta's son Jamey Hemings, whose father was
Samuel Carr's brother, Peter.

And in the hierarchy of slavehood I stood at the pinnacle, even before Elizabeth Hemings, for I was the

"favorite," the untouchable. I was far above the station of
the other slaves. Accountable to no one except the master.

"I cornered the bastard!"

I smiled at the recollection of James returning tri-
umphantly from Philadelphia and reading to me the written
promise: "That if the said James shall go with me to
Monticello in the course of the ensuing winter when I shall
go to reside there myself and shall there continue until he
shall have taught such person as I shall place under him
for the purpose to be good cook, this previous condition
being performed, he shall thereupon be made free and I
will thereupon execute all proper instruments to make him
free. . . ."

Why was he so childishly proud of that piece of paper?
Why hadn't he simply stolen himself?

"He would have freed you anyway, James," I said.

"No, he wouldn't. I'm the best cook in these United
States. Even now, he would keep me if he could. He's
kicking himself already over this piece of paper!"

"What will you do, James?"

"The first thing I've got to do is cook my last meal at
Monticello and get out of here!"

"Who have you chosen?"

"Peter, of course."

"Good," I said. "A position as powerful as that shouldn't
go out of the family."

He looked at me. "You are your mother's daughter,
all right," he said.

"The master will miss you."

"I've already given him six extra years of my life.

"The master," he said. "You always call him that even
with me. With that French accent of yours. I call the
bastard Jefferson or TJ when we are alone or with other
slaves, and half the time I call him that to his face if no
strangers are present. But I have never heard you refer to
him as anything else except 'the master,' except that you
make it sound like an endearment. . . . No wonder he
loves you. If you can take the most ruthless word in the
English language and turn it into an expression of love . . ."

I turned away. It hadn't been so long ago that he too had
called him "master." Did he really believe that that piece

of paper erased a word he had mouthed since he was a child? I knew my brother so well. He was so vulnerable. Let him call my lover bastard if it made him feel better. We were all bastards after all, weren't we? We stared at each other.

"He is not God, you know."

"Isn't he, James?"

"Only God deserves to be loved."

"That may be so, but once you have loved a man, it is difficult to love God."

I caught his hand and studied him tenderly.

He was twenty-nine years old now. His beauty had matured. The soft curly hair was denser and thicker. I could no longer remember it with powder. The high-bridged Wayles nose and the perpetual sneer of his perfect mouth gave him a foreign look. His face fascinated women, both black and white, and it was just as well he was leaving this place, I thought. In the years since our return to Monticello, he had made no connection, of this I was sure, although I knew that many overtures had been made to him by women. I wondered, as I already had in Paris, if he had ever loved a woman.

"*Je t'aime*, Sally," he said suddenly.

"Ah, darling James. *Moi aussi.*"

He gave me a kiss, but I felt we were miles apart, countries apart. He will never understand, I thought.

"Help me," he said.

"Yes," I answered.

"I need you."

"I know. If only he didn't need me more . . ."

"Are you sure he does?" he asked.

"I think so," I whispered.

"God help you if you are wrong," he said.

"And God be with you if you are right, James."

We saw little of each other after that.

In my mind, he had already gone from this place.

Adrien Petit came back. He had been persuaded by my master to leave his beloved Champagne country and his mother and make the dangerous journey to America. He brought to Monticello a thread that connected Marly and Virginia, a link to past happiness and a promise that more would come. We slipped back into our old relationship, Petit and I. He was kind to me. Though unshockable, he was nonetheless shocked by Virginia. He could not reconcile himself to slavery and slaves.

Thomas Jefferson began to make drawings for a new house which would rise on the foundations of the old mansion, and the whole plantation was alive with plans and planting.

We planted charlton, marrow fat, blackeye and green peas, Windsow brown, Lima, Allegheny and soup beans. We raised peanuts and cabbage, shallots, sorrel, cresses, garlic, white mustard, pineapple, green, Venice and watermelons. Figs and hops, strawberries and gooseberries, sage, balm, mint, thyme, lavender, tansy and rue blossomed. We nursed cuttings of lilac, jasmine, white honeysuckle, yellow honeysuckle, Athala, gelder rose, wormwood, Southernwood, rosemary, poplar, Lombardy, Balsam and periwinkle. We harvested Kentucky coffee, Missouri maurus, East India asparagus, Irish potatoes, Palermo broccoli, Spanish broom, Lily of Canada, Pride of China, Cherokee rose, Indian peas and Jerusalem artichokes. That year Thomas Jefferson seeded and plowed and laid out two thousand cuttings of weeping willow.

He lived on his horse. He even measured his fields for planting on his horse. He would estimate his distances on Brimmer, who stepped a yard in two strides.

In the nailery, Moses worked with Bedford John and Bedford Davy, as did the two brothers James, Phill Hubbard, Bartlet, and Lewis. All were young boys between the ages of ten and twelve. The nailery was on Mulberry Row, not more than sixty feet east of the Southern Breezeway and within shouting distance of the mansion, where there was an avenue of stables, slave dwellings, workshops, forges, and storage houses.

The Hemingses who did not stay in the Big House all lived and worked there, along with the white workmen who now thronged the grounds in preparation for the renovations. Naked children mingled among the blacksmiths and the horses. The clanging forges and the nailery worked all day long next to the steady thump of the weavers' looms where the young girls toiled.

In June we began to cut wheat at Shadwell and in early
July we cut wheat on this side of the river.

Our reapers were Frank, Martin, Phil, and Tim.
Ned, Toby, James, Val, Bagwell, Caesar, and Lewis.
The younger boys were George, Peter, and the two
Isaacs.
Our gatherers were Isabel, Ned's Jenny, Lewis,
Jenny, Doll, Rachel, Mary, Nancy, O, Betty, Molly,
and Lucina and her sisters.
Our stakers were great George, Judy, Hix, Jamy,
Barnaby, Davy, and Ben, Iris, Thamer, and Lucinda.
Our cradlers were John, Kit, Patty, the two Lucys,
Essex, Tom, Squire, and Goliath.

We treaded at Monticello with seven horses, their flanks
turning silver with sweat. The spicy, inexpressible fragrance
of bruised and trampled chaff rose on the heavy air, im-
pregnating hair and skin. The hoarse cries of the reapers
fluttered over the ocean of not yet harvested grain like the
mobs of crows which circled in formation as the stocks
rose like sentinels in the half-reaped fields. The earth
seemed to roll over and sigh with each slash of the scythe,
its voice too, woven into the din of the reapers. All seemed
to be of one plan and one motion: the burning sun, the
earth turning, the wheat slumping under its own weight.
Great George constantly mended the cradles and grinded
the scythes that were never still. Their steel glint was visible
for miles; flecks of silver paper against the high-noon
gold. Each day, Nance, Mary, and I distributed the supplies.
For every family unit, we gave out four gallons of whiskey,
two quarts of molasses, one smoked and one fresh meat
with peas.
We worked. My kin, my fellow slaves and I. We worked
from sunup to sundown. We worked so that all, according
to my master, would move in exact equilibrium. No part
of the force could be lessened without it having an effect
on the whole, he said. No hand could be stilled without
retarding the scheme of things. And nothing could
jeopardize his main design or delay it. This was his law:
the vast rolling motion of this human machine moved

according to the blueprint he had laid down for it. And if a bent back had straightened and a head shaken sweat like a wet dog, and an eye had stared into the sun, and a mind or a heart wondered if this was the way God meant things to be; my master would have said yes. For wasn't he God at Monticello? And if one loved the man, one could still hate the God.

We stood there on the mountain, silently savoring our last month of solitude before the August company arrived and Martha and Maria came home. The deep mulatto clay gave gently underfoot, tender and softened by the constant spring rain. It would be a wet summer, with twice as many wet days as in common years. Our feet seemed literally to have taken root. A burst of fragrance, probably from a flowering bush disturbed by our movements, enveloped us.

My lover came around and stood near me. Here we were both married to two things. This place we loved and the love of this place.

"Wife," he said.

"Master," I replied.

"A girl this time," he murmured as he took me in his arms and then turned me around. "However far you can see, it is all Monticello," he said. "I solemnly promise you there will never be a white mistress here."

I pressed myself into the broad chest behind me. My master might own Monticello and my mother might run it, but in my secret heart, Monticello was mine. There had been only one white mistress of Monticello, the first Martha, buried at the foot of the mountain under a pale white stone etched in Latin. And now, there would never be another. It was this strange legacy I now claimed from her.

There will never be a white mistress here.

The inky seal of his voice followed me through the gardens, along Mulberry road, into the workshops of my brothers, it spilled out onto slave quarters that dotted the mountain side like white pigeon pairs, it seeped through the constant noise of the rebuilding and construction, it mingled with the low songs of the field hands, and the evening conversations of their cooking fires. It haunted me from the vistas stretching limitlessly on either side of the mansion. It shimmered on the bristle of the scythed wheat fields and the plains hunkered down in cotton. It echoed below his leveled off mountain onto the curl of the Rivanna River meandering through the virgin forests towards the sea. I imagined the Atlantic, and beyond the Atlantic, Marly. It dimmed.

There would be no white mistress at Monticello. He had promised.

CHAPTER 25

JULY 1795

Going out into the open air, in the temperate, and in the warm months of the year, we often meet with bodies of warm air, which, passing by us in two or three seconds, do not afford time to the most sensible thermometer to seize their temperature. Judging from my feelings only, I think they approach the ordinary heat of the human body. Some of them perhaps go a little beyond it . . . but whence taken, where found, or how generated? . . . They are most frequent about sunset; rare in the middle parts of the day; and I do not recollect having ever met with them in the morning.

THOMAS JEFFERSON, *Notes on the State of Virginia*, 1790

. . . blind obedience is ever sought for by power: tyrants and sensualists are in the right when they endeavor to keep women in the dark, because the former want only slaves and the latter a plaything. The sensualist, indeed, has been the most dangerous of tyrants, and women have been duped by their lovers, as princes by their ministers. . . .

MARY WOLLSTONECRAFT, *Vindication of the Rights of Women*, 1792

"What do you think you're doing?"

I had not expected him back from his ride for hours. He found me sitting in his room. The only private place in the mansion. I had taken some of my letters out of my secret place and was reading them.

In two strides Thomas Jefferson was upon me.

"I thought I told you to burn my letters." He was furious. The two familiar lines of rage etched themselves between his eyes. "I don't want any letters of mine lying around, do you hear me?"

They were not his letters, they were mine. It said so

right there in black and white. "Sally Hemings." My letters were the only thing that existed outside him or myself. Sometimes I didn't even bother to read them as I knew them by heart. I simply stared at my name.

"I always kept your letters in Paris. In a little silk envelo—"

"You promised! Damn it, Sally, this is Virginia, not Paris! It's dangerous keeping letters. I told you to burn them. I'll never write you another letter if you don't destroy them."

"I would have to forget you to burn them."

"If you don't do as I say, I'll never write you another letter!"

"I won't do it."

"If you won't, I will."

He picked up a handful of my letters and strode toward the fireplace.

"You burn those letters, Thomas Jefferson, and you'll sleep alone."

He hesitated a moment and then he threw the letters onto the smoldering coals. In a flash I was beside him. I shoved him out of the way. The letters were already going up in flames. I pulled them out with my bare hands.

"Sally! Darling! You'll burn yourself!"

He lifted me up from my knees and his heavy boot came down on the flames, until he had stomped out the fire. He then bent and with his own hands pulled the charred letters from the ashes.

"Here are your letters."

I took them with my good hand.

"At least promise me you'll burn them when I'm dead," he pleaded.

"Or when it is over," I said.

"It will never be over until I'm dead."

I put the letters in my petticoat pocket.

"You've hurt yourself."

"It's nothing I'll have some blisters tomorrow."

But a sharp pain shot through my right hand, making me stumble. Before I fell, he picked me up in his arms and carried me to the bed, where he stared at me for a long time, then slowly his head came down toward me. I reached up with my left hand and untied the ribbon which

held his thick hair. The eyes above me were dark. I
recognized the pinch of suppressed fury, and as always, the
inner turmoil.

I felt myself being lifted and borne toward him. He
tugged at my knot and it fell undone in his hands. He
gathered my hair like a bouquet into a cushion under
my head and locked his hands into it. His lips came down
on the white scar at my temple.

The letters. They were were all of the fragile self I had
so painstakingly built in Paris. And he wanted to burn
them. He strove as if he wanted to undo the small part of
myself I had managed to build these past years. He didn't
have to remind me that this was Virginia. Virginia. Virginia. And it would be Virginia forever. Virginia. That's
why I clung to my letters. But now we no longer remembered if it was Paris or Virginia.

"What shall we do about your hand?" he asked gently.

"Ask Mama," I said. When he returned, he had a poultice
from Elizabeth Hemings. It smelled of mint and honey.
He dressed my hand and let me go to sleep.

Virginia. I knew that what had happened to us in Paris
could never, never have happened in Virginia.

August brought the girls back. Martha was with child. I
was to accompany Maria to her first ball. I looked forward
to that evening. As I had not left the confines of Monticello
for more than four years, I wanted to see the new fashionable dresses, the carriages, the decorations. I wanted to
hear the music, see the latest dance called the *mazurka*. I
had been out of touch with even the small world of Tidewater, Virginia, for too long. I sat with the other servants
and watched Maria dance.

Dancing was one of the things I most regretted. I had
loved it since my first awkward tries with Martha in Paris.
I remembered learning how to surrender to that eternity
which was the first note of music. I could be anything I
wanted for as long as the music played. And tonight the
music played and played.

There were as many servants milling around as there
were guests. To us all, whites and slaves, the ball was a
chance to break the isolation and monotony of living on

far-flung plantations all the year; to see new faces, new dresses, new horses, to catch up on Tidewater gossip.

I fingered the bright-yellow bandanna tightly wrapped around my head and savored the soft night breeze in the lavish gardens of Prestonfield Plantation. The dresses were more daring than any I could have imagined. My mother was right. There were new dyes and there was more gauze, more silk, and less satin and velvet. The crinolines were ridiculously large, giving the ladies the appearance of watermelons.

I gazed at everything with new eyes. Through the tall square-paned windows I looked at the swirling figures inside. I contemplated this world of exquisite food and delicate music, of graceful dances, of laces and satin, plumes and powder and perfume, of polished cherrywood floors, and crystal chandeliers.

Why, in the midst of happiness, must I be reminded of Paris? Look at them! I had heard about the Quadroon Balls of New Orleans where the white people were being mimicked, so here these provincial whites were trying to mimic Paris. I sneered at the pretensions of Virginia gentry. I had known real splendor! What was I doing in this backwater . . . this tomb?

After all these years, John Trumbull was coming to Monticello. I didn't know whether to hide or greet him as a friend. A dinner had been organized for him, and included in the guest list was my master's choice for Maria, Mr. Giles, a senator from Virginia. Thomas Jefferson wanted him as a son-in-law, and he spent his time around Monticello that summer courting Maria; but in the meantime Maria had fallen in love with her cousin Jack, the same Jack who had helped me to lure her on the boat to Paris. Isaac and I commiserated with poor Master Giles as he was kindly but firmly rejected. Maria was too terrified to tell her father her choice, and begged me to do it for her.

The night John Trumbull came, I spied on the dinner. It was not the first time I had spied on my master's dinner guests. I did it constantly. Later, in the privacy of his bedroom, we would discuss the guests, their personalities, and their intrigues. Thus my political education continued despite my isolation. What I didn't learn from spying, I would learn from my mother and the other slaves. They were a constant and reliable source of gossip and funny stories that kept my lover entertained.

The dinner with John Trumbull turned into a veritable disaster. No sooner was the company seated than a lively discussion of the character, conduct, and doctrines of Jesus began. My master sat smiling and nodding as Master Giles, a freethinker, led the argument. I could see discomfiture and then shock on the face of John Trumbull, who defended his faith as best he could. The Massachusetts-accented voice I remembered so well rose in indignation over Master Giles's raillery. Then he addressed my master:

"Sir, this is a strange situation in which I find myself; in a country professing Christianity and at a table with Christians, as I suppose, I find my religion and myself attacked with severe and almost irresistible wit, and not a person to come in my defense but my friend Mr. Franks, who is himself a Jew!"

For just a brief moment his outburst seemed to have some effect on the company. The conversation became subdued. I could hardly hear what was going on. But then Maria's suitor returned to the attack and burst out with as broad and unqualified avowal of atheism as I had ever heard. John Trumbull was almost in tears. He seemed to look directly at me, but I knew he couldn't see me.

"The man who has made the previous statement is perfectly prepared for the commission of every atrocious action by which he can promise himself the advancement of his own interest or the gratification of his impure passions, provided he can commit it secretly and with a reasonable probability of escaping detection by his fellow men."

I froze. No. It was not possible that he saw me. Not even with his artist's eagle eyes. In his fury they seemed more crossed than ever. He rose. Thomas Jefferson remained seated, not saying a word. John Trumbull addressed Master Giles for the last time. He seemed to be addressing me.

"Sir, I would not trust such a man with the honor of a wife, a sister, or a daughter. . . . Our acquaintance, sir, is at an end."

My friend John Trumbull. My hand reached for his

miniature. John Trumbull driven from our table. I remembered my last words to him at Cowes. "God bless you," I had said. God. Why had my exquisitely mannered lover allowed such a scene at his own table? I was appalled. Of all things to offend a gentle friend on his religion at one's own table! I clutched my locket. Now people would say Thomas Jefferson was an atheist! Trumbull had left the table. It was a dangerous thing to do, I thought, humiliate a man in public. In the past years I had learned enough about politics to realize that one never knew when one might need a friend. Enemies were expensive. Politicians could only afford so many. . . .

That night, I asked him why he had allowed John Trumbull, whom he had adored in Paris, to leave his house and his table angry. My master showed no surprise that I had listened in on the dinner.

"I didn't feel like being diplomatic," he said to me. "I'm finished with politics. I have no more need to be polite."

"But why let people think you don't believe in God?"

"I don't care what people think anymore," he said bitterly. This was more than the disappointment of three years in Philadelphia!

"What is it?" I asked in alarm.

He was trembling. "It's nothing. It reminded me of a mistake I once made. Early in my political career, I gave up what I most deeply believed in for the sake of not provoking people. I vowed never to do it again."

He turned toward me. "Why shouldn't Giles have said what he thought? At least he had the courage to say what he means, which is more than most people in the world do. . . ." He looked at me. "What is it?" His pale sapphire eyes had turned their strange night-blue color. "You. You were three years old then. Your brother Robert was with me in Philadelphia."

I turned toward him instinctively.

"They had given me the Declaration of Independence to draft. At thirty-three! I was very young and very passionate," he said slowly. "I poured my soul onto sheet after sheet. I wanted to place before mankind the common sense of the subject, in terms so plain and so firm as to be undeniable. After all, I was fighting for our lives and those of our family, and the families of all the other rebels—

because that's what we were then, rebels, insurrectionists. We all stood to be hung and quartered and it was up to me to explain ourselves to the world. . . . I set to work on it in a little brick house at the southwest corner of Market Street and Seventh. After a week or so of work, I copied off a rough draft and took it to Dr. Franklin and John Adams. John Adams liked it. Dr. Franklin had more than forty corrections, but he softened it with his story about the hatter. . . ." My master smiled. "That was mild compared to what happened in the Continental Congress. It was the third of July. My declaration was ready for a hearing by the gentlemen in Congress. The secretary, Mr. Thompson, began to read my draft aloud. At first everything went well. Several of the members nodded. I was congratulated on my felicity of language. They got to the end of page one. Some delegates were deeply moved. Franklin leaned over and said, 'I wish I had written it myself!' Then the secretary began to read the facts, the nearly thirty accusations against George III. Thompson came to the last charge. I had left it to climax the list of grievances. . . . The delegates had criticized certain phrases. . . . 'King' was used in place of 'Tyrant,' and so on. Every change hurt." He smiled. "I was young. I sat in the back of the room with my thermometer on the windowsill outside. I was next to Dr. Franklin, who dozed off every now and then. There was little time to lose. We had to sign the Declaration. The revolution was already in motion. Your brother Robert waited for me outside. I was much worried about my own standing at the Virginia Convention. I feared to be knifed out of Congress. Martha was expecting our child, and I had not heard from her in three weeks. My mother had gone to her grave only three months before. I sent Robert twice a day for the mail, but there was never anything. Not a word since I had left Virginia. . . . The secretary read the last charge against the king, which was that he had waged a cruel war against human nature . . . the enslavement of the Negro people."

I held my breath.

"With the exception of South Carolina and Georgia, everyone was in principle opposed to slavery. Benjamin Franklin was the president of the Pennsylvania Society

for the Abolition of Slavery." His voice broke then and
took on the charred husky tone of real defense.

" 'I think it too passionate,' somebody said.

" 'Turgid.'

" 'Irrational.'

" 'A tirade.'

" 'Completely irrelevant.'

" 'Too strong for such a dignified document,' said another. 'It's a philippic,' said somebody else. The Reverend
Witherspoon questioned its accuracy. 'After all,' he said,
'the traffic existed long before George the Third was born.'
Then Edward Rutledge of South Carolina said that the
question of slavery should be determined by the states
themselves. The Virginia delegate said, 'It concerns not
only the importing states, it concerns the whole union.'
'What enriches a part enriches the whole,' said Rutledge.

"At that all bedlam broke loose.

" 'It is dishonorable,' put in the Maryland delegate.

" 'Honor has nothing to do with it,' said the South Carolina delegate.

" 'In time,' said Lynch, the delegate from Georgia, 'it
will disappear of its own accord.'

" 'Neither morality nor wisdom have anything to do with
this,' Rutledge declared. 'Interest and interest alone is the
governing principle of nations. If the gentlemen from New
England will consult their own interest, they will not op-
pose the importation of slaves. New England is the chief
carrier! Who builds the ships? Who sails them?'

"John Adams was mortified, because he knew this was
true. So did Samuel Adams. The arguments ran back and
forth. Robert was waiting outside with the package of new
gloves I had bought for Martha. I had bought her seven
pairs. The two Adamses descended on me.

" 'The whole passage will have to be cut or South Carolina will never agree to the declaration,' they said.

"Benjamin Franklin opened his eyes long enough to
agree with them, and to say the passage would destroy our
still precarious unity.

"I was so young. I listened to the debate swirl around
this resolution in silence. I never once defended it. I didn't
think it was proper for me to defend my own declaration. I

was upset. I had submitted my draft . . . if the Congress
chose to mutilate it . . .

"I had taken no part in the debate and had tried to keep
calm. I prayed the passage would not be cut. The temperature at three o'clock was seventy-six degrees." He brushed
his hand across his face. "To preoccupy myself, I took my
new thermometer out of its box for another reading, but
my hands were shaking so, I dropped it. It fell and broke
on the floor. I covered the fragments with my handkerchief. Dr. Franklin had been observing me under his half-
closed eyelids. I suppose he took pity on me. 'Come to my
house tonight,' he said. 'Sally's making a wonderful dinner.'

"Those were his last words I remember. Sally was his
daughter.

"You were three years old . . .

"The next day I took my seat again in the last row. I
kept my eye on the Southern delegation: Rutledge, Middle-
ton, Lynch, Gwinnett, Hall. . . . Washington was named
commander-in-chief of the American armies that morning.
Dr. Franklin kept pressing upon me the need for an agree-
ment on the declaration. I wished mightily for George
Wythe . . . any ally—but he had been detained in Williamsburg. He would arrive when it was all over," he said
bitterly.

"The Congress skipped over the passage on slavery and
read the closing portions. I sat and marked the mutilations
on my own copy. After the final paragraph had been read
and revised, they took up the passage on slavery again. I
listened in silence to the appeal to God, to reason, to
humanity, to future generations.

" 'National sins will be punished by national calamities,'
somebody said.

"All through the afternoon they droned on. Everybody
was restless. The flies from the stables across the street
tormented us. The declaration could not be postponed. The
news from New York was bad. Washington was in trouble.
Staten Island was taken. The declaration was vital. Nothing should jeopardize the main design or delay it further. If
the passage in question blocked the road to unity, it would
have to be cut.

"The honorable gentlemen from the North were confused. 'Compromise,' 'Yield,' 'Hope for the best,' 'Concensus,' 'Delay,' 'Fight the war first,' 'Time,' 'Shipping interest.'

"Where was majority rule? I thought. But I was silent. Franklin was silent. Sherman was silent. Adams was silent. And Rutledge held the trump card: secession from the not even formed union. . . . John Adams looked at his watch. I looked around me. Everything in the room, the smell of sweat and tobacco, the heat, the flies, the Northerners, the Southerners, Adams, Hancock, Franklin, said, 'Let's worry about slavery another day . . . let's get out of here'." He smiled.

"I remember everything hurt. My eyes. My neck, my head, my stomach hurt." He paused. "The clause reprobating the enslaving of the inhabitants of Africa was struck out in complaisance to South Carolina and Georgia," he said quietly, but his voice shook. He passed his hand in front of his face again, as if to wipe out the last weary arguments.

"What an incomprehensible machine is man! Here we were, rebels, all of us, depriving one-sixth of our population of the same liberty we were fighting and risking our heads for!"

"But you think black and white can never live in peace and equality here."

"I would have sent them home."

I sat stunned. I tried to embrace the immensity of what he had just told me. I grasped at the easiest thing to understand: that three years after I was born, he had tried to rescue me. He had truly tried.

"I have often thought," he whispered, "if my declaration had been adopted as I had written it . . . you would not be here, for there would be no slavery in America, no slaves."

In the terrible silence that followed, how I loved him.

Then I did look at him. He had turned on his side. His voice was muffled.

"From that day I vowed never never to put myself in that jeopardy again. I vowed never to raise my voice in defense of myself or my principles—especially about *that*. I washed my hands of it! I vowed to let the Almighty, if there is one, do his own work!"

There was only silence in the room. His brow, his cheeks, his lips were relaxed. He had fallen asleep.

I snuffed out the candle.

We would never speak of Philadelphia again.

CHAPTER 26

CHRISTMAS 1795

On what consists the greatness of a despot? In his own intrinsic merits? No, in the degradation of the multitude who surround him. What feeds the vanity of a patrician? The consciousness of any virtue that he inherits with his blood? The list of his senseless progenitors would probably soon cease to command his respect if it did not enable him to command that of his fellow creatures.

FRANCES WRIGHT, *Views of Society and Manners in America*, 1821

Perhaps the condition of women affords, in all countries, the best criterion by which to judge the character of man. Where we find the weaker sex burdened with hard labour, we may ascribe to the stronger something of the savage, and where we see the former deprived of free agency, we shall find in the latter much of the sensualist.

FRANCES WRIGHT, *Views of Society and Manners in America*, 1821

Holding the great iron ring which housed all the Monticello keys, Elizabeth Hemings hurried down the whitewashed breezeway between the kitchen and the main house. The keys, her badge of authority, jangled in rhythm with her brisk step. The cooking odors of her domain followed her halfway down the main hall. There was only one thought in her mind: her son James was to be set free the next day, Christmas 1795, more than five years since his return from France. He had served his master while he had been President Washington's secretary of state, she thought, and Thomas Jefferson was finally living up to that piece of paper James had made him sign . . . now that his younger brother Peter knew all about the art of French cooking.

Elizabeth Hemings nodded in satisfaction. Two freed, she thought, and five to go. . . . Five only because she knew her daughter had surrendered to her love for Thomas Jefferson with such abandon. But he was as faithful to her daughter as a bridegroom, thought Elizabeth Hemings. Martha Wayles Jefferson had been dead thirteen years now and the master gave no indication of replacing her with another white wife. Thank the Lord. Not that they weren't after him, poor man.

As she hurried along the passage and came into the dining room of the mansion, the sounds of hammering and sawing assaulted her. After everything he had promised, Thomas Jefferson was tearing up the house again, one day before Christmas! And Sally Hemings was no help at all, egging him on in all those ideas.

Elizabeth Hemings's face softened at the thought of the new baby; a girl child, Harriet, more beautiful than Sally, more beautiful than anything she could have imagined. . . . There was another new baby over at Edgehill, too. Martha Jefferson Randolph had delivered promptly every year since she had fled Monticello into the arms of her cousin Thomas Mann.

She liked Martha and wished her well, but her departure from Monticello had been a great relief. It left Sally Hemings mistress and, through her, she, Elizabeth Hemings, continued to rule. Elizabeth Hemings bumped into Big George.

"How's ol' Jimmy holdin' up?" He smiled at her. "You'd think this here's a daughter's weddin' the way Masta Jefferson a carryin' on."

"It ain't every day that the masta goes around freeing people, Big George. He ain't been none too generous with this here freedom you might say." Elizabeth Hemings smiled wickedly. Her son Robert was the only other slave she knew of that Thomas Jefferson had ever freed, and he had bought his freedom with borrowed money.

"Bett and Queenie out there, Big George," she called after him. "You get them to help you get out all that heavy silver, you hear? Get it all out. Sally tends to dress a table tonight you ain't never seen the likes of!"

When Elizabeth Hemings entered the hall of the west portico, she found her daughter on her hands and knees, arranging the velvet drapery and the presents at the foot of the Christmas tree. With characteristic quickness of movement, Sally Hemings spun on her heels and was on her feet by the time her mother reached her side. She was now twenty-two years old, and twice a mother.

"Everything is ready for tomorrow, Maman."

Elizabeth Hemings nodded at her beautiful daughter and winced at her "Maman." She had affected it ever since her return from France, and Elizabeth Hemings didn't like it. She had never dared tell her daughter this, however, so she continued to sprinkle her conversation with French expressions. Elizabeth looked up at the immense tree.

It was the tallest Virginia pine they could find on the slopes of Monticello, and it almost toppled over with the weight of the decorations, many of which her master had brought back from France. The French had taken up the Anglo-Saxon habit of decorating Christmas trees with a fervor and imagination that had outshone the often modest homemade decorations that were traditional in the United States. The French decorations gleamed like jewels and were the special joy of her daughter, who had taken it upon herself every year to trim the tree. The delicate silk balls with their silver pom-poms, the crystal snowdrops and lace snowflakes and the spun sugar James had spent a whole day creating, mingled with the cloved oranges and the pine cones. The top of the tree touched the ceiling of the entrance hall where tomorrow the white family and all the house servants would gather around after dinner for the distribution of presents.

"Tomorrow is going to be one happy day, daughter."

"Oh, Maman, James will be free at last! If it hadn't been for me, he would have been free years ago. I . . . I was so sure that things were going to turn out differently."

And what about you? Elizabeth Hemings wanted to say, but she held her tongue.

"How's little Harriet?"

"She's fine, Maman. I just left Suzy's cabin. She had finished nursing." Her daughter's dimples flashed in a quick smile of excuse. Elizabeth Hemings was silent. She loathed the fact that her daughter would not nurse Harriet. Her daughter knew this. She had given her to a newly delivered young slave who worked in the cotton mill to wet-nurse while she bound up her breasts in the French fashion to get rid of the milk.

"Bring her into the house, daughter. She can sleep with me. I'll get John to bring in her cradle. Suzy can come in to nurse hers and yours together."

"But I enjoy . . ." Sally Hemings began.

"Now, daughter, it's decided." Elizabeth Hemings had spoken.

Sally Hemings dropped to her knees to straighten a fold of velvet drapery at the foot of the tree. She had no intention of giving up Suzy's nursing.

"Let Big George do that, Sally," Thomas Jefferson's musical voice rang out behind them as he strode into the hall from his study.

"I much prefer to do it myself, Master. The crystal snowflakes from Paris are so delicate, and we can't get any more. I found some we didn't use last year. Martha will be so surprised. . . ."

"And how is Harriet?"

"Harriet is fine, Master. I've just come from her."

Elizabeth Hemings turned away. The look she caught between the two people embarrassed her. She didn't understand it. She never would.

Christmas Day that year of 1795 was warm and sunny. It was almost four o'clock when Big George and Martin slipped away from the dining room, where the white people were lingering over the last meal James would cook at Monticello. He had helped me light the hundred Christmas tree candles. James, Ursula, Peter, and my mother were in the kitchens sweating over and admiring this last triumph of James's: the rich turtle soup swimming with tender croissants, the New England lobster and Maryland crab, their shells dressed with butter and hollandaise sauce, served stuffed with tiny shrimps and fried oysters; a roast pork fragrant with fresh herbs, stuffed as he used to do it in

Paris, with walnuts and mushrooms, and its own deep fried chitterlings. Then came the game: tender pigeon and pheasant baked in pastry; wild hare in the mustard sauce my master so adored. Endless vegetable platters followed: candied and spiced yams, dark wild rice, pumpkin pudding, steamed mustard greens, carrots in a white sauce, winter celery, okra and red cabbage. The company groaned as new plates of hot biscuits and corn bread arrived. Now there were only the dozens of desserts. James had outdone himself. All kinds of pies ended the feast, along with profiteroles and the fashionable new French dessert: ice cream. Toasts of fine Burgundy and clarets, more groans, cries for the "Chef," and the meal ended.

There had been eighteen white people at the table with as many servants, one behind each chair for this special dinner. When the banquet was over, the company filed in from the dining room, flushed and happy. Big George gathered all the servants and the increasingly homesick Petit for the celebrations that were to follow. The children of the house, both black and white, were holding on to their mothers or their nurses. Although part of the house was already being torn down, the central hallway was still intact; its pale-blue damask gleamed in the reflected candles we had just finished lighting. The late-afternoon sun and the glow of the Christmas-tree candles imparted a golden haze to the entire company. The sculptured busts of Voltaire, Lafayette, and Washington seemed to be staring down from their pedestals.

I stood to the left of the master, with the other slaves in a semicircle. Martha stood to the right of her father, the white people curving in an arc to her left completing the circle.

Outside the sun was setting. The plantation slaves were gathering two hundred strong. Their good-natured conversations wafted through the glass doors of the vestibule toward the circle around the pile of packages. The black half of the circle faced the other half, the white half that was in turn closed by Martin and the ten-year-old Michael Brown, son of George Wythe and his freed mulatto mistress, Lydia Broadnax. His father had acknowledged him publicly as his freed slave, son of his housekeeper. All of

Albemarle County, however, knew the truth, for he did
nothing to hide either his pride or his love for his only son.
Michael had been brought so that he could enjoy the celebrations and stuff himself with Christmas dinner with the
other slave children in the kitchens.

As I stood, the two-month-old Harriet in my arms, the
five-year-old Thomas Hemings clutching my skirts, I became only one in the web of blood ties that weaved itself in
and across and around the two parts of the circle, binding
one half to the other in arabesques as twisted and complicated as the hanging strands of silver cord on the tree
above us. My mother had gathered nine of her fourteen
children; facing her were two of Master Wayles's daughters. Elizabeth Hemings was either mother, stepmother,
grandmother, aunt, or great-aunt to practically everyone
present. To those she was not actually related to by blood,
she was related to by bonds of property. This kingdom was
hers, and she ruled as queen mother, a force of life to be
revered and reckoned with by both black and white. She
had loved, reared, nursed, birthed, served each person in
this room.

There were no secrets for her here, neither heart nor
body that she did not hold the key to—just as her iron ring
held the key to every room and closet in Monticello. In her
arms was one of Martha Jefferson's children.

My eyes went now to the white side of the circle and my
two half sisters, Tabitha Wayles Skipwell and Elizabeth
Wayles Eppes. It was Elizabeth who had sent me to Paris
with Polly Jefferson so long ago. I caught the eye of Martha, standing next to her husband, Thomas Mann, whom
she had loved for such a short time and who was now
sinking into the melancholy which would lead him to insanity. Had she rushed into marriage, two months after we
arrived from Paris, in order to escape me and her father's
connection with me? I wondered. If so, she had been mistaken in her father's hold upon her, for though she lived at
Edgehill, forty miles away, she clung to Monticello. Pity
rose in me as I surveyed Thomas Mann Randolph. His
bulk was growing with each year, along with his violent
temper that had become legend in Virginia. His drinking
sometimes sent his desperate wife and children scurrying to
safety at Monticello. He was now looking at his wife with

that same baffled, expectant expression with which my brother had sometimes looked at me. They both knew no other man would ever supplant Thomas Jefferson in either her heart or mine. And it was driving Martha's husband crazy.

Next to Thomas Mann stood James Madison, small, round, birdlike, timid, and insignificant—a schoolteacher dressed for a funeral, Elizabeth Hemings once said. He gazed in silent adoration at his unexpected prize, his bride the widow Dolley Todd. It was said that Madison—to his great surprise—had captured his new bride from the attentions of Aaron Burr. She stood beside him, resplendent in rose satin trimmed in silver, a gray chiffon scarf was tucked into the low-cut bodice that revealed a splendid bosom, and her eyes roamed restlessly over the assembly, not liking very much what she saw.

James Madison, I thought, was a real politician. He would succeed where my master—fastidious, uncompromising, stubborn, proud—never would. Politicians, I had long decided, should not be very bright, or at least should not think very much. And, I thought, if I were free . . . I gazed at the glorious Dolley Madison. She reminded me of certain French ladies I had observed. There was the same cynicism hidden under the soft feminine manner, the same ability to manipulate, even this rustic company, to shine, and put herself in the best light. There was a sharp mind behind her pretty appearance. She had, I sensed, the ambition to succeed. Dolley Madison would succeed because she had no competition. And envy, mingled with the constant ache of my own deprivation, invaded me.

My dress. It was six years old, the last of the dresses from Madame Dupré. I gazed at the emeralds glistening in the earlobes of James Madison's wife and at the matching bracelet on her plump arm. A wife, I thought. A true wife. Recognition. Nothing delineated me from the other servants except my position of honor next to the master, the tiny ruby earrings fastened in my ears, and the heavy silver locket around my neck. I lifted my chin.

George Wythe looked proudly at his mulatto son, who had the same round face, the same soft intelligent eyes as his father. Michael Brown was splendidly dressed, in the Quaker fashion, his shorts in buff with white stockings. His long brown uncut curls reached his shoulders and hung loose, giving him an angelic, princely look. My mother adored him and envied his education. He excelled in Latin and Greek, mathematics and astronomy taught him by George Wythe, who was determined to prove him brilliant not only beyond his color and station but beyond his age as well, and there was the wanness of overwork about his face.

Next to Master Wythe stood Polly, and next to her our cousin Jack Eppes. From the frightened child I had escorted to Paris and the uncertain adolescent that had returned with me, Maria had become the serious and remote beauty who stood timidly beside the man she deeply loved, and had been afraid to tell her father she wished to marry.

All last year, after her return from Philadelphia, I had nursed her through illness after illness. She had inherited the health of her mother, and her delicacy. Her mother had loved and accepted my mother and her children as part of her inheritance. For Maria, too, the Hemingses had always been a part of her life, and she had long ago acknowledged that still another Hemings, the one she loved best, held a permanent place in the affections of her father.

It was Petit who now joined the circle between Martin and George Wythe, unwittingly attaching the white half of the circle with the black. Our eyes met. Affection? Pity? Horror at this Monticellian "family"? He shrugged and with a wry smile looked at Martin, his black equivalent.

Thomas Hemings tugged at my skirt and his father's hand came down on his head in a caress.

My brother moved next to me. I shifted two-month-old Harriet, whom I held in my arms and reached down for his hand. It was cold. He was trembling violently. I increased the pressure of my hand in his, hoping to quiet him while the distribution of the presents went on. Then I registered the movement the other side of me. My master began to speak. He began to announce what I couldn't, yet must, believe: the emancipation of my brother. James had won. He was being given at last what he had vowed never to steal. But the speech was ringing with phrases which under the circumstances were self-righteous and pompous. I felt humiliation for James and embarrassment for my master.

James's mouth twitched downward as he whispered to

me, "I should have blackmailed him years ago . . . I notice
he doesn't mention anything about back pay." James's salary had stopped the moment he set foot in Virginia. "This
morning he gave me thirty dollars and a horse."

". . . with a flare of genius for the culinary arts and the
temperament—or I should say the temper—that goes with
it . . ." Thomas Jefferson was finishing his speech, "he has
served me faithfully, devotedly, and unselfishly in his craft
and art, and I am loath to part with him. He shall ever
have in my heart and my affections a special place, just as
his brother Robert does for all of us here, and I am sure
there is not a person present that does not wish him every
happiness in his new and justly deserved . . . *freedom!*"

I looked up at my brother, who was almost as tall as my
master. This ceremony, I had been shaken to find, not only
released him from his long bondage as a slave but from the
bonds of a vow which had kept him in chastity all these
years. It had been last summer when I had finally gotten
the courage to ask him about a wife. He had laughed in my
face. "Since when do slaves marry?"

"A wife is a wife whether she is married or not."

"You think I would spill my seed as a slave! To father
other slaves! You think I would enrich some white master
by breeding more slaves for him. If I spill it, it will be as a
free man who can father free children. This I vowed long
ago. In Paris. I vowed I would never touch a woman as a
slave. My life has been celibate, sister," he had said. "I
have never known a woman."

I looked now into those clear eyes. They looked over my
head to hold those of his ex-master, in a gaze of such love
and hatred that Martha and I, the only persons present
whose eyes had not strayed from James Hemings, lowered
our heads over our respective babes in arms.

Thomas Jefferson was thoroughly moved by his own
speech. He blinked back his tears and turned away from
James. Petit, to Thomas Jefferson's surprise, was crying.
He felt a small hand on his sleeve.

"They are waiting for you, Master," a voice said softly
just as the excited drone from outside swelled into a babble
of cries: "Presents! Presents! Master. Master . . ." He gave
the signal for the company to pass through the glass doors

of the hall onto the west portico and stood facing the
multitude gathering in front, as a cry—half-cheer, half-
plea—went out from the throng of slaves, now jumping
up and down in anticipation and cold.

Sally Hemings and Martha started to distribute the
Christmas bundles. Martha handed out the clothes. His
slave wife handed out the presents, the sweets, the cider,
and whisky.

The lines seemed never ending, yet Thomas Jefferson
knew that his Farm Book was mightily depleted of the
names of many of his slaves. Secretly, he had had to sell
more than a hundred slaves to cover outstanding debts that
went back twenty years, and still the end was not in sight.
He had been forced to sell Elk Hill—the estate he had
wanted to give to Maria as a wedding present—for ready
cash. The debts he had undertaken had mounted, with
accumulated interest, to an unbearable load. In desperation, he had sold slave upon slave to meet the claims upon
him. His son-in-law had attended to the details, so that
nowhere did his name appear on the sale of his property.
Yet the results had been disappointing. He had averaged
only about forty pounds a slave; there had been a time
when a good Negro had brought upward of two hundred.
He had even been compelled to break up one family, something he hated to do, simply because the male was too
valuable and essential. He had asked his brother Randolph
to buy the wife and children or, failing that, to sell them to
some good master in the vicinity, so that they might remain near their husband and father. No others, he had
instructed, were to be sold under any circumstances, in the
immediate neighborhood.

Thomas Jefferson looked out with emotion over the
heads of his slaves. There would soon be a mortgage on all
of them in order to finance the rebuilding of Monticello.

CHAPTER 27

SPRING 1796

I always had a fancy for a closet with a window I could
more peculiarly call my own.

ABIGAIL ADAMS

I bent over the fine-lined drawings on the blue-squared
French architectural paper of my master's new plans for
Monticello. I leaned over his shoulder. As he explained to
me how he was to change my house. Now was my chance
to ask for what I wanted. The demolition had already
begun, with his workmen prying loose three to four thousand bricks a day; the noise, the confusion, and even the
danger at times resulted in achieving what war and revolution had never been able to produce in my mother. She
would cry every day. Most of the household was camping
out. Only his bedroom and study had any semblance of
order, and it was here, before his drawing table, that he
was seated while I stood behind him, my arms about his
neck on a fine spring day. He had made great plans for his
house. He had in mind to remove the second-story attic
and spread all the rooms on a single floor. In place of the
attic, he wanted an octagonal dome, like the one on the
Hôtel de Salem in Paris that we had visited so many times.
Around the interior of this dome would be a mezzanine
balcony, thus providing privacy for the bedrooms intended
for his white family. In his own apartments on the ground
floor he envisioned a double-height ceiling with a skylight
and a bed alcove between the bedchamber and the study
accessible to both, and with a passage between them. To do

this, he must demolish the fireplaces that stood where his
bed would stand.

I had never asked him for anything before. Even now,
with a new life in my womb, pressing into the solid warmth
of his back, his hands encompassing mine, my lips on his
hair, I hesitated, but the closeness and his excitement at the
new changes gave me courage. He shifted his good hand to
hide his infirm hand, as he was wont to do.

"What is it?" he asked, as if he sensed my agitation.

"I should like you to design . . . to build a room for me."
I went on quickly, before he had time to respond. "A secret
room adjoining yours where I may pass to and from without crossing the public hall where anyone who happens to
be about may see me," I said. There was not a servant or
member of the household who did not know that only I
had access to the apartments of the master. I was mistress
of his bedchamber and his wardrobe. His premises were
forbidden to all, including his daughter. Yet I felt naked
every time I had to enter by the public hall, always full
of people: visitors, workmen, servants, relatives. It would
be so easy to find me a little space of my own somewhere. I
longed for the shadowed recesses and the vast apartments
of the Hôtel de Langeac with its endless attic rooms, secret
corridors, unused apartments. Here, every space was occupied by slave or master. Twenty servants ran in and out
of the main house, not counting all the other people, and
even once a horse. . . . I recounted all this without stopping, as if I would run out of courage before I ran out of
breath. Only the ticktock of the French clock broke the
sound of my breathing. Outside a whippoorwill trilled.

"You shall have your room," he said.

I waited for him to tell me where and how, but he said
no more. There was a mischievous look on my master's
face, as if he had had in mind to build me a room all
along. I raised him from his seat, put my arms about his
waist, and kissed him.

That same spring Thomas Mann Randolph and Martha
went to Warm Springs, leaving their children at Monticello. The servants of Edgehill were whispering that ever
since the birth of Thomas Jefferson Randolph, their master

was losing his mind, driven by the dark forces that seemed to overtake all the Randolphs in their prime. He and Martha had traveled as far away as New York seeking relief, and Martha had turned more and more to Monticello and her father for solace and comfort. Polly, who was now at home, my mother, and I would care for them. There had been many a time when Martha would take refuge in Monticello, having run away from her husband.

"What are you going to do about Martha coming here so often?" said Elizabeth Hemings.

"What can I do? She's her father's daughter, and Monticello will be hers and Polly's one day. It is her right. Besides, she's lonely, I think, and unhappy."

"Poor man, he can't help his sickness. First thing, she won't have a husband."

"I think that would suit her just fine," I answered.

"Would it suit her father as well?"

A throb of jealousy sounded deep in me. Elizabeth Hemings always knew where to probe for her answers.

"I think it would. He needs her. He dotes on her and he loves her." I didn't add, "more than he loves me," but I thought it. "He doesn't like his son-in-law," I added.

"Well," my mother said, "he is not the first hard-riding, hard-drinking, evil-tempered bad Masta Randolph these parts have seen. Think on his cousin John Randolph of Roanoke. Rumor has it he don't have no head for business. Thomas Jefferson be well to put this plantation in other hands than his. Seems he's practically ruined."

"It's Martha's dowry they are living on."

"That's so, now."

I sighed. "As if you didn't know, Maman!"

"Well," chuckled my mother, "we got to keep our white folks informed and—"

"And spied upon twenty-four hours a day," I said.

"Don't we belong to them twenty-four hours a day?" replied Elizabeth Hemings. "When they give us a few hours' freedom every day, we'll give them a few hours' peace."

"You'll never forgive me for coming back, will you? Or dragging James back here for all those wasted years. . . ."

"Daughter, all that's history now. What's left is between you and Thomas Jefferson. James is free. He's over there in France, cooking for them nobles like he dreamed."

"I forgot, Maman."

Elizabeth Hemings looked at me without understanding.

"It's harder, Maman, to forget freedom than slavery. Over there, I had forgotten what it was like, if I ever knew. You raised me as free as any white child in the Big House. I came back to that, not to my real condition."

"You came back because of that child."

"No, Maman, I came back because I didn't remember who I was."

"You remember now, don't you."

"Yes."

"And the masta didn't do much reminding, did he?"

"I don't think he truly remembered, either. We were like children. He with his illusions, and I with mine."

"You were a child, then, true; but he had no excuse except his own selfishness."

"It wasn't true selfishness, Maman. White people are different from us."

"They ain't different, daughter, they simply expect to get what they want or what they need in life, that's all. It never occurs to them—as it *always* occurs to us—that they won't get what they need, nor what they want. You want to stroll away? Nothing stopping you."

"Nothing?"

"He wouldn't pursue you. There's enough gossip already."

"I think he would."

"Never, daughter, no matter how much he wanted to. His pride would stop him."

"His pride is great, Maman, but not as great as his passion for owning things. I belong to him. I'm his, and no other man's. And he'll keep me. He's given up too many things he's loved in life."

"Got to let you go if the Lord claims you."

I got up and walked toward the warmth of the smoldering kitchen chimney. I had come for company, as my master was out in his fields. I hadn't wanted this conversation. For years, I had been avoiding this conversation. . . .

"Being free isn't so important I'd die for it," I said, and turned to face her.

"Don't tell me freedom ain't worth dying for! Black people dying left and right, in the fields and on the ships, being beaten to death for not yielding, being hunted like dogs for strollin', being killed for standin' up like men and women instead of grovelin' like dogs! Don't give me any of your lip about 'not worth dying for'! They's even white folks—abolitionists who's risking their lives—their white lives for black people, helping them run. And you, you with your pride! Thinkin' that slavehood would never touch your precious body, or your precious spirit, that it would not hurt you and damage you and change you. . . ." My mother's face had darkened. It always changed colors when she was in a rage. "Pride has given you a worst burden than any field hand out there, because theirs can be lifted, but yours never will. Thomas Jefferson playing father to you, me spoiling you like I didn't know your color. If you had stayed here, you would have learned. . . . Oh, Lord Almighty, how I wish I had never put you on that boat!"

My mother had grasped my wrist with her strong rough hands and had drawn me toward her. I looked at her without expression. I had long ago abandoned myself to that particular joy of not being responsible for oneself. I had struggled against everything that surrounded my master and was hostile to me. I had overcome the fearful disgust which his situation as a master and mine as slave inspired in me.

"If you don't want it for yourself, at least get it for your children!"

"I have, Maman. I have the promise."

At that moment, I didn't care about that. I still had not accepted the great ring of household keys, which was my badge of authority, from my mother. I let her cling to it. The warmth of the fire stole under my skirts and up the back of my legs and spine. He would be coming home soon. I looked at my mother with impatience, as she continued to hold on to me.

"What if he grows tired of you?" my mother asked.

"Then," I answered, "I just might think about dying for

freedom." I smiled, and my mother released me. I looked
down at my wrist and saw the rosy mark left on my skin
by her fingertips.

"Sally?"

I had been reading a letter from James. I turned toward
him. He was almost shouting, the demolition of our walls
making it virtually impossible to be heard.

"I want to transplant all the rhododendron along the
south hedge. I was going to tell Giovanni to do it, but I
wanted to ask you what you thought."

"What does Petit think?" I asked.

"He said to ask thee."

We fell into speaking French.

"I liked them where they were," I said. "And what will
thou do with all the babies in the nursery, then?"

"Find a new place for them. I thought to make an alley
at the end of the formal garden."

"Oh, no." I hesitated, then called him by his name. He
seemed pleased, and laughed out loud. I had pronounced
his name as it was said in French, dropping the "s." *To-
mah*.

"Always call me thus," he whispered.

He held out his arms. I looked up at him.

"Dearest, then go to Giovanni and explain to him exactly how you want those flowering bushes planted, and in
what sequence. I have no more time. I'll be back late. I am
seeing Wythe. Tell Mammy Hemings. . . ."

"Mammy said to tell thee that Ned's Jenny has laid in
with a boy called Joyce."

For a moment there was a shadow in his eyes, like a
cloud passing before the sun.

"Good. I'll record it in the Farm Book tomorrow. . . .
Thou mustn't wait up for me, my love."

But I always did.

It was more than a year before I had the room I could
call my own. But true to his word, he built it. A tiny
winding stairway led from the foot of his bed to a narrow
passageway over the top of his bed alcove which ran the
length of it and was lit by three round windows giving onto
his rooms. The shape of the windows had been inspired by

the painting of Abraham and Hagar he liked so much, as
well as those for my room. My room was octagonal, hidden under the eaves, and looked westward over the mountains. There I waited, accumulating my account of hours.
My small treasures from Paris filled the room: the onyx-
and-bronze clock, my Paris sofa and bedstead, the copper
bathing tub that Joe Fosset had copied for me, my chests
full of dresses I never wore, my linens, my bolts of fine
silks and cambrics, my books, my guitar. There I was free,
solitary, away from the multitude of the mansion. I savored entering his inner sanctum by my own stairway.
Only in my official capacity as slave and mistress of his
wardrobe did I enter by the public hall on the ground
floor.

Only after he had built the miniature stairway to my
room did he discover to his dismay that the two new wings
of his mansion had no stairs at all! He quickly ordered
my brother John to add a stairwell to each wing. It was
barely wider than my own—a mere two feet across—and
had to accommodate not only the bulk of his masculine
company but the hoopskirts of his females. I thought of
the great stairway at the Hôtel de Langeac, that monument
of rose marble I had fled down that March morning eight
years ago. Only my secret room, with its passageway and
tiny staircase, resembled the great house of Paris, and it
linked us to the past. Soon our private existence would give
way once again to the demands of the public and of power
but, for a while at least, I was safe, happy, hidden, and
loved.

CHAPTER 28

PHILADELPHIA, MARCH 1797

"There is nothing I so anxiously hope as that my name may come out either second or third—the last would leave me home the whole of the year, and the other two-thirds of it. . . ."

With these words, our happiness in retirement came to an end. On Christmas Day 1796.

My master was now the second vice-president of the United States. So loath was he to leave home that he considered having himself sworn in at home in Virginia. As for me, I was in mourning. My third child, Edy, had not survived her first months, and now came the blow that I would lose my master again to his old mistress, politics. Neither Martha nor Maria was to go with him to Philadelphia for the inauguration. To cheer me, he offered to take me with him for the ceremonies.

I looked forward to the eleven long days of journeying; anything to rouse me out of my deep depression. Perhaps I would have news of James, from whom I hadn't heard in over a year.

We departed. Day after day, new landscapes sped by as we traveled farther north. We passed Ravensworth, and Montpelier, Dumfries, Elkridge, and Georgetown. We had taken the Paris phaeton, and Isaac and Israel as outriders were charged with the extra horses. We were drawn by the six beautiful bays of Monticello. On the second of March, after leaving Chester, my master tried to obtain a public carriage to carry us to Philadelphia, but none was to be had. We delayed until evening, with the intention of entering the city in secret, but the yellow-and-lilac carriage with

the Monticello coachman had been recognized and our
arrival had been reported by messenger. As we entered the
city, we were greeted by a large, roaring crowd carrying a
banner proclaiming: "Jefferson, Friend of the People," and
by a company of artillery that fired sixteen rounds of am-
munition in salute. A cold dread seized me, and I clutched
at my master's sleeve and buried my face in his shoulder. It
had been almost eight years since I had come down off the
mountain that was Monticello. I was once again out into
the world. That mountain on which I had spent almost all
my existence had rolled away like a great stone covering a
tomb and let in the light and air of the world, and this
world was pounding on the sides of the carriage and
screaming slogans and love as my master laughed and dis-
engaged his arm from my clutches, the better to lean forward toward the window and show himself. Burwell, who
was inside the carriage, stuck his head out the other side
and watched Davey and Jupiter soothing the frightened
horses, smiling, and waving at the crowd as if they had
been born to do it. I peered out nervously behind the bulk
of Burwell onto a sea of white faces cut into by the booted
and spurred legs of our outriders. I had not seen so many
white people at once since Paris. I remembered James's
description of the Bastille mob and the crowds, and I saw
myself in the Paris streets. That memory became one as I
glimpsed these friendly Americans come to acclaim their
vice-president. Had I forgotten, on my mountain, that the
world was made up of white people? This howling, laughing, unruly crowd was the white world. I uttered a small
cry and clutched at Burwell as I had at my master, but he,
like his master, was only interested in those faces swarming
around us. He shrugged off my hand and ignored me.

The next day I roamed the streets of Philadelphia, a city
that seemed to be made up of only one color and one
material: red brick. The streets as well as the houses were
made of it. The wetness made the bricks slippery underfoot
and, several times, Burwell kept me from falling. We
strolled down Market Street looking into the shop windows, at the street vendors and the newspaper sellers. I
looked for my master's little house at Seventh Street, noisy
and filled with young boys, both black and white, selling

broadsides and pamphlets and newspapers, all proclaiming
to have the story on the first succession of the presidency
of the United States. Burwell brought several of them for
the plantation.

In the course of our walk, Burwell would point out the
freed men as they crossed our path, and I couldn't help but
stare at them. They were all wearing neat clothes, and
conveyed the feeling of self-confidence. I knew, of course,
that in Charlottesville there were many freed people of
color, but this was the first time that I had looked into
the faces of Negroes who had never been slaves. Some
seemed rich, the women with long elegant skirts trailing the
sidewalks, accompanied by dignified men in dark broad-
cloth and snowy linen. I had put on my best dress, and
although it was years out of fashion in Paris, it was not
noticeable here. I was looking forward to seeing the elegant
ladies tomorrow in their fine gowns, cloaks, hats, and
gloves.

The day dawned clear and sunny. We followed our master, walking to the Senate building, where the swearing-
in ceremony was to take place. I strained my hearing to the
utmost, but was still unable to make out one word, either
of the speech or of the prayer he offered for the country. It
was the first time I had ever heard my master speak in
public, and after the first few words his voice lost all its
musical resonance, and became little more than a husky
whisper. In order to learn what he had said in a public
speech, one had to have recourse to the printed speech in
the newspapers. After giving his prayers for the happiness,
peace, and prosperity of our country, he led the senators
and the crowd to the House of Representatives, where
Master Adams was sworn in. It had been almost ten years
since I had last seen John Adams from the back window of
the phaeton taking Polly and me to Paris. He had not
grown slimmer with age, and where he had been square
and stout, he was now round and fat. With his prim countenance, long, pinched nose, and tiny piercing blue eyes, he
resembled nothing so much as a Virginia hare in his pearl-
gray frockcoat, waistcoat, and breeches. I felt an old surge
of affection for him, wondering what my life would have
been if he had sent me back to Virginia that summer long

ago. Abigail Adams was nowhere to be seen. Had she not come to honor her husband on this day?

As I looked around, I realized that there were practically no women at all. All the fine ladies I had hoped to see had stayed home and this gathering looked as if there were only men in this United States.

At the side of George Washington was his slave Samuel, as old and stony as his master. President Washington was dressed all in black: a tall old man with an old-fashioned powdered wig with rolled curls at the sides, and with cold, small blue eyes set in a face so white it seemed blue. The nose was large and his lips were so thin they were invisible until he drew them back in what was meant to be a smile showing his large, black false teeth, which were famous. Now and again he waved stiffly at the crowd, and as he did so, exhibiting his black smile in a pure white face, the slave at his side would also smile, exhibiting his pure-white smile in a black face. The crowd cheered the outgoing president and tears began to slide down the face of the president and that of his slave shadow Samuel. John Adams made a fine speech in his harsh Massachusetts accent. He too was greatly cheered. To this day, I wonder why Abigail Adams did not come to see her husband made president of the United States.

Standing outside the Senate House after the ceremony, Burwell and Jupiter at my side, I looked over the now dispersing assembly, trying to recognize friends of my master whom I had seen at one time or another at Monticello. Suddenly I noticed a short, handsome man. He was magnificently dressed, wearing buff, with yellow lace showing at the neck and wrists.

His curly black hair was pulled back from an abnormally high forehead, the pallor of his skin contrasting with the jet-black hair and eyebrows that were arched in a quizzical expression over deep brown eyes. He headed directly toward us, stopping once or twice to greet people who hailed him, turning swiftly from one side to the other on the balls of his feet in a dancing motion that was most graceful. Finally, he was upon us.

"Davey Bowles! Jupiter! The imperturbable and good Jupiter! Miss? . . ."

"Masta Burr, suh. A glorious day for the Republic, suh. You looking for Masta Jefferson, suh? He went with a group of gentlemen over to the Representative House . . . suh."

Jupiter stepped protectively in front of me as he made his speech. Jupiter was the same commanding height, as well as the same age, as his master. He towered over this Master Burr, who came up to his chest.

"Why isn't Bob Hemings here, Jupiter? Where's that boy?"

"Robert Hemings, he freed, Masta Burr, suh, like James. He done bought his freedom from Masta Jefferson so's he could join his wife and his daughter in Richmond, who's slaves of Master Strauss there. Masta Jefferson, he signed his manumission papers on Christmas Day '95. He regretted thoroughly leavin' Masta Jefferson, Masta Burr, but he jus' couldn't prevail upon hisself to give up his wife and his daughter."

"Well, I wish him well, Jupiter."

"Yassuh."

Aaron Burr didn't take his eyes off me. He waited patiently, apparently used to Jupiter's evasions, and said nothing.

Finally, Jupiter, after more rambling conversation that astounded me by its servility, gave in.

"This here child, she's a servant of Masta Jefferson, too. She's a Hemings, and Burwell here is her nephew. She's called Sally Hemings of Monticello," Jupiter added unnecessarily. It was the longest speech about me that I had ever heard Jupiter make.

"Another Hemings of Monticello! Good God, how many of you are there in this family? And how is James, by the way? I heard he went back to France. Mr. Jefferson's dinner parties haven't been the same since. As a matter of fact, he has spent the last year trying to steal other people's cooks! And this girl, surely she's not a field hand now, is she?"

"She's mistress of Masta Jefferson's wardrobe, suh," Jupiter replied grandly.

This man called Aaron Burr turned his black and burning gaze on me as if I were standing before him naked.

"The . . . mistress . . . of . . . Thomas . . . Jefferson's wardrobe . . . Jupiter?" he uttered slowly.

His eyebrows arched almost up to the hairline of his wide high forehead and gave him the appearance of Satan himself. His eyes raked me with such a mixture of contempt and lewdness that my blood turned cold. Never had a man looked at me thus. I was trembling. When I met his gaze he insolently held it. He threw back his head and laughed—a high, tinkling, peculiar laugh that was most unpleasant. I decided then and there that I detested Master Aaron Burr.

"From the way he dresses, Jupiter, I didn't think he had a wardrobe, let alone a mistress of it. Except for today," he added, "as he is looking most elegant in French blue, possibly because he has his mistress here to dress him . . ."

I felt Jupiter tense.

"Je vous en prie, Monsieur. Je suis la femme de chambre de Mademoiselle Maria Jefferson," I interrupted coldly in French. I don't know why I did it. I was flushed with anger and I was glad my face was half-hidden by my hat. Master Burr was as astonished as if a dog had started to speak Latin.

"Ah! Que je fus inspirée. . . ."

"Quand je vous recus dans ma cour," I replied.

It was the first lines from an aria that Piccinni, the singing tutor to Marie-Antoinette, had written. Marie-Antoinette was rumored to have sung it in public to her lover, the Count Fersen, at one of the famous parties at Trianon. It had been made into a limerick by the Parisian populace. Everyone who had been in Paris just before the Revolution knew it by heart. I couldn't help smiling at his astonishment, and he smiled back at me; a wide, handsome wicked grin. I blushed, sorry that I had smiled at him despite myself.

"Vous parlez très bien le français," he said with his heavy American accent. *"Vous avez bien dit, une servante de Maître Jefferson? C'est a dire, une esclave?"*

"Oui, Monsieur," I replied.

He looked questioningly at Jupiter, then at Burwell, neither of whom answered since they had not understood what we had said. Burwell too had put his "don't-ask-me-I-

just-a-poor-darky" expression on his smooth golden-brown
face.

*"Eh bien, ton maître a tant de choses à célébrer en plus
de son poste comme vice-président . . ."*

"Que Dieu le protège dans sa tâche," I replied, curtsying
low and in the French manner.

"Bien dit—well said, indeed. That God protect him.
From his enemies and his friends."

So this was my master's rival, I thought, the rich and
famous lawyer from New York, Aaron Burr. I loathed
him.

"Burwell, take your aunt out of this mob. Jupiter . . .
Davey, Mademoiselle Hemings of Monticello . . ." Again
he drew out the words sarcastically.

Outrage filled my breast. If I had been white, he would
not have dared address me so, servant or no servant. Despite my rage, I curtsied low, and to my surprise, he bowed
expertly. He spun on his heels in a curious dancing movement and walked jauntily away. He spoiled the effect,
however, by looking over his shoulder at me, and promptly
bumped into a tall handsome man who, Jupiter whispered,
was Alexander Hamilton. The comic effect of the formidable Master Burr falling over himself in his attempt to
get a last look at me didn't dispel my hatred, nor the sense
of dread the crowd had evoked in me. "Enemies?" I had
thought that in all this great crowd there were only friends
and followers of my master. Who could be an enemy of
Thomas Jefferson and why? Who could wish him any
harm? Certainly my master had complained at times about
the envy and the malice of political life, but mortal enemies seemed impossible to conceive. Master Jefferson, the
absolute ruler of Monticello, was so gentle, so serene. He
was surrounded by love. Could he be surrounded here by
people and forces he could not control? People that could
thwart his will as easily as he could that of his servants? I
thought of the newspaper articles I had read in the past
few days. Yes, there were people here he could not rule,
could not order, could not even fight or convince, who
were as intelligent, as rich, as powerful as he. There were
friends whose support he would need to seek. Mysterious
enemies from whom he had to defend or protect himself.
And, above all, there was the "public": that dangerous and

volatile mass that one could call neither friend nor enemy, for it could change from one day to the next. And this "public" had been given the name "The People" by their government, thereby making it one body, one will, the sole source of power that the great sought with such tenacity. "The People" now stood milling around the blood-red courtyard; "The People" brushed up against Jupiter, Burwell, and me as we stood to one side of our carriage. "The People" could destroy my master. And if my master was destroyed, what would become of me? It was then that I understood that my master's enemies were mine as well. That, in this white world, I had nothing but enemies.

"Jupiter, I'm going into the carriage. I feel faint."

As Jupiter helped me into the carriage, he said, "I expect that Thomas Jefferson don't want you out here minglin' with this mob, being scrutinized. I don't think he'd like the idea of you being exposed to this riffraff. He expected you to go home after the ceremony. You can see there ain't no ladies here." With that he slammed the door of the carriage.

". . . and, I told him, my inclination would never permit me to cross the Atlantic again."

I stared at him. With one willful declaration, the spoken and unspoken promises of the last eight years were broken. All my dreams of ever returning to France had vanished. Even now, with James gone without me, and with two children to raise, buried deep, I had always hoped to return to Marly. Now that subject was closed forever.

Three days after the inauguration, my master, accompanied by Jupiter, went to a dinner given by Master Washington. Despite hopes by everybody of a reconciliation between him and the new president, Adams, it had been evident at the dinner that their relations were so cold and so singular as to foment gossip even among the servants in the kitchens. Servants industriously discussed every aspect of the political situation. They sometimes seemed to have more information than the actual participants in the feuds and intrigues that evolved. Jupiter was not surprised, therefore, when his master returned from the dinner in a rare rage that only he and I were ever permitted to witness.

His face was flushed way beyond its usually high color, and he tore at his cravat so brutally that he practically strangled himself. His long legs paced the floor of the tiny room, shaking the floorboards, and his voice trembled with anger.

"The first and only thing John Adams proposed to me was that I return to France!"

He then let out a stream of imprecations against his old friend Adams; against Hamilton, Knox, Pickering, Burr, and the others. They were all against him. I memorized the names. So, I thought, these were my master's "enemies." In great agitation, he called for Jupiter to get a horse saddled, then changed his mind. He sat down long enough for me to pull off his boots. He stood up in his stocking feet and let loose another string of insults.

"If John Adams and his inherited Federalist cabinet think they can shut me out of the government, they had best think again!"

His huge fist came down on a small table beside the bed, smashing it to pieces.

My brief excursion into white America was over.

When we returned to the mountain, from Philadelphia, the mountain was in bloom.

He stayed home for almost the whole year.

At the end of the following summer, Maria Jefferson married her cousin Eppes in a small ceremony, amidst the demolition work going on over our very heads at Monticello. The couple would reside at Bermuda Hundred, more than a hundred miles away. For her wedding, her father gave Maria twenty-six slaves, seventy-eight horses, pigs, and cows, as well as eight hundred acres. Our good-byes were tender, for Polly had always treated me as a friend. We had managed to forge an unwritten truce that placed our love for her father as security against our love for each other. There were no secrets between us. When I showed her the room connected with that of her father's, her sigh of relief was as great as mine.

"Oh, Sally, how very nice!"

"He changed his apartments last year to accommodate it, and Joe and John are building the staircase."

"It means you no longer have to cross the public hall to enter and leave."

We never mentioned why this new arrangement would be better for all concerned. Nor would she ever mention this new arrangement to her father or ever allude to it.

"Remember, in Paris," I said, "all the secret stairways and rooms in the mansion? How we would imagine romantic stories about them?"

"We were so young in Paris," Polly said.

"You still are, Mistress. Seventeen is a wonderful age. . . ."

I had a safe harbor at last. But a mother is never safe. My master had been home for almost five months, Polly was still on her honeymoon, when rumors of an epidemic spreading up from Charlottesville struck terror in the heart of every mother, black or white. Both Tom and Harriet fell ill. Martha's daughters were sick at Edgehill, as well as half a dozen slave children. During the next weeks, we worked without sleep, nursing the children, Martha traveling back and forth between Edgehill and Monticello. Dulled by exhaustion, shedding bitter tears, Martha and I watched my little Harriet, only two summers old, slowly suffocate to death.

I laid her next to Edy, in the slave cemetery. Four of his white children lay under their stones in the white cemetery. The dividing line did not even stop at the grave. But what did it change? They were all his children, and they were all dead.

Harriet's death brought me low, undermining the fragile movements of still another new life in my womb. The winter reminded me of Paris in '88, long and cold and nothing like normal Virginia winters, with candles burning in the afternoon, keeping everyone, slave and white, indoors. My first born, Tom, survived, and I clung to him with all the desolation I felt that winter.

Martha, who had lost a daughter at the same time I had lost Edy, raced back to Edgehill and her children in mortal fear, leaving me alone.

Only one living child left, except the one in my body. I kept Tom indoors the whole winter, never letting his sturdy red-headed figure out of my sight. My heart pounded at every cough, stopped at every complaint.

At the end of March, I sent word that my time was approaching. A few days later, a sofa came made of fine mahogany with carved legs and back in the Jacobean style; a feather mattress and down coverlet of silk arrived as well. He had not forgotten me. When I wrote that I was safely delivered of a boy, the reply came back, "Name him Beverly," and I did.

Not long afterward a harpsichord arrived from Philadelphia. Martha came up from Edgehill to see it almost immediately. I looked with envy on her four healthy children. I too would have had four . . .

"It is for Maria, you know."

"Yes, so I understand."

Martha didn't mention the fact that Maria no longer lived at Monticello, but away at Bermuda Hundred. I was delighted with the harpsichord.

"It is a charming one, I think," she said, "but certainly inferior to mine."

She was looking not at the harpsichord, but at the white, blond, blue-eyed slave child I held in my arms . . . her half brother.

CHAPTER 29

MONTICELLO, OCTOBER 1800

What security for domestic purity and peace there can be where every man has had two connections, one of which must be concealed; and two families. . . .

HARRIET MARTINEAU, *Society in America,* 1837

The organ of justice, is the couple considered as a personal duality, forming by the contrast of attributes a complex being, the social embryo. . . . Nature in man and woman is not by consequence, the same. Moreover, it is through him that the conscience of both of them opens onto justice, each one becomes for the other at the same time witness, judge and a second self. Being in two personages, this couple is the real human subject.

PROUDHON, *Pornocracy or Women in Modern Time*
[published in 1875]

The Richmond Jail, Sept. 13, 1800

SIR,
Nothing is talked of here but the recent conspiracy of the Negroes. One Nicholas Prosser, a young man who had fallen heir, sometime ago, to a plantation within six miles of the city, had behaved with great barbarity to his slaves. One of them, named Gabriel, a fellow of courage and intellect above his rank in life, laid a plan of revenge. Immense numbers immediately entered into it, and it has been kept with incredible secrecy for several months. A number of swords were made in a clumsy enough manner out of rough iron; others by breaking the blade of a scythe in the middle, which thus made two swords of a most formidable kind. They were well fastened in proper handles, and would have

cut off a man's limb at a single blow. The conspirators
were to have met in a wood near Prosser's house, upon
Saturday before last, after it was dark. Upon that day,
or some very short time before it, notice was received
by a fellow, who being invited, somewhat unguardedly,
to go to the rendezvous, refused, and immediately
informed his master's overseer. No ostensible preparations were, however, made until the afternoon pre-
ceding the night of the rendezvous, and as the militia
are in a state of the most contemptible disorganization,
as the blacks are numerous, robust, and desperate,
there must have been bloody work. But upon that very
evening, just about sunset, there came on the most
terrible thunderstorm, accompanied with an enormous
rain, that I ever witnessed in this state. Between
Prosser's and Richmond, there is a place called Brook
Swamp, which runs across the high road and over
which there was a bridge. By this the Africans were of
need to pass, and the rain had made the passage im-
practicable. Besides they were deprived of the junction
and assistance of their good friends in the city, who
could not go out to join them. They were to have
attacked the Capital and the penitentiary. They could
hardly have failed of success, for after all, we only
could muster four or five hundred men of whom not
more than thirty had muskets. This was our state of
preparation while several thousand stands of arms were
piled up in the Capital and penitentiary. I do not pretend to blame the executive council, for I really am
not sufficiently master of the circumstances to form an
opinion. Five fellows were hung this day and many
more will share the same fate. This plan was to massacre all the whites, of all ages and sexes, and all the
blacks who would not join them; and then march off
to the mountains with the plunder of the city. Those
wives who should refuse to accompany their husbands
were to have been butchered along with the rest, an
idea truly worthy of any African heart. It convicts
with my knowledge that many of the wretches, who
were, or would have been, partners in the plot, have
been treated with the utmost tenderness by their
owners and more like children than slaves. . . .

I read through the rest of the letter, which dealt with general political opinions, and to the name of the sender: Thomas T. Callender. I fixed the name in my mind, then handed the letter my master had asked me to read back to him.

"I suppose you already know all about it," the familiar voice added with something like sadness.

Indeed, the slave intelligence had brought the news long before now, and the story of Gabriel Prosser was already legend.

Davey Bowles had brought the first news and told me of the uprising. Gabriel Prosser and Jack Bowler had been the leaders of the insurrections. Gabriel, a handsome, twenty-four-year-old giant of six-foot-three and his comrade Jack, three inches taller and four years older, had organized more than a thousand men in Henrico County. Brilliant and literate, he had carefully planned his rebellion. Gabriel's wife, Nanny, had been active as well, as were his brothers Solomon and Martin. They had all been betrayed by a fellow servant called Ben Wolfolk, who had heard of the conspiracy through two loose-mouthed slaves, George Smith and Samuel Bird. The insurrection was to have taken place on the first of September; the rendezvous for the rebels had been a brook six miles from Richmond. Eleven hundred men were to have assembled there and were to have been divided into three columns. All were to have marched to Richmond under the cover of night.

The rebels had counted heavily on the French, whom they had understood to be at war with the United States, for the money that was due them, and that a warship, which would help them, had landed at South Key. If successful in this first stage, the penitentiary in Richmond had enough arms, the powderhouse was well stocked, the capital contained the state treasury, the mills would give them bread, the control of the bridge across the James River would keep off enemies from beyond. Thus secured, they had planned to issue a proclamation summoning to their standard of red silk, with the words "Liberty or Death" printed on it, their fellow slaves and humanitarian whites. In a week, they had estimated they would have had fifty thousand rebels and could have taken other towns. In case of failure, they were to retreat into the mountains, as the rebellious slaves of Santo Domingo had done.

There had been intimations all summer of insurrection in Richmond, and the white table talk had been ominous with it. Yet the attack itself had surprised and shaken them. Why? I wondered, when they all lived, black and white, with this threat every day of every year. The whites had been surprised and unprepared. Only treachery had prevented success—treachery and God, for the appointed day had been prey to the most furious storm ever known to Virginia's memory. Why? I asked myself again and again. A tempest had burst upon the land instead of insurrection. The governor of Virginia, Master Monroe, had called in the United States Cavalry and the hangings had begun. I looked at the date on the letter. It was already outdated. Gabriel Prosser was already dead. Captured by treachery on a schooner in Norfolk, he had been brought back to Richmond in chains. There he had manifested the utmost composure and taking all the responsibility onto himself, had conducted himself as a hero, and had made no confession. Now, I looked at a fourth letter. Master Monroe was writing to Thomas Jefferson for advice. How to stop the hangings? More than thirty-five had gone to the gallows, and the Richmond jails were groaning with prisoners. They had suspended the trials. If they hanged everybody, they would annihilate the blacks in that part of the country.

"I think there has been enough hanging."

Why, when he kept so many things from me, did he want to share this particular burden? Did I not already have enough to bear? He knew that I could never come down on his side in this.

My lover looked at me with surprise.

"You know about the hangings?"

"Yes."

"You know how many?"

"Rumor has it forty or fifty, with hundreds waiting to be tried."

"Governor Monroe doesn't know what to do. Here, look at this."

I read Master Monroe's letter.

"All I can say is," I said, "you can't kill every slave in Virginia."

He got up from his desk and came toward me. "No," he said slowly, "you can't kill every one." He took the letter from my hands and went back to his desk. "When to stay the hand of the executioner is an important question. Those who have escaped from immediate danger must have feelings which dispose them to extend the executions. . . ."

"I still say there's been hanging enough. You can't kill everyone."

I thought of the new seed planted in my womb. A new slave.

"You must understand," I began, "they are not felons or common malefactors, but persons guilty of what our society obliges us to treat as a crime, and which their feelings represent in a far different shape—"

"I know this," he interrupted. He was turned away from me, the frightened, imploring letter of Master Monroe still in his hand.

He turned toward me but did not approach. He was afraid of me. He could forget in private, but he could never forget in public.

More to himself than to me, he said, "It is certain that the world at large will forever condemn us if we indulge or go one step beyond necessity."

At the word "necessity," I looked into his eyes but said nothing.

"Our situation is indeed a difficult one," he continued, "for I doubt if those people can ever be permitted to go at large among us with safety."

"Then exile them! The French and British do so," I begged. "Those people" were my people! Even as we spoke, he forgot. Banishment. Was that not James's choice? I pressed my palms to my womb. If I could save one . . . just one of them.

"I have thought of it," he said. "Surely the legislature would pass a law for their exportation, the proper measure as you have pointed out on this, and . . . all similar occasions."

I thought again of Gabriel Prosser. He had died on the gallows with ten of his men and with hundreds in the Richmond jail waiting to be tried and hanged, but they, the slaves, didn't believe it. Already there was a song that had started somewhere on some plantation, and was now winging from slave quarter to slave quarter. Prosser, the song went, didn't die on the gallows, but escaped with the help of a young slave boy named Billy. He lived to rise again. We were not about to let Gabriel Prosser die. He would rise again. Another black man would rise to take his place just as he had at Santo Domingo. My master looked down into my eyes.

"Exile them," I whispered.

Relief broke over his face. "Thank you," he said, and his eyes were filled with an ineffable tenderness. He, for the first time in his life, had a glimpse of the terror of slavehood and loving me he had acknowledged this terror. On this mountain, his eyes seemed to say, we can hold everything at bay, even this.

Shyly he reached out and touched me. He still seemed afraid of me. "Let me work now," he said.

I suffered his touch, but my mind was ablaze. There were so many things I wanted to say.

I turned and left him to his letters. I climbed the miniature stairs at the foot of his bed to my room. It was not until my master had left for Philadelphia, the balloting for the presidency still in doubt, that I heard that the last of Gabriel's condemned rebels had been reprieved and banished from Virginia by James Monroe.

I had not pleaded in vain.

CHAPTER 30

OCTOBER 1800

God from the beginning, elected certain individuals to be saved and certain others to be damned: and that no crimes of the former can damn them: no virtues of the latter save.
                                                    THOMAS JEFFERSON

James came home. He had arrived from France more than a year ago, and we dreamed to hold him at Monticello until the summer. He had seen his ex-master in Philadelphia.

"Thomas Jefferson says my journeys will end up on the moon! If only it could be so, for I am tired of this earth and its inhabitants!"

"When did you see him? How is he?"

My brother looked at me in disgust.

"He is fine. Embroiled in politics, as usual, and complaining about it, as usual. Burwell sends his love. Your master has no stomach to govern men. He says, 'I leave to others the sublime delight of riding the storm, better pleased with sound sleep and a warm berth below, with the society of neighbors, friends, and fellow laborers of the earth, than of spies and sycophants. . . .' So, I guess he misses you, sister. He can't decide whether he wants to be vice-president or not. Certainly, according to the newspapers and the backstairs, they are giving him a hard time. He looked so worried and despondent, I proposed that he join me on my next voyage to Spain to forget his troubles."

"Spain!"

Both Elizabeth Hemings and I exclaimed at the same

time. We were sitting in one of the cellars next to the
kitchens where it was cool. We had stuffed James with
everything good we could find to eat in the pantries. He
was wearing the latest French fashions and looked splendid. Men no longer wore breeches, but long pants, slender,
and tight, and tucked in tall boots. The colors had changed
as well—no more rose satin or pale-blue silk. Frock coats
were shorter, fuller, in dark colors with high collars and
white linen swathed the chest and neck up to the ears.
James no longer wore his hair long; it was cropped short in
a mass of curls.

"But why Spain?" we asked.

"And why not Spain? As I told your master, it is the
only country not fighting, or getting ready to fight, with
France! Don't think that France is any party since the
Revolution; we had only the beginnings of it that October
of eighty-nine, and the stories we've heard here are nothing
compared to the reality. When I arrived in France, I had
hoped to find work with one of the great houses I had
known when we were there. Only I learned that most of
the great houses were closed, or gutted and burned, their
owners and occupants either in exile or gone to the guillo-
tine, like the poor king and his queen. And the 'citizens,' as
they call everyone now, were looking askance at the servant class as well. Many cooks' and valets' heads came off
along with their masters'. Petit knew what he was doing to
leave when he did.

"Once Robespierre was dead, it was thought that the
bloodletting would be finished, but it goes on even now.
There is civil and foreign war. Everyone is attacking
France or getting ready to attack her. Because of the up-
heaval, there had no been no planting and therefore no
harvest. There is no bread and no money. People pray only
for a deliverer. The Estates General is paralyzed. Everything—everything is chaos, yet your Jefferson still hopes
for victory for the Revolution. Nothing but a miracle will
save France now. Never did I think the fine house of the
old Comtesse de Noailles on the Ile Saint-Louis would be
gutted and burned to the ground; as well as the Hermitage,
and the Tuileries Palace. There was no trace of the Bastille,

but think on this: they destroyed Marly as well. Nothing is
left."

Marly. So it too was gone.

"And all of Master Jefferson's friends?" I asked.

"How changed their fortunes are now! Lafayette is in a
prison at Magdeburg. Madame de Corny is a widow and
has retired to Rouen with a pittance she salvaged from her
jewels. Mrs. Cosway has gone into a convent at Genoa.
Monsieur de Condorcet escaped from a hanging indictment, and is a fugitive. The Duc de la Rochefoucauld was
torn to pieces by a mob before the eyes of his mother and
wife. Those who have not been separated from their heads
are either in exile or in prison. The Directory could well
use the Bastille we tore down!" James licked his lips.

The recital of murder and trials went on long into the
night. We listened at first with horror and interest; then
numbness set in as the litany went on and on. James took
delight in the demise of one great aristocrat after another.
His hard eyes glinted when he told the tales of the Terror
and Jacobins and finally Robespierre's death. Now there
was the chaos and civil war of the Directory.

"We Americans didn't have a revolution worth talking
about," James continued. "We're just as much slaves now
as in 1776! We're just as much slaves under a vice-president and a president as we were under a British governor.
They still import as many slaves into this so-called Republic. If the French could make an insurrection with stones
and pitchforks, why can't we?"

"James, hush your mouth!" Elizabeth Hemings cried.

But there was no master here to overhear what we said.
I was the mistress of Monticello.

"I'm trying to say, Mama, that there are thirty thousand
slaves in the state of Virginia alone. In South Carolina, we
outnumber the whites. . . . Thirty thousand Virginia slaves
. . . that's an army. You realize that? An army!"

My mother rose as if to block the very words out of
James's mouth. But who was listening?

We moved outside and I watched the mountains turn
gold, red and silver as the sun dipped. James's eyes glowed,
feverish as ever. The low-hanging smoke from the slave

fires dimmed the pink of the sky, and the buzz of night creatures mingled with the droning of James's familiar voice.

What did I really feel? Horror, vengeance, delight, sorrow, indifference . . . yes, indifference was the closest to this tight stony feeling that pushed itself up into my heart.

"Lord, you know that sounds like some slave revolt!"

"That's what I mean, Mama, if you could see what the Revolution—theirs, not ours—brought down as we saw it, then you would know that anything is possible!"

"But them aristocrats," my mother said slowly, "was weak."

"And our masters are strong? Those white people were just like us; militia and passes, and lynchings . . . Just like us, Mama! Can you understand a little of what I'm trying to say to you?"

"I understand more than you think, James Hemings. I understand when you talk about revolution and how many slaves there is in Virginia and how our masters with all they privileges ain't no stronger than that King Louis. I understand you just like anybody got two cents' worth of brains understands you. But I know what we *ain't* got, and what we ain't got is a leader to lead us. A Moses. We ain't got him. He ain't come and unless he do, we ain't going nowhere. You talking about people who followed because they was *led*. I'm ready to follow, but who's going to lead? All the white folks get together even if the poor trash can't stand the rich white folks. They get together from all the plantations to put it down. Make an example of the leaders, put the fear of the Lord into everybody. France got some troubles on its hands, and I don't think what they be needing is a pastry cook. What they need is somebody, one body to pull their coals out of the fire, not their petit fours. . . ."

"I don't intend to go anywhere near an aristocrat or a citizen, for that matter," James said, "but where there's war, there's money. That I learned from our politicians and bankers up in Philadelphia. And I intend to make a fortune. I came back for just one reason—to get my sister. You coming, Sally Hemings?" James's voice cracked onto the still air like thunder in my ears and I sat up struck by it.

"Come with you?" I whispered.

"Nothing stopping you," he said.

"Nothing . . . except two children."

"Leave them with Mama and come back and get them, or take them with you. I don't care which."

"You don't know what you're saying, James. I couldn't—"

Without warning, James's face contorted with rage. "Mama, listen to her. You hear her! Mama!" It was a scream. "Eleven years and she hasn't learned anything! After all the promises in Paris, it took him seven years to free me, and I got thirty dollars and a horse. I traded freedom for promises, because I thought he loved me: a few cooking lessons in Virginia, and I ended up giving him seven years of my life for thirty dollars and a horse, and I even said 'Merci, Monsieur.' He promised her her children would be free at twenty-one, pokes out her stomach with his bastards, says he loves her, and she says, 'Merci, Monsieur.' Fool!"

"Coward!" I screamed. "Afraid to steal yourself! Why didn't you run? Why? What stopped you? And now, look at you! More than five years of freedom and what do you have to show for it? Nothing!"

"And you do? I suppose. You could have made more in a bordello!"

"What do men make of the world for women except a bordello!"

"And you revel in it!"

"Men revel in it! Lovers and husbands, brothers and uncles—you all revel in it! My whoredom is yours and you know it!"

"I know it," he cried, "and it never leaves me, even in sleep. I want only to forget it! To leave you to it, if you want it!"

"Then leave me to it. Leave me, leave me!" I screamed.

"I'll never leave you to it as long as I have breath in my body, as long as I dream at night."

"We all have dreams," I said deliberately. "You think yours are special, but they are not. I've had enough of chasing eleven-year-old dreams of Paris."

"You sound just like him. 'Enough of chasing rainbows . . .' Stay where you are. Lay up money. Be a good ex-slave. Make something of yourself. And I look at him. I look at those cold blue eyes and I say, 'You've already made something of me . . .' and the bastard doesn't even understand what I'm talking about."

"James, you got to stop hating yourself." This was Elizabeth Hemings speaking. Her voice trembled in a way I had never heard before. My brother's violence had undone her. I realized she was afraid of her son. She who was afraid of nothing.

"Mama, you ain't got no idea what hate is," James said.

"I guess I ain't," replied my mother.

"Women! Somebody cover you with dung and you wipe it off, wrap it up and start crooning a lullaby over it."

"You better go on back over there across the water, son."

"I'm going, Mama. I just want to know, for the last time, if she's coming with me." He turned to me and his eyes were dark burning holes and the look in them was the same he had turned on my master that Christmas Day five years ago.

"You coming, Sally Hemings?"

"No," I said.

"I'm never coming back here for you again. Save yourself, sister."

"No, James."

This time I could not keep the pride out of my voice. Was I not the legatee of my half sister? I had love. Did I not have a room of my own? I had privacy. Did I have a white mistress? No, I did run this place. Had I not saved ten black men from certain death? I had power. How could my brother speak of saving myself. I had no need to.

James looked out. The sense of desolation he had carried all these years enveloped him with the familiarity of an old friend. Loneliness. Dislocation. Thomas Jefferson's pompous proclamation had no more freed him than his own impotent declarations in Paris so long ago, he thought to himself. No piece of paper ever would, he had finally realized. Happiness had dissolved before him. The future no longer stretched before him full of hope, but swerved back onto itself and his past. He was not free. Only if he took

Sally away . . . freed *her*, would he feel truly emancipated. Why, James wondered to himself, did he need the freedom of Sally Hemings? He looked at his sister. Suppose she never left Thomas Jefferson? Never left Monticello? What would become of him, James, who needed her freedom more than he needed his own?

James left Virginia for Spain on an English ship out of Norfolk sailing for Gibraltar. At the end of December, his letters began to arrive. Sometimes his "You coming, Sally Hemings?" would echo like a heartbeat on the page after page of fine script full of adventures and descriptions, plans, hopes, and dreams . . . always dreams, and the culmination of those dreams, always just one more letter away.

Many times that winter I thought of Richmond and Gabriel Prosser. The state capital was guarded these days by armed and uniformed sentinels and a permanent cordon of bayonets. This was the lasting memorial to Gabriel's defeat. The insurrection hung over the valley and all that was in it which was his.

I thought about what my master had said:

"An insurrection is easily quelled in its first effects, but far from being local, it will become general and whenever it does, it will rise more formidable after every defeat until one will be forced after dreadful scenes and sufferings to release them in their own way. . . ."

"And how?" I had asked.

"I don't know, but if something is not done, and done soon, we shall be the murderers of our own children. . . ."

Had he known what he was saying? I felt a numbness come over me.

"You must be chilled, my dear," he had said with a concerned voice. "Shall I ask Jupiter to come and light a fire for you?"

He could speak of murder and his children, and then his slave Jupiter . . .

The summer of 1800 that had just passed so quietly at home was also the summer that was, ballot by ballot, crowning my lover president of the United States. The scent of power had seeped into the mansion. The house had been abuzz with messengers, letters, newspapers, and visitors.

It seemed to me an omen that the duel for power between Thomas Jefferson and Aaron Burr came to an end while Jupiter lay dying. The faithful Jupiter was fifty-seven years old and he shared his birth year with his master, whom he had served since the age of fourteen. The handsome black face, gray now with illness and impending death, flooded with joy as I bent over his still bulky and powerful form to whisper the news of his master's presidency.

"I knowed from de beginnin' at Willam' an' Mary dat Masta Jefferson was gon' be first in de lan'. . . ."

The words in their soft slur escaped me at first, and I bent closer to the pain-racked body in order to hear.

"Uncle Jupiter, I have greetings for you from Master Jefferson. He says you get well and he bring you up to Washington City to the president's house. . . ." I slipped into the slave dialect: "He say you younger than him by four months and you ain't got no business gettin' all sick without his permission. And you shore ain't got no permission to lay out and die on him. . . . He says ol' Davey Bowles, he can't drive his bays like you. Say he tearin' up dem bays, dat young pip . . ." My eyes filled with tears as I soothed the old man, the soft Virginia drawl falling as easily from my lips as the French I sometimes spoke with Polly. "Full-blooded bays, Masta Epps bought fo' Masta Jefferson's carriage in Washington. You'll be seated behin' dem, Uncle Jupiter. . . . They's de mos' spirited, de mos' showy, de mos' beautiful. . . . They cost de masta sixteen hundred dollars. Best horses in Washington . . . first in de lan' . . ."

We had called the black doctor from Milton and the white doctor from Charlottesville. My mother had strained her knowledge of herb remedies to the limit, but nothing had helped.

"Uncle Jupiter," I said softly, "you wan' som' milk bread? Try a little, Mama made it jus' fo' you. . . ." But he could not hear my words; my mother closed his eyes, and, on either side of him, Martha and I knelt. I was going to have to write my master that his beloved Jupiter was dead.

The news of Jupiter's death spread throughout the household, and then out toward the slave quarters and outlying plantations. The slaves began to gather for the wake, a low moan lapping up the mountain from the underside of Monticello.

It was at the funeral of Jupiter that most of the slave population learned that they were now the property of the President of the United States.

once the world behind that façade, which had fallen to

CHAPTER 31

MONTICELLO, 1801

When he came home for the first time as president, except for Maria, who was too ill to come to Monticello, everything on his mountain was safe and at peace.

He was proud. He was loved, not only in his own domains but by the whole nation.

We watched a rainstorm break over Shadwell, far in the distance. From the north terrace, we could see the gray mists resting on the range that stretched for forty miles to the Chesapeake Bay. In the distance, we could see the low-hanging clouds of a spring storm, which looked like a theater set to the two of us standing in the weak April afternoon sun.

He had built not only power last summer but his mansion, which had taken its final shape. I could feel its space, every foot of its masonry, every inch of its brick and mortar, behind me like a fortress. He had overlooked no detail, had underplayed no effort toward perfection. He had goaded his master builders, John and Joe, into a sublimity of effort. His long-accumulated books, paintings, sculptures, and instruments—some of them in their cases since our return—had at last found their proper places. His curtains and draperies, china, silver, Persian rugs, linens, clocks had also been incorporated. His plants, his trees, his roses stretched in gigantic patterns on the west and south sides of the mansion. The house stood, a one-story brick building facing west, surmounted by an octagonal dome that camouflaged its second story, while the terracing and sloping of the mountain camouflaged the understory. The beautiful and perfectly proportioned façade, with its Doric columns and heavy cornice and balustrades, looked over the vast lawns and gardens down onto the valley, and out onto the world. Behind that façade, which had taken so long to build, his slave and white families lived with his other possessions.

He looked down at me. "Look at the rain clouds," he said. "It rains, it storms, and yet we feel not one drop."

"It thunders, too," I said, as the first rumblings of the spring storm's fury was carried over the distance of the mountain.

"And it lightens as well," he laughed as the sky beyond us burst white. "Yes, we are not lit by it."

"And thank God," I said.

We stood watching the shower. The servants would be lighting the candles in a little while and setting the table for eight places, even for his solitary dinner, in the rosewood-paneled dining room off the center hall.

I knew what he was thinking.

His Eden was complete.

In another month, there would be a new addition to our family. He wanted a girl, so I prayed for one, for him. A president's daughter.

"If it is a girl, name her Harriet, after our Harriet," he had said.

"And if it is a boy?"

"Then name him James."

I knew he was happy. I begged him to await the birth. He had never been present at the birth of any of my children. Again, he left me to the final weeks of waiting.

On the eighth of May, the very anniversary of the birth of his last child by my half sister Martha, whose death had begun the journey to my destiny, I gave birth to my fifth child.

I named her Harriet, as I had promised.

My mother was not pleased. "Martha Jefferson did the same thing," she said, "and she lost both of them Lucy Elizabeths. Don't name this daughter Harriet, Sally."

"Her father wants her named Harriet. He's lost one Harriet, and he wants another. This one will survive."

"Not for you or him to say if she gonna live or die. God has still got some rights, even in Virginia. Masta may be president, but he aint' got that last power—life and death, and well he should know it!"

"You're just superstitious, Maman, it doesn't make any

difference what her name is. You sound like one of those
Indian squaws who dress their son up like a girl so that
God won't know he's a male."

Yet, even as I argued with Elizabeth Hemings, the sense
of doom that had plagued me since Gabriel's insurrection
took hold of me. I looked down on the ivory-skinned,
auburn-haired infant sleeping in my arms, another Harriet,
and pressed her to my breast. She would survive. And she
would survive to live free.

"My Martha named that second Lucy Elizabeth after
the dead one, when I told her—"

"I don't care what you told your precious Martha
Wayles. I don't care what Martha Jefferson did or didn't
do. I'm not Martha Wayles. I am me! Martha Wayles
Jefferson is nothing to me, nor do I want her to be."

"She's your sister, if you like it or not, and I told her—"

"Mama! I don't care if she was my sister or not! She has
nothing, *nothing* to do with me or my children. This is my
Harriet. Mine and Thomas Jefferson's."

"This is the first time in my life, daughter, I ever heard
you call him by his name." There was amazement in her
voice. "Lord, child, what's the matter? I know who you
are, I know you not your half sister. I'm your mother, not
hers, though it's true I loved her. But you can't ever say I
loved her more than I love you."

"You did, Mama. Admit it. You've said it a million
times. Your white daughters. Your sweethearts."

Anger now hung like a cloud between us. I had hurt her.
But I had not been able to stop myself.

"No, child," she said, "it's not like you say. I guess I am
like that Indian squaw. I pretend I love you less so that
God won't punish me by bringing hurt on you. I'm only
afraid for you. You won't fight for yourself. You won't
protect yourself. I only want that. That you fight for yourself and your children, that's all. I didn't mean no offense."

We looked at each other. She didn't understand. I was
fighting. I was fighting him. I was fighting love, slavery,
and Virginia.

"No, Mama, you never mean any offense," I said.

"But, daughter, you might suckle her yourself and not
give her over to a wet-nurse like you did the others."

I tightened my hold on Harriet. Martha Randolph was pregnant and ready to bear. My mother always made it a point to remind me that Martha nursed all her babies.

"Now don't go getting resentful about nursing," she said, as if she had read my mind. "You careful, it won't hurt your bosom any. Martha Randolph done suckled all her children, and she still got a beautiful bosom. Pretty enough for any man to lay his head on."

I don't know why, but I started to cry. Sobs of rage and scalding resentment shook me. What did I want? He loved me. What did I want? He listened to me. What was it then I wanted?

My mother took me in her arms. Her face next to mine was dark and cloudy.

The summer meant the return to Monticello of my master's white family. Thomas and Beverly were swept up in the ever-increasing swarm of children, slave and white, that mingled in total freedom all the summer months. My Thomas, red-headed and gray-eyed, romped on the west lawn with Thomas Jefferson Randolph, red-headed and blue-eyed; and the Randolph girls, all dark like their father with his Indian blood. Anne and Ellen found in blue-eyed Beverly the perfect doll. Martha Randolph had proudly announced to my mother, much to her vexation, that she was again "expecting." My mother had wanted only me to give birth this year.

A test of power at Monticello between Martha and me had been postponed by the simple expedient of letting my mother keep the huge iron ring of house keys that hung at her waist. My mother, now sixty-six, knew her position as dowager queen could not last much longer. Nevertheless, while she ruled, she ruled, and it was to her that all the children, Martha's and mine, turned to as ultimate arbitrator and bounty-giver. I knew my mother secretly feared that I would never have the will to fight for Monticello. She had often said that once she let the reins of power go, it would be Martha, not me, who would take her place. But she didn't know that Monticello had been promised to me by my master.

It was bad enough that I could not take my place at the

head of the table at Monticello. But that Martha should
wear the keys . . . never!

The summer was hot and humid. The heavy perfume of
jasmine, honeysuckle, and peach blossoms exuded a sweet,
deep, dangerous sensuality. It was the heat, I suppose, and
some mysterious chemistry that seemed to combine into a
volatile mixture of sullen arrogance and irritability. The
mountain reeked of that climate that bred fevers and sudden violence.

Both Maria and Martha were coming home to give
birth. Maria arrived first. She was enduring her second
difficult confinement, still a semi-invalid, suffering the
complications of her first child's birth. She brought, as
usual, her own servants. They were Monticello slaves that
had been given to her on her marriage and who found their
friends and family again. They included her personal maid,
her coachman, her cook, her outriders, her nurse, and
several of their children.

Next came Martha Randolph, heavy with her sixth
child, along with all her children, Anne, Thomas Jefferson,
Ellen Wayles, and Virginia. Both her husband and Maria's
were in Washington City and would arrive in August with
their body servants, coachmen, horses, and luggage.

I greeted my nieces with my babe in arms. We were
genuinely glad to see one another. The winter had been
long and lonely. Maria, ill all of the time, isolated at Bermuda Hundred, enjoyed the added attention, the music,
the conversation, and her father's triumphal presence.
After only five years of marriage, her bright beauty had
washed away to the almost transparent delicacy of a much
older woman. As for Martha, her big-boned and robust
body had already settled into middle age. Her face had
hardened with the bitter struggle against her husband's er-
ratic and increasingly uncontrollable behavior. After several years of relative lucidity, Thomas Mann Randolph was
again slipping back into the melancholy and depression
which were the harbingers of his insanity. All the weary
travels from doctor to doctor, from cure to cure, had not
helped him. More and more Martha looked forward to
summers at Monticello with her father. Like him, she too

suffered from violent migraines that disappeared only on the mountain.

There were now thirty-two servants for six white people, including the children. Before the summer was over, there would be as many sleeping guests.

We settled into our positions, re-establishing the old accommodation and bonds among ourselves. We girded for the arrival of the men, who must at all cost be recaptured, comforted, redomesticated, and spoiled after their long absences. The air, as always, again became heavy with jealousies and unrealized dreams.

All this would focus itself on Thomas Jefferson. All the loves and hates and jealousies of Monticello would gravitate toward its center, my master. Calm and possessed, he would ride above the often stormy, half-smothered passions that struggled around him, both at home and in Washington; and by his fierce will, would repress any open violence. He would turn a deaf ear to the problems of all of the women on the mountain. And we dared not intrude upon him. He wanted peace. And he wanted his façade of perfection. He would not tolerate less. And I, I tolerated Martha and Maria on their summer visits, but they were not the mistresses of Monticello. I was. That was our covenant. He had promised.

Even before the men's arrival, the first bad news of the summer had filtered into Monticello. Danby Carr, the youngest of the hot-tempered Carr brothers, had been involved in a duel. He had severely wounded his opponent and had been arrested. Danby had rowed across the James River in the early dawn, cocked his pistols at a friend, and half-killed him, then had gone bragging all over Milton and Charlottesville on the quality of his pistols and the cowardliness of his target. Peace? If Thomas Jefferson thinks he is going to have peace, I thought, he had better think again. Depressed, I began trying to keep order among the slaves, to find rooms for the ever-increasing white family, which now included the Carrs and Jefferson's sister, a poor relative. I suppressed the dark foreboding of the months to come and lifted my own burdened and disappointed heart to my task.

* * *

The August sun beat down on his back and bared head. It was the second time he was riding up his mountain as president. He had taken his saddle horse and mounted up at Shadwell, leaving the phaeton with Davey Bowles and Burwell, and had gone galloping ahead, his still reddish hair brushed back by the wind. Thomas Jefferson returned depressed and convinced that his robust constitution had finally failed him, stricken with a dysentery that had not left him since he had taken office. He had also begun to keep track of the deaths of the signers of the Declaration of Independence with the same precision as he noted the singing of Dick, his mockingbird.

The death of Jupiter had struck fear into his own heart. . . . Not without bitterness, he remembered that neither Martha nor Maria had written to congratulate him on his election as president. He had won by a hairbreadth over Burr, and now he would have to crush his power as well as the lingering residue of Federalist influence.

Thomas Jefferson looked up at the tall Virginia pines. He was haunted with death. The bursting mountainside underlined the tragedy of that other summer, so many years ago, when his great love had let life go, after giving birth to a girl child, now also dead. It was the nineteenth anniversary of Martha Jefferson's death. And now, in fear, he clung to the image of his slave wife who gave birth easily.

He reined in his bay Wildair, and sat slumped under the arched green vaults of his own forest, the bridle paths leading up the west slope, etched by the years of riding his own favorites. The dappled sunlight played about his broad shoulders and the flanks of his horse.

He had left Washington City in a state of weariness. His illness, the unfinished president's house, the strain of political life had taken a toll on his state of health. His migraines, which had not tormented him since he had left France more than ten years before, were plaguing him again. His estates were slipping, and the Wayles legacy of debt was still not resolved. Yet, he thought, raising his head, the mountain was still there; a young mother waited for him at the top; his two daughters, and his grandchildren were within his embrace. He dug his spurs into the

sweating flank of Wildair, urging him faster and faster up
the mountain.

My master returned with the news that James was back
on these shores. James had written to me all last year, wild
incoherent letters filled with impossible dreams of fame
and fortune, as he wandered from one European capital to
another in the wake of refugees fleeing the wars of Napoleon. He still begged me to leave Monticello. Like some
flying eagle, he had dipped and swooped above my head,
rattling my nest with the beating of his wings, always with
his lure and song of freedom. But I had known he would
be back. For some unknown reason, he kept returning to
Virginia. Almost as if he were compelled. James had
turned his back on his former master, and had refused to
come to Monticello, or even send greetings to me, his own
sister.

The master ensconced himself in his private apartments, reading and writing in the morning, appearing for
dinner, then riding out for hours in the afternoon. Only I
was allowed entrance into his chambers where he worked,
often morose and depressed. Yet, he appeared without fail
at the supper table, cheerful and serene.

All the children, black and white, competed for the attention and love of the master; all fought for their places in
the sun.

In August, Martha went into labor. The double-faced
clock on the east patio rang hour after hour, as the birth,
despite the ease of the previous ones, proved to be a long
and difficult one. My mother and I sat on either side of
Martha's plank as the midwife, Ursula, struggled silently to
bring forth the new life. Martha's labor had begun the
night before, and now, well into the end of the day, her
eyes were glazed with pain and exhaustion. Our dresses
clung to us in the August heat, but we could not throw
open the windows that were sealed shut, nor douse the fire
that burned in the hearth. Martha moaned, filling me with
dread. I thought of Maria, no more than a month away
from her travail. I had so begged Maria to attempt no more
children, just as my mother had begged Maria's mother
before her; but now there was no time to think of Maria.

There were only Martha's moans, and finally only her
screams; almost eighteen hours after the first pains, the girl
child came at last.

Downstairs, the white family waited as I descended to
announce the birth of a girl, who would be named Virginia. During the long hours of labor I had a premonition
of the awaited test of power. Two days after Virginia's
birth, when Martha's milk had not come, it happened.

"You will wet-nurse Virginia, Sally. You have plenty of
milk." Before I could answer my mother answered for
me.

"There's no need for that, Mistress. There's two newly
delivered slave women. I'll send for Sulky for you."

"I don't want Sulky, Mammy Hemings, I want Sally.
She will be the one to nurse Virginia. After all, she doesn't
have anything else to do!"

"But, honey, your milk will come, it always do, and
meanwhile Sulky, she much better, she's—"

"I said I want Sally to do it."

My mother shrugged and turned away. This was between Martha and me. She watched with horror as I took
the white infant, and with tears of rage streaming down my
cheeks, pressed her to my breast.

Virginia's birth was celebrated for two days. The school
bell rang, the slaves were issued whisky and the children
candy; the white family celebrated with French champagne
in a state of happy relief.

It was in this festive atmosphere that Danby Carr at-
tempted to seduce my sister Critta. Critta belonged to Peter
Carr, who was the father of her children, and neither of
the other Carr brothers had ever dared to coerce my
haughty and beautiful sister.

I was sorting linen with Elizabeth Hemings when Critta,
pale and distraught, burst in on us.

"Mama, Masta Carr messing with me!"

My mother didn't look up from her sorting.

"Which Masta Carr?" she asked.

"Danby!"

We both knew the danger. Danby had always been jealous of Peter over Critta. Now he was bloodied, he had
decided to challenge him, and Samuel, the eldest brother,

was probably egging him on. Danby had just fought one duel. . . . Trouble. They were spoiling for trouble.

"He put his hands on you?" Elizabeth Hemings asked.

"Not yet."

"He going to?"

"He got a mind to. You know what Masta Peter do to me, he find out?"

"Did you tell him yourself?"

"Tell him?"

"Tell, tell on Danby? Tell Masta Peter he messing with you?" Elizabeth Hemings looked into my sister's hazel eyes. She was beautiful, but not too bright. Disgust drew down the corners of Elizabeth Hemings's mouth.

"It's the only way, Critta, 'less you want real trouble."

"I ain't looking for no trouble," Critta said. "I just want to be left alone."

"Well, you ain't going to be left alone with them boys around. Just try to stay out of their way. Don't get into any close quarters with him. Stick close to Masta Peter."

"But Peter's going to Richmond tomorrow."

"Then come stay with me. You can stay in my room. Don't sleep alone."

"He set on it," Critta said.

"Well, he can get set off it. Them nephews got enough slaves in trouble around here, including you."

"Why you suppose all a sudden? . . ."

"Jealous of Peter, feeling his oats with his dueling, showing off to Samuel—how should I know what goes on in white men's heads?" The helplessness of the situation caused a tremor in the hand Elizabeth Hemings placed on my sister's shoulder.

"If worse comes to worse, I'll tell Masta Jefferson. There ain't nothing else I can do to protect you from a white man. Best you tell Peter first, then, if that don't work, I'll tell Masta."

"They'll fight," Critta said.

"Better they beat on each other than you! Let them kill each other." Anger shook my mother's voice.

"But what old Masta going to say he find out Danby and Peter fightin' over me?"

"There's going to be hell to pay," Elizabeth Hemings said grimly.

I could see Critta hesitate.

"I'll tell him," Critta finally said. "I'll tell him he come messing with me, I'll tell his brother."

"They'll all get thrown off here they make a ruckus. . . ."

Elizabeth Hemings looked at me after Critta had left. I could tell what she was thinking. Bad blood. Bad blood between brothers. Bad blood between Martha and me; all the pauper relatives feeding off the larder. . . . She began to count up the supplies the household had gone through this summer, then stopped. She started to laugh. She sat down hard and laughed until the tears poured down her face.

"White workers running rampant like a herd of goats through the slave quarters, relatives eating me out of house and home, and everybody come to me . . . the head slave in the harem! I hope . . . I hope Peter Carr beats the tar out his brother!"

Elizabeth Hemings looked up at me. I didn't know if she was laughing or crying.

The fight between Danby Carr and his brother over Critta started in the ice cellar, where Critta had been cornered by Danby. Her son Jamey, who had gone to fetch his father, witnessed the fight of his father and his uncle over his mother. Critta was hurt in the fracas, having been pushed against a wall. Her wrist was broken and she had begged Martin to take Jamey off to Pantops after Jamey had tried to attack his father. Critta took shelter with me, and Maria promised she could go back to Bermuda Hundred with her when she returned. Critta went back to Peter Carr, and Danby left for his plantation.

Maria's baby came at the end of September, and, as feared, the birth was long and difficult and the child feeble. I didn't think there was that much blood in a human body, as we fought to stem its flow with teas and herbs. Finally, a doctor was called, and he recommended more bleeding to "rid" Maria of poisons that might lead to infection. On this murderous note, he left, after conferring with a distraught husband and father, who declined to follow his advice.

Little by little Maria fought her way back, willed to live by my mother and me, but the child continued to suffer convulsions. I took the infant Francis to my own breast as well.

No sooner had we suffered through Maria's recovery, as if God's own vengeance was sweeping down, a plague of the dreaded whooping cough swept through the children on the hill. Once again all of the women on the mountain were waging the fight against death to the children. All grudges were forgotten then as we joined in the struggle to preserve the fragile lives.

This time no child perished.

Exhausted, we parted, Martha and Maria returning to their plantations, Critta gratefully going along with Maria, leaving Elizabeth Hemings and me alone on the hill to face the winter. Anything the winter would bring, I thought, would be better than the summer just past. But I was wrong.

The preparations for Christmas were under way; my chests of decorations had been taken down from the attic, the housecleaning and baking already started. I was sitting, playing the new harpsichord, when I heard the strangled cry of my mother and the heavy spurred boots of Davey Bowles, who had ridden two days without stopping from Washington City to arrive before the letter.

I had seen Davey Bowles lips moving, but it seemed to have taken forever for the words to reach me.

It was the fourth day of December 1801. Davey had come to bring the news of James's death.

James had hanged himself with a bloody sheet in a lonely waterfront rooming house in Philadelphia. He was already buried in unconsecrated ground up North. There had been no belongings, no letter, no message. Only John Trumbull's silver-framed portrait of me and a small silver dagger were found near his bedside. Davey handed them to me in silence as I stood screaming James's name over and over again until I sank to my knees. For a long time I remained kneeling. Then I raised my hand.

From this day on, I vowed, I would live in perfect slave-hood, in perfect love, and this slavery and this love would be my strength and my fortress; never would he forgive himself or his world for it, and never would he escape from it. It would be the master who would be branded and bonded to me forever. I would turn love against the possessor and daze him into the everlasting hell of guilt! I vowed Thomas Jefferson would see only what he wanted to in the silver-and-gilt mirror of my love and, with that reflecting force, I would strike him down, blind him, commit arson against him. And what arm would he have against it? If I could not hate him, I would kill him with love. And if I could not kill him, I would maim him forever, cripple and paralyze him, so that he would have no possibility to walk away from me, no voice to deny me.

Thomas Jefferson would no longer be able to live without me.

A ruthless joy took hold of me. I rose and fled from the room and from the mansion out of doors.

I swung around, my back against the deep many-hued valley with its army of black pines, and faced the impeccable whiteness of Monticello.

James's death seemed to herald the final calamity that was to befall us.

CHAPTER 32

NOVEMBER 1802

Let Dusky Sally henceforth bear The name of Isabella And
let the mountain, all of salt Be christen'd Monticella
                                    JOHN QUINCY ADAMS, 1803

But what have I done to make them hate me so?
                    MARIE ANTOINETTE, *Correspondance secrète*, 1785

If there is any country on earth where the course of true
love may be expected to run smooth, it is America.
                HARRIET MARTINEAU, *Society in America*, 1837

THE RECORDER
Richmond
September 1st, 1802

It is well known that the man, *whom it delighteth the
people to honor,* keeps, and for many years past has
kept, as his concubine, one of his slaves. Her name is
SALLY. The name of her eldest son is Tom. His features
are said to bear a striking though sable resemblance
to those of the President himself. The boy is ten or
twelve years of age. His mother went to France in the
same vessel with Mr. Jefferson and his two daughters.
The delicacy of this arrangement must strike every
portion of common sensibility. What a sublime pattern
for an American ambassador to place before the eyes
of two young ladies!

If the reader does not feel himself disposed to pause
we beg leave to proceed. Some years ago, the story had
once or twice been hinted at in *Rind's Federalist*. At

that time, we believed the surmise to be an absolute calumny. One reason for thinking so was this: A vast body of people wished to debar Mr. Jefferson from the presidency. . . .

The establishment of this SINGLE FACT would have rendered his election impossible.

By this wench Sally, our president has had several children. There is not an individual in the neighbourhood of Charlottesville who does not believe the story; and not a few who know it. . . .

Behold the favorite, the first born of republicanism! The pinnacle of all that is good and great! In open consummation of an act which tends to subvert the policy, the happiness, and even the existence of this country.

'Tis supposed that, at the time when Mr. Jefferson wrote so smartly concerning negroes, when he endeavoured so much to *belittle* the African race, he had no expectation that the chief magistrate of the United States was to be the ringleader in shewing that his opinion was erroneous; or, that he should choose an African stock whereupon he was to engraft his own descendants. . . .

Mute! Mute! Mute! Yes very Mute! will all those republican printers of political biographical information be upon this point. Whether they stir or not, they must feel themselves like a horse in a quick-sand. They will plunge deeper and deeper, until no assistance can save them.

If the friends of Mr. Jefferson are convinced of his innocence *they* will make an appeal of the same sort. If they rest in silence, or if they content themselves with resting upon a general denial, they cannot hope for credit. The allegation is of a nature too *black* to be suffered to remain in suspense. We should be glad to hear of its refutation. We give it to the world under the firmest belief that such a refutation *never can be made*. The AFRICAN VENUS is said to officiate as housekeeper at Monticello. When Mr. Jefferson has read this article, he will find leisure to estimate how much has been lost or gained by so many unprovoked attacks upon

J. T. CALLENDER.

"James T. Callender." I repeated that familiar name once again. "James T. Callender."

My mother burst into tears.

"Sweet Jesus! You mean that's printed in the newspaper for everyone to see?"

"Not only *The Recorder*, Mama, everywhere in Virginia, by the *Examiner*, in the *Virginia Gazette* in Lynchburg, in Fredericksburg, in Philadelphia, in Washington City, in New York." I had left out the political parts she couldn't understand.

"But what does it mean, daughter?" For once, my mother didn't know what to say.

"It means, Mama, that they are attacking the master through me, to hurt him. They accuse him of many more dreadful things than miscegenation. They accuse him of being a coward, of trying to seduce another man's wife, of being an infidel. . . ."

My voice had broken. In truth, I knew so little, entombed here at Monticello. Maria and Martha certainly knew more, but refused to speak. Even Maria. So we remained in our cocoons of silence, not able to comfort one another. For once, the slave intelligence had been silent. Yet the plantations all knew. My shame was the common knowledge of every field hand in Virginia. The intelligence passed from those who could read to the multitudes who could not.

"And Thomas Jefferson, up in Washington City? What does he say?" my mother wanted to know.

"He doesn't say anything, Mama. He doesn't even know that I know about the newspaper articles."

"He ain't said *nothing* to you?"

"No."

"And to his friends? . . ."

"He has kept his silence. He has said nothing to no one."

"But it can't go on like this! He will sell you and the children . . . out of Virginia. O God, have mercy on us!"

"God," I said, "has nothing to do with this."

My mother looked up. "And Martha?"

"She knows as much as I, or perhaps more, but she is as silent as her father."

"And Maria?"

"Maria, too, is silent."

"All are silent?" my mother asked. Her voice was small in the empty, white-draped room where we sat facing each other, mother and daughter, two generations of white men's concubines.

"Oh, no. His friends are rallying around him, denying everything. Denying that I exist. Calling Callender the most foul and blasphemous slanderer ever to be born. Meriwether Jones, the editor of the *Richmond Enquirer*, has wished Callender in Hell by means of the James River. He's the one who wrote: 'Is it strange, therefore, that a servant of Mr. Jefferson's at a house where so many strangers resort, who is daily engaged in the ordinary vocations of the family life, like *thousands* of others, should have a mulatto child? Certainly not....' "

My mouth twitched. *Certainly not.* I thought of my sister Critta, my half sister Mary, my mother's daughters, Nance and Betty. I thought of my mother, Elizabeth, and of her mother, the African. I thought of all black bondswomen everywhere in the South at God's and Fate's mercy. Thousands.

"But he, the masta, says nothing?"

"Nothing, Mama. Even this summer, when we were all ignorant of the danger, there were hints in the newspapers, but it is this one, Callender's story, that has caused all the furor."

There had been others, more serious because they had been closer to home, I thought. Callender was a foreigner, a Northerner, an enemy. These other men were friends and neighbors. The editor of the *Frederick-Town Herald*, for example, had been seen in Charlottesville, by Burwell and Davey Bowles, asking questions of servants and neighbors and townspeople and of the small outlying farmers who got their wood from Monticello. All those who had known my master from birth knew who I was. They knew who my mother was. There was one calumnious article after another, the most recent from the *Virginia Gazette*, whose article had asked the same questions and got the same answers. *"Why have you not married some worthy of your own complexion?"* one had written in an editorial.

Then there was the ballad called "Black and White" that had appeared in Boston and Philadelphia in April.

A statesman so great, and a damsel so neat,
Convers'd about things where they were;
They ogl'd and chatted, and made it quite late,
Tall Tom was the name of the statesman so great,
And *Sally* the name of the *fair.*

And now says *Tall Tom*, since to-morrow I start,
With a message for Washington city,
I cannot help saying before I depart,
I fear that *Tom Paine*, with his air and his art,
Has made, or will make, an attack on your heart
And enter it even to pity.

Do you mean to affront me, the *fair Sally* said,
I ne'er heard the like in my life.
For if you be living, or if you be dead,
I swear I will never love one in your stead;
I'll be constant and true as a wife.

Behold me, *false Ethiop*, behold me he cried,
Learn the *cause* and *effect* of this evil,
"God grants, that to punish your falsehood and pride,
"My ghost, with a message from hell cut and dried,
"Should come at this moment, stand close by your side,
"Then carry you off to the devil."

Thus saying, his arms around poor *Sally* he grip'd,
Tho's she screech'd to the *people* around,
Her throat from one ear to the other he rip'd,
He pull'd out her tongue, through the floor then he slipp'd,
And never since that has been found.

Twelve times in the year when the moon is at full,
And mortals are snoring in bed,
Her sprite haunts that place all cover'd with wool,
And patiently waits for her *Thomas* to pull,
The tongue by its roots from her head.

Two hundred new slaves with a leap and a pride,
All dance round a high blazing fire,
And when to the end of the circle they come,
They drink out of warming pans full of hot rum,
And this is their toast, "here's success to *Tall Tom*,
"And the devil take *Sal* for a liar."

My eyes filled with tears. I heard my master's voice: "Tell me who die . . . who marry, who hang themselves because they cannot marry. . . ."

I stared at the white back of one of the draped pale damask armchairs from the *hôtel* in Paris, and fondled the richly carved wood.

"I believe he will never say anything to anyone about me."

"Daughter, you don't understand white men. They loves you. Sometimes all they lives. But when you go up against they real life, they white life, white friends, white children, white power, you got to lose. You got to be cut down. You got to be put away. Thomas Jefferson's real mistress is his politics. It was that way with Martha and it's that way with you. Nothing will stand in the way of that. No woman will ever keep him from that. Even a white wife would not have been as bad as this. . . . He will send you away. He has got to do it. His white folks will destroy him if he don't. At least he has got to say what is true is not true. . . ."

"He will not lie, and he cannot avow, so there is nothing left except silence," I said.

"Silence," Elizabeth Hemings spat out into the white room, "or sale."

For one moment my heart seemed to stop as she uttered the dreaded words. Sale! Had I lived too long in Monticello, hidden, petted, spoiled, and loved? Had I forgotten it was love that ceded, and not the white world? Then I said:

"He will not sell me, Mama. And he will not abandon me or send me or the children away. Not for me, not for his daughters, not for his friends, not for his enemies, not even for the presidency."

"And why, pray, daughter?"

"Because he cannot live without me."

It was true. I had made it so. This had been what I had wanted. There was no triumph, no smugness, no pride; there was not even joy in my voice. Only the reality of how it was between us.

"He cannot live without me." The words fell like pebbles in the room. They seemed to take a long time to reach my mother, as if they had been thrown down a deep well. But the words struck the sides of my being like flint against flint, and, like flint, struck fire in me. I had won.

"I'll have the keys to the mansion now, Mama."

After a moment, my mother unfastened the great iron ring with its score of keys. The dull glint of forged iron struck the light. Their metallic music was the only sound in the room except for the tick of the clock. I knew she would never understand. Why now? Why at a time when we had been betrayed by servants and neighbors, why, when everything was lost, when I should be fleeing for my life and those of my children, when I should be paralyzed with fear, why had I decided to stand, when I had never stood before? She would never understand. Yet I knew I was right. This was the line. This was the battle. This was the test that Thomas Jefferson would have to pass. If he passed this trial, it meant victory for us. A feeling almost of elation filled me. We had the power of love on our side. We were stronger and better than the monstrous iniquity we had sprung from. I held out my hands. My mother placed the mass of iron into them. I took the keys and weighed them, and then, without a word, attached them to the black ribbon at the waist of my black-and-white calico dress. The keys hung low and nestled into the folds of my skirt. Elizabeth Hemings recognized the orderly transition of power just as my master did; that day, Monticello had passed from one ruler to the next. Her reign was over.

"We wait, Mama," I said a moment later, "in silence. We wait and we let them rant and rave. But, if they really want to hear about Southern gentlemen and Negro mistresses, we have some stories to tell, no, Mama? We can start with John Marshall, the chief justice of the United States. Virginians talk in their sleep, you once said, Mama. And who hears them? Their servants."

Elizabeth Hemings looked at me with dawning respect. I hadn't spent three years in France for nothing.

"Now you know why Martha and Maria have left for Washington, when they have always refused until now," I said.

"To dampen the scandal by their presence."

"Yes. And to keep Dolley Madison from the head of the presidential table."

"I never could figure why they both left."

"Now you can. And now, I want the word spread among the slave population. My name is never again to be mentioned. Nor those of my children. To anyone black or white. I do not exist anymore, nor do my children. My name on our people's lips is forbidden. Forbidden! Spread it among our people, black and white, on pain of being fired or sold. And tell Jim I want to see him."

I dismissed my mother.

It was only when Fanny and Edy returned from Washington that I learned the amplitude and the viciousness of the campaign which had raged about us. It was from Fanny that I heard the part of a poem by the famous Irish poet Thomas Moore that referred to me, and that was making the rounds of the kitchens and salons in Washington and Virginia, in New York and Baltimore, in Boston and Philadelphia.

Fanny, who could write, had copied it out on the back of a sheet of butcher's paper in her large childish scrawl:

> The patriot, fresh from Freedom's council come,
> Now pleased retires to lash his slaves at home;
> Or woo, perhaps some black Aspasia's charms,
> And dream of freedom in his bondsmaid's arms.

I stared at the large printed letters. Freedom. What had I won? I had bound him to me as surely as I was bound to him. Nothing could change that. Not poems or ballads, not slander or insults, not the crudeness of mankind. My tears fell on the oiled paper and rolled off, making no mark, just as I made no mark on the surface of the world; except for these lewd cries of indignation, crude obscene scrawls, smirking winks of slander and perfidy.

Fanny's excited voice dented my thoughts.

"You is the most famous black lady in the whole United States! I tells you, you is famous! I saw a letter about you in a Philadelphia newspaper, but it was too long and hard for me to copy it. And in Washington—you is the talk of the town! But we servants don't say nothing about what we knows, or don't know. And poor Masta Jefferson—as if every Virginia gentleman that holds the title ain't messed with a black mistress. Why they family gives them one at sixteen or seventeen. How can they expect that they don't cherish them later? I do declare, white people are one strange breed of humanity. They do everything they want and then cry distress when what they *do* gets around to people who don't do it, because they ain't got it to *do* it with! I do declare, I'm glad I got me a black husband. A good black man. And don't have to be sniffing after no white masta who is hell on earth!"

My mother looked at the bisquit-colored Fanny.

"Yo Mammy," she muttered.

"Yourn," replied Fanny, evenly, without blinking.

She was a match for my mother, and she knew it. Not only did she have the estimable advantage of being cook at the President's House, she could read and write as well. Fanny held Elizabeth Hemings's eye, but, before the onslaught came, I stepped between them.

"Enough, Fanny," I said. "I know you and Davey so tried Master Jefferson's patience with your squabbling that he sent for Mister Bacon to sell you both in Alexandria." I looked at her. "I trust you begged your way back into his good graces, since you are standing here and not on an auction block."

"I hear it's mostly died down," Fanny said contritely. "I expect it's finished, Sally. But Lord knows, you sure made a stir! You can't imagine. . . . Them white folks is outraged."

"Then let it be finished, Lord God. 'Cause we is sick of it at Monticello," Elizabeth Hemings said as she took Fanny by the shoulders, and with a slight push, propelled her toward the door of her kitchens.

He still would sell a slave in pique or to assure his domestic tranquillity. He was still white. He was still the master. And he was not the same in his white world. My master amongst white Americans was not the man I knew. I wished he would come home. I wished he would come home where he was safe and loved. People, I thought wearily, like horses, tire; and the uses of silence born and bred into every slave, would serve me well.

CHAPTER 33

MARCH 1803

Love is, in a great degree, an arbitrary passion, and will reign, like some other stalking mischiefs, by its own authority, without designing to reason.

> MARY WOLLSTONECRAFT, *Vindication of the Rights of Women*, 1794

> *Duty's a slave that keeps the keys,*
> *But love, the Master goes in and out*
> *Of his goodly chambers with a song and shout*
> *Just as he please—just as he please.*
> DINAH MARIA MULOCK CRAIK (date unknown)

It was March before Thomas Jefferson arrived again on his mountain. His slave family rushed to greet him. Thomas, Beverly, and Harriet. He seemed to hesitate in greeting them, then he saw her. She approached timidly.

"Thomas," she said softly.

"Thine own," he replied, adding his harsh short laugh.

"Thomas. Thomas. We . . . thou cannot. The risk . . ." But the risk has already been taken. And pride had sealed it. They had won.

"The thermometer at sunrise today, my darling, was thirty-four degrees. I have marked it in my book. I have taken it every day for the past four months and I didn't drop the thermometer once."

His voice was husky and scarred as it was that day in Paris. She began to cry. She knew he would listen to no one, accept no advice, no opinions, nor have this passion discussed, revoked, diluted, appended, crossed out, objected to, or any part of it destroyed. She would not be excised. She would not be censored. She would not be discarded. She would remain at Monticello.

There was irony and love in his voice:

"Hold, little one," he said. "The peach trees begin to blossom and I see the well has plenty of water in it after having been dry for eighteen months."

She pressed her head into his chest, and his great hands came up and cupped her skull. Her tears wet his vest and shirt. Here was her victory, written in his haggard and loving face. They were like the lone survivors of an earthquake. It had shaken the mountain, but the mountain was still there.

Thomas Jefferson sat making delicate sketches of the plan for his new pleasure ground: a grove of the largest trees, shaded with poplar, oak, maple, linden, and his beloved ash trees. A green labyrinth, which had at its center a small temple: a safe place.

His troubles were far from over.

This trip was to try to avoid the possibility of a duel with his old friend John Walker over his wife. Callender had not stopped his pen. With the aid of the Northern papers he had enlarged its scope to include the Langhorne letter to George Washington involving his nephew Peter Carr. Then there was the everlasting charge of atheism, of Jacobinism, and now the threat of publishing his letters to John Walker over something that had happened thirty-three years ago! It was insane.

"Why have you not married some woman of your own complexion?" The Virginia Gazette.

He ground his teeth. Why? "Tell me who die," he thought, "who marry, who hang themselves because they cannot marry. . . ." He prayed that Sally had not seen most of what had been written about them. He came home feeling defeated. Everything reminded him of his two families and the problems they faced. The presence of Maria and Martha in Washington last winter had dampened all but the most infamous gossipmongers. They had not deserted him. He had his explanation with them and now he must arrange a meeting with his injured friend and avoid a duel at all cost. He had already talked his son-in-law Thomas Mann out of a duel with his cousin John

Randolph for the sake of Martha; now Madison must do the same for him. He could not leave either his white family or his slave family unprotected by his death.

Thomas Jefferson looked up at his slave wife as she entered his rooms. She appeared terribly small to him and fragile.

She wouldn't know the worst!

The following day James Madison arrived at Monticello. He was bringing good news. He had interceded in Thomas Jefferson's favor, and there would be no duel.

"I cannot tell you how relieved I am, Mr. Madison, with the outcome of this unfortunate affair . . . and how I thank you."

"Mr. President, I don't think Mr. John Walker was any more anxious for a duel than you."

"My dear Mr. Madison, I've never even held a pistol in my hand. The very idea of one man murdering another in the name of injury is insanity. We already have enough ways of men killing men without inventing an etiquette for it."

"The law of Virginia 'honor' is a rather crude one, sir."

"Mostly the law of vanity, dear sir. I am a simple man. I accept with relief your intervention in this senseless affair and am quite satisfied that Mr. Walker has accepted my apology."

James Madison noted a slight hesitation. Thomas Jefferson was anything except a "modest" man and "insanity" or not, he was a Virginian brought up in its codes and mores. The Walker affair had distressed him much more than he was willing to admit. And his vanity had indeed been touched. There was yet one more thing.

"As for the other calumny . . ." began James Madison, "I believe Mr. Monroe would be happy to take her."

Madison couldn't bring himself to say Sally Hemings.

"Take her?"

Thomas Jefferson swayed slightly and the blood rushed from his face.

"Temporarily, of course," added James Madison, alarmed at the sudden pallor of the man standing before him.

"Take her where?"

"Why doesn't she . . . I believe . . . she has a sister Thenia at Mr. Monroe's. She could . . . retire there with her children until the time when—"

James Madison raised his eyes from the silver buttons on Thomas Jefferson's waistcoat and looked directly into his eyes. How could Thomas Jefferson not know in what political danger he was? He, James Madison, simply had the duty to warn him that Virginia would not tolerate, even from Thomas Jefferson, certain unpardonable things. He had to understand.

James Madison involuntarily stepped back. The cold blue eyes had now turned a deep aquamarine.

"The Hemingses are mine," said Jefferson. "All of them. I will deal with them personally."

"I didn't mean to presume . . ." began Madison. He concentrated on controlling the tremor in his voice. He brought his handkerchief out of his waistcoat and mopped his brow. He had gone too far. Too far for his own good. Relieved, he realized that Thomas Jefferson had already dismissed the subject. His face had taken on the serene expression Madison knew so well: his public face. The flash of his inner turmoil had been suppressed. Thomas Jefferson seemed even taller to Madison as, towering over his small person, he took him by the shoulder and flashed one of his rare smiles. The sudden intimacy made Madison blush.

"We have come this far, Mr. Madison. But we still have a long road to travel . . . full of the most dangerous ruts for the carriage of State." Thomas Jefferson's smile disappeared. "You know, Mr. Madison, how I feel about your rightful place in the political scheme of things. . . . I'm an old man. Compromise comes hard to me, but you have a brilliant talent for negotiation. A nation isn't shaped in a featherbed. . . ."

Madison started. It was a strange choice of words, but Thomas Jefferson didn't seem to notice.

"Shall we get back to the important issues of the day? Put this demeaning and ridiculous affair behind us. You have a long way to travel, my dear Madison. After all, we can't disappoint Mrs. Madison, can we? She's dead set on

redecorating the President's House. And God knows, it
needs it!"

Both men laughed.

The night before he left the safety of Monticello for
Washington City, Thomas Jefferson sat alone in his study
and brooded on what he had written in his account book in
August 1800. He knew now that there would be no duel,
thanks to the sturdy and tenacious Madison. Callender
could be silenced—the others were mere copiers. He could
end the outcry in the Republican press; if only his friends
could end the clamor in the Federalist press.

He must bring his families through the crisis of Callender but he must navigate the United States through the
bloody aftermath of Napoleon and the specter of his troops
arriving at the Mississippi; he must control an undeclared
war on Tripoli; cope with the Indian boundaries which
were constantly violated as the nation pushed them farther and farther West; he must reduce the public debt,
distribute the surplus in the Treasury—at least, at last,
the slave trade was outlawed; and he must bring to a successful end the secret negotiations with France for the
purchase of Louisiana and mount his expedition to the
Pacific. He had already chosen his secretary, Meriwether
Lewis, as head of the expedition, and he would take back
to Washington City his new secretary, Lewis Harvie, who
was loyal enough to have threatened to kill James Callender.

Callender. His Judas. Sally Hemings was only a pretext.
Before he had left for Washington, he would put down his
for all to see. He had also made a census of his family.

He lit his candle in the darkening study, opened his
account book and wrote:

A CENSUS OF MY FAMILY

Males:	free whites under 10	2	*Females:*	3	4
	10 under 16	1		0	1
	16 under 26	3		1	4
	26 under 45	1		0	1
	45 upwards	1		0	1
Slaves:	93				

Shortly after Thomas Jefferson had returned to Washington I looked at his account book and found the pages open to the census he had written in it of his family.

I stared at it for a long time, and then softly closed it. My master had counted Thomas, Beverly, and Harriet as free and white.

Our love had been denounced and we had been betrayed in Virginia. Even now, the hate, the epithets made me shiver. Did he think I hadn't heard them all? *Slave, whore, slut, concubine, Black Sal, Dusky Sally, paramour, blackamoor, wench, a slave paramour with fifteen or thirty gallants of all colors, including Thomas Paine, black wench and her mulatto litter, mahogany-colored charmer, Monticellian Sally, Sooty Sal, black Aspasia* . . . nothing was too horrible for me: my heart cut out, my tongue pulled out by its roots, my body burned, my throat slit from ear to ear, my soul sent to everlasting Hell. Perhaps they would at least triumph in sending my soul to Hell, but for the rest it was too late. My master and I were both anchored to a past and a passion nothing could disavow. I had prayed for proof and he had given it to me.

He had paid the worst of all possible prices: public humiliation. To have been scourged at the public whipping post for slaves would have been easier for him than that price: the loss of his public image, the façade he cherished almost as much as he cherished the façade of Monticello.

He had paid. There was something he could do: remain silent. And this silence would be payment. Payment for my servitude, which he would not change. Payment for our children, whom he did not recognize. He had paid with a kind of helpless, bewildered pride, for I was Monticello.

CHAPTER 34

MONTICELLO, 1803–1805

"Familia" did not (originally) signify the composite ideal of sentimentality and domestic strife in the present day philistine mind. Among the Romans, it did not even apply in the beginning to the leading couple and its children, but to the slaves alone. Famulus means domestic slave and familia is the aggregate number of slaves belonging to one man. . . . The expression (familia) was invented by the Romans in order to designate a new social organism the head of which had a wife, children and a number of slaves under his paternal authority and according to Roman law, the right of life and death over all of them.

FRIEDRICH ENGELS, *The Origin of the Family, Private Property, and the State*, 1884

God forgive us, but ours is a monstrous system, a wrong and an iniquity! Like the patriarchs of old, our men live all in one house with their wives and concubines: the mulattos one sees in every family partly resemble the white children. Any lady is ready to tell you who is the father of all the mulatto children in everybody's household but her own. Those, she seems to think, drop from the sky.

MARY BOYKIN CHESTNUT, *A Diary from Dixie*, 1840–76

Oh, how can you thing of slaves and motherhood! Look into my eyes, Marianne, and think of love.

KATE CHOPIN, "The Maid of Saint Phillippe," 1891–92

The news of the Louisiana Purchase came like a bolt of thunder at the beginning of the summer. The guns were fired in Richmond, the bells rang, and there was great rejoicing. The news of Master Monroe's success in Paris caused a sensation all over the nation and made him the hero that would someday make him president. My master had doubled the territory of the United States, purchasing the whole expanse of Louisiana and the Floridas for fifteen million dollars.

"Typical of Thomas Jefferson," Elizabeth Hemings declared, not without pride, from the vastness of her kitchens. "He sets out to buy four acres and a mule, and ends up with a plantation and a herd of cattle!"

"No, Mama. He set out to buy New Orleans and he has ended up buying an empire."

Now that we had weathered the worst of Callender and the Federalist newspapers, it seemed we had reason enough to celebrate. On the sixteenth of July, the cabinet agreed to the purchase of Louisiana, and on the seventeenth, Meriwether Jones danced a jig on the west lawn of Monticello. It was not to celebrate the Louisiana Purchase but to celebrate the death of James T. Callender. He had been found, dead that morning, in the James River, drowned in three feet of water.

A year passed. A year free of scandal, although *Monticellian Sally* still rose now and again in the press.

My master won his re-election by a landslide, losing only four electoral votes out of one hundred and seventy-six, and not one for Aaron Burr. It was his moment of greatest triumph, for he knew, if he ever was to know, that the whole nation loved him. I felt keenly the pleasure of his triumph. Gone were his protests of disdain, his abhorrence of public office, his flight from using power. Truly, this outpouring of love and gratitude was enough to turn the head of a man who, more than anything else, loved to be loved.

His sixty-one years lay lightly on his shoulders. His hair was now gray. His troubles of five years ago were gone with the daily horseback riding in which he indulged. His skin was clear and high in color. His thick neck and wrists gave an impression of great physical force, even though his frame was slender, long and shackling. His feelings ran strong and deep, buried under the surface of a seemingly sunny and even-tempered disposition, but I knew him as he was: passionate to the point of cruelty, sensitive to the edge of brutality, eager for approbation to the limits of honesty, constant in love, lonely behind his façade of perfection, and imperfect in his fear of loneliness. Our fate had been tested by scandal, our love tempered by it. And our family grew like a many-rooted oak on our mountain. We were safe. Or so I believed.

In the spring they brought Maria up the mountain on a litter made out of rope and wood borne tenderly by Burwell, John, Davey, and Israel. She was dying from the complications of childbirth.

"Things change, only to remain the same," he said, standing framed in the doorway of her room. And it was true that it was now I rather than my mother who nursed and fed and washed and tended Maria, and it was my son Thomas who stood with Maria's son, Francis, wide-eyed in the hall.

The horrible ulcerating breast was surely gangrenous by now. The pain so intense that even laudanum gave no ease. In the afternoon, when the pain seemed the worst, I would sit for hours holding Maria in my arms, and thus her father would find us when he came to the door of her room to stare silently. He had withdrawn in a solitude with his books and his horses, as if they could nullify the fact of Maria's agony. But her agony was not to be nullified, neither by him nor me nor Maria.

I would brush her long auburn hair that fell to her waist, still lush and luxurious, until it began to come out by the handful. This I tried to hide from her, saving all the long strands, as the hairdressers in Paris used to do, to supplement the natural hair of their mistresses with chignons and poufs.

A nauseating sweetish smell clung to this exquisite woman not yet twenty-six, and I desperately changed her three or four times a day. She who had never been overly fond of dress or ornament was calling for her jewels. She who was always vexed by allusions to her beauty now required them from me, her sister, her husband, her father.

After her husband's visit, for which she would endure hours of toilette, she would turn her face to the wall and cry. As for her son, she would not let him enter her room.

My own anguish lay buried deep within me. I was only
waiting.

The day was fine and hazy, with a mist that hung low,
even in the afternoon. On the mountains, with their tops
bright with sunlight, every blossom and bush pushed its
way toward the warmth of the sun. Suddenly, there was
only the sound of my own breathing in the room. It was so
still that I looked at the sealed window to make sure that
the sun, the sky, and the unfolding nature were still there.
And then I knew why it was so silent.

She had died. Without a word, her hand in mine. I too
made no sound. No sound the human voice could make
could express the pain I felt. I stayed beside her a long time
before I finally rushed from the room to inform the small
group that was still at supper: her husband, her son, her
father, her sister. Then I returned to the room to wash and
bathe her for the last time. Like my mother before me, I
wept, for now I could weep as I wrapped her in white linen
and then covered everything in the room. I descended into
the garden, and with Wormley, I cut every spring flower
there was, leaving not one remaining in all the vast gardens
to insult her death with its life. I filled her room with them,
scattering them on the beds, and blocking the light with
them.

Only then did I allow her white family into the room.

We stood staring at each other over the fresh grave of
Maria and that of her child, who had succumbed to convulsions.

Maria's death settled between us like a hungering beast,
separating us from each other, ugly and terrible. Fear
descended upon us, and over her grave we clutched at life.
We clung to each other in our despair and our grief and we
hurried back up the mountain as if the Reaper himself
were pursuing us.

A new life was made that day, for my third son, Madison, would be born nine months afterward to the very
hour. . . .

The second four years of my master's mandate began.
For the second time, he had walked to the Capitol flanked

by excited crowds and popular acclaim. For the second time, he delivered an inaudible speech to the gathered crowds, and again it was only the next day when they were able to read it in the newspapers that they knew what he had said.

Aaron Burr killed Alexander Hamilton in a duel at Weehawken in New Jersey, a misty July dawn in 1804, but my master's country was at peace except with one nation.

An irresistible current moving west was making it a white man's country. The white man was crushing the Indian as he crushed the slave under the heel of the boot he placed on every inch of soil he could tread. The land which now stretched from the Carolinas to Vermont, and from the Atlantic shore to the Appalachian Mountains contained, according to the new census, five million whites, two million slaves, one million mulattoes, and an undetermined number of native Americans.

In the past four years, my master, as president, by fair means and foul, had transferred fifty million acres of Indian land from their sovereignty to the United States, paying a total of one hundred and forty-two thousand dollars; one-tenth of a penny an acre, or as he said, the equivalent of one hundred and forty-three prime male Negro slaves.

For another four years, he would be lost to me and Monticello. I was barred from the President's House. But I determined one day to set my foot on its planks. Davey Bowles brought me secretly, at my stubborn request, to Washington that winter. I traveled by night in a curtained carriage, and slipped into the mansion by the servants' entrance. It was more than ten years since I had ventured from Monticello.

Shielded by the Monticello servants there, hidden during the day by Burwell, I roamed at night the unfinished cavernous rooms that I knew I would never see again. I noted the fixtures, the hangings, the paintings, and the stiff old-fashioned furniture that had been installed by the Adamses. After the elegance of the Hôtel de Langeac, the President's House seemed crude, barnlike, cold and dismal. The roof leaked, there was no heat, the stairway sagged, gloom and dust were everywhere. Even Thomas Jefferson had an unkempt, run-down appearance.

The large kitchens, where Edy and Fanny worked with
Peter, were the only cheerful rooms in the whole house. I
visited Petit, who was installed in Georgetown, a gentleman farmer, and Davey Bowles managed to take me out
driving in one of the carriages to see Washington City.

It was a place of incredible distances, interspersed with a
few scattered buildings; a quagmire of mud when the sun
shone, and a sea of frozen ruts during the winter nights.
The gaunt wooden skeleton of the Capitol building rose
like a gallows on the hill, while swarms of workmen and
slaves struggled in the soft earth with the enormous white
stone that had begun to sheathe it. Surrounding the Capitol
was the Federal City, which consisted of seven or eight
boardinghouses, the best being Conrad and McMunn, and
all of them brimming over with senators and representatives. There was a tailor shop, a shoemaker, a printer, a
washerwoman, a grocer, a stationer, a dry-goods establishment, and an oysterhouse.

This, then, was the new capital of the United States. The
swamps on all sides emitted the putrid odors of decay and
a rancid fog hung over the city half the time, as the
inhabitants fled at the first hint of the malarial fevers that
periodically swept the city.

I inspected the half-finished Capitol, where John Trumbull's paintings would hang; the mansions surrounded by
wastelands stretching down Pennsylvania Avenue to
Georgetown reminded me of those that had been con-
structed back when I was in Paris on the Champs-Elysées.

The Champs-Elysées. It stretched dimly now, its per-
spective fifteen years behind me. The fashionable golden
and white buildings that had been so "modern" then must
have already settled into old-fashioned respectability. Respectability! I laughed to think what the Federalists would
think of Sally Hemings in the President's House. But such
was my master's popularity that even if I had been found
out, no one would have now dared to print the story.
"Dusky Sally" was as dead as James T. Callender.

But, as fate would have it, just before I was to return
with Davey Bowles to Monticello, I met in the confines of
the gloomy mansion the only person in Washington sure to
recognize me: Dolley Payne Todd Madison. She, who already considered the President's House hers, had come

in, unannounced, by the kitchens, and surprised me in the company of my master.

"Why, Sally Hemings of Monticello!"

I remained silent.

"What on earth are you doing in Washington? Have you deserted Monticello for the kitchens of the President's House?" Not at all shocked, she had remarked my condition.

"Another Hemings for Monticello? Good! We need all the little pickaninnies we can get these days. . . . And if it is a boy, could I ask you to name it Madison, and you'll have a fair gift for the name, too! I promise you." She looked at my master. "Might she do that, Mr. Jefferson? Name it Madison if it's a boy, and Dolley if it's a girl? now don't you say no. . . ."

The flat pasty face with its upturned mouth smirked with malice. The tiny bead-eyes sunk into the flesh of her puffy face matched the necklace around her fat short neck. She was no longer a beauty, Dolley Madison. Ensconced in the ruffles and frills she loved, always in pastel colors that did nothing for her complexion, which had turned sallow in her middle age, she resembled nothing more than a multi-colored cabbage.

My master stood helplessly and more than a little foolishly aside. He was the President of the United States, yet he could say nothing.

I bided my time while she took her revenge. Her marriage to Master Madison had not produced children, and her bitterness and disappointment in this made her more cruel perhaps than she would have been had she been a mother. Well, I thought, why not? Madison was a fine name, and I truly liked Master Madison, but no child of mine, I vowed, would ever be named Dolley.

In the dim, drafty hallway, we circled one another like antagonized she-wolves—the rough floor planks cut into my slippers. I kept my eyes on the neatly shod feet of Dolley Madison. Her boots were pale-blue suede. I kept my eyes down, but I staked my territory. Even if I had been white, I would have been trespassing, but being black, I was an invader of all that was sacred.

She stepped back out of my circle, our pact made. A name for silence. That she should symbolically try to take the seed planted in my womb which rightfully should have been planted in the womb of a white woman—in her womb—was her duty. Mine was to survive and prevail without murder. We both did our duty.

Madison Hemings was born the following January, on the nineteenth day of that month, a bright, sandy-haired, and gray-eyed boy.

CHAPTER 35

MONTICELLO, 1806–1808

The Southern white woman is the chief slave of the master's harem.

DOLLEY MADISON, 1837

I was amazed to see called black and treated as such: children as white as myself.

LE COMPTE DE VOLNEY, *Monticello,* 1776

"Jamey done 'strolled.' "

"What?"

"He gone. Masta, Jim, Bacon, whole plantation knows where he is but ain't nobody going after him. . . ."

As usual, it was Elizabeth Hemings who had the news of Jamey's flight first. Critta's son was now seventeen, the same bitter, bright, violent seventeen that his namesake, my brother James, had been. I wondered when Jamey had decided to run away. Was it when he had witnessed his father and his uncle fighting over his mother? Or had it been that lonely winter when he had been left on the mountain while his mother had fled to Bermuda Hundred with Maria?

For the first time in his life, Thomas Jefferson had had a slave, James Hubbard, flogged severely in public, not just because he kept running away, which he had done with regularity now since he was twelve, but because he kept running away from *him.* . . . Yet he must have known in his heart that this one would never be a slave again. He would die first—die being beaten or die running. I, who had written his pass for him, had accepted that. Why did my master not accept something so simple? There came a

time in some men's lives when they were simply no longer
slave material. If that meant that they were dead men, well,
they were dead men. That's all. The imponderable and
excessive rage of masters at fleeing slaves mystified me. It
was not just a matter of losing valuable property. They all,
including my own, acted so abandoned, ready to kill rather
than love again. What was it the slave did to the master's
pride, I wondered, for him to be so mortally wounded by
flight?

"Thomas, you know that Jamey's gone?"

"Yes. Who told you?"

"Mama, of course."

"There were some Mohicans in the neighborhood, and
he stole off with them, or was stolen by them!"

"Ran off with the Indians?" I asked it innocently, but he
knew as well as I that it was the route many escaping
slaves took: refuge with Indians. If they could reach an
Indian nation, it was the safest and surest route to freedom.

"They will probably take him across the Mississippi or
to another tribe who will get him to Canada. I doubt if he
will stay with them. He is white enough to pass for white,
so let him stroll."

There was no rancor in his voice, but the chill of deser-
tion was there. Even for Jamey. Jamey had chosen freedom. My master no longer "loved" him enough to go after
him. I breathed a sigh of relief. He would not send the
patrols after him. Thomas was now seventeen. When had
he realized that the master was his father? And how long
did I have before he too would stroll?

I did not have long to ponder Jamey's flight, for hard on
his disappearance came an event that underlined the mortal
danger we lived in on our mountain: a double murder. It
was a murder that struck special terror in the gentry—
poisoning, the one killer all Southern whites lived in dread
of. More than one Big House cook had been hanged in
Albemarle County on suspicion, or conviction, of poisoning her white folks.

It was my mother who brought me the news: George
Wythe, Liddy Broadnax, and their son Michael Brown had
been poisoned,

"Well, like the Richmond papers say," she announced,

"it happened a little more than two weeks ago, that is the poisonings happen then, 'cause Masta Wythe, he just died. The bells in Richmond was a-tolling like the end of the world, but poor Michael, he died more than a week ago after horrible suffering. They cut him open—the doctors—and they found the inflammation in the stomach and the bowels that's caused by yellow arsenic, like Wormley use for the moles and groundhogs."

Michael Wythe Brown, two years younger than my Thomas, was now dead. He had been here for James's Christmas emancipation. I picked up eighteen-month-old Madison. There were now two Madisons. Martha had named her last son Madison to cancel out mine in the affections of his father. White vengeance had many faces.

"And what are they saying in the Richmond kitchens, Mama?"

"Well, Masta Wythe's nephew George Sweney been charged with murder and the white folks is up in arms and having a fit. You know how scared they is of poison with all us cooks. . . . Ain't nothing caused such a sensation in Richmond since the British. You know old Masta Wythe considered a saint in Virginia. You know how well loved he was, how mild and kind and how he done served on the Continental Congress and signed the Declaration of Independence, and served on the High Court and all. . . . Well, he done wrote a will giving his house to Lyddy Broadnax and his property and half his bank stocks to his son Michael Brown. The rest of his money he left to his nephew George Sweney, with the regulation that if Michael died before Sweney, Sweney would get Michael's part, too. Lyddy says Sweney found out about the will the night before Whitsunday, the twenty-fifth. Masta Sweney came as he sometimes did when Masta Wythe was at court, and went to his room and found his keys of his private desk. He opened the desk, and when Lyddy went in she found him reading a paper that her masta had told her was his will. She done tied it herself with a blue ribbon.

"Well, in the morning, when breakfast was nearly ready, Masta Sweney came into the kitchen. Lyddy said he went to the fire and took the coffee pot to the table while she was toasting the bread. He poured a cupful for himself and then set the pot down. She saw him throw a little white paper in the fire. He then drank the coffee he had poured for hisself and ate the toast with some fresh butter. He told her goodbye and went about his business. She didn't think there was anything wrong then. In a little while, she heard old Masta Wythe's bell. 'Lyddy, did I leave my keys in my desk yesterday, for I found them there last night?' he said to her. And she said, 'I suppose so, Masta, 'cause I saw Masta George at the desk reading that paper you gave me to put there. Masta George said you had sent him to read it, and to tell you what he thought of it.' Old Masta Wythe said, 'I fear I am getting old, Lyddy, for I am becoming more and more forgetful every day. Take these things away, and give Michael his breakfast, and get your own, Lyddy.' She gave poor little Michael his breakfast and as much coffee as he wanted, and then drank a cup herself. After that, with the hot water in the kettle, she washed the plates, emptied out the coffee grounds, and scrubbed the coffee pot bright. By that time she was so sick with cramps she could hardly see, and Lord, she was poisoned and her son and her master as well. And now they're both dead and Lyddy Broadnax wish she was. Her son—her only son—dead. And they had had such hopes for him. Wasn't no boy in Richmond educated like Michael. Masta Wythe didn't spare nothing for his education. And freed him too, from the beginning, and Lyddy as well. He had the finest books. . . ."

For the first time I saw fear in my mother's eyes.

"Who did she tell all this to, Mama?"

"Well, first to the doctor, Foushee, then to the other doctors who opened up poor Masta Wythe and found the same inflammation as in Michael. Then she had to tell it to the Court of Examination. This was after Michael died. Before then she was suffering something terrible and Michael was suffering worse than either her or Masta Wythe. She was so sick that she didn't even know when her son died. It was the Sunday after the poisoning that Masta Wythe, dying himself, found out his son just died. He cried out, drew a long breath, and said pathetic-like, 'Poor boy.' Well, it seems that Masta Wythe immediately called for his will to change it, since he knew by then he was mur-

dered. 'I am murdered,' he said, and he struck George
Sweney from his will. 'Let me die righteous,' were his last
words."

The cords on my mother's neck stood out. Her eyes
seemed to be on some horrible object far in the distance
coming toward her. Her hair was a silvery white, her skin
darkened by age, but hardly wrinkled. Rather it seemed
solidified. It was neither flesh nor stone, but a thin, fragile,
paperlike substance hardly covering her bone and muscle.
Her eyesight was intact and she had all of her teeth.

"But that George Sweney, he'll hang for it, won't he?"

"I think not, Mama. Black people and mulattoes can't
testify against white people. Lydia Broadnax can't accuse
her son's murderer."

"No! It ain't true!"

"Thomas Jefferson made the law himself. He and
George Wythe."

"No! Lord God. Lyddy. Lyddy."

"There's no sense calling on God. He only takes white
men's testimony," I said with bitterness.

"Oh, Lord Jesus Sweet Saviour have mercy on us black
women," she moaned.

My heart burst. Mama, after seventy-three years of
slavery, still believed in justice. She rose, her body quivering
with age and fury; I looked at her helplessly. I could do
nothing for her. Just as I could do nothing for myself.
Thomas. Michael. Beverly. Madison. What protection did
we have from white vengeance?

"Darling," Elizabeth Hemings whispered suddenly, her
face gray with fright, "you think they'se trying to kill us
all?"

The deaths of Lydia Broadnax's son and lover destroyed
my mother. Her spirit broke. She who had always been
envious of Lydia's freedom and privilege and her son's
education, she who had made freedom and recognition
for herself and her children the supreme goal in her life,
now saw that being free did not lead one from the dangers
of blackness.

All her life, she had urged me to get freedom for the
children; to strive for that magic circle which she thought
was safety, only to find that there was no safety for us

anywhere. There was only one escape from white will and white justice. And she decided to take it.

"Think I'm going to die now," she said simply one day, and she folded her apron and took to her bed. She refused her food. "They" were trying to poison her and she decided to die before she was murdered.

Martha and I spent the days of the summer watching and listening as she strained toward death, her life running out in rivers of words. And, to the end, she clung to the idea that somebody was trying to poison her. We did everything. We ate her food in front of her. Both of us. Martha. Me. We fed the children out of her refused plate. But she opened her mouth only to speak.

"Put your hand on my chest and push down," she had finally whispered. "My heart won't stop beating."

By the end of August, Mama finally won her battle to die. She was buried in the slave cemetery. I was now all alone and the second legacy of blood and kin fell upon me: not only to love but to survive.

I did not know how my master had taken the death of his well-loved friend and benefactor until he came home for the summer after the murders. He had not written from Washington City of the death of his professor, and it was only upon his arrival that I fathomed his grief and his shock.

I learned that he had been mentioned in Wythe's will. He paced the floor as he told me:

"Such an instance of depravity as has been hitherto known to us only in the fables of poets."

I said nothing. George Wythe had flaunted Michael's intelligence, his education, his beauty, had freed him and, by making him his heir, had advertised his parentage for all to know. Against the most sacred law of the South . . . he had gone against the rules and he had paid with what he had loved most: his only son died before his eyes.

"When I think that we all gathered at the Washington Tavern in the capital in March, less than a year and a half ago to celebrate my second inauguration, and John Page asked George to retire and then proposed a toast to him, praising his wisdom and integrity as a magistrate, his zeal and disinterestedness as a patriot!" My master shook his head. "The hall resounded to nine cheers . . . as many as were given to me—" His voice broke. "He left me his library, his scientific instruments, his silver cups and walking stick—" He paused. "And he had made me a guardian of Michael Brown. . . ."

Oh, God, I thought, not only had the quiet, mild-mannered George Wythe advertised his miscegenation by leaving an inheritance to his yellow son, he had advertised the plight of Thomas Jefferson by placing a yellow boy under his guardianship.

By the time the trial began in September, it was famous throughout Virginia. Edmund Randolph, Martha Randolph's cousin by marriage, defended George Sweney. The outcome was as I had predicted. For the murder of George Wythe, signer of the Declaration of Independence, codifier of the Virginia laws, judge in the High Court of the state, George Sweney was acquitted for lack of evidence, despite forged checks in his uncle's name, despite the arsenic found in his room, despite the eyewitness account of Lydia Broadnax, who was never allowed to testify. If it took only a few minutes for the jury to return a verdict of not guilty of the indictment of murder of George Wythe, the indictment for the murder of Michael Brown was dismissed without a trial. For the forged checks in his uncle's name, George Sweney was convicted and sentenced to six months' imprisonment and one hour's exposure on the pillory in the marketplace in Richmond, but he never served even this sentence.

George Sweney was free. Mama, Wythe, and Michael were dead, still freshly in their graves that September day when I stood posed to mount the staircase to my room. I still remember his voice.

"How painful and melancholy to reflect that a man so pure, so upright, so virtuous, and so beloved should have met an unnatural death."

A flash of disbelief went through me. I turned and almost stumbled. He was lying to himself! He was going to lie to himself even about this! Oh God, when would we stop the lies.

"Unnatural death!" I screamed. "It was murder. *Murder!* Don't you understand? Oh, Thomas, can't you face your white race this one time?" He looked up. There was actually surprise in his eyes.

Remember Callender! Remember, Goddamn you, Thomas Jefferson! Remember the hate, remember the filth, remember Callender dead in the mud of the James River! This is what you can expect from your white world. Death and hatred and damnation for you, for me, for the children!

"Free us! Free us! Free us, Thomas!"

"I would have to banish you from me . . . by law, and I cannot. . . ."

"Oh God, how can you keep me . . . us, in such an abomination?" I stood, my back to the staircase as he came toward me.

"By loving you," he said quietly.

"Why do you do it?"

"Because I love you."

Love me and remain a slave.

"And what do you wish me to do about that?" I whispered.

"Love me."

"You think love pardons everything."

"Does it not?" he replied gently, reaching for me.

"Have I not loved you since I was a girl of fifteen, Thomas?"

Love me and remain a slave.

"This is the only way I have to love. This is the only way I have to love and protect you. This is the only way I have to keep you safe."

"The only way?" I whispered. "But you are the President of the United States!"

He said not a word. He had turned stone-white. I reached up and brought his face down to mine, searching his eyes for hope. But I found none. There was no safe place for us. He could no more protect me than my mother could! He thought my safety was in slavery. She had thought it was in freedom. Now I knew that both of them were wrong. His country hated me and my race enough to do murder. His friends had sanctioned the killing of the man Thomas Jefferson had loved like a father. And his son. If they had done this to their own . . .

What would they do to me?

And my children?

White America meant to destroy me, my lover, and my children. These people meant murder. Lydia had known it. Mama had known it, and now it would be my turn. I was alone. I could expect no help from Thomas Jefferson. He had been warned, and he had chosen to disdain this warning; but I vowed never to forget it. Never. There would be no freedom, no recognition, no emancipation, no flight, only stubborn silence would rule our lives from this day hence. If I had ever hoped that somehow, someday, my lover, who stood before me like a monument, would avow his yellow children, I laid that hope to rest in the graves of Michael Brown and Elizabeth Hemings. As for me, I could no longer afford his grief, his misery, his plea for forgiveness. Their deaths had unearthed the long forgotten specter of emancipation and his abnegation had sealed it.

I would not be destroyed, I would survive. I would survive Marly, mother and master.

He began to cry in rage and I took him in my arms. So he too had thought we had a safe place.

That winter, he unleashed the Embargo of 1807 upon the country after the frigate *Chesapeake* was attacked by the British.

"Now they have touched a cord which vibrates in every heart," he said. "Now is the time to settle the old and the new."

The embargo lasted two years and ruined Virginia.

Once more he stubbornly proposed to a stubborn Congress the prohibition of the African slave trade. He welcomed home with joy Meriwether Lewis, returned safely from his expedition in Louisana. And he tried Aaron Burr for treason.

The bitterness and resentment I felt against my lover, against my fate, I turned against Aaron Burr. When there were so many white men to hate, why did I choose Aaron Burr? Was it because of that one frank stare of lewdness that day in Philadelphia? Was it because he was the first man, black or white, who with one look of contempt had insinuated that my whoredom was of my own asking?

I hated him. I badgered my master for news as he sought affidavits against Aaron Burr from New Orleans to Maine, from Indiana to New Jersey. I wrote to him constantly, always stressing the danger of assassination from this man, of the duel with Hamilton, of his hatred, of his threat to my master's power. And he wrote meticulous letters home describing his progress in gathering evidence. He commanded me to burn the letters. But these letters, like all the others, I vowed to keep until my dying day.

Aaron Burr was brought to Richmond for his trial, which had the air of a country fair. People swarmed into the city. Balls and dinners were given in his honor. He strode the streets with his daughter Theodosia on his arm, the immaculate dandy. Besides himself, his defense lawyers were Edmund Randolph and George Wickham, the defenders of George Sweney. The trial opened with a hundred government witnesses, and my master's arch enemy John Marshall presiding. I followed the trial passionately, but like the trial of George Sweney, the outcome had been predetermined by Chief Justice John Marshall. The jury returned a verdict of "not guilty because, not proven guilty."

The great treason trial was over. And by the end of that trial, in January 1808, the African slave trade was abolished. I was again with child. My seventh. The next May I gave birth to a son, whom I called Eston, my only child born in the presence of his father, who celebrated his birth as if he were white.

CHAPTER 36

MARCH–OCTOBER 1809

Here arise questions of value, tact, and tolerance. . . .
For what, one must ask at last, would these Southern
ladies and domestic slaves have known and felt about their
being relatives? And what would it have meant for
Jefferson whose only son died unnamed at the age of
three weeks, to send into safe oblivion, a mulatto son who
is said to have looked very much like him?

ERIK H. ERICKSON, "Dimensions of a New Identity,"
Jefferson Lectures, 1973

There is love-making and love-making in this world.
What a time the sweethearts of that wretch, young Shakespeare, must have had. . . . The poor creature that he left
his second best bedstead to, came in second best all the
time. . . . Fancy people wondering that Shakespeare and
his kind leave no progeny like themselves? Shakespeare's
children would have been half his only; that other half
only the second best bedstead's. What would you expect
of that comingling of materials?

MARY BOYKIN CHESTNUT, *A Diary from Dixie*, 1840–76

Thomas Jefferson Hemings and Thomas Jefferson Randolph raced each other down the mountain to greet their
father and grandfather. My master's second term as president was over.

Bareheaded, their identical red curls flying in the March
wind, the cold and speed raking their already high color,
the two boys made for Shadwell, four miles away, as fast
as they could without crippling their horses.

I was thirty-six; Thomas, nineteen; Beverly, almost
eleven; Madison, four; Eston, one; and their sister Harriet,
almost eight. Martha was also thirty-six; Jeff, seventeen;

Anne, eighteen; Cornelia, ten; Ellen, thirteen; Virginia,
eight; Mary, six; her Madison, three; and Benjamin, one.
Maria's only child, Francis, was eight. Nineteen years of
childbearing.

The children were scattered on the steps of the mansion,
Randolphs and Hemingses mixed together, as always. The
boys were fair, their bright, red-blond and auburn heads
like wild poppies among the dark heads of the girls, who
took after Thomas Mann, except for Harriet, who had the
thick red hair of her father.

Both Thomas Jeffersons had fled out of the schoolroom
when Jim, the overseer, brought the news that the master
had already arrived on horseback at Shadwell, and was
riding hard through the March snowstorm for home. The
boys, blinking back the glare of swirling snowflakes which
lay on their shoulders and their horses' flanks like powdered sugar, raced to meet the returning ex-president halfway down the mountain. With shouts of joy we could
hear all the way to the mansion, they had accompanied
him the rest of the way to Monticello, riding on either side
of him, pressing jealously as close to him as their horses
would allow.

In a mist of fine snow, the whole household of Monticello stood on the west portico waiting. Besides myself,
Martha, and our families, there were the household slaves
and their children. Everything had been ready for weeks.
Wormley had been working by torchlight in the gardens to
get all the tree planting done. Five hundred peach stones
had been put in and as many pecans, new English turf
planted for seedlings, every blade of winter grass mani-
cured, every hedge, every bush, every flower bed in the vast
gardens dug, raked, nourished, and attended to. A week
had been spent hog-killing, the butcher planks running red,
the house resounding with the high-pitched cries of the
black-and-white Calcutta hogs, each weighing between
three and four hundred pounds. Peter had sweated over the
mincemeats, sausages, bacons, hams, pickled ears and skin,
scrapple, and hog fat for soap and candles. In the house,
Critta, Mary, and Edy had shined floors and polished silver
for a month. There had been a great deal of sewing, too. I
had wanted a new dress as had Martha, Anne, and Ellen,
and all the other children. Six seamstresses had been kept

busy for a month. Ursula had sorted, mended, rewashed, and used up seven kegs of starch on the household linen. I had left nothing to chance, the house sparkled, candles burned, and I stood watching the young men and their famous father and grandfather ride toward me. It had been eight years. Thomas Jefferson was coming home forever.

Shouts, cries, and kisses greeted the master of Monticello as he dismounted.

"How you all." He laughed. "Peter, what have you got good?"

"Masta, I got guinea hens and *carré* of lamb. I got rabbit in mustard, the way you like it, and Masta Meriwether Lewis's mother done sent over three of her hams for you!"

Everybody burst into laughter as he grabbed Eston, tottering on unsteady legs, and swung him around, sweeping him off the steps, and into his arms.

After that, there was bedlam as the children, black and white, tumbled down the stairs of the portico to greet the riders. Thomas Hemings beat Thomas Randolph to the reins of his father's horse. He was half an inch taller than his father, with the same luxurious red-auburn hair, blue eyes, rangy loose body, which was still awkward and uncoordinated from the growth of the past year.

Every summer for the past seven years, when the hordes of visitors descended on the estate, Thomas had been sent away to a neighboring farm almost fifty miles away, returning again only for the winter. This year would be the same, and the precious month before June would be the only ones in which he would see us until Christmas. But then, this Christmas would be different, I thought. This Christmas Thomas Jefferson would be home with his sons.

James Madison was now president. Dolley Todd Madison was finally mistress of the President's House, I thought, smiling. My master had been forced to borrow eight thousand dollars from Mrs. Tabb in order to pay his overdue bills before leaving the capital, according to Burwell. His inheritance of debts over eight years in the President's House was horrendous and his embargo against England and France had ruined him. It had hit the Southern states even worse than the mercantile states. His friends, the Virginia plantation-owners who had counted themselves

rich, found themselves, like him, with useless assets on
their hands, and a pile of debts. My master's tobacco was
worthless; wheat had fallen from two dollars a bushel to
seven cents; land values had been completely swept away.
The only wealth that remained were slaves. The only in-
dustry that seemed destined to survive in Virginia and reap
sickening profits was the breeding of slaves for inland trade
to the deep South. He had returned home penniless and
depressed. The Louisiana Purchase was the only thing he
could take real pleasure in.

Meriwether Lewis's mission, in the beginning, had been
a secret one. Under the guise of exploring the Territory for
"literary" reasons, Meriwether and William Clark were to
open up British territory for private traders, since they had
been forced out of business by government traders on this
side of the Mississippi and had been resentfully inciting
discontent among the Indians. Why not, Thomas Jefferson
had asked himself, divert their hopes of profit in the direction of the Missouri River? He could kill two birds with
one stone: the government traders would be left in undis-
puted possession on this side of the Mississippi, with the
aim of bringing the Indians into debt and forcing them to
sell their lands; while the dispossessed private traders could
open up new land for trade which now went to Great
Britain. If traders went, settlers would not be far behind,
and the Territory would become white instead of red.

He had needed someone he could trust for the expedition, someone who could combine daring, prudence, woods-
manship, surveying, familiarity of the Indian character,
with a good knowledge of botany, natural history, mineralogy, and astronomy. What better choice than his brilliant secretary Meriwether?

My son Thomas had dreamed day and night of that
expedition, had begged his father to let him go, although
he was much too young. Meriwether Lewis had chosen
William Clark and his slave York to go with him. For two
years and four months, they had toiled and marched the
uncharted wilderness. Of this my master was proud. But
even this happiness, we were to discover, was mortgaged.

It was at the end of summer, the September golds and
oranges already turning into October's reds and browns. As

if in a dream, repeating itself, I heard the heavy tread of
Davey Bowles in the hall, the strangled anguished cry, only
this time it was a male cry. I had time only to turn to see
Thomas Jefferson burst into his study, his face contorted
with grief and incomprehension.

Meriwether Lewis had committed suicide in Tennessee.
He was dead at exactly the same age as James. The cold
terror of that self-murder ran through me as I stared in
fearful apprehension at his wild grief.

James gone. And Maria. Jamey. And Michael. And
Mama. And now Meriwether. Death lay around our feet,
like the neat piles of raked leaves Wormley had left scattered on our lawn. Thomas Jefferson had turned away
from me.

I knew how much my master had liked Meriwether
Lewis. He had taught him surveying, as my master's father
had taught him. He had taken him on as private secretary,
and it had been Meriwether who had assuaged the loneliness of the sinister President's House in Washington City.
He had introduced Meriwether into the circles of power,
and when he had needed a leader of the expedition to the
Pacific, who had he chosen out of his "family" but Meriwether? He had thought of the danger, I knew, but had
refused to shield a "son" from becoming the first to explore
it simply because of his own fears for safety. And Meriwether had done him proud. He had become a hero and
my master had covered him with honors, made him governor of Louisiana. And now Meriwether Lewis was dead
by his own hand: Accused by James Madison, another
"son," of mismanaging Louisiana. As dead as James, and
for reasons perhaps as unknown.

"All my hopes were in Meriwether. He was the last.
Why must I always lose what I love? Why can I never hold
what I cherish? Why have I no sons of my own?"

His words stunned me. What about the census of his
family? I had seen it with my own eyes.

I said quietly, "But you have four sons."

Could not Thomas or Beverly be instructed in botany, in
astronomy, in surveying; could not Madison or Eston learn
natural history, mineralogy, Indian affairs? I wanted to
scream.

He took a long time to answer me. "I don't have four sons. You have four sons."

Silence.

I had burned for him and I had birthed for him. Seven times I had descended into that valley from which neither his wife nor one of his daughters had returned. And my sons stood as testament and hostage to a body I could never call my own. I felt an explosion of insulted motherhood, all red and brown, like the leaves scattered on the lawn outside the window.

His back was turned to me. My eyes sought the iron poker lying within my reach near the chimney. I wanted to strike that broad blue-sheathed back. I wanted to strike and strike again, with all my strength, to smash him. Oh God, I wanted to kill him, for now, after all these years, I understood what he had understood from the beginning, but had not had the courage to tell me. He had renounced his sons from the day of their birth!

The red and brown were swimming now in patches of blackness, like a flickering candle. Snatches of darkness overtook the colors. I reached for Joe Fosset's iron poker. The master had no sons, the slave had sons. The white man had no sons, the black woman had sons. It was she who had lusted, not he. She who had seduced, not he. No, Beverly or Thomas or Madison or Eston could not be instructed in mineralogy or botany, in Greek or Latin, in music, in architecture, in natural history, in astronomy. They would never count as real sons.

Never.

Then why had he clung to us all these years. Why had he bound us soul and flesh to him? Why had he not relinquished and freed us? And why, why had I stayed?

Love me and remain a slave.

Now the colors had darkened.

The iron poker gleamed dull and lethal. His back was still turned to me. In my mind's eye I struck and struck and struck. I wanted to see the look of surprise as he turned to defend himself. I wanted to see terror and disbelief in those innocent eyes. Then I wanted the poker to smash that high-arched nose, to see that expression of mild benevolence disappear under blood. I wanted him dead.

All the colors became that almighty color: black. I wanted him dead.

I felt horror for us all. Master. Concubine. Bastards. I no longer had the strength to lift Joe Fosset's poker over my head.

I didn't—would never—have the courage to kill Thomas Jefferson.

But I would free his sons.

I put my mind to it methodically, as if making up a household inventory. When would Thomas Jefferson Hemings "stroll" away? How much money did he need? How much did I have? Could I sell my sapphire bracelet secretly in Richmond through Burwell? Would he or would he not say good-bye to his father? Where would he go? Who could I trust to help him? Did it really matter that he was nineteen and not the "promised" twenty-one? He was white enough to pass for white, as his father had said of Jamey. Would he leave Monticello a white man? Could he do it to save himself?

No, Thomas Hemings would not say good-bye to his father, to be charmed or willed or loved out of going away. Yes, he would leave Monticello a white man. At the top of my stairs, I stared into the mirror, just as I had one day twenty years before in Paris. The long Calvary of the renouncement of one child after another was beginning.

But the departure of my eldest son did not go as I had planned. I had not planned that he would meet his father unexpectedly on his stolen horse, with all the money I had in the world on the Fourth of July.

The father and son met on the wide front lawn of the west façade of the mansion, under my window, each on horseback. Thomas Jefferson was hatless as usual, his fine sandy-gray hair lifted in the breeze, wet from the summer dawn; my son's deep auburn hair was wild and thick as his father's. They seemed almost a double image, the same long, pale faces, stubborn chins, and pale hooded eyes.

They faced each other for a long moment, their horses stock-still under their expert hands. So still that they resembled two equestrian statues in the pink morning; sculpture erected to commemorate some long-ago and forgotten heroic deed. A slight movement of the horses, nervous and ready to run, shattered the illusion. They rose in their saddles as one and drew together in an embrace that lasted a long time. It was Thomas who broke the hold of his father, who then spun his horse and sped away at a reckless gallop on sloping terrain, taking a nearby hedge on a jump that would have unseated anyone except him.

My son reined in his horse, frightened by the sudden movement, and sat a long time looking after the vanishing horseman.

I gazed at my own reflection distorted in the thick glass. I placed my hands in front of me, between myself and the windowpane. They were soft, strong, and steady. On my left hand, I wore a wide yellow band of gold. Wife. My hand came down upon the window hard, but it would not shatter.

Thomas Jefferson Hemings turned and looked back at the columned façade. In something like a salute, he raised his arm as he turned and rode away down the mountain.

PART V

1834
Albemarle
County

CHAPTER 37

DECEMBER 1834

The female slave, however fair she may have become by various comminglings of her progenitors, or whatever her mental and moral acquirements may be, knows that she is a slave, and, as such powerless. . . . She has parents, brothers, sisters, a lover, perhaps, who all suffer through her and with her.

MARGARET DOUGLASS (from prison), 1853

Though the effects of black be painful originally, we must not think they always continue so. Custom reconciles us to everything. After we have been used to the sight of black objects, the terror abates, and the smoothness and glossiness, or some agreeable accident of bodies so coloured, softens in some measure the horror and sternness of their original nature; yet the nature of their original impression still continues. Black will always have something melancholy in it. . . .

EDMUND BURKE, "On the Sublime and Beautiful," 1756

Sally Hemings closed her eyes and remembered. The smooth eyelids slid over the dark openings set like caves in a clay mountain, leaving the pale oval countenance flattened and glowing like a polished bone in the dark of an unearthed grave. In the cabin, the fine French clock of onyx and bronze struck the hour, then ticked over a new minute of silence. In her mind she saw her son ride away.

She rose from where she was sitting and went over·to the light. Carefully, she untied the black velvet ribbon she wore around her neck, and opened her locket. She took out the lock of red-auburn hair and brushed it with her lips. Then she stared at the painted image in the locket for a long time. Tomorrow was another son's wedding day.

Scrupulously, with the edge of her muslin scarf, she wiped the tears that had fallen onto the portrait. Then she replaced the bright lock within and closed the case, the fine mechanism of the lock giving her a moment's satisfaction.

She stared out of the window, remembering another December more than twenty years before. Another kind of "black death." The December of the murder at Rocky Hill, in 1811.

"T.J.'s dead sister, Lucy's boys, Lilburn and Isham," her sister Critta began, "been condemned for killing, and dismemberin' Lilburn's body servant, George, out there in west Kentucky. The news is just reachin' Virginia."

Critta had sat in the darkness of her secret room at the top of the staircase and told her the bad news from Kentucky. That was the reason why her master had snatched her up, along with Fanny and Burwell, and fled to their newly finished house at Poplar Forest. Away from the mansion.

"Last December, on the night of the fifteenth, Lilburn decided to chastise his slave George and ordered a bonfire built in the meat house of the plantation, and ordered all his slaves present. There, Lilburn and his brother Isham had two slaves tie up that poor boy, not two years older than Beverly, and then laid him on the meat block. First people thought Lilburn was only going to whip George. 'Hand me that ax,' Lilburn told his brother. Then the people thought Lilburn only going to chop off a finger or an ear, or maybe a whole hand or foot. But Lilburn first cut off the boy's two hands and flung them into the fire and then cut off his feet. Then the people knew Lilburn's goin' to kill his slave. Lilburn started chopping and the people started groaning. Lilburn continued on and the people fell silent. Lilburn cut away at that living boy; the forearms, then the limbs and still that boy lived, but only the head and torso, alive and screaming, although those that heard that sound said it weren't no more a human sound. That boy George so strong cause he been beat so many times. He must have smelled his own flesh frying in the fire. Some say Lilburn chopped the head from the body, others say he threw George into the fire and burned what was left of his slave alive. All this because George broke a favorite milk pitcher of his dead mother. All this because Lucy Jefferson Lewis's linen kept gettin' ripped and her aprons kept disappearin', and her dishes broken."

Critta had paused. Sally Hemings stared at the trickle of saliva that had formed at the corner of her sister's mouth. Wasn't it James's dream that Critta was telling her? James's dream that she'd known in her bones for twenty-four years. Was she mad, her sister?

"And then people wailed into the night, and of course, according to them superstitious slaves, they done stirred up nature itself because an earthquake, they called it the New Madrid, an earthquake now rocked the Mississippi and it flowed backward, turned red, and overrun the banks, and all the ground shook and trembled, and windstorms came, and lightning, and all sorts of strange occurrences came on that night; and Lilburn's wife went mad with the knowledge of what he done, and fled to her brother's, and her ravings brought Lilburn and Isham to their ruin. . . . The slaves buried what was left of George, and Lilburn locked up his raving wife in the house. But the sheriff of the county came around asking questions, and when Lilburn's hound dog dug up a jawbone, and the sheriff seen it was a human jawbone, he got the Lewis slaves and made them tell where they had buried George, then he made them dig up the rest of George's charred bones. Lilburn and Isham were arrested for murder and taken to Salem and indicted."

There had been a small sigh of exhaustion, and Critta had stared out the window for a long time saying nothing. Winter still lay on the land. The Blue Mountains were shrouded.

"The sheriff released them two brothers," Critta had continued, "on bail of five thousand dollars to await their trial, but Lilburn made a suicide pact with his brother to shoot each other over the grave of their mother. Isham fired and Lilburn he fell dead. Isham fled, but he was captured after a few days. He was tried for his brother's murder and sentenced to be hanged. But before they could hang him, he escaped and is still not found."

"And this is true, Critta?"

"As true as death, sister."

"And how . . . how do you know?"

"How could I not know?" Critta said in disgust. "White people knows. So it follows that anything they know, we know."

"But how?"

"Lilburn and Isham's father was in Virginia at the time. The Lewis slaves, they all knew. Then it come in from the West on the slave intelligence, the trial in the newspapers. Only reason you ain't read it is that Masta Thomas hid the newspapers. White people don't know how many slaves can read. White people going around tiptoeing and whispering and slamming doors in their servants' faces and locking them, and shutting their mouths in front of the servants. As if we wouldn't know of it! They sat around here with blank faces with you and Masta Jefferson gone. He high-tailed it out there to Poplar Forest with you, like he could get away from it. Silence when you entered a room. Looks. They really think we don't know what's going on."

She had stared at Critta. Her master had said nothing to her all those days. Had Burwell known? Fanny? Had he really thought she would not find out? Or had he simply decided to let someone else tell her? He had not had the courage to tell me, Sally Hemings thought. But then she had never had the courage to tell him of James's nightmare either.

"For weeks," Critta had continued, "when any of the house servants entered a room, the conversation stopped. I swear I will never understand white people. Do they really think their lies fool the people who serve them? They go around whispering 'Not in front of the servants,' yet they done butchered a poor boy in front of the servants! They commit their crimes in front of the servants. They commit murder in front of the servants!"

Sally Hemings stood up, trembling, blocking the light, drawing in the room with her breath. She stood against the window as she had stood in the doorway of her cabin the day the census taker had come up her road. Except that now the violet was outside. The deep shadows of a sunless afternoon. The clock ticked over another moment of silence.

"You! You don't know *nothing* about slavehood," her sister had said. "You brush your skirts against it, that's all.

Petted and pampered and hidden and lied to. . . . Buried
alive by your lover! You ain't never puked from the smell
of whiteness . . . begged God to take this cup from you. . . ."

"Critta," she had said, "you are crying. . . ."

"Aw God, have mercy on us! Lord Jesus Christ in
Heaven, have mercy!"

"Critta. . . ."

Sally Hemings' face was seamed with rivulets of tears.
They fanned out like delicate transparent lace on ivory
satin.

Critta had accused her of not knowing anything about
slavery. But she had known everything there was to know.
Critta had been ill-used. She had been raped and scorned.
But Critta was she and she was Critta. They were and
always had been one and the same, and they in turn had
been one with every black field hand bent over the tobacco
and cotton that had kept their white family in *servants*. Yet
what had they known about their *servants*? She knew
everything there was to know.

The *servants* surprised the master at stool and fornica-
tion, childbirth and menses, in every secret intimacy. They
knew if he was clean or filthy. Everything that was spotted,
soiled, unwashed, creased, rumpled, worn and discarded,
they picked up, and washed, folded and mended, and laid
out anew for him. They knew if their master slept alone or
not, and with whom. They recognized his waste and his
possessions. They knew the true color of his hair and the
true age of his sorrows. They saw him in fear and pain,
jealousy and anger, lust and happiness. They knew his
bastards, because most times they were their own children.
Their master's footsteps were as familiar as their own, his
voice recognized in the midst of company.

They saw him fight vice or honor it, swallow truth or
pronounce it, flatter for power, gossip for amusement, wife-
beat for amusement, flog out of viciousness.

They knew if he destroyed out of envy or built out of
pride. They knew his station in life and how he came to it.
They knew if he hoarded his money or spent it, honored
his debts, believed in his God. They smiled at his follies,
laughed at his jokes, defended his reputation, nursed his
children, despised or respected him as they pleased, obeyed
him if they were compelled, ignored him when they had a

mind to. They brought his children into the world, laid out
his dead, buried his forgotten, hid his sins from the world,
even from God—if they could. But not even they could
always do that. And still the master thought he could speak
the truth only out of their earshot, *never in front of the
servants.* . . .

Sally Hemings drew in her breath just as the hour struck.
The jerking shadows of the firelight etched into the shadows of her face. The horror of the murder had lost the
allure of memory and stood exposed before her there on
the cabin floor—the dreadful amputated stump of slavery
itself.

She and Critta had stood that day, servant to servant,
concubine to concubine, and had been one with their
mother and their mother's mother and *her* mother. One
long line: The African and the beast hunter Hemings, the
housekeeper and the slave master Wayles, the slave mistress and the American Jefferson. . . .

He had not told her. His hands had been bloodied with
his kin's crime, and not only had he pretended not to know
it, he had pretended that she would not know it. Those
hands that had drawn her and had known her in all the
secret places had not revealed his white secrets. And hers?
Had her hands revealed her black secrets? James's nightmare? Her hands that had soothed and caressed, had they
been any less bloody? Didn't she have James's blood on her
hands? On those immaculate hands she had kept so soft for
him. And Critta, had her hands been free of blood? Had
they not served the same murderers? And the slave boy
George, hadn't he lain down on the meat block for his
masters; and his fellow slaves, hadn't they tied him up and
looked on and kept silent?

How many had they been to witness murder? How many
of them had been grown men? How many of those grown
men would it have taken to overwhelm two white men and
their guns? How many had thought only about their own
flesh, their own sons; their precious flesh opening under a
steel ax, their blood spraying like mist onto the heated air;
their heart carved out on the butcher's table.

They were all bloodied, thought Sally Hemings. The
whole race was bloodied. Not only with the real blood of
suffering, the real blood of chains and whips and hatchets,

but the blood of race, polluted, displaced, and disappearing in rape and miscegenation, and cross-ties of kin—that fine lace of bastardy that stretched across the two races like the web of a spider filled with love and hate—claiming cousins and nephews, daughters and sons, half sisters and half brothers. . . . The whole race was bloodied, the whole race had served with bloodied hands and had wiped them on their masters.

They had washed and scrubbed and polished and glazed, but how could they, bloodied as they were, have cleaned anything? How? Sally Hemings's mouth formed the word, but there was only silence, and a lonely woman in a cabin on the boundary of Monticello.

She had never revealed to Thomas Jefferson that she had known about Lilburn and Isham. But she had turned away from his hands that day. From his touch. From his "darling." And if she had told him, what would he have said? *That it had had nothing to do with them.* He would have spoken about "the insanity of mankind." He had always taken things out of the specific, out of reality and made an abstraction of them. But men were real. Blood was red. George and Lilburn and Isham and James and Meriwether were not merely "mankind." They had been his blood. If he hadn't been responsible for his own blood, for his own issue, for his own race, then who had been responsible? So she had left it unsaid. She had forgiven him for so many things. Why not one more?

And the years had passed like seeping water from a drying well. Silence between them. A whole kingdom of silence.

The peeling gray mansion of Monticello stood bleak and deserted on its mountaintop while the wind howled and snow swirled around it.

Sally Hemings sat until she could no longer see her hand before her face, and then she rose and went out into the snowstorm, hugging her shawl, her skirts dragging in the white satin layer of crystals beneath her feet.

She went to her henhouse to gather some eggs, and on her way back she saw him again ahead of her, breaking pane after pane of silvery light, and then she knew that the circle was closed. It had been twenty-four years since

Thomas Jefferson Hemings had strolled away, thirty-one
since James had died, and forty-four since she had last
seen Marly. Should she hurry to catch up with him, she
thought, stay twenty paces behind, or return to the mansion?

In the white mist, breathing softly, Sally Hemings listened to the coursing of her blood. She pressed her hands
against her womb, and whispered, more to herself than to
the dark figure, who, after all these years, still strode his
Elysian fields:

"Tell me is it not true, love, that I was never happy. . . ."
But she knew then, she had made her pact with the infer-
nals. The number of kisses it might take to redeem her now
was beyond even the power of Thomas Jefferson.

"Martha gone and sold Monticello, Mama."

Mama?

"Mama, Monticello's sold! To tradespeople in Charlottesville!"

Madison Hemings was desperately trying to pull his
mother back from her reveries. She was standing in the
December evening. It was six o'clock. She was chilled yet
she would not move. He tugged at her, shaking the delicate
snowflakes that had settled on both of them.

He had helped pull a drowned man out of the Ravina
once. He remembered the incredible weight of that water-
logged body—it seemed a hundred times the weight of a
normal man. He remembered the pull of his muscles, the
strain, the ache to drag the broken body up on the bank,
and how he had stood there breathless, staring at the
bloated shape, heavier than lead and no longer human.

"Mama?"

Sally Hemings felt herself being wrenched upward by an
incessant humming in her ear, like a dying fly at the onset
of winter. It was her son Madison.

"What did you say, Madison, honey?"

"Mama! I said Martha done sold Monticello to the
druggist named Barkley in Charlottesville for his business
and two thousand five hundred dollars. The price of three
slaves! Ain't the Randolphs' no more. Ain't Papa's no
more!"

Madison was shocked. For the past five years, only the mansion itself and grounds surrounding it had remained: empty, deserted, decaying, but still theirs, a link to the past. In the spring, they would have been going up to the cemeteries to clean and weed and replant. . . .

"Mama, you be careful going up there to the cemetery, 'cause you'll be tresspassing now. . . . Every time you pass the boundary line, you'll be trespassing. . . ."

Sally Hemings stared up at her gray-eyed son. So much like James . . . the same cat eyes. He had filled out in the past year. The ranginess and some of the violence was gone. Mary McCoy, she guessed. Madison and his black freeborn Mary McCoy. They would marry tomorrow. She stared up at him, but she didn't have to ask if it was true about Monticello. She knew it was. The mansion. Houses died or were killed, just like people. She felt neither pain nor sorrow. The last link with the world was gone. She could drift now, she felt light. As light as snowflakes drifting.

The weight of that house, which had been on her shoulders since she was seventeen, slipped off.

PART VI

1812
Monticello

PART VI

1812

Monticello

CHAPTER 38

SUMMER 1812

Love songs are scarce and fall into two categories—the frivolous and light and the sad. Of deep successful love, there is ominous silence.

W. E. B. DU BOIS, *The Souls of Black Folks*, 1953

Sally Hemings stood in the middle of Mulberry Row. Her hands were on her hips, her face protected from the sun by a wide-brimmed hat. Around her, children, dogs, chickens, horses, and slaves swarmed and threatened to capsize her not more than a hundred yards from the Big House. She surveyed what the summer of 1812 had wrought. Her body was tensed and leaned slightly forward.

Along Mulberry Row, there continued the incessant thump of the nailery, the weaving cottage, the blacksmiths' and the carpentry shop. From the stables came the sound of snorting, restless animals. The stables held stalls for thirty-six horses, and they were full, with the rest tethered on the pasture land behind. Bacon, the overseer, had given up trying to feed the forty carriage horses of the guests. He had begun to cut down on the feed, but the master had reprimanded him severely for it. Edmund Bacon had just arrived in the kitchens with a wagonload of his wife's mattresses to supplement the depleted resources of Monticello. Every bed was full and in the upper rooms and attic, mattresses were strewn everywhere; servants slept on the floor on straw pallets in the hallways and corridors, which were so narrow Sally Hemings had to step over sleeping bodies every morning to get to her smokehouses and larder.

Larder, she thought. Edmund Bacon had killed a whole beef day before yesterday and it was completely gone! Like hordes of boll weevils, the summer company had gone through their supplies like a field of cotton, leaving nothing in its wake. They had come from everywhere: Richmond, Charlottesville, Louisville, Alexandria, and a dozen other places farther away.

About the middle of June, the travel would commence from the lower part of the state to the Springs, and there would begin a perfect throng of visitors. Whole families came with carriages, riding horses, and servants, sometimes like now, three or four gangs at the same time. Their carriages and buckboards lined the mile-long road to the house, and they stayed and stayed, from overnight to all summer: not only family but friends, neighbors, sightseers, and even total strangers. A dog yelped around her skirts and she gave him a hard kick. The table would be set for forty tonight, and the children, white and black, would eat in the kitchens.

She saw three housemaids coming from the washhouse farther down the road, their arms full of snowy, newly washed and ironed linen. A footman was following with two mattresses on his head.

Sally Hemings yelled at him. How many times had she told him not to carry mattresses on his nappy head! To tie it with a clean rag! He turned, stuck his tongue out, and continued on his way. Two other housemaids came by her carrying slop jars, a small child, who was crying, trailing one of them. Around her wafted the cooking odors of the midday meal, savory and pungent in the torpid air; farther down Roundabout Row, in one of the slave cabins, somebody was cooking chitterlings from the freshly killed hogs.

After Thomas Jefferson's return from Washington City, she had stood under the shade trees on the east lawn and watched Martha Randolph, with her wagon train of household goods, and all her children, make her way up the mountain for good. She had finally come to stay, she with her brood of children and her mad husband. Not that her family had had any place else to go. They had become penniless, with debts so overwhelming they could barely pay the interest on them. Thomas Mann had excelled his father-in-law in spending money and raising debts. She wondered if Martha were pregnant again. Thomas Jefferson had pleaded with her. What was he to do? Let them starve? Leave Martha, his only living child, at the mercy of her husband? His only living white child? And since then there had been no mistake about who was now mistress of Monticello. Thomas Jefferson had broken his vow. He had brought a white mistress back to Monticello: his own daughter.

"But you promised me!"

"Martha isn't a 'white mistress,' for heaven sakes, she's my daughter . . . your niece, our family!"

"And who runs Monticello?"

"Martha does."

He had said it. And he would not be moved on this; she knew him too well. There was an air of indifference about him now, a calm produced by the gratification of every wish. Beneath the suave manners, the glacial serenity, the almost deferential politeness, remained that special Virginian brutality that came from the habit of despotism and privilege, of never being crossed, of handling blooded horses, controlling ambitious men, ruling your own small kingdom, and contemplating your own place in history. He had forgiven himself everything, and he didn't care if she forgave him or not. He was letting the Almighty do His own work. But she had kept the keys.

"Sally Hemings, what on earth are you doing standing out there in the hot sun with your hat on when you know I need you right this minute, you hear me?"

I hear you, Martha. I barely hear you over all this racket; this noise and heat and running back and forth and hammering and yelling and screaming and crying and playing children, and horses and cows and chickens; but I hear you, thought Sally Hemings, and I'm coming. Just don't rush me, not today.

It was the anniversary of her mother's death five years before. She would never forget her. An image seared her and then dissolved. What was a black woman's life? What was a woman's life? Sally Hemings decided to ignore Martha's summons for the moment. She let the waves of noise and smells ride roughshod over her, hardly caring, because in a few days she and her master would escape from the crowds to their unfinished hideaway, Poplar Forest, leaving Martha to cope with feeding, housing, and entertaining almost fifty people.

When, she thought, were people going to stop persecuting Thomas Jefferson with their "most felicitous and cordial and heartfelt thanks for your hospitality"?

They were officeseekers, relations, friends, artists, biographers, young Daniel Webster, Madison, Monroe, foreigners, natives, the famous, the near great, nonentities, and total strangers. They pretended to come out of respect and regard for him, but she thought that the fact they saved a tavern bill had a good deal to do with it. She was tired of seeing them come and she was tired of waiting on them, and, most of all, Monticello just couldn't stand the drain much longer!

There were several ladies, parasols in hand, strolling along the edge of the west lawn not fifty yards from her, and on it, a dozen children, mostly Randolphs and Hemingses, were playing blindman's bluff. She looked up. At night the very floorboards of the house seemed to sag under the weight of humanity housed within. Maids and footmen and butlers, many of them promoted only for the summer crowd, broke the dishes, scorched the linen, mislaid the supplies, dropped the platters, and were slow as molasses to obey. This summer had seemed worse than any other. Her master seemed more withdrawn than ever, Martha more present.

Let Martha lead the table at Monticello and preside over this madhouse, she thought. They would go to their hermitage for half the summer and all the fall, in their new octagonal brick house, and laugh and talk and tell old tales. She smiled.

"You know how many names they got for Papa's chamber pot?"

"Beverly!"

"Well, Mama, it's true. I heard Mammy Ursula talking to Fanny the other day 'cause little Ned had an accident, 'cause he fell asleep."

"What?"

"Papa's *State of the Union* came out and spilled all over Ned's head!"

Beverly had begun to laugh. He had a laugh like his father's, she thought, short and abrupt, and likely to bring tears to his eyes if prolonged. Sally Hemings had laughed as well. Her lover had built an inside toilet, which was the object of much mirth among the household slaves. He had invented a way to move his chamber pot by a system of ropes and pulleys and wheels along a tunnel leading from the house to an opening in the ground about twenty-five feet away. It had been christened "The Underground Railway," over which traveled his "runaways." She and the other household slaves had elaborated on the theme until now there were "inaugural addresses" pronounced "in-all-urine-ass-dresses," "states of the union," "cabinet meeting," "Federal Reserves," "Treasury bonds," "ultimatums," "levees," and "Indian Treaties."

"Aunt Bett found a new name," Beverly had continued. "She said they were his "manumission papers." But in that case, he ain't *shat* in a long time!"

"Beverly!"

"I named it his *Declaration of Indepen—*"

"Beverly!"

"Now, Beverly, you want a good switching," she had said to his grinning face. But she had been laughing too hard for him to believe her. Blasphemy! She had tried to explain to her sisters how the mansion on the Champs-Elysées had been of the most modern construction, and had had as well as bathrooms, *lieux anglais*, or indoor water closets.

"That may. be very well and good in Paris, France, honey, but trouble is, sister," Bett Hemings had said, "once this thing gets out there, there is still got to be a slave standing there ready to catch it, and empty it! Typical that Thomas Jefferson can't invent nothing that don't have a slave on the receiving end of it. . . ."

She saw him now in the distance saddling up one of the bays he loved so much. First thing he had done when he came back from Washington City was to build a new carriage. John had built the body, Joe Fosset had done all the ironwork, and Burwell had painted every bit of it. Only the plating had been done in Richmond, and a finer carriage there was not in Albemarle. That carriage, with its four bays, Diomede, Brimmer, Tecumseh, and Dromedary, each pair guided by a slave, with Burwell outriding on Eagle, was some pretty sight, almost outshining in splendor his cousin John Randolph's, with his blooded horses and his slaves following with perhaps a dozen more.

The Randolphs.

They were the bane of her existence.

The Randolph blood.

It was the tragedy of her life.

Without it, Martha might never have returned to Monticello and Thomas Jefferson.

Without it, she and Martha might have lived out their lives apart.

The Randolphs, and God knows there were enough of them, were strange people. John Randolph was one of the most eccentric men who ever lived, and Thomas Mann Randolph was well nigh his equal. Like two identical steers. Having Thomas Mann on the mountain permanently didn't make her sleep any easier. Thomas Mann didn't like it any better—living with his father-in-law and watching his wife worship the ground her father trod on, any more than Thomas Jefferson liked his son-in-law drinking and acting crazier and crazier. But Martha was in such bliss to be back up here, she didn't seem to notice that her husband was crazy. Jim, the overseer at Legos, had told her the other day that Thomas Mann had driven Dromedary over to Edgehill and right into a row of haystacks, just like that. Scattering them in all directions and covering himself with straw. When he had reached the overseer and finished his business, he had calmly declared that he thought an old bull must have gotten into the wheat field, 'cause he had seen a good many shocks overthrown and scattered on his way over. As serene as you please, when he had done it himself, she thought. The overseer had laughed, because he knew Thomas Mann Randolph was crazy as a loon! Burwell said he had seen him take Dromedary's tail and run him up the mountain as fast as he could. And he was in money trouble too. Bad. Selling his slaves for cash.

Then there was Anne Cary, Thomas Mann's sister. She had been brought to trial for infanticide with her cousin and lover Richard Randolph. That had rocked the gentry!

Her thoughts were interrupted by the screams of the half-naked children who came racing by her, Ceres, the bull terrier, on their heels. Sally Hemings looked up into the lacy greenness of the immense ash trees that shrouded the Big House in shadow—trees planted by her lover before she was born. She loved these trees. Encompassing her in their soft violet shade, they seemed to stand between her and the world. Protecting that strange love which was her secret and her burden.

A dull pain struck her temple. She was almost forty years old. If she lived as long as her mother, there was as much of her life behind her as in front of her. And in those forty years she had had to learn slowly, like her mother before her, like every female before her, the uses of love.

And Martha. Everything would be all right, she thought, if only there were not two mistresses at Monticello, as if there could really be two mistresses of anything.

CHAPTER 39

SUMMER 1812

Thomas Jefferson was happy. He had deeply missed the pleasures of Monticello. He had missed his slave wife. How many times when he had been away from her had he imagined his hands riding over that beautiful body, seizing it as if it were handfuls of his own buff clay Monticello earth; the fragile woman's landscape of her turning, twisting, rising, and falling under his hands; the long black hair winding like a tributary of his own Ravina River; the golden eyes which turned dark amber in heat, shining upon him like his own Virginia sun, steady and enervating. Those eyes, this mountain, his friends, his neighbors. They were the places he really felt safe. The mansion, his mansion, was finally finished. His burden of state, his presidency, was over. Only his university remained to be built now, and his family to care for: slave and white. He thought of Anne, soon to be married, and dismissed Sally's son Thomas, who had deserted him. He turned and beckoned to Beverly. Often, for the last year or so, he had seen Beverly waiting, as he was now, saddled up, hoping to be invited. And sometimes, when he really didn't feel like being alone, he would take Beverly along with him. Isaac, who held his horse, looked up at him and then over to Beverly, who sped to join his father.

As young as he was—thirteen and a half—Beverly was a splendid horseman, thought Thomas Jefferson. He rode almost as well as Burwell, and certainly better than anyone near his age at Monticello. Sometimes, when they raced, he would rein in Brimmer and let Beverly win. Sometimes. Beverly had grown so much in the past year, the boy's height would equal his own.

The two bright heads met in the light, Beverly's hair brighter and blonder than the fading, graying mane of his father. The two bodies were cast from the same mold with their heavy, awkward necks and wrists, their huge hands, and their long legs. Beverly flushed with pleasure and adoration as they rode off silently together. He had taken to riding the fields, asking questions, demanding—yes, demanding—instructions, begging to be taught, calculating, planning, counting, pleading for more knowledge. His father had been surprised at the astuteness of his questions, his quick mind, his grasp of trade, banking, interest, exports, tariffs, yields, crop rotation, loans . . . everything seemed to fascinate him.

His mother had begged that he be allowed to go to school with the Randolph boys in Charlottesville, if only as a body servant. She had not succeeded in this, but he had finally agreed that Beverly could be tutored secretly after classes by the instructor there, Mr. Oglesby. He was proud of Mr. Oglesby's report on Beverly's progress. Beverly was the only boy he allowed the freedom of his library. Even his grandson Jefferson had to ask first. What power there was in teaching, he thought. His dream now was a university in Charlottesville and he was determined to build it.

Yes, thought Thomas Jefferson, his slave wife would forgive him in time for Martha. He had no choice, and he had wanted his daughter with him. Peace. He was home. He had returned to the scenes of his birth and early life, to the society of those with whom he was raised and who had always been dear to him. The long absences, the pomp, the turmoil, the bustle, the splendor of office had drawn but deeper sighs for this place; he longed for private life, friends, and family. He had laid down his burden of power and hoped only that he had obtained for himself the approbation of his country, he mused.

He reined in his bay and waited for Beverly.

Thomas Jefferson's knees and thighs increased the pressure on his mount as Beverly reached him. Then, as they moved together, he cast a sidelong glance at his slave son. The clear, handsome profile was a replica of his own, even to his color. Love. God knows, he loved the boy's mother. Cherished her. He was bonded to her. She owned him just as surely as he owned her, the only difference being that her possession of him was a gift while his was a theft.

He was stirred as always by the thought of her fragility . . . her smallness, her smooth round skull he could cup in one great hand, the voice, that lovely voice. . . . He never ceased to be amazed at her beauty that seemed to deepen year by year. She was more beautiful now than at twenty, he thought. As for his own age, he wore it lightly, despite his attacks of rheumatism, his constantly aching right wrist, his bouts of dysentery. His wife had been dead for twenty-nine years, and this woman, whose image was before him in her plain blue gown, he had loved faithfully, with a mixture of guilt and passion, for more than twenty-three years.

Beverly, he thought, would soon be a man. He stared at his second son. A wave of love and bad conscience overwhelmed him.

"And how are your studies coming with Mr. Oglesby?"

"Fine, Master, sir."

"He's treating you well?"

"Oh, yes! He's very kind, Master. He's . . . wonderful to me, Master, sir."

Thomas Jefferson felt a pang of jealousy. It was the Charlottesville schoolmaster Beverly adored, not he. This Scottish schoolmaster was opening the door of the world to him, leading him, not he. . . .

"Come to my study this afternoon, Beverly. I have some books for you."

"Thank you, Master, sir. Shall I come before my classes?"

"Yes. You can show them to Master Oglesby."

He took a deep breath but the pain remained. Why didn't this son, whom he had never called son, and who had never called him father, love him?

Martha Jefferson Randolph was four weeks into her twelfth pregnancy. Twenty years of childbearing, and her eldest about to marry. She sat at the downstairs window of the salon and watched her father ride away with Beverly Hemings.

She wondered where Jeff was. Of course he was in school, she remembered. How stupid. Jefferson was eighteen now, a gentle boy, but not a Jefferson. Simply a Virginia gentleman without any special talent. Soon he would carry on his fragile shoulders the responsibility of the whole estate. Not only his father's affairs, which were in a dreadful state, but his grandfather's as well. Martha shuddered. How would he hold up under such a burden? If only Thomas Mann . . . But Thomas Mann was lost to her, to everyone. He had turned on his family. His delusions of persecution had cast her out. He accused her and the whole family of the most detestable crimes. Yet, he slept in her bed every night, got her with child every year, and made her life hell. She only hoped that Anne would do better. She didn't trust the handsome, rich, well-born Bankhead. She prayed that Anne would never live to regret her choice.

Why did she feel so old? She smoothed back a strand of hair, already turning gray, into the indifferent coiffure of the morning. She was only months older than Sally. Yet Sally's face was unlined, and her body seemed as fresh as it had been in her eighteenth year. Her own body felt used and abused, and she knew she had a slovenly air about her. Even her father had said so in so many polite words. Since then she had made a special effort to appear not only neat but with some style, especially at dinner.

Martha felt a burst of loneliness. She tried to conjure up the image of her mother, dead now for twenty-nine years. The unclear face of her mother flickered briefly before her. After Martha Jefferson's death, her father had gone on a rampage of destruction. There remained no vestige of her portraits, letters, journals, accounts, diaries . . . everything went. He had never forgiven her for dying and leaving him. But she, Martha, had forgiven her. She strained to remember the face of this woman before the time when, sick and wasted, she had bound her father to a vow which had kept him wifeless and her motherless.

Then, Martha Randolph realized, she did look into the face of her dead mother every day. When she looked into the face of her slave, her aunt Sally Hemings. She had realized it even in Paris, although she didn't know how long it had been evident to her. There were differences, but there were the same eyes, the same small stature—so different from her own—the same dreamy look, the same

steely submission that masked the same taste for luxury
and powerful men, except that her slave had more of a
taste for politics than her mother had ever had. And if this
is what she saw when she looked at Sally Hemings, what
might her father see? She would give all of Monticello to
be as adored as that. Or would she?

Martha Randolph shifted the weight of her awkward
body. She picked up her sewing. Two things Sally Hemings, for all her resemblance to her mother, could never
be: she was not white and she was not free. She, Martha,
was mistress of Monticello now, and she would rule here,
she vowed, until the day she died. Her father could have
his pleasure. She would have Monticello, and her children
after her, and her children's children. Monticello would
descend upon her children unto the third and fourth generations, she thought proudly.

Sally Hemings held her straw hat in one hand and
shaded her eyes with the other. She watched Beverly Hemings ride down the mountain with his father. The small
head glistened in the slanting sun, the smooth brow furrowed with the effort of following father and son as far as
she could see. Sally Hemings was in the summer of her life.
There was a voluptuous richness about her. The yellow
eyes had darkened to gold with a glint of steel, and the
ivory skin to a delicate amber. The soft, pointed chin and
dimpled mouth had the set now, not only of authority but
of confidence. Her children were all born. Each birth had
been difficult, but she had always recovered quickly. She
had inherited the robust constitution of her mother and the
vicious will of her father, so that pain had never stopped
her from anything.

Thomas Jefferson was sixty-nine years old. Their passion, she knew, would diminish. She would not regret it.
He had been an amazingly virile and passionate man, and
their life together had been rich and full. But the body
tired. The body simply refused. She would never take another lover. She had been one man's only. His. And if they
were now like father and daughter, their contours, she
thought, would always blend into that entity which was the
human couple.

The summers seemed to pass more quickly. Europe was at war. Her beloved France was at war. The United States and its territories were at war with England. James Madison had been re-elected. Her master had reconciled with John, but not Abigail Adams. And now there was a fourth generation of Hemingses on the mountains. Little Sally Hemings and Maria Hemings, as well as her Harriet, had been sent to the weaver's cottage to learn to spin this summer.

She looked out over the land. They plowed in terraces now, following the contours of the hilly land instead of the straight rows up and down which had allowed the precious soil to run down into the river. Black hands plowed horizontally, following the curvatures of the hills and hollows on dead level; each furrow acting as a reservoir to receive and retain the rainfall. At least, thought Sally Hemings, in point of beauty, nothing could exceed that of these lines and rows winding and unwinding along the landscape. She stood contemplating it all for one more moment, and then, with that quickness of motion her lover had always remarked, she swung around, the heavy iron ring of keys at her waist jangling like a tambourine, and entered the mansion.

CHAPTER 40

WINTER 1819

Beverly Hemings's eyes roamed the hilly, hard-to-work
farmland that stretched to the east. It had once been
worth fifty to a hundred dollars an acre, but now with the
Panic, it was worth barely twenty. His father was in money
trouble. It had dawned on him more than three years ago,
the day they had packed up his library and shipped it up to
Washington City, the library that had been Beverly's only
real education, aside from Mr. Oglesby.

My father needs money, he had suddenly thought. That
realization had brought terror with it. Money troubles for
the master meant only one thing for the slave—the auction
block. His hands had trembled as he, along with Burwell,
Harriet, and his mother, had carefully wrapped and packed
the books into the cases that had been prepared by his
Uncle John and Dinsmore, the master carpenter. The Randolph girls—Virginia, Cornelia, and Ellen—had helped as
well. When they had finished all the packing, there had
been sixteen wagonloads of books—three thousand pounds
each—forty-eight thousand pounds of his father's life.
Each book had been handled, read, and touched by him.

No, Beverly was sure, he would never have sold his
library, even to the United States government, if he hadn't
needed the money desperately. The British had burned the
Library of Congress when they had burned the Capitol
during the war. He remembered with what horror and rage
his father had received the news, and now all his books
were leaving. . . . Beverly had burst into tears; his grief was
not only caused by the sudden loss of "his" books but the
meaning behind it all. His father had let him take out his

favorites from the lots, but had made him promise never to reveal this to a soul.

"If everyone were allowed to take out their favorite books, me included, I would have nothing to sell to the Congress. . . . You understand, Beverly, I have made a promise. I can't except anyone from the rule, even you. . . ."

From that day on, Beverly had had only one thought: how to keep his father, and thus himself and his family, safe from the threat of financial ruin that seemed to hang like a pall over Monticello. He had studied and looked and listened and planned and prayed as he saw the net drawing tighter and tighter around them all. And now the Panic had made everything ten times worse. There was real fear in the air.

Beverly Hemings stood watching the cavalier tear across the furrowed field just below the slope where he had set off his balloon. He laughed. He knew well who it was by the checkered black-and-white gingham coat with the huge metal buttons on it, the size of a dollar. The pantaloons were of the same material. The rider, mounted on a bay— Eagle, he guessed—was going at great speed. He was hatless as usual, his very head seemed on fire as his white hair caught the golden light, and he had a lady's parasol, probably Mama's, thought Beverly, stuck in his coat behind him and spread over his head to protect him from the sun. Beverly's heart filled with a kind of ironic tenderness. For his father.

It was now ten years since he had ridden home from the presidency. The time it had taken Beverly to grow up. His mother had not so much grown older as lighter, Beverly thought. Not so much in color; as a matter of fact, her beautiful face had grown darker—and not so much in authority either, for her presence was still as formidable as ever. Rather, there was about her a gradual disappearance . . . a seeping invisibility, so that even as he heard her voice, as sweet and thrilling as ever, with its soft lilt and slight foreign sound, it was as if it were coming to him disembodied.

If his mother was as transparent as a looking glass, his father glowed like the sun in it. He, Harriet, Thomas, and the younger boys seemed not even to have been created by this golden monster on his blooded, dangerous horse, and his mother, as still and deep as a reflecting pool. He didn't understand either of them. They were beyond mortality. They were like stones or trees. One couldn't rile against stones, could one? One couldn't curse trees. Beverly flung his fair hair out of his eyes. They were the strangest couple he had ever encountered, his mother and father. His tragic, terrifying parents.

Perhaps she is a miracle, he thought, to have loved him and to have survived this long. But now Monticello needed another miracle—no disembodied voices, no guardian angels, no supernatural beings were going to resurrect this place or save it.

Jeff Randolph was fighting mightily to keep Monticello from bankruptcy, but he was fighting a losing battle. The unprofitable condition of Virginia estates in general, and his father's in particular, had left it next to impossible to avoid ruin, especially with the failure of the banks. It was he who helped Thomas Jefferson Randolph run the plantations, now that his father had put his affairs in the hands of his grandson.

All the planters had been in bondage to the banks, which held tons of paper on every plantation in Virginia, and this would continue unless some change took place in the mode of working them. What the estates needed was a complete reorganization, away from agriculture and slave-breeding. The unprofitable land should be sold and the money invested in the developing cities of Richmond and Fredericksville. Lumber should be their staple crop, not slaves; they should be supplying the fast-growing cities with lumber, and making investments that would make possible the exploitation of the thousands of acres of forests that belonged to them. Beverly was certain they had the means to save Monticello and make a fortune to boot. But no one would listen to him. It seemed so simple to him. His father didn't want to be a slave-breeder, didn't want to live off the labor of slaves. Instead of slaves working in wheat, tobacco, and cotton fields, whose crops were at the mercy of Northern bankers and boll weevils, they should have freed men, each with their family, housed in community housing, working for wages in Monticello lumber yards, nail factories, iron works. . . . Goodness knows, they had labor!

With the rendezvous of the boats from western Virginia only a few miles away at Milton, they could ship thousands of tons of nails, thousands of cubic yards of good Virginia pine to the newly building cities, the settlements of the Louisiana Territory, not to mention the rebuilding of Washington City. And what about wagon wheels?—with the iron, the lumber and the manpower available, they could make millions of wagon wheels for the West. It just took a little business sense, something his Virginia aristocrat cousins knew nothing about. The nail factory, for example, was ludicrous. Run by an illiterate slave and a dozen children. It should be twenty times bigger, run by a foreman, white or black, it didn't matter, with men and the latest tools and forges. They had the land to build a real factory, not those miserable cabins they called a factory. White people were settling the Territories, and white people needed nails, iron pots, wagon wheels, farm tools, ax heads. And why not? Iron parts for the new steam engines, rails for the new steam carriages.

Beverly stopped abruptly. This was a good way to go crazy, he thought bitterly. He was nothing. A slave chattel. Why was he standing here watching his eccentric father ride, dreaming of a fortune in nails and lumber?

Yes, he would leave him in the end, this man whom he hated. Whom he wanted to adore. He had no choice. He was outlawed from him by his mother's blood.

His father dismounted next to him. It always amazed Beverly that he was taller than his master, as broad, and now, with the years piled on Thomas Jefferson, stronger, much stronger.

"Thank you, Beverly. You, Isaac, be sure to wipe off Eagle. Wipe him down and rub him good. He's as tired as I am."

"Yessa, Masta."

Beverly had waited almost an hour for his father to return. He had wanted to talk to him about his ideas for the nailery and the south forests. But now his courage faltered. He knew that the only thing his father really wanted to talk about was his university. The university that he, Beverly, would never see the inside of, except as a carpenter or floor polisher.

Last year he had ridden out with his master, his Uncle John, and the white workmen and slaves to commence the building of the university. Bacon had fetched a ball of twine from Davey Isaacs's store in Charlottesville, and his uncle had found some shingles and made some pegs; and they had all gone out into the fields that had belonged to Master Perry, now the grounds of the University of Virginia, and struck out the foundations of the building.

His father thought he could build a university that would take his mind off his decaying fortune, his mortgaged estates, his terrifying debts. His father would go on talking about his university in his presence without the least acknowledgment that every word was like an arrow in his breast: the new professors, the new buildings, the library, the rotunda, the future students . . . while he was trying to think of something that would keep Monticello from being sold out from under his father's . . . seat, Beverly thought grimly, and them along with it!

"Well, come, Beverly, if it can't wait. You've been standing there on one leg. Where's Jeff? What did he send you to tell me?"

Jefferson didn't send me to tell you anything, Father, thought Beverly. Jeff doesn't know how or what to do to save you. But I do. If only you would listen. I do. Me. Your bastard.

"Well, now, before you start in, Beverly, go fetch Jeff and see if you can find Joe and John. I've just been over to the university and I've got some new things to discuss with them. John has got to agree to do the planking the way Dinsmore says. I know it will be more expensive that way, but in the long run we'll save on nails."

Thomas Jefferson turned and looked Beverly in the eye. Their eyes were level; they were the same blue; there was the same frost in them that hid their real feelings from the world. Both pairs of eyes turned dark when anger or contradiction plagued them, as both reflected the rarity of their intellect. A kind of sullen brilliance rotated between father and son like a planet.

"Well, boy, what are you waiting for? Find your uncles!"

"Yes, Master."

Beverly caught the smell of horse on his father. He needs a bath, he thought.

He turned away. What had he hoped?

"Did you know that Beverly has been absent from the carpenter's shop for about a week?"

Thomas Jefferson, who had just returned from James Madison's Montpelier, looked up with surprise into the face of his overseer of thirteen years, Edmund Bacon. He asked Bacon to repeat what he had just said.

"I said, did you know that Beverly has been absent from the carpenter's shop for about a week?"

Thomas Jefferson thought for a moment that Bacon had left the door open behind him and had let in a blast of cold December air. He knew that Beverly's origins were no secret to Edmund Bacon. His overseer had waited a week to tell him of his son's disappearance and now he stood before him, his face a mask betrayed by the anger and incomprehension in his eyes. When would it end, this deceit that even servants judged? This unbearable waste?

It was the beginning of 1822, and his university was entering the last stage of completion. In another year or so it would open its doors to fifty or sixty young men. His dream was almost within his grasp. He opened his mouth to ask for details, to demand why he hadn't been informed before, perhaps even to send Bacon looking for him, but to his surprise he found he was speechless.

Beverly. His beloved Beverly had "strolled" without saying good-bye. Had deserted him when he needed him most. And what about Oglesby? If Beverly had been absent from the carpenter's shop, he had been absent from his tutor's classroom as well; but Oglesby had not sent word that he was missing.

When Beverly had stayed beyond his twenty-first birthday, he had somehow felt that this slave son would remain by his side, that this one was more his than the others. He was a brilliant boy, and it had grieved him that his education had not been what it should have been. Oh, he had given him Oglesby and books, but the recognition, the incentive, these he had withheld. Just as he had withheld the love he had felt for his son. Out of pride, he thought.

"You knew he was leaving?"

Thomas Jefferson was standing in the room of the mother of his runaway son. He had waited until now to confront her—he had wanted to confirm Beverly's absence with Oglesby and be sure that she had known Beverly was gone.

"Yes," she answered.

"Why didn't you tell me?"

"Because he didn't want you to know."

"Why?" he exploded. "I would never have stopped him from leaving!"

"He knew you would never stop him from leaving . . . because of your promise. That is why he didn't want you to know . . . he didn't want your permission."

Sally Hemings was guessing. This flight was one she had not planned. She didn't know why Beverly had suddenly decided to stroll. He had simply given up. Given up loving or hating his father, she didn't know which, and left. Before her master had left for Montpelier, he had sold twenty men, women, and children to his son-in-law Jack Eppes for four thousand dollars. His son-in-law had agreed to let the families remain together and to turn them over with the grounds to his son, Francis, when he came of age. In this way, Beverly's cousin, Mat, thirteen, was to become the property of his white cousin Francis, also thirteen years old.

Then, over at Edgehill, Thomas Mann sold Fennel's four-year-old Ely to Edmund Bacon for two hundred dollars. One day Fennel came home from the fields and his daughter wasn't there anymore. His wife lay in a faint; their baby girl had been sold away from them. Fennel had come riding from Edgehill to Monticello to recover his daughter from Edmund Bacon. When Bacon had heard Fennel was coming, he pleaded with her to calm him, as "he didn't want to harm him."

She had heard Fennel come howling down Mulberry Row as door after door closed upon his terrible face—the face of a man already dead, for wasn't he here to kill the white man who had bought his daughter or the one who had sold her? He had been pursued all the way from Shadwell by the black overseer, Jim, who had caught up with him almost in front of Elizabeth Hemings' former cabin. He had clubbed Fennel to the ground, and then had taken him tenderly in his arms. A ring of black men stood watch while Fennel had howled his grief into the night, within hearing distance of the Big House, howled like an animal, like the wild wolves that sometimes came up to the very doors of the slave cabins. His cries had washed over Monticello, over her and her children, safe within the mansion. Finally, dazed and beaten, Fennel had been lifted gently and flung over Jim's horse, and Jim had taken him back to his plantation.

That was when Beverly had left.

"Where is he?"

Sally Hemings was too tired to be frightened by the tone of her lover's voice. The violence of it was like a taste in her mouth. What could he do to her that he hadn't already done? She waited while her lover struggled to bring himself under control. She waited as she always had, supple and coiled and ready to spring to the left or the right, or fling herself down the center of his fury, depending on how it struck.

"I won't tell you," she said evenly, "because he doesn't want you to know where he is. He doesn't want any help from you. He's gone. North . . . as a white man. Of all your sons, he is the only one who hates you."

Thomas Jefferson stared at the woman who had been his mistress for thirty-five years. He would never completely understand her. She had raised these slave children, and if this son hated him it was because he had been taught to hate.

His long, gaunt figure moved quickly as he raised his slave wife from her chair. He knew now why this sensation, this chill, this sense of jeopardy was so familiar to him. He had never known, all these years, if one day he might not wake up, or come home, and find this woman gone. He drew her to him and looked into the eyes, which burned back at him like the sun.

I will free his sons.

Then she broke.

"Oh God, another gone!"

"And thank God for it," said Thomas Jefferson.

He felt his own throat go dry as he watched her strain away from him, watched her tremble once more above the abyss of contradiction which was their life together, peering over the edge into that moment he knew would come one day; when he would no longer be able to hold her, when she would choose to follow Beverly.

The woman looked up at the man.

Thomas Jefferson braced himself, as the small body he held against him crumbled, the tiny hands raking and clutching the material of his frock coat.

"Sally. Mother. Don't cry. Please don't cry." He was disconsolate. His face was a mask of helplessness, bewilderment, and rage that resembled nothing so much as that of the slave father Fennel.

CHAPTER 41

SPRING 1822

The Spring cut through her like the memory of a lover's quarrel. The May sun was high in the sky as she wandered down toward the sheep pastures, taking the shortcut through the sparse woods on the east slope. The moss had turned from silvery gray to emerald green and the ground under her feet was covered with white clover that looked like new-fallen snow, except that the earth was warm, not cold, and it was May, not December. New life was reaching out, claiming its inheritance. The earth, in its eagerness, was warm enough to walk barefoot. She stood among the black pines and inhaled the spring silence, opening her mouth wide in a soundless scream.

Thomas Hemings had given his father a grandchild, a white grandchild. Her son had secretly announced the birth of a little girl to her. A little white girl.

God, stand up for bastards, she thought. She shook her head. Martha had finally abandoned her husband. Thomas Mann Randolph had been elected to the governorship of Virginia, to everyone's surprise, and Martha had refused to accompany him to the governor's mansion in Richmond, preferring to remain with her father at Monticello. She had finally made her choice between husband and father.

Also, to everyone's surprise, Thomas Mann had proposed a plan for the emancipation of all slaves in Virginia and their deportation out of the state. Crazy Thomas Mann Randolph had had the courage to do something that his father-in-law had never dared. The proposition was defeated in the House of Burgesses. Thomas Jefferson had remained silent on the issue. Her sons had been beside themselves. The enormous prestige of their father could have saved the bill, they were sure. But he had said nothing to help his son-in-law.

It was the last thing he could have done for his slave children. It was the last thing he could have done for his precious Harriet, his only other daughter.

Harriet. Didn't he know he would lose her, too? More, even than his sons, she was lost to him. His darling little girl.

Sally Hemings came out of the woods. She saw her daughter converging on her from the direction of the house. The daughter had seen the mother and now she hurried. She didn't want to face her. Not now. But it was too late to escape back into the green. She stood and watched.

She could almost imagine that it was Maria who came running, so light and young and fragile and like her, except in height, was the young girl who approached. Harriet was now nineteen. She ran with her sunbonnet in her hand, and the light struck her auburn hair, which her mother had never cut and which was drawn back in a long braid reaching to her waist. As she ran, she held her head down under the weight of it. When the young girl stopped before her, there was only the slightest blush of pink under her cheeks.

"Mama . . ."

Sally Hemings looked into the emerald-green eyes of her daughter. She was out of breath and very beautiful. And she, the mother knew, was next.

Her twenty-first birthday.

Beverly had been gone for almost six months.

This would be her last ball as a slave. But Harriet Hemings expected to attend others on her own. The music of the slave orchestra wafted out over the expanses of lawn and jasmine bushes, the banks of roses and flowering magnolias of the Prestonfield Plantation. In the light from the tall windows of the ballroom sat an assembly of maids, carriage boys, valets, body servants, drivers, outriders, lackeys, footmen, and mammies: every shape, age, condition, and color of slavehood. Slavehood. She would peel it off like a dirty petticoat. She had been raised like a lady by her parents, educated with her cousins, and then, to her shock, had seen her adored playmates turn into masters overnight. Nothing would ever erase that pain. But then her mother had explained to her who she was and what would eventually happen to her.

The magic of her twenty-first year, when she would be freed. Free, as her father had promised her mother long ago in Paris.

And so she had played the game, but always in her mind was the knowledge of her reward, the breaking of the evil spell cast on her by . . . by whom? Whose fault was it that she was a slave? Her father's? Her country's? God's? Her mother had never been able to explain this to her satisfactorily, and she had never dared ask her father.

Hope had been her birthday. Now she was slave about to be free, black about to be white; girl about to become woman; without a past, about to be given a future; all for her birthday. She looked up at the sky. The moon was no more than a white sliver in the immensity of blackness. And what if the sky were white and the moon black? she thought.

Harriet had come into the circle of light from the ballroom windows, where she stood with the rest of the servants, entranced with the scene unfolding inside. The slave orchestra broke into a sprightly quadrille. Without the knowledge of the dancing white people it was playing Gabriel Prosser's song. Harriet shook her head and laughed with the rest of the servants while the whites continued to dance. Wasn't it typical, she thought, of white people to dance to a tune they didn't even know the words of. The whole South was dancing to a tune they didn't know the words of. The ladies and their escorts swung and looped, turned, skipped, grouped, and regrouped, forming circles and breaking like water on a creek bed.

Harriet's slender foot tapped to the music; her lips began to move. Suddenly, someone caught her from behind and swung her around. The maids and the lackeys had begun to dance in the circle of white light. They would continue to dance as long as their masters, far into the night, laughing and flirting, cooler outside than their sweating masters inside. They would outlast them, and then have to drive them home, undress them if they were drunk, wash them if they puked, pick up their clothes where they had dropped them, and put them to bed.

Harriet's skirts bobbed and swayed as her feet kept time and she sang the words of Gabriel Prosser's song:

There was two a-guarding Gabriel's cell
And then more in the jail about;
And two a-standing at the hangman's tree
And Billy was there to get Gabriel out.

There was musket shot and musket balls
Between his neckbone and his knee,
But Billy took Gabriel up in his arms
And he carried him away right manfully.

They mounted a horse and away they went,
Ten miles off from that hanging tree,
Until they stopped where the river bent
And there they rested happily.

And then they called for a victory dance,
And the crowd they all danced merrily:
The best dancer amongst them all
Was Gabriel Prosser who was just set free!

Harriet Hemings carried a razor-sharp stiletto deep in her petticoat pocket. It had been her Uncle James's. She would kill the man, black or white, who tried to force her. As her Uncle John had explained how difficult it was to kill, she had decided if she could not kill, then she would maim. She would die, but there would be one slave, or one master, who would never rape again.

She was going to be free. She was going to choose her husband. She was going to be married in a church. And she was going to her husband a virgin. She picked up her skirts and whirled in familiar black arms.

Everything was ready, and soon she would leave. It was November, already six months past her birthday. It was as good a time as any. Her mother had been working on her trunks for over a year. She had sweated and sewn until her hands were raw and swollen. Not only her mother, but her Aunt Critta, Aunt Bett, Cousin Betsy, Aunt Nance, Mammy Dolly, Cousin Ursula. Her Uncle John had made her three wooden trunks of the finest rosewood, with leather and copper fittings, lined in scarlet linen. Little by little, the trunks had been filled with dresses, linens of all sorts, petticoats, underwear, sheets.

Her mother had cut up everything she owned, either for the material or the trimmings. Even her yellow cloak had been torn apart, cleaned and recut into the most elegant yellow-and-black-velvet redingote she had ever seen. Her mother didn't dare let any of the white women of the house see it, for fear it would be confiscated. It was her strolling trousseau.

Her mother.

A slave inherited the condition of the mother. Was it her mother's fault that she was a slave? But why was her mother a slave? Wasn't that her father's fault?

More than any of her brothers, she had endured her temporary evil spell, her temporary slavehood, if not happily, then without rancor, and without suffering, grooming herself for the moment she would shed it, as her father had promised.

What no one had told her, and what she had had to fathom for herself, was that there was no freedom without whiteness; that to shed her slavehood was also to shed her color. If she were to escape the dangerous, persecuted, and harassed life of a freed slave, she would have to pass from one race to the other, from black to white.

Her mother.

Her mother still lived on memories of France while sitting in her secret room at the top of the mansion at Monticello, year after year, unable even to call her body her own!

Harriet Hemings had seen that room. It was filled with private treasure: silk dresses and petticoats, satin and kid shoes, and gloves, muslin and lawn dressing gowns, books, sheet music, a beautiful onyx pendulum clock, a green morocco leather chest, tooled in intricate designs and filled with linens, silk, and lace. There was also a delicate French writing table, a *coiffeuse,* bolts of velvet, and, most extraordinary of all, a hammered copper bathing tub called a *baignoire.* Her father had made a drawing of the *baignoire* her mother had used in France and Joe Fosset had built her one. All jammed into this one room: a whole secret life, full of beautiful treasures.

Most of it would be hers, her mother had told her. It was, she had reminded her daughter, her only dowry. She didn't need to indulge in her passion for beautiful clothes and beautiful things any longer.

Harriet Hemings was young and she was selfish. She would not throw away the gift of freedom as had her mother. She would grab it and run. Harriet's heart was heavy as she thought about the stagecoach that would take her away from everything she loved. But unlike her brothers, she would say good-bye to her father.

Adrien Petit had already arrived from Washington City to escort his former master's daughter to Philadelphia. He had left Monticello long before she was born, but Harriet had heard all about the indomitable Petit in Paris, in Philadelphia, at Monticello. Now her father had asked him to come and get her, and as a last service to his former master, he had arrived: a prosperous gentleman farmer and caterer, and, if the truth be known, richer than his former employer by many thousands of dollars.

Petit had prospered and bought land cheap around Washington and watched it double, then quadruple in value as the city thrived. He had tried, in the beginning, to persuade James Hemings to join him as a partner and chef, but James had had other ideas and had finally left for Spain, saying he would never live in a slave country again. Petit had wondered why James ever returned. But when he learned of James's death, he forbade himself to ever wonder again.

Petit sat now with his former master, receiving instructions about his daughter's settling in Philadelphia.

"You 'strolling,' Harriet?"

Madison Hemings was seventeen years old, tall and rangy with the bitter, suppressed violençe of his uncle. He was trembling with rage.

"Yes, Madison. I'm leaving at nightfall."

"You going to pass for white?"

"Yes, Mad, I'm going to pass."

"Father knows you strolling?"

"Yes, Mad. He's arranged everything. He sent for Monsieur Petit to come and fetch me to Philadelphia."

"Who's that? A friend of Papa's? You got any money?"

"Papa, he gave me fifty dollars, and Petit, he's seeing to the rest."

"You know how much you worth on the slave block, Harriet?"

"Oh, Madison, don't. Mad. Mad."

"You worth a pile of money, sweetheart. I tell you. You a *fancy*!"

"Madison . . ."

"I tell you Father could get five thousand dollars for you on the block! Five thousand dollars in New Orleans . . . at one of those Quadroon Balls . . ."

"Oh, Madison. Don't cry. I love you so. I'll always love you. Do you think it's easy to leave you? If I don't take this chance, what other chance do I have? What future if I don't?"

"You'll be alone with no family, Harriet . . . the end of Mama. You're deserting her."

"I know, Madison, but I'll always be a part of you. I'm *you*; *you*. I'm your sister. I'm your flesh and blood, and I'll always be, no matter what happens. No matter how far away I go. I'll never forget you."

"Yes, you will."

"Madison, please. Don't be so hard. Don't be so hard on me . . . I'm a girl . . . a woman. You don't know what it means to be a slave woman. Wait until your turn to stroll comes! Perhaps you'll understand better."

"Never. I'll never pass. It's worse than being *sold*. Selling yourself for whiteness."

"Perhaps when your turn comes, Madison, you can have your freedom without stealing it!"

"Perhaps when my turn comes, I can even kill for it."

"I have no choice, Madison."

"Five thousand dollars you worth to some white man . . ."

Madison's voice followed Harriet as she turned and walked away from him down Mulberry Row. When she was out of sight, Harriet leaned against the nearest cabin and was violently ill. But she refused to weep.

Harriet found her mother in a wheat field, far from the house, beyond the orchards. She was standing facing east toward the Chesapeake Bay and the sea two hundred miles away, as if she could see the tall clipper ships in the harbor. She did not turn as Harriet approached.

"Mama?"

"*Laisse-moi.*" Sally Hemings spoke the French she had taught her daughter.

"Mama, the carriage is waiting."

"I know. *Laisse-moi*, leave me."

"*Au revoir, Maman.*"

Sally Hemings remained staring toward the sea. Her daughter walked around her as if she were a monument of stone, until she faced her.

"*Je t'ecrirai, Maman. . . .*"

"*Oui. Ecris-moi.*"

"*Tu ne viens pas?*"

Sally Hemings looked at her daughter as if she were mad. The yellow light of her eyes struck Harriet like a lighthouse beam.

"*Non, je ne viens pas.* I'm not coming . . ." her mother said.

She knew Harriet's father would sit down at his writing table this night. He would light his candle and meticulously inscribe in his Account Book, "Run" after Harriet's name, just as he had written "Run" after Beverly's. As with Beverly, he would put the date, she decided, since the age of flight had been written long ago in their heart.

Harriet's father was waiting for her when she arrived at the carriage. It was almost dark. She had changed into her traveling clothes, the yellow-and-black redingote. Although she was almost as tall as Martha Randolph, she had to stand on tiptoe to embrace her father. She felt the frailty under the still imposing height and breadth. He was old, her father. Almost eighty, and she would never see him again. He trembled, and she held him fast, much longer than she had intended. She caught his scent: old wool, lavender, ink, and horse. When she saw him crying, she averted her eyes, but they met those of Petit, so she bowed her head and waited for her father to gain control of himself.

Harriet was young, and her young heart hardened with childlike logic. Why was he crying now? Now, when it was too late? What did he expect? Why hadn't he cried twenty-one years ago when he could have saved them all? She would never understand him. Had he thought that because he was Thomas Jefferson he would not have to pay someday?

She would start her new life without home, without family, without friends. She would be white. White. For the rest of her life she would live this lie. She would live in dread, on guard against slips, against chance encounters, against a keen eye. She was, after all, a runaway slave. A fugitive. Madison was right. It was worse than being sold away, she thought. She could meet her kin over the grave of her mother and still she could not recognize them. She would not even be able to stand over her father's grave and grieve. And what of her white family? She could no more recognize the whites than the blacks. This was the price.

Harriet's green eyes turned hard. So be it. Don't cry. Don't cry over it. Crying was done with forever. She was white now. She had nothing to cry about.

Adrien Petit looked on the scene with much the same horror as he had looked on the Christmas emancipation of James Hemings twenty-eight years ago. But, perfect servant to the last, he showed nothing. He was stunned by the beauty of this daughter: a wilder, more violent beauty than that of her mother. She had inherited the looks of her mother, and the flamboyance of the Jeffersons and the Randolphs; their height, their big bones, their presence. The combination was so remarkable it was difficult not to stare at her. She had her father's incredible hair and his creamy complexion, unvexed by Thomas Jefferson's freckles. Her eyes were a perfect combination of the yellow of her mother and the blue of her father. She had his pride, his stubbornness, and his vanity. This one was hard. And she was superb. She would never cry, and she would never bend. She would die first. How could his former master bear to lose her?

He understood that she would now pass for white. She would have to change her name, he supposed. What would she call herself? Harriet Petit, perhaps. . . . He flushed as if he had said it out loud.

He was leaving America for good—rich, old, and still a bachelor. He would return to the Champagne region and live out the few years remaining to him. He would not mind at all leaving his name behind.

Harriet Hemings lifted her head and looked at her father for the last time. She wanted to tell him that she was his. His daughter. She would always be his daughter. But she said nothing. Then she turned her gaze, hard and candid and green, on Petit, imploring him to take her away from this place forever.

He straightened instinctively under the command of those eyes, then bowed and helped her into his carriage. His last service to Thomas Jefferson.

Darkness was descending as they drove down the mountain.

Adrien Petit and Harriet Hemings rode away and never knew that within hours of their departure, Thomas Jefferson slipped on a decayed step of one of his terraces at Monticello, breaking his forearm and dislocating the bones of his right wrist for the second time.

Harriet would not have known its significance, and even Sally Hemings, rushing to the aid of her injured master, could not have savored the special irony of this fall. Only Petit, opposite a violently trembling, but dry-eyed young orphan, would have remembered his master's original fall from grace, in the Paris of Maria Cosway, the year of Our Lord, 1787.

CHAPTER 42

OCTOBER 1825

"Sally!"

It was Martha's voice, sharp with anxiety. I didn't know why I had come down the east stairs from my room as if I had been summoned, but I was in the hallway when she called. I saw her leading her father from the dining room, where he had—as usual—been entertaining a group of young students from the University of Virginia.

The door had been left ajar, and I could see the assembled young men, several of whom I didn't recognize.

As was his custom, Thomas Jefferson's place had been set separately, at a small table which was now empty, the chair pushed back. The young men were all on their feet, and several were peering anxiously through the opening of the doorway.

"Sally, he's been taken with a malaise," Martha said.

"No, Martha, I'm perfectly all right now."

"Here, let me help you."

He leaned heavily on me. I felt the tremor of his hand on my shoulder. How fragile and weak it was. Those hands that had had so much strength, that had guided, shaped, designed, and caressed. Now they rested, palsied and without weight, on my shoulder. I turned my back to open the door, and slowly we made for his room across the hall.

"Get Burwell," he murmured.

Burwell's gone to Charlottesville, I thought in panic as I looked over my shoulders beyond the open door into the glare of the candle-lit dining room.

Then I thought without surprise, He is dying.

* * *

From Harriet's departure on, misfortune had plagued us. No sooner had my master recovered from his fall from the terrace than he had ridden and had been thrown again by Brimmer. Stubbornly, he had ridden once again, and this time it had been Eagle that had slipped while fording a river and my master, entangled in the reins with his crippled wrist, had almost drowned. Next had come a fever that had confined him to his bed for three weeks. Then a flash flood had swept away the dam he had been building for over a year. He began to sink under the weight of his debts, which seemed to have no end. He had had to borrow from his son-in-law Jack Eppes and had pledged Varina, Martha's estate. Then his eldest and favorite granddaughter, the lovely and gentle Anne, whom we called Nancy, died, believed by everyone to have been killed by the brutality of her husband. Charles Bankhead, a young, handsome aristocrat, had turned out to be a drunkard, a bully, a coward, and a wife-beater. Many a time one of the overseers, or Burwell himself, had saved her from a beating by her husband.

Six years earlier, Jefferson Randolph had accosted Bankhead on the courthouse steps in Charlottesville and accused him of abusing his sister. Bankhead had responded by stabbing Jeff several times with a long knife. When Thomas Jefferson had heard the news, at nightfall, he had mounted his horse and galloped down the mountain the several miles to Charlottesville. Then, before I could stop Beverly, he, too, had saddled up and ridden out to find his father. "He'll kill himself in this weather," he had said. Fear in his face, he had taken Brimmer and sped. When Beverly arrived at the store where Jeff had been taken, he saw his father kneeling by the head of his wounded grandson, weeping. Jefferson Randolph had been conscious and when he saw his grandfather crying, he too had started to cry. Burwell and Beverly had watched in silence. Jeff, unlike his sister, had survived.

It was Eston who rode out after Thomas Jefferson now, fearful that he would come to some harm. He would ride down to his university that Eston and Madison had seen the inside of only as carpenters. . . .

In one way or another, all my master's "sons" had for-

saken him. Thomas Mann in insanity, Bankhead in brutality, Jack Eppes in premature death, Madison and Monroe
in ingratitude, Meriwether Lewis in suicide, Thomas Hemings in flight, Beverly in whiteness. There was only Eston
who remained a son. And in his hurt and melancholy and
loneliness, he had shown more affection and tenderness to
Eston than to any of our other children. He had given
Eston Maria's pianoforte, encouraged his music, paid for
his lessons; given him and Madison a plot of land of their
own to earn money. Madison had become a fine fiddler,
but even this tired and tardy recognition left me unmoved.
I was like a piece of ground too long soaked with water
which remains damp and cold even when the sun appears.

In the end, it was the master who sought his sons and
their love, their attention, who wanted more from them
than was his due; for if he had loved them, had he trained
them as sons, a fierce and loyal love would have been his.
His white grandchildren would never be able to give him
the special kind of desperate love his yellow children would
have laid at his feet. His grandsons were, after all, one
generation removed from his flesh. Madison, Thomas,
Eston, and Beverly were the sons of his passion.

At the end of 1824, one man who could remind him of
our beginnings arrived at Monticello.

Resplendent, Lafayette returned again in February to
Monticello, at the end of his triumphal tour of America,
where he was laden with honors and voted by Congress
two hundred thousand dollars and a township of land in
appreciation for his services to the country during the Revolution. For my master, it must have been a bitter mockery
of our own desperate situation.

General Lafayette's first visit to Monticello had had the
aura of an official visit. There had been more than three
hundred people present to witness the two old men shuffle
into each other's arms, tears flowing.

The crowds had gathered outside on the west lawn that
day to see with their own eyes the meeting of the two
heroes of the Revolution. The fastidious and luxury-loving
Lafayette had not changed his tastes, nor his mode of
living, I saw, French Revolution or no French Revolution.

As the elegant carriage rolled onto the flattened clay and sand, a dapper, finely dressed Lafayette had descended amidst cheers.

The last visit was quiet and more intimate, the true closing of a circle begun so long ago, the rendering of accounts, toting up of long-lost memories.

It was during this second visit that I made the acquaintance of Lafayette's companion, the mysterious Frances Wright. She sought me out, eager to speak. Frances Wright, a rich, well-born orphan of Scottish descent, was rumored to be General Lafayette's mistress and had been his constant companion for several years.

She was twenty-nine-years old and Lafayette sixty-seven. The thirty-two years difference between her and her general was three years more than the difference between me and my president. She too had to fight Lafayette's daughters for a part of his affection, and if she had begged him either to marry her or adopt her, as was rumored, it was in the same futile hope of legitimate protection for her love as I had dreamed of for mine, and with the same despair.

Frances Wright was as tall as Martha Jefferson. Her hair was magnificent, but she was not especially pretty. Her fortune, her education, her unmarried state had given her a freedom and an independence unheard of for a woman. There was about her carriage, something of the radiance of a young man unafraid of whatever fate had in store, and confident that she would overcome whatever it was.

She did not seem in the least affected or aware of my position, or my color. I sat and listened as she outlined her ideas on emancipation, not only of slaves but of women. She was the first abolitionist I had ever met. I longed to speak to her of Thomas, of Beverly, of Harriet, but they were no longer Thomas, Beverly, or Harriet. They no longer existed in my world. They existed in the white world now, and I had no right to speak of that world to anyone, white or black.

One day, Frances took my hand and spoke to me passionately.

"Merely freeing and enfranchising the Negroes is not enough for them to participate in a free society. Only after they have been given some education and trained to support themselves can their freedom be meaningful."

She spoke with fervor of the communities set up by two men in Pennsylvania, Robert Owens and George Rapp. She spoke of helping slaves and whites alike live on a basis of equality, somewhere in the West or South, paying with her own fortune, where the slaves would be not only freed but educated. Blacks and whites would go to school together, people would be free to love and marry whom they chose. She also spoke to me about a woman called Mary Wollstonecraft, an Englishwoman, who had written a book on the emancipation of women called the *Vindication of the Rights of Women.*

"More than ever, it must be proved that black and white can and must live together," she lectured. "Since the Missouri Compromise, we have a country that is divided between slave and free societies. It cannot and will not endure thus. . . ."

It was the first real courage I had ever encountered in a woman. Frances Wright evoked a vision of life I did not recognize, and it seemed just as well that my life's illusion was near its end.

"Oh, Sally Hemings, let's understand what knowledge is . . . let's clearly perceive that accurate knowledge regards all equally. Truth is the same for all humankind; there are not truths for the rich and truths for the poor, truths for men and truths for women, truths for blacks and truths for whites, there are simply TRUTHS. . . . At least this much I have learned. While you are bound can any American woman say she's free? Can any American woman say she has *nothing to do with slavery?* And can you, Sally Hemings, say you have nothing to do with us? With me? We are all you and you are we . . . and THAT'S the truth.

"Nowhere outside my investigations of the rights of slaves could I have acquired a better understanding of my own rights . . . womanhood's own rights. The anti-slavery cause is the high school of morals in this land. The school in which human rights are more fully investigated and better understood and taught than in any other. Is this country a *Republic* when but one drop of colored blood shall stamp a fellow creature for a slave? . . . Is this a *Republic* while one half of the whole population is left in civil bondage . . . sentenced to mental imbecility?"

I smiled. Oh, if only Harriet could hear her, I thought. "You don't count the bonds of love and passion as one more bondage? You, a modern woman?"

Frances Wright smiled back at me. It made her face beautiful.

"Love and civics unfortunately don't necessarily go together," she sighed.

Later that year, she purchased two thousand acres of land for her new settlement of Nashoba, fourteen miles from Memphis, Tennessee, and there she put her ideas on women and Negroes and education into practice. When her experiment failed, her name would become, as mine had once been for the public, equal to every vice, and she would be denounced as "The Great Red Harlot of Infidelity," just as I had been denounced as "Black Sal." Her name, as mine had been, would be coupled with the unspeakable crime of miscegenation.

At the same time that Lafayette left America and Frances Wright left Virginia, Jeff Randolph tried to organize a lottery of our estates to satisfy my master's creditors. Timidly, he had showed me his letter to the Virginia Legislature for permission for the lottery, carefully enumerating his services to the nation.

Thomas Jefferson begging! I wept. "Why not ask John Adams?" I asked. But he shook his head slowly. The nation and Virginia had forgotten him. He was too proud to ask Adams. His son, John Quincy, was now president of the United States, and who knew how John Quincy Adams felt about Thomas Jefferson?

Thomas Jefferson would die thinking his lottery was going to save Monticello. And he died hard, just like Elizabeth Hemings.

He had persisted in riding to the very end. Isaac and Eston would lift him up on Eagle, aged like him, and he would ride out alone, with Eston or Burwell or Isaac following at a safe distance to watch over him. He would be out for hours, his white hair whipped by the wind, his coattails flying. When he no longer could ride because of the terrible pain, he semireclined on his couch, unable to either sit, lie, walk or stand.

"The doctors are trying to keep the old man alive until the Fourth," Burwell said on the third of July. "I don't think he's going to make it."

"I swear he will," I replied.

On that day, it was Burwell who had understood and lowered his head. When Burwell left the room, I realized I would soon have to give my master up to his white family, which was gathering. Martha, who was at Varina, would never make it up the mountain in time.

He was mine alone.

"The letters," he murmured.

So he had not burned them all.

I went to his desk and opened the drawers one by one. Mementos, locks of hair, a ribbon of mine, secret things I had never dreamed of, faced me as each drawer opened and closed. I spied a soft lock of fine blond hair. Which dead baby was it? I fell upon a packet of my letters.

"You found them?"

"Yes."

"You know . . . what you must do . . . Please?"

It was the first time he had ever addressed that word to me.

"Ask Burwell to do it," I whispered, "for I cannot." I backed away from the desk.

He reached out his right hand and clutched at my skirt. The twice-broken wrist was doubly twisted with arthritis, the hand atrophied. I slipped to my knees to come closer to him and looked into his eyes. They were the eyes of a young man; the same sapphire blue as always. One dies with the eyes one had as a child, people say. Even when the body is unrecognizable with illness and age, eyes are the eyes of childhood.

"Did you love me?" he asked.

After thirty-eight years he still had to ask.

"Lord, keep me from sinking down. . . .

"Lord, keep me from sinking down.

"Lord, keep me from sinking down," I repeated over and over again into that silence. A whole kingdom of silence. A whole world of silence.

When Burwell entered the draped study, there were tears streaming down his face.

"He left everything to Jeff Randolph. Madison and Eston are freed by his will. They are left under the guardianship of John, who is also freed. Joe Fosset is free . . . so am I."

I stared at Burwell, waiting, but he stood there, his face contorted, his hands hanging loosely at his side, a look of grief on his face which resembled nothing if not stupidity. Still I waited. Waiting was my natural condition.

"He didn't free no . . . women."

I smiled. So he held me even in death. I had guessed as much when I had not been summoned to the dining room. I sat smiling. My smile must have been as stupid to see as Burwell's grief.

The death of a master, good or bad, is always a catastrophe for the slave. Sometimes he grieves out of real affection for the dead master, but mostly he grieves for the state of his future, which from that moment on is as vague and dangerous as his first journey out of his mother's womb.

Death of the master meant sale, separation from the land, from friends, and, if there were any, from wife and husband. And most of all, from children. The white family always took these outpourings of grief as proof that they were beloved, or of how much the dead master had been.

The Randolph family assumed as much, though here there was true grief as well. My master had been a "good master." The Randolphs were genuinely moved by the sorrow and mournings of the Monticello slaves. What they did not know, however, was that the slaves knew very well that Thomas Jefferson had died penniless, bankrupt, with a lottery on his land and his creditors hounding him to his very last breath. And they knew, too, that sooner or later Monticello, as had his other plantations, would fall.

It came sooner rather than later.

At Christmas I found Martha alone, standing in the threadbare blue salon, her heavy silhouette against the light, her white hair making an angry halo around her head. To my surprise, this day she had on gray silk, not black, an old dress, let out and pieced to accommodate her bulk. As I stood waiting for her to speak, I thought of our lives. We were only nine months apart, and I looked into the fifty-five-year-old face, so familiar to me, even more than in youth—a female replica of her father's face.

Age had marked it as it had not my own. The fair and fragile skin was etched with a thousand lines around the mouth and eyes, the skin crumpled like linen, the mouth drawn down in unhappiness. Tiny red veins, broken under the skin, gave it a flushed appearance. Her blue eyes had been burned gray by some internal fire. I could hardly see the eyes, so pale were they behind the spectacles she was now forced to wear.

My mistress. Had her life been so much different from mine? Or as happy, for that matter? Slave or free, white or black, women were women and they were indentured to husbands, fathers, brothers, children, in sickness and in health, in death and life, to pain and pregnancy, work exhaustion, grinding solitude, and waiting. Ah, God, above all, waiting. It was all in Martha's face.

I waited. I knew what she had to say to me. I was to go on the block. The rumors were no longer rumors. In less than a month, Monticello and the remaining plantations would be auctioned off and everything on them, including the seventy-odd slaves. The inventory had already been taken by Jeff. I was listed as worth fifty dollars. And Martha? Was she worth any more than I? The domain we had struggled for in an undeclared war that had lasted thirty-eight years was no more to be fought over. It lay under our feet and hung over our heads, a decaying, awful parody of its master and builder.

This, then, was the last battle.

If the power had been hers, I thought, the endurance was mine. My face, I knew, was without line or crease; my complexion clear; my hair still black and abundant; my figure, except for a thickening at the waist and ankles, the same.

Martha took off her spectacles, which left scarlet bruises on her nose and brow.

"Ah, Sally."

"Martha."

We stood facing each other, sentinels to four decades of lies.

"I have something to tell you . . . such terrible news. . . . I don't know just how to . . ."

I waited for her to finish speaking. The words droned on without meaning. I then found myself staring at Martha in disbelief as she continued.

". . . and as he instructed me, you were to be freed within two years of his death, as soon as Eston was of age and could act as head of the family. I thought . . . forgive . . . that this day . . . that today was a good day. . . . Eston will be twenty-one in a few months . . . until then you may stay here, at least until July, as the house will not be sold, but you must know, since you people know everything, that the auction is the beginning of the year."

The date of the auction! Her voice suddenly reached me, clear and fraught with meaning.

"We cannot hold out any longer, Sally, and I dare not wait any longer to give you your papers. I hereby free you as my father wished, but could not acknowledge for . . . reasons of his own. He asked me to tell you this. He petitioned me, begged me, to free you. And for his sake I do so."

Here she paused, waiting for me to make the proper gesture. But what gesture was there to make? I knew of none.

"You have nothing to say?" she asked.

"Nothing."

"Nothing?"

"Nothing," I repeated.

I thought of my mother and her mother. It would have been slavish to have said anything. And I was not her slave.

"I think you could at least express your thanks. He petitioned me, but only I have the power to make you free. I could have allowed you to be sold on the block with all the rest!"

I stared at Martha. Did she really think she had the power to free *me*? Free *me* with a piece of paper, when I couldn't free myself with all the total yearning of a whole lifetime?

"Martha, I have no thanks to give. You cannot free me. Even *he* could not free me. He couldn't free me living, he couldn't free me dying, and he can't free me dead. He did what he had to do, as have you and I. I am an old woman, Martha, worth fifty dollars, and you are as worthless. Our lives haven't been all that much different, and death has us both by the hair. Can we not at least explain ourselves one to the other before it's too late?"

"You think I'd ever *explain* myself to you? I would rather die." Martha's voice was strangled with anger.

"Recognize that—" I began.

"Recognize! Do you think I'd ever recognize you? Recognition for the harm and slander you caused an innocent and great man?"

She would lie to herself to the end. She waved the white envelope in the air above my head like a child's gift.

"A thank you from the family?" It was our family she spoke of. "Recompense from the family? A souvenir from this house? A silver watch, perhaps?"

"Everything I'll ever need in recognition I've had, and souvenirs I have more than enough, even to silver."

What I did then, I don't regret, but it was a gesture as futile as our lifelong lies. I did it in cold anger and hatred of that white power she waved over my head. I pulled out the locket with the miniature John Trumbull had given me at Cowes and showed her his face: the same face in miniature that Martha always carried with her, the image she thought was hers and hers alone, I had carried for thirty-seven years around my neck.

The lock of his hair, blood-red, slipped from its place and fluttered to the floor. She made a gesture as if to stoop and catch it, then straightened with a sob, almost touching me. I fell back. Lie, I thought, lie to yourself, for it is your only hope. Deny me if you wish. Deny me with your last breath, your last cent, for in time, in this land, it will come to that.

"He loved me more than you! He loved *me*! You are nothing, you black slut! You slave whore! You know your children are not his! Never! They'll never be his!"

"Perhaps, but I was his. He loved me, Martha. It is not out of vanity or pride that I say it, but that was how it was between us. We loved. It was all that mattered."

"How can you speak of love between a master and a slave . . . between a hero and chattel?"

"We had no need to speak of it. . . ."

"You were nothing to him! A convenient slave paramour, a . . . receptacle!"

The evil words clattered like iron nails in the coffin of silence. There was nothing but pure hatred between us now. Martha's face pressed into mine and I looked into its decay as if in a mirror. Those eyes would not leave mine. She would not leave me in peace. The breath. The feverish face. We were like two bitches worrying over a rotting and long-dead carcass. Didn't she understand that it was over?

Then she drew back. Dread seized me by the throat like some wild animal. She was going to tell me something.

"Didn't you ever love me?" she whispered.

It was the same thing her father had asked. A wild, uncontrollable desolation bore down upon me. A howl like that of a wounded dog caught in my throat. When . . . when would they understand this farce and this tragedy? I knew that only the one who stopped loving, who stopped needing love, would survive. And hate seemed to drop over me like a veil. Love had left me, and hate had filled that space. The grief and loneliness without him; the empty meaningless days and nights dissolved like dry straw. Hate lifted me up in a kind of exaltation. The white envelope which said I was free but which I knew would never really free me remained in her hand.

I didn't need anything anymore. I didn't need Martha. Martha needed me to free, but I didn't need Martha to free me.

I, like my mother and her mother before her, had survived love.

CHAPTER 43

NOVEMBER 1826

Notice from Richmond *Enquirer*, 7 Nov. 1826
EXECUTOR'S SALE

On the fifteenth of January, at Monticello, in the county
of Albemarle, the whole of the residue of the personal
property of Thomas Jefferson, dec., consisting of valuable negroes, stock, crops, etc., household and kitchen
furniture. The attention of the public is earnestly invited
to this property. The negroes are believed to be the most
valuable for their number ever offered in the state of
Virginia. The household furniture, many valuable historical and portrait paintings, busts of marble and plaster of
distinguished individuals, one of marble of Thomas Jefferson Ceracci with the pedestal and truncated column on
which it stands, a polygraph or copying instrument used
by Thomas Jefferson for the last twenty-five years, with
various other articles useful to men of business and private
faculties. The terms of the sale will be accommodating
and made known previous to the day. The sale will be
continued from day to day until completed. The sale being
inevitable is a sufficient guarantee to the public that they
will take place at the times and places appointed.

[signed] THOMAS JEFFERSON RANDOLPH
Executor of Th. Jefferson dec'd.

It has long been known that the best blood of Virginia
may now be found in the slave markets. . . .

FREDERICK DOUGLASS, 1850

Thomas Jefferson Randolph, better known as Jeff, sat in
his grandfather's study, his long legs stretched out under
the old man's writing table. He was the image of Thomas
Jefferson.

He stared at the laboriously written inventory. It was
pitiful, he thought. Not more than five years ago, these
people would have brought four or five or even ten times
these amounts. Of course, the most valuable slaves were

not at Monticello, but at Poplar Forest, where they were about seventy odd who would bring in money as prime laborers. The Monticellian slaves were all more or less fancies, high-yellow or white slaves, highly trained, but they were too old. He had never known Monticello without them.

He had lined them all up on the west lawn, practically in front of the window he was now gazing out of, and had gone around from one to the other making the inventory with Mr. Matter, the auctioneer. His nurses, his playmates were all there. He had taken out his own slaves—Indridge, Bonny Castle, and Maria—and those of Aunt Marck's, which were the most valuable, except for Davey Bowles. Damn! Davey Bowles should have been able to bring at least two thousand. . . . He had passed each familiar face, some so dear to him, that tears had welled in his eyes. When he had stood before Fanny, he had wanted to throw himself in her arms bawling.

Mr. Matter had kept apologizing for the low estimates, explaining that the bottom had fallen out of the market in the past year and that prices had plummeted almost eighty percent! At least they would keep the house with one miserable acre. That was all.

His eyes roved to the miniature staircase at the foot of his grandfather's bed. The passageway would be sealed at the request of his mother. Only the tiny staircase would remain. No one had taken the trouble to explain the relationship between the Hemingses and the Randolphs, but children had a way of finding out what they wanted to know, thought Jeff. Like the day of the inventory when he had looked into the eyes of Sally Hemings. He had heard Mr. Matter's automatic whisper:

"Age?"

"I reckon between fifty and sixty," he had answered.

"Fifty dollars," Mr. Matter had said.

And Sally Hemings had said, "Oh my husband," looking straight at him.

She had said it, damn it. Clear as a bell. Only once, but he had heard it. When he had told his mother of it, she had shrugged and said that Sally's mind was probably wandering with the shock of the sale. She had never had a husband. Then his mother had announced that she was freeing

Sally Hemings because his grandfather wanted it that way. It meant they would have to petition the Virginia legislature for her to remain in the state—dangerous.

Of course, Sally Hemings hadn't said those words to him, for her eyes had been fixed on the Blue Ridge Mountains, and they had had the most unearthly yellow glow. God damn! . . .

Barnaby	$400	Davy	$500
Hannard	450	Zachariah	350
Betty old woman	no value	Nace	500
Critta	50	Nance an old	
Davy senior (worth		woman	no value
nothing)	250	Ned	50
Davy junior	250	Jenny (of no value)	
Fanny		Moses	500
Ellen	300	Peter Hemmings	100
Jenny	200	Polly (Charles's daughter)	300
Indridge (the younger)		Sally Hemmings	50
Bonny Castle		Shepherd	200
Doll (of no value)	—	Indridge the elder	250
Gill	375	Thrimston	250
Isaac an old man	0	Wormsley	200
Israel	350	Ursula	
		and her young child	300
James	500	Anne & child Esau	350
Jersy	200	Dolly 19	300
Jupiter	350	Cornelius 17	350
Amy	150	Thomas 14	200
Joe to be free in July		Louisa 12	150
next	400	Caroline 10	125
Edy & her child Damie	200	Critta 8	100
Maria 20		George 5	100
Patsy 17 or 18	300	Robert 2	75
Betsy 15	275	Infant valued with Ursula	
Peter 10	200	its mother	60
		I have omitted Aunt	
Isabella between 8 and 9	150	Marck's and mine, also	
		the 5 freed ones	
William 5	125	The ages are set down as	
Daniel 1½ Lucy's child	—	near as I can come at	
		them without the book	
Good John, no value	—	Johnny to be emancipated	
Amy same	—	July next	300
Jenny Lewis (of no value)	—	Madison same	400
Mary (Bet's) young		Eston same	400
woman	50		
			11,505

[signed] THOMAS JEFFERSON RANDOLPH

CHAPTER 44

JANUARY 1827

The dismantling of Monticello by the slave auction of 1827, the abomination of the sale of my kin, the ticketing and labeling and pricing of every stick of furniture, every sheet, every curtain, every dish, every book, painting, sculpture, each clock, vase, bed, table, horse, mule, hog, and slave that had been Thomas Jefferson's; that had been he, himself; all his parts and pieces, his choices, his favorites, his ears, his hands, his eyes, was the sorrow and pity of my life. His life had been parceled and lotted and priced by the auctioneers who thronged through the house. His life's bits and pieces probed and handled, weighed and inspected. Everything, animal and human, including my own flesh.

I despised the steaming crowd that had gathered round the west portico of Monticello that January day, come to bid like vultures on the carcass that had been a man and his house. If only he had not loved everything so much! If everything had not been love and memory as well as collection!

People arrived by the wagonloads. A country-fair atmosphere reigned as the prospective buyers strolled in and out of the barns that held the slaves, and the house that held the objects, their flyers in hand, inspecting objects tenderly accumulated in Paris; a house of brick and wood assembled by my kin; the brilliant English gardens, now brown and colorless; and the orchards, now leafless and barren; and beyond, the rolling fertile fields, woods, cascades, and rivers. Already the deep black lands of Pantops and Tufton, Lego, Poplar Forest, Bear Creek, Tomahawk, and

Shadwell were gone, now the humans attached to them were going. One thousand four hundred and fifty lots had been auctioned off that day, forty-two hogs, fifty sheep, seventy cattle, fifteen horses, eight mules, and fifty-five humans from Monticello—more than half of the slaves were my sisters, brothers, cousins, nieces, nephews. And one hundred and twenty from Bedford.

The crowds had begun to assemble early that day. They had come from as far away as Kentucky for a chance to buy prime black flesh, livestock, or an object that had been, as I had been, a possession of Thomas Jefferson. There had been that same lewdness in the air, that same miasma of death and contempt and titillation that always accompanies the trial, judgment, and condemnation of a man's life. Around me festered the curiosity about the great, the aura that sets some men above others and brings out that predatory hatred of the common for the extraordinary.

My master had left debts of one hundred and seven thousand dollars. Martha and Jeff had struggled valiantly to save Monticello, selling off all the other lands and plantations; the lots in Richmond and Charlottesville, everything. But everything had not been enough. The gods had demanded and got all but the mansion of Monticello.

Strangers had roamed his precious gardens, treaded his polished floors, inspected his linen, looked into his barns and the mouths of his slaves, pinched velvet and flesh, sniffed tobacco and the smell of human sweat, hefted samples of cotton and the private parts of male field hands, rubbed their hands over the woolly rumps of Merino sheep and the heads of pickaninnies, discussed the qualities of Monticello blooded bays and Monticello pure-bred bodies.

Hatted and veiled, my identity hidden behind my color and the name of "Frances Wright" of Tennessee, I had roamed the crowds that day as a freedwoman, despite the danger, willing myself to engrave every moment in my memory, hoping to save one or two of the children, and vowing never to forget the sale of Thomas Jefferson.

"If you don't be good, I'll tell Master, and he'll sell you to Georgia, he'll sell you so fast . . ."

How often had those words struck terror in a slave

child's heart? How long, how much longer, would they
continue to? He had been good, but he would be sold
anyway.

"What do I have, whatdo I have, whatdoihave for this
lot number thirty-four, three prime male field hands,
twenty-six to twenty-nine, broken here at Monticello, in
perfect health, no scars, bruises, defects *of any kind*; never
been whipped, docile, strong, perfect for breeding. What
am I bid, whatamibid, three hundred, four, four fifty. Do I
hear five? Five, five twenty-five, six, six, six. Do I hear
seven? Yes seven, seven twenty-five, seven fifty; only seven
fifty for this prime lot, three . . . ladies and gentlemen,
three prime Monticello slaves, three for the price of one.
Ladies and gentlemen, I ask you, is this the best you can
do? Eight, eight fifty do I hear nine? Nine, do I hear
nine, nine, nine, nine—going once, nine going twice, nine
going three times—sold, sold to the lady for nine hundred
dollars. Prime, male house slave, thirty-two years old, Israel, father of seven in the next lot, locksmith and metal-
worker. Prime, housebroken pickaninnies, a lot of seven.
Just a few years and they'll be prime field hands or house
servants, healthy stock, no blemishes, light-skinned. Do I
hear five hundred? Five hundred once, five hundred twice,
five hundred three times. Sold! Sold! Sold! A female,
twenty-nine years old, breeder, light-skinned, seamstress
and cook, perfect for a housekeeper for a young gentleman; may I start at four hundred? Four hundred fifty?
Elizabeth, Israel's wife. Do I hear four? Four, four fifty,
five . . . female slave, fifteen, guaranteed virgin, healthy,
bright, best stock of Monticello, trained as a house servant.
Priscilla, Israel's daughter.

"Do I hear three hundred? Three hundred. The best
stock at Monticello. Docile, perfect for a lady's maid. Only
five hundred dollars. Ladies and gentlemen, Christmas was
a week ago! I cannot let this prime female go for less than
three fifty. Do I hear three fifty? Yes, three seventy-five.
Do I hear four? Four. Four. Do I hear four? Sold to the
gentleman for four seventy-five. Dolly.

"Prime first-class female. Cook. Thirty-six years old;
served at the President's House in Washington City. Pastry
and all-around cook. Do I hear one hundred dollars? Two?

Do I hear three? Three for this treasure trained in French *cuisine*. Of impeccable stock, guaranteed fertile, mother of three. Three fifty, do I hear four? Four fifty, do I hear five? Five fifty once, five fifty twice, five fifty three times. Sold to the lady for five hundred and fifty dollars. Fanny. One big black healthy mammy trained as washerwoman, mid-wife, and pastry cook. Weighs in at two fifty (laughter). House servant for twenty years. Sixty-two years old, ladies and gentlemen, I won't lie to you, but she still has some good years in her. Loves children, mother of eight herself. All them children in lot fifty-six hers! Loyal, honest, clean house mammy. Do I hear thirty dollars? Thirty-five, do I hear forty? Fifty? Do I hear . . . fifty it is. Going, going gone. Sold. Sold. Doll.

"Now here's a perfect lady's maid, tall, beautiful, bright, breeder, a child sold along with the female, two months' . . . one lot, ladies and gentlemen, one lot. Ursula.

"Twenty years old, Ladies and gentlemen, look at that body. Born to breed. Look at those breasts. Ladies and gentlemen, do I hear four fifty? Do I hear it? Do I hear five? Five for the lot, ladies and gentlemen. Buy her and get the sire of the next lot. Do I hear five fifty? Five fifty, once, five fifty twice, five fifty three times. Going, going, gone."

Critta's Milly, sold to Mississippi. James Hubbard sold to Kentucky. Washington Hemings, my nephew, sold to West Virginia. Critta had fetched one hundred dollars despite her age. Nance, six hundred and fifty dollars with two adolescent grandchildren thrown in. Betsy, her daughter, sold pregnant at one thousand to North Carolina. Betsy's husband brought five hundred, sold to Georgia. Isaac brought seven hundred and Wormley six hundred. Davey Bowles, the highest price of all, one thousand dollars, sold to New Orleans.

At the end came the "extra articles" prized because of their beauty, their color, their training, their pedigree. The white Hemingses came under that category . . . all my sister's children. Lilburn, Henry Randell, Martha, Maria, Dolly. Peter Hemings, as a first-class chef, brought five hundred. His twin boys brought seventeen hundred for the pair.

John had given his seven hundred to a white man to buy

his son, and Joe Fosset bought his wife for nine hundred fifty, and his mother, Mary, for twenty-five dollars. My room, with all my possessions, had been sealed. Only later would John be able to retrieve them. I had only the clothes on my back. But I had the locket. If only I had tried to sell it. The little money I had with me, I had hoped to buy one or two of the children, perhaps Critta's ten-year-old Nancy, or Rachel's six-year-old twin girls. I wanted to save one or two small children, my sister's children being grown and too expensive. I hadn't realized that they would not be sold one by one, but in lots. In lots of three or four children for two to four hundred dollars. Too late, I realized I had not enough money to buy a lot. Too late, I realized that the locket was my condemnation to everlasting hell.

I had stood like a survivor of a shipwreck who had managed to be pulled ashore and lay half-drowned on the rocks. The worst was the end, when the leftover children and women were sold in lots away from their husbands, or mothers, or children. The screams of the children, the cries of the mothers, the groans of the fathers and husbands rang in my ears.

Then I saw him before me on the block, unclothed, his lean, naked, white body covered with its soft red down as I had seen him when I was a young girl; the wide square shoulders; the long, heavy-wristed, heavy-thighed, heavy-angled body with its powerful neck supporting the delicate head; the leonine burst of thick auburn hair. A white, male, shorn of his gifts, his power, his possessions, his history, his family, his children, his lands, pale and vulnerable. Thomas Jefferson.

I heard the auctioneer droning—"Prime male, unusually strong, intelligent, trained as a carpenter, a gardener, a horse trainer, a secretary, a musician . . . useless in the fields, but a good breeder. Going once, going twice, going three times. Sold! Sold for seven hundred dollars. . . ."

PART VII

1835
Albemarle
County

CHAPTER 45

JUNE 1835

St. Claire laughed. "You'll have to give her a meaning or she'll make one."

HARRIET BEECHER STOWE, *Uncle Tom's Cabin*, 1852

Philadelphia, July 4th, 1776

He has waged cruel war against human nature itself, violating its most sacred rights of life & liberty in the persons of a distant people who never offended him, captivating & carrying them into slavery in another hemisphere, or to incur miserable death in their transportation hither. This piratical warfare, the opprobrium of INFIDEL powers, is the warfare of the CHRISTIAN king of Great Britain, determined to keep open a market where MEN should be bought and sold. He has prostituted his negative for suppressing every legislative attempt to prohibit or to restrain this execrable commerce, and that this assemblage of horrors might want no fact of distinguished die, he is now exciting those very people to rise in arms among us, and to purchasing that liberty of which *he* deprived them, by murdering the people of whom he also obstruded them; thus paying off former crimes committed against the LIBERTIES of one people, with crimes which he urges them to commit against the LIVES of another.

THOMAS JEFFERSON

The Declaration of Independence, 1776

(Excised from the final draft by consensus)

Nathan Langdon released the pressure of his thighs and reined in his horse. He had just taken the rotting dilapidated barrier on the western slope of Monticello at full speed, and now he rested in the cool, vaulted overgrown forest, still criss-crossed with Thomas Jefferson's bridle paths.

It was the first time he had returned home for the summer in two years. The handsome face and the pure gaze were slightly touched with the cynicism of his profession. He was a Washington lawyer now, considered one of the best, and he was Washington-wise and Washington-weary, full of compromise, adroit at survival, and totally successful. The beautiful mouth revealed a line of disappointment. There was no more black or white in his life, only infinite shades of gray.

As the brilliant June light filtered down, flecking the fair hair and the flanks of his mount, Nathan was suddenly invaded by a pervasive, unfounded premonition of disaster, a rising dread as he continued up the mountain to the mansion.

When he came to the leveled-off clearing at the top of the mountain, he stared in horror at Monticello. It stood naked. The lofty elegant shade trees that had protected and surrounded it for seventy years had all been cut down, the stumps still white, raw, and ugly. Even in his shock, Nathan Langdon's legal mind registered the fact that he was trespassing. Monticello had been sold last year to a pharmacy shop owner in Charlottesville, the new rising race of a new era: that of the common man.

Nathan stared at the decaying gray façade. It was deserted. Burwell's paint had peeled off, Joe Fosset's iron balconies were rusted and crumbling, John Hemings's shingles were warped or missing. It no longer belonged to Sally Hemings. Langdon smiled. It no longer belonged to the heirs of Thomas Jefferson. Why did he always think of it as belonging to Sally Hemings instead of the other way around?

It was now five years since his first meeting with Sally Hemings. Four years since his banishment. He had learned nothing more of her than what he had known from the beginning. He had encountered only evasiveness and omissions.

Terror seized Nathan. If this is what they had done to what had been Thomas Jefferson's mansion, what had they done to Sally Hemings?

Langdon started down the mountain toward her cabin, fighting a rising anguish. Where was she? What had become of her?

He rode within sight of the tiny cabin but he didn't dare approach. The old yearning returned, something—as infinitesimal as a rustling branch or a leaf, or the wind, or a pebble beneath his mount's hoof, or the sound of his own heart beating—held him back.

In the distance he saw the small figure emerge from the house. She was alive. Who was it, he thought, who had said: . . . *and then consider what mere Time will do . . . : how if a man was great while living, he became tenfold greater when dead. How a thing grows in the human imagination when love, worship and all that lies in the human heart is there to encourage it. . . . Enough for us to discern far in the uttermost distance, some gleam . . . in the center of that enormous camera-obscura image to discern that at the center of it all was not a madness and a nothing, but a sanity and a something.*

He watched her as she stood, her arms wrapped around herself. And as he watched her, Nathan Langdon felt the gulf between them. It had grown, he realized, with the years. Even as he stood there unknowing, the distance separating them was a canyon, a bottomless crater, a fissure in the earth, uncrossable, unbridgeable, unfathomable, unforgivable. The sound of summer thunder rolled over the Blue Ridge Mountains, a distant prediction of turbulence to come. What Nathan Langdon did not know is that the turbulence to come, which he would witness in sickness and despair, would claim the lives of three of Sally Hemings's grandsons. A bitter struggle that would cost five hundred thousand lives. One life lost for every slave freed.

Sally Hemings stood in the violet rectangle of her cabin, her arms outstretched, her palms pressed against the oak doorframe, the dark shadows framing the still lovely face. She contemplated the cherished and familiar landscape. It calmed her. The lush Southernness soothed her nerve ends, the colors washed over her flesh so long contorted and deep with memory. Memory had no shame. All were equal before it. Then she stepped outside. Her body dove into the languid summer landscape like a swimmer, and her head lifted as if she sensed a presence. She looked toward the Blue Ridge. But all she saw was the dark-green forest and luminous sky and all she heard were the sounds that summer makes.

She had never reached out beyond her triple bondage. She had clung stubbornly to the only thing she had ever found of her own in life: love, and love had been more real to her than slavehood. And she had survived both. This was the truth of her life.

Sally Hemings closed her eyes against the sunlight and against the blinding pain in her head. She stood in her own embrace, triumphant; beyond love, beyond passion, beyond History.

And surrounding the two solitary figures, lost in the vast intractable wilderness of the American landscape, was the infinite chiaroscuro of silence, where all biographies become one.

She picked up her skirts and started up the mountain toward the safety of her beloved shade trees, just as, with a kind of violence, the census taker turned away and headed back down her road.

AFTERWORD AND ACKNOWLEDGMENTS

Although a bibliography would be long and out of place here, I feel I must acknowledge certain published and scholarly works not previously mentioned and without which this book could not have been written. They are not, of course, responsible for any errors, interpretations, or misinterpretations I have made.

First, Fawn Brodie's book, *Thomas Jefferson, An Intimate History,* and her two articles published in *American Heritage,* "The Great Jefferson and Taboo" and "Thomas Jefferson's Unknown Grandchildren."

Second, the memoirs of Madison Hemings, of Edmund Bacon, of the ex-slaves Israel Jefferson and Isaac Jefferson, as well as the diaries of Aaron Burr and John Quincy Adams.

Third, the letters of John and Abigail Adams and the Family Letters of Thomas Jefferson, his Farm Book and his Account Book.

An unpublished paper at the University of Virginia Library by Jean Hanvey Hazelton, "The Hemings Family of Monticello," must be mentioned, as well as the Jefferson Lectures of Eric Erickson at Princeton University; Cornel Lengyel's *Four Days in July, The Autobiography of John Trumbull* and the Nathan Schachner biographies of Thomas Jefferson and Aaron Burr.

Lastly to be mentioned: *The Jefferson Papers* of Julian Boyd and his article "The Murder of George Wythe," published in the *William and Mary Quarterly; Thomas Jefferson, The Darker Side,* by Leonard W. Levy and the catalogue and the exhibition, "The Eye of Thomas Jefferson," organized by The National Gallery, Washington, D. C.

My last acknowledgment is to a nineteenth-century novel, *Clotel, or the President's Daughter,* published in England in 1853 by William Wells Brown, a runaway slave, considered the father of the Afro-American novel. Although I read the original version only after I wrote this book, I was touched to the quick by the recognition of cadences, themes, wellsprings of feeling that are the roots of Afro-American writing. That the theme of this novel, the first black novel published outside the United States, is the same and was written by an expatriate in the true sense of the word, only brings the circle full round. I would like to thank the Schomburg Collection of Black Culture, my researcher Rother Owens, my secretary and editorial assistant Carolyn Wilson, Victoria Reiter, Mary McCarthy, Lynn Nesbit, my family and my friends and my editors.

SOURCE DOCUMENTS

Census Entry, Albemarle County, 1830 (*Courtesy of the Microfilm Division, The University of Virginia*)

Letter from Thomas Jefferson to Francis C. Gray, 1815 (*Writings, Thomas Jefferson [Monticello Edition], Lipscomb and Bergh, Volume XIV, pp. 267–71*)

Memoirs of James Hemings, "Life Among the Lowly," Pike County (Ohio) Republican, March 13, 1873

Passport issued by Louis XVI for Thomas Jefferson, Maria and Martha Jefferson, James and Sally Hemings, 1789 (*Manuscript Division, The Library of Congress*)

Description of harvest at Monticello, List of Slave Workers (*Thomas Jefferson Garden Book [1795–96]*)

Promise of Emancipation of James Hemings, 1793 (*Writings, Thomas Jefferson, Philadelphia, September 15, 1793, Boyd, 18 vols., Princeton*)

Two letters from James T. Callender to Thomas Jefferson, 1800 (*Manuscript Division, The Library of Congress*)

"The President Again," by James T. Callender, *The Richmond Recorder*, 1802 (*September 1, 1802, Archives, The Virginia State Library*)

"Black and White Ballad": Portfolio April 9, 1803 p. 120, Reprinted from the *Boston Gazette*.

The Census of My Family, Farm Book, Thomas Jefferson, 1807 (*Thomas Jefferson, Farm Book, 1807, Massachusetts Historical Society*)

The Slave Inventory and Advertisement of Slave Auction, Monticello, 1826 (*Courtesy of Jefferson Papers, University of Virginia Library, Manuscript Department. Notice from Richmond Enquirer, November 7, 1826, courtesy of Jefferson Memorial Foundation, Monticello*)

Excised portion of the Declaration of Independence, 1776 (*Manuscript Department, The Library of Congress*)

The Story
All America
Took To Its Heart

live out the few ... ...ing him. He would not
... ... leav...
Harriet H... ... ...d at her father
... the last t... ...at she was his
... daughter. She would alw...s be his daughter. But she
...d nothing. Then she turn...her gaze, hard and ...

A Woman of Independent Means

A Novel by
**Elizabeth
Forsythe
Hailey**

THE SPLENDID
NATIONAL BESTSELLER

"Nothing about it is ordinary . . . irresistible."
Los Angeles Times
"Bares the soul of an independent American housewife . . .
a woman to respect . . . a writer to remember."
John Barkham Reviews

AVON $2.50

WIM-7/79